By the dawn of the 14th Century, the Crusaders' Order of the Knights Templar was well on its way to the control of Europe— enormously wealthy, a secret society stronger than many monarchies. By the middle of that century, it was brutally suppressed on the confession of some of its members that it was a conspiracy intending to conquer the world at the orders of a demon named Baphomet.

That is history as our Earth knows it.

But the only sort of "demon" enlightened modern men would recognize would be an extra-terrestrial voyager with the tools of a higher technology than medieval men knew.

And what if Baphomet had been just that?

Who then would have called the tune?

PIERRE BARBET is the by-line of one of the most popular science fiction writers in France today, and it is also the *nom de plume* of a distinguished doctor of pharmacology and authority on many branches of medicine. A devoted sf enthusiast, he is particularly proud of these novels which he regards as his first and most detailed "historicals" and into which he poured a great amount of research.

Among the novels made available in English translation by DAW Books are:

GAMES PSYBORGS PLAY
THE ENCHANTED PLANET
THE NAPOLEONS OF ERIDANUS
THE JOAN-OF-ARC REPLAY

COSMIC CRUSADERS

by

Pierre Barbet

Two complete novels:

BAPHOMET'S METEOR
Translated by BERNARD KAY

STELLAR CRUSADE
Translated by C. J. CHERRYH

DAW BOOKS, INC.
Donald A. Wollheim, Publisher
1633 Broadway, New York, N.Y. 10019

BAPHOMET'S METEOR

Translated by Bernard Kay

DEDICATION

Au docteur Jean-Claude Laburthe, historien érudit, dont es conseils m'ont été précieux pour la rédaction de cet ouvrage.

En témoinage d'une ancienne et sincère amitié.

—P.B.

Prologue

October, 1118 A.D.

High in the azure sky of Cathay, a meteor left behind a long silvery trail, clearly visible in the bright sunlight.

Near Troyes, as night fell, a harsh north wind assaulted Grand-Orient Forest, already stripped of its golden finery. Far off, the plaintive yelping of dogs following the scent of some quarry could be heard.

Suddenly, a black shape rushed from the bramble thickets. It was that sturdy solitary, a wild boar with long, thickset hair, which fled for its life. It appeared exhausted, slaver drooling from its mouth where two sharp tucks gleamed, the cleft of its right forehoof rent by a sharp branch.

Then quiet returned.

A few lingering leaves fluttered to the ground. Then from the coppice a horseman charged into view, in full cry, his horse streaming with sweat, its muzzle frosted with foam. In front of him, the dogs—dead tired—kept their noses to the ground, following the still fresh scent of the beast.

They came from the direction of Beaulieu and made off toward the meres in the heart of the forest, great somber pools of stagnant water filled with rotting leaves. There, the full-grown yet young boar still fled before them but with his pace now slowed. The four hounds, their tongues hanging, gained ground.

As the hunter glimpsed his prey, a weary smile etched itself on his lips.

Well now, he thought, *not this time will Hugh of Payens again return empty-handed. By my faith, a fine animal! I wager he'll defend his life dearly.*

7

Watchfully, the hunter lowered his short hunting spear, ready to strike if the boar did an about-face. On his left, the waters of a pond reflected the bloody rays of the setting sun.

At that instant, a flash of lightning lit up the yellowing leaves that carpeted the ground.

The dogs howled in terror. The horse, startled, swerved unexpectedly, unseating and throwing its rider. In his fall, his head struck the trunk of an oak tree and he lay motionless on the ground, his arms spread, a little blood running down one cheek, torn by a bramble.

Long minutes passed.

Finally Hugh sketched a movement with his right hand, then regained some consciousness and sat up, still half insensible.

It was already night and the full moon washed the undergrowth with a pale luminescence.

Suddenly, a wet raspy touch brought him to his senses— one of the dogs licking his wounded cheek.

With aid of a nearby tree trunk, the horseman got to his feet and ran an exploratory hand over his head, grimacing.

Apparently nothing was broken.

Painfully, Hugh of Payens knelt again, made the sign of the cross and gave thanks to God.

After that he felt better and took brief stock of his situation. The dogs surrounded him, watching with almost human expressions and whining uneasily. The horse grazed placidly on the sparse grass at the edge of the pool.

The hunter frowned as a strange object caught his eye. An enormous, rusty metal sphere emerged from the black waters and, wonder of wonders, its upper dome seemed to rotate slowly.

Hugh crossed himself again without effect. The vision did not disappear. Then, as the dome continued its movement, a distinct groove appeared in the metal surface. Abruptly all movement ceased and, as the sphere rocked gently, a circular opening from which a scarlet glow emanated was disclosed.

Prepared for anything, Hugh seized the dagger fixed at his belt. The enraged dogs snarled, showing their fangs, but they kept at a respectful distance as though realizing they lacked the size to confront the unknown peril which the roseate opening represented.

Step by step, they retreated, contenting themselves with

challenging growls. Instinct warned them of the approach of some mysterious danger.

Then a strange silhouette, not clearly visible in the pale moonlight, emerged from the sphere.

Horrified, Hugh of Payens finally made out the diabolic figure. He rubbed his bulging eyes with his left hand as if to assure himself that it was no more than the question of a nightmare.

But, no! He was not dreaming. A few steps in front of him was a deformed, bearded being with a smooth, hairless cranium that bore two short horns. Clawlike fingers still gripped the metal edges of the opening.

The monstrous dwarf was obviously stark naked. Two womanish breasts swelled on his chest. Short wings stood out behind his shoulders.

Exactly like the pictures in the missals! A demon incubus vomited up from hell to tempt the souls of Christians. . . .

Again Hugh crossed himself and mumbled prayers, but the being would not be exorcised. Instead he emerged even further from the orifice of his strange habitation.

Two eyes, glittering like live coals, fixed the knight, who could scarcely bear the unwavering gaze. He had an impression that the malefic pupils emitted flames that pierced his brain, having access to his most secret thoughts.

Futilely, he tried to dismiss the whole thing as some kind of nightmare, but the monstrous creature was all too real.

After seconds that seemed like centuries, he felt the unclean spirit pervading his being. Strange thoughts imposed themselves on his mind. The demon was speaking to him!

"Fear nothing, you miserable creature, riveted to this backward planet, I an not Satan. . . . I come from beyond immeasurable reaches of space, and from a world much more highly evolved than yours. Unfortunately, an ion storm crippled my spacecraft while it was orbiting close to your star. And here am I, shipwrecked on this minute planet in an unsalvageable vessel, without a means of communicating with my own kind. . . . Still, you have no reason to fear me. On the contrary, if you will agree to follow my instructions, you will become rich and powerful, and you will command even kings themselves."

"Your speech is the same as that with which the Prince of Darkness tempted our Lord on the mountain in the desert.

May you not be the angel, Lucifer, the fallen one who desires only to lead men to their ruin?"

"Come now, let's leave fairy tales to little children. If I were the evil one, I would seek to lead your king astray, not some obscure knight. No, Hugh of Payens, I am only a living being, come from the stars after a long and difficult voyage. Nearly all the delicate mechanisms of my small spacecraft have been destroyed by this catastrophic landing. However, I still possess powerful weapons that would allow me to destroy you without difficulty. See for yourself. . . ."

On these words, the creature pointed a gray tube toward a huge oak. Hugh could not say from whence it came, but when a blue-green flame sprang from the humid trunk, he shuddered in terror as though lightning had just struck close beside him.

"Well, what do you say to that, knight? This tube could reduce you to ashes, you and ten like you, but I would never use it against you for you can render me an inestimable service."

"Speak. If what you want in no way puts my immortal soul in peril, I shall obey you."

Hugh was beginning to relax.

After all, this strange creature seemed in no way troubled by his signs of the cross. Besides, did he not wear about his neck a venerable relic that would suffice to make all the demons in hell flee, braying like asses?

"There is substantial recompense," continued his interlocutor. "We will reach an agreement. All the more because I ask very little: each day your manservants must place provisions near this pool. Then they must leave and not return. I, for my part, am ready to make you and those who follow your instructions masters of the world."

"Bah! You are poking fun at me. . . ."

"Not at all. I will give you gold: for me the dream of your alchemists is a reality. With this metal you can buy lands, impose your will on kings. And even, should you so desire, raise armies to do battle under your command."

Hugh felt temptation growing inside him.

If this creature spoke the truth, he, poor knight of the House of Champagne, would acquire riches and renown . . . a petty nobleman could not hope for an equal piece of good luck. Gone would be the bleak winter nights when one counted the bushels of wheat, asking oneself if there would be enough bread until the next harvest. Over and done with the hard labor around the ramshackle familial manor. No more coats worn threadbare, nor tattered doublets. From the very moment he could be done with hunting to assure a roast for the meager seignorial table. He could have serfs and game-beaters for his own pleasure. And yet, the torture with red-hot pincers for all eternity! If this creature were lying, if he were indeed the demon tempter . . . then Hugh of Payens would lose his immortal soul!

Suddenly an inspiration swept away his scruples. These riches, promised to him alone, why not consecrate them to a noble cause and thus assure his salvation? The deliverance of the Holy Sepulchre, for which legions of Crusaders had given their lives, was a thing accomplished, but King Baldwin needed assistance to defend Jerusalem against the assaults of the infidels. . . .

Since 1113, the Hospitalers had fought at the side of knights of all nations, but with resources insufficient for the task. Why not assist them? Better still, why not found a new monastic order that would have as its sole reason for being the defense of the Temple of Jerusalem?

Yes! He would set up monasteries in France and in neighboring countries. He would recruit and train knights who would consecrate their lives to the struggle in the Holy Land, who would go to Jerusalem to offer assistance to King Baldwin II. Surely Geoffroy of Saint-Omar, Andre of Montbart and other knights would support such a project with enthusiasm.

That settled it. He would accept.

"Well, knight, you have decided?"

"I will gladly feed you as long as you wish. On the condition, you understand, that you do not ask the impossible of me. Tell me your name and put your hand in mine: thus we will seal our agreement forever."

"Call me Baphomet!" The dwarf laughed derisively and extended a scaly palm.

Hugh felt a deadly cold seize him on contact with the stranger. Without doubt this being was real. He felt the grasp of a hand. . . .

"It is good," declared the knight, crossing himself. "By the

Lord Jesus, who died for us on the Cross, I swear to obey your orders scrupulously."

"Excellent. To begin, you are going to give me your water bottle and the provisions you have in your saddlebag. My food synthesizer was destroyed and I must content myself with frightful nourishment. After that, you will go and gather around you eight companions, gentle knights like yourself. You will betake yourselves to Jerusalem, abandoning your wives and children. The gold you leave behind will console them during your absence. The king will agree to entrust you with guarding the route taken by the pilgrims, which passes through Jaffa. He will also bestow on you the freehold of a part of his palace located on the exact site of the ancient Temple of King Solomon. There you will establish the rules of your Order before the Patriarch of Jerusalem. After that, an illustrious knight, Hugh, Count of Champagne, will join you."

"How can you already know my desires and be so well-informed about our Holy Land, you who claim to be a stranger?"

"Fortunately, not all the equipment in my ship was destroyed. I still have a device linked directly with my brain which permits me—within limits—to see the future. Your thoughts are known to me, of course. But that is not all. In eleven-twenty-eight you will return to France. From here, you will go to England to enlist new recruits. The Council of Troyes will definitely confirm the rules of the Order of the Temple. Finally, a saintly man, Bernard, will lend you his assistance. Your power will then be great and the white mantle of your knights will be saluted with respect. In due course you will return to the Holy Land, paying your respects to the Bishop of Avignon on the way, after which, in the company of Fulk of Anjou and his forces, you will engage in many a hard-fought battle. The glory will reflect on the Order and your converts will become innumerable."

"Lord!" cried the knight, quite dazzled. "What have I ever done to deserve anything so marvelous?"

"You have gladly helped a creature in need. God is rewarding you for it by my agency. Listen to me a little longer. Near here, you will set up several Commanderies for the purpose of protecting this forest: at Beaulieu, Pinay, Royson and Bouy. On your death, the date of which I will not reveal to you, you will bequeath our secret to your successor, the Grand Master of the Order, who must swear to carry out every point of your agreement and, like you, jealously guard knowledge of my existence. Wherever you may go, you will take with you a kind of magical statue which will allow you to communicate with me, even when you are in the Holy Land. Bear well in mind that its existence, too, must be kept absolutely secret, for it will destroy itself, if the gaze of one unauthorized should fall on it. I have said enough to you. Later on, I shall place at the disposal of the Grand Masters other devices, powerful weapons and subtle machines which will allow you to overcome all adversaries. For the moment, content yourself with this gold; you might turn the destructive engines that I possess against me."

Hugh could say or do nothing. His head reeled, his eyesight blurred. Was he, after all, dreaming? And yet, Baphomet was holding out to him a block of yellow metal, as promised.

With a mechanical gesture, he detached his water bottle, flung down the saddlebag containing his provisions, then seized the ingot. Its weight surprised him, but its luster was that of good alloy. This creature from another world kept his word.

"Do not forget," warned the dwarf, "Tomorrow, at the same hour, those who serve you must place food and drink beside this pool. I need strength to undertake repairs on my ship."

"I shall take care always that you want for nothing," the knight stammered.

"It is well. Before you leave for the Holy Land, come back here to get the effigy which will allow you to stay in communication with me. And, above all, be discreet. . . ."

With these words, Baphomet reentered the curious abode.

The cover slid across the opening, sealing it. Then the sphere sank slowly under the black waters of the tarn.

Thoughtfully, the knight placed the precious ingot in a leather pocket of his saddle, then mounted his steed and, following the dogs, disappeared in the night mist.

Thus, Baphomet, an explorer lost in the galaxy without hope of return, because a space-time tornado had cast him far from his homeland, had established the basis for an empire of which he intended to be the sole master.

The robot-images introduced into each Commandery would be the means of ensuring his hold on humanity through the intermediation of the Templars.

One day, perhaps, some patrol from his faraway planet would discover him. At such a time, he would be able to bring to his leader an empire already subjugated, and he would be showered with honors.

Chapter I

1275 A.D.

William of Beaujeu, Grand Master of the Temple, had every reason to be satisfied. The Commanderies of France, England, Italy and Spain were flourishing. On the other hand, the situation in the Holy Land was disturbing.

Leaning over the stern rail of the ship, William thoughtfully contemplated the attenuated wake of foam on the jade and emerald billows.

The weather was magnificent: weather such as only the Mediterranean can offer its faithful admirers. Birds, flying nearly level with the crests, foretold the approach to land.

Some cable-lengths apart, ten other vessels, loaded to the brim with chargers and the provisioning necessary to an army, scudded along before a stiff breeze.

Beside the Grand Master was another high dignitary: Peter of Sevry, Field Marshal of the Temple. The latter contrasted with William to an astonishing degree: while the first, thin and ascetic, seemed the classic figure of a friar-knight, the second—a thickset and rubicund giant—appeared tailored for the good life and gallant company.

On the bridge, behind them, squires and knights chatted in high spirits, all cheered by the imminent arrival of the convoy. This crossing had been achieved under the best of auspices: favorable winds, clement weather and not the slightest harassment by Saracen vessels.

Before long the gray line of the shore appeared on the horizon: Cyprus, the marvelous island, the veritable paradise protected by the billows from pagan armies, where the

Crusaders, weary from combat, found peace, calm and repose in an enchanted setting.

This sight, announced by the lookout, was greeted with the cheering of all the passengers, knights and bondmen, who rejoiced at the thought of regaining solid ground. The old hands praised the merits of this white city to the novices, the charm of its palaces, its baronial halls, and the sweetness of its nights.

Their enthusiasm seemed to bring the Grand Master from a dream. He stood to his full height and sighed: "Well, my worthy Peter, you have nothing to say?"

"I was respecting your silence, master. . . ."

"And I appreciate your thoughtfulness. You know my projects are vast and ambitious. This time, thanks to the reinforcements we bring, to the gold and abundant provisions, I hope to finish once and for all with that accursed Sultan of Egypt, Bibars. . . .

"That demon has taken Caesarea, Jaffa and Antioch from us! May he burn forever in the flames of hell. Now we hold only Tripoli, Acre and Sidon; little enough compared with the flourishing realm of old. That is reason enough for taking the offensive once more. . . .

"By the Christ who died for us on the Cross, I swear to you that the wretch will not profit from his conquests much longer. In the hold of this ship we bring powerful weapons that shall occasion him some Gehennas. However, the time has not yet come. Before that, we needs must settle some differences on this fair isle of Cyprus."

"You are thinking of the throne of Jerusalem, master?"

"Most certainly. King Henry III of Cyprus plays no part in my plans. Let his damned soul be the puppet of the Hospitalers. Charles, Count of Anjou, will suit our convenience much better. Thanks to heaven, I bring enough gold to establish him on the throne. It is also reported to me that Bohemond VII, Count of Tripoli, does not like us overmuch. What do you say to Guy II, of Jebala, to replace him?"

"Djebail? They say he is well-disposed toward us. . . ."

"I am certain of it. And, once my supporters are assured, I can throw myself into an assault on those places which Bibars wrested from us in unequal combat. Soon, my brother, we will enter our castle at Safad once more, and the one at Beaufort, too."

"I pray the Holy Spirit to aid you, master! However, the pagans are without number and we are but a handful, for it is useless to count on much support from the Hospitalers; the knights of your cousin, King Philip of France, are something less than certain, as are the forces of Edward I of England. . . ."

"I overlook nothing. Nevertheless, thanks to Mary, Star of the Sea, who brought us safely to port, I am in possession of some weighty arguments. You know what Greek Fire is?"

"Indeed, I do. Those flaming balls of naphtha have been the cause of enough ravages in our ranks!"

"Well, what would you say to spheres of flame a thousand times more destructive—the fire of hell itself let loose on the ranks of the Saracens?"

Peter of Sevry made the sign of the Cross.

"Only the devil can command such power, master. . . ."

"There you are mistaken, Peter. Satan has nothing to do with the matter. Our Baphomet has such engines. Until now, he has not entrusted them to us, fearing that we might make evil use of them. This time, he agreed to grant me this supreme power. I described to him the desperate situation of the Holy Land, and our successive reverses touched him. In his goodness, he condescended to give me one hundred fires wrenched from the sun. With them, I am strong enough to convince the Franks and the English. A discreet demonstration will take place at the proper time. I wager that after having proof of its force, they will agree to unite with us."

"I am completely astounded, master. . . . Is this the fruit of some new alchemy?"

"There you ask too much of me, Peter. Baphomet gives me not one hint of his magical secrets. The gold with which he supplies us is fine-grade ore; no one has ever found any fault in it. This fire from the sun exists. I, myself, have seen its consequences. Unfortunately, I have no idea how it is compressed into the metal spheres which, strangely enough, are cold to the touch."

"In faith, these are great wonders! But would it not be prudent to keep the matter secret so that no word of it may reach that miserable Bibars?"

"You are right, Peter. Only the Commanders and the dignitaries of the Order will know of the existence of this magic fire. However, while we are at Acre, I shall have a demonstration for Otto of Granson, Commander of the men-at-arms of the English king, as well as John of Grailly, who leads the French Crusaders. In this way, I shall persuade them to join our forces. But a truce to discourse, brother; here we are at the quay. Let us pay a visit to noble King Henry. . . . Our gold will suffice, I hope, to establish the young prince of Salerno, Charles, on the throne of Jerusalem."

A gangway had already been lowered but, to the disappointment of the Brothers of the Order, all landing had been forbidden.

William wanted to reach Acre as soon as possible, so only the Household of the Grand Master was authorized to go ashore.

A majestic procession formed on the quay: at its head, the Baussant standard, black and white with a cross gules crowning all. Behind it came William of Beaujeu, followed by his faithful Marshal at Arms, both astride magnificent, jet-black chargers.

A few paces behind them, the Seneschal, second only to the supreme leader, moved at the head of the Household, properly so designated, where were found the Brother-Chaplain, two knights chosen for their feats in battle, a scholar well-versed in the scriptures, two Brother Sergeants, a Saracen scrivener whose richly embroidered silk cape contrasted with the sober white mantle of the Brothers of the Order.

Four Turcopoles, the farrier, the cook and the squires kept their respective distances.

Finally, ten Brothers, formerly noble knights, followed by their sergeants, brought up the rear of the column.

As it passed, the Cypriots paused, filled with admiration for the exalted demeanor of the Templars, for the beauty of their steeds, the brilliance of their new armor. A group of children, shouting and singing, followed them all the way to the royal palace.

William's stay there was extremely brief.

Before midday he left the royal enclave to repair to the Commandery, where, after a frugal repast, he heard vespers before reembarking. The flotilla forthwith took to the open sea, sailing before the wind toward Acre.

Five other vessels had joined the convoy to avail themselves of its protection.

There were, therefore, sixteen in all that hove to, after a short crossing, near the fortress-home of the Templars, situated close to the sea in the port of Acre.

It was noon and the heat of the sun at its zenith was oppressive. The Templars and their squires streamed with sweat under their armor. However, the Turcopole slaves immediately began unloading the invaluable cargo contained in the bulging bellies of those ships come from overseas.

The Grand Master and his escort soon arrived at the Commandery where Theobald Gaudin, Master of the Acre Templary, awaited them.

Four large wooden coffers banded with iron were stowed in a safe place; then the knights were able to take some repose in the coolness of the vaulted chambers.

This arrival filled the hearts of the inhabitants of the city with joy. They were greatly relieved to know that they were protected by fresh, well-armed troops. The huge amounts of provisions unloaded assured them that they would be well-fed in the case of siege.

For a long time, Acre had lived under the constant threat of the Mameluke army. It was rumored that Bibars had at his disposal forty thousand knights and one hundred thousand foot soldiers. What could the twenty thousand inhabitants of the city hope for? Even protected by the thick walls, they feared—with reason—finding themselves submerged by such a tide of humanity.

The Accursed Tower, key to the fortress, had been hastily reinforced, but Bibars was a known expert in the art of siege. His war machines, his engineers, his miners, would work swiftly to breach the walls. This done, even the bravery of the Christian knights would be incapable of resisting the onslaught of the Mamelukes.

The arrival of the Grand Master and his knights doubled the numbers of the cavalry, bringing it to more than two thousand. The foot soldiers now numbered almost twenty thousand. Little enough for combat on the open field, but it could be hoped that a siege by the Saracen army would be effectively resisted. Even the Grand Master of the Hospitalers was not unhappy at this influx of Templars, whom he customarily treated as rivals rather than as allies. At least he recognized their bravery and, in this desperate situation, any reinforcements were welcome.

The visit of the Templar Seneschal, the following morning, surprised him not at all. He willingly agreed to betake himself to the Templary, there to discuss "important questions concerning the safeguarding of the city."

When he arrived in the chapter room, he found an old acquaintance in the person of the giant Swiss, Otto of Granson, a mercenary in the pay of the English king, whose broad shoulders accentuated the lofty stature and the elegance of his neighbor, John of Grailly.

The Hospitaler's observant glance noted a strange circumstance.

Usually, at such meetings, all the dignitaries of the Order, Commanders and knights, were present. This time the number of Templars was reduced to a strict minimum: the Grand Master, his Seneschal and his Field Marshal.

Taking care not to seem to notice, he greeted the assembly with, "In the name of the Father, the Son and the Holy Ghost." This done, the monk-soldier took his place at William's right, while his own Marshal, Matthew of Clermont, moved to stand behind him.

The Grand Master of the Temple knelt and pronounced a brief prayer:

"May the grace of the Holy Spirit assist us. Lord Jesus Christ, Saint Peter, eternal and omnipotent God, wise Creator, giver of all things, benevolent guardian and well-beloved friend, pious and meek Redeemer, mild and merciful Savior, I humbly pray and beg of You that You shed Your light upon us. In the name of Mary, Star of the Sea. Amen."

After this, he rose and regarded each of his guests with eyes as piercing as those of an eagle, then declared:

"Good gentlemen, Brother Hospitalers, I have asked you here today for the purpose of claiming from you all the assistance that it is lawful for you to grant me, for I held high hopes; soon the Holy Sepulchre will be in our hands. . . ."

The most profound astonishment showed clearly on the faces of all present. William had never had a reputation for jesting. Consequently, they could only ask themselves if the Grand Master had not suddenly gone mad.

John of Villiers, Grand Master of the Hospitalers, made himself their spokesman by objecting:

"This is marvelous news, noble brother! Pray heaven that you are right. . . . Unfortunately, such an ambition seems to me less than reasonable. Our numbers scarcely suffice to defend this city, and you talk of going out to conquer Jerusalem. . . . Your words demand some explanation, because my limited understanding cannot fathom how you envisage such an achievement."

William smiled craftily. He was awaiting the final astonishment of his visitors and took a wicked pleasure in doing so.

Husbanding his effects, he continued:

"By all the Saints, the Archangels and the Host of the Blessed, I swear to you, noble friends, that within thirty days the Holy Places shall be free of the vermin that now overrun them. And I am going to give you proof of it, if a jaunt to the heights of Toru doesn't frighten you."

Hospitalers and Commanding Officers consulted each other with swift glances. Nothing stood in the way of such an outing. The surroundings were safe: not one enemy horseman had been reported. Finally, they signified their acquiescence with a nod of the head.

The seven knights left the cool of the chapter house regretfully and went into the burning courtyard where their steeds, led out by the squires, awaited them.

All, however, were anxious to learn what miracle could truly inspire their host to hold such designs.

They did not have long to wait.

A quarter of an hour later, William reined in his horse on the summit of a low hill overlooking Acre and the neighboring countryside.

On his right, about a hundred meters away, was a rocky eminence, at which he pointed.

"Look closely at those stones, gentlemen."

Everyone stared intently in the indicated direction.

"Now place your gauntlet in front of your eyes and do not, under any circumstances, remove it."

Whereupon, the Templar, using both spurs, raced away toward his target. Drawing a sling from one of his saddle-holsters, he placed a grayish sphere, about the size of a fist, in it. Then he threw this projectile with all his might and, wheeling abruptly, fled at a gallop from the spot hit by that inoffensive-appearing ball.

Some seconds later, a blinding light burst from the ground. Rocks showered around the knights, some striking their shields, while an appalling explosion almost deafened them.

Shocked, they stared in the direction of this apocalyptic thundering, holding their rearing mounts with difficulty.

A high column of dust in the shape of a mushroom, whose revolving summit rose rapidly, hid the point of impact.

As the slight wind drove it inland, they saw that a vast crater had unquestionably replaced the outcropping of stony crags.

For a long time the deafening echoes of the explosion reverberated among the hills, then silence fell once more.

"By Saint Gorge!" growled Otto of Granson. "What kind of lightning was that?"

"Saint Dennis preserve me!" John of Grailly whispered. "How can you talk of lightning from a cloudless sky? The earth just vomited the fire from its entrails. . . ."

John of Villiers did not utter a word. He urged his horse at a trot toward the smoking crater, stopped some distance from it and contemplated the molten pit for a long time. Then, shaking his head thoughtfully, he rejoined the little group of knights, crossing himself repeatedly.

William still wore his ironic smile. Without seeming interested in the general consternation, he whipped his horse to a trot and headed back toward the Commandery.

A difficult task lay ahead: he was going to find himself faced with divergent interests; how could he reconcile them with his own?

Minutes later the seven knights reentered the cool of the chapter room.

Without delay the Grand Master of the Hospitalers launched into a harsh diatribe.

"Noble Brothers," he began angrily, "the faith and abnegation of the Knights of the Temple have already been placed in doubt by certain individuals. Though it is far from my intentions to accuse their leader of dealings with Satan, nevertheless this fire surging suddenly from the rocks irresistibly makes one think of demoniac intervention. Never has man raised up such infernal flames, unless by devilish incantations. I acknowledge that this is an all-powerful weapon whose effects on the pagan hosts would assure us certain victory. But, in your soul and conscience, Brother William, can you swear that you would never use it against Christians in order to become supreme master indeed? Further, can you prove to me that our Lord Christ would approve of such a lightning bolt, even against the Saracens? Have you envisaged the use that could be made of it, should it fall into ambitious hands? Hurled from the sky on some unfortunate city, it would reduce ramparts and houses to nothing. All inhabitants, the lowly and the exalted, would be killed without distinction. No, William! By heaven, I adjure you to destroy these evil devices immediately, for if you do not, you put your immortal soul in peril!"

The Grand Master of the Templars had let his dangerous rival speak without interrupting. He had blanched with rage at the accusations brought against the Holy Order which he represented, but had succeeded in containing himself. Now he exploded:

"By Christ, placed on the Cross for our transgressions, you are going to take back your offensive words or, if not, you shall smart for it. How dare you doubt my Brothers or myself? Never have we had any ambition other than to deliver the Holy Places and to establish the True Faith throughout the world. You know our motto: *Non nobis, Domine, non nobis, sed Nomine Tua da gloriam!* We have no wish for glory; all our actions have as their object only the glory of the Lord! You seem to be saying that springs forth by power of the Evil One. Very well, in that case, the Holy Relics, the consecrated wafer, would have power to extinguish it on the spot. I, myself, have made the test and I can assure you that they are without effect. . . . It is nothing more than the end result of some alchemy, strongly hermetic certainly, but with nothing of the demoniac about it. I swear it by the Virgin Mary!"

The Hospitaler appeared unconvinced. With contracted brows, he pondered the matter.

At that point, John of Grailly intervened politically:

"Noble sires, I have been—I admit it—dumbfounded by the power of the weapon demonstrated for us by the Grand Master. At the time, those flames made me, also, think of some intervention by the Prince of Darkness. However, after some reflection, I am convinced that this is only a kind of Greek Fire. Our ruthless adversaries have never hesitated to use the most savage stratagems against us. Have you forgotten the pots filled with deadly vipers that were hurled into our ranks? The quicklime thrown out over the assailants of their castles? The poison placed in the water holes? Well then, in all fairness, I ask why we should not treat them in the same way. As far as I am concerned, I am certain of the purity of our Brother Templar's intentions; never has great power been placed in better hands. The noble William of Beaujeu promises us never to use this subtle fire except to annihilate our opponents, to reconquer Jerusalem and to propagate the True Faith. For my part, I am ready to place the fullest trust in him. It goes without saying that he needs must keep us informed of his intentions and of the way in which he proposes to use our troops. Under those conditions I am ready to assure him of the complete support of King Philip's men-at-arms. However, since all labor merits recompense, it seems to me that the lands and castlewards liberated should be divided in all equity among the knights who participate in the combat."

"By my faith, this speaks of gold," thundered Otto of Granson. "All useful work does merit wages. I am ready to send my valiant knights to storm Jerusalem on the condition that some stronghold be ceded to my worthy sovereign, as is proper and fitting."

"This is a matter that calls for further thought," the Grand Master of Hospitalers interjected. "But first of all, calm your temper, noble William. Casting doubt on the virtue of the Knights of the Temple was farthest from my thoughts. My words only reported the gossip, the 'they say' talk that is heard in the courts of France and Italy. Even though this manner of snuffing out human lives is repugnant to me, I am forced to recognize that, after all, it is only a question of infidels. I would like, nevertheless, to hear from my Brother William's own mouth what his intentions are concerning this campaign."

"I take not of your words with joy, brother. It goes without saying that the Templars have never thought of appropriating the Kingdom of Jerusalem and the castlewards or principalities belonging to it. All who take part in the action will have the right to a recompense in proportion to the assistance given. Here and now I make a solemn promise to restore to our Brother Hospitalers their former castles. Later, when our troops shall have liberated the Princedoms of Tripoli and Antioch, I swear to place again in your hands, noble Sire of Villiers, the fortress Krak, which belongs to the knights."

"Well spoken!" trumpeted John of Grailly. "On these conditions, the support of King Philip's knights is assured."

"And that also holds true for those of England!"

The Grand Master of the Hospitalers thereupon rose and solemnly clasped William of Beaujeu in a brotherly embrace. In the closeness of this reconciliation, the resemblance between the two monk-soldiers became even more striking: the same height, the same ascetic slenderness, the same gray eyes, cold and calculating, the same toughness of a soldier disciplined by years of battle, and also the same mystical gleam in each glance. Then both turned to the situation in hand.

"It only remains to draw up a plan for the campaign," the Hospitaler observed. "Our battle forces are still weak despite the powerful weapon you possess. No doubt you have thought of this."

"Indeed I have," William affirmed. "Here are my suggestions born of long sleepless vigils. As of this moment, we have available two thousand knights and twenty thousand foot soldiers and horsemen, all seasoned and courageous. Our troops will follow the seacoast, in the direction of Pilgrim Castle and Nablus. Bibars will not believe his ears when he hears the news; his army will come out to meet us. Only then will we use the magic fire. We will fight with our spears and swords during the first skirmishes but, when the main body of the Saracens is brought up, the flames will send them to hell."

"Wisely thought out; the power of the weapon must not be unveiled prematurely."

"And the provisioning?" interposed the Marshal of the Hospitalers. "Those devils will do everything possible to cut off our rear guard with their cavalry."

"I have thought of that, Brother Matthew. The vessels that brought me here will also follow the coast, assuring both assistance and control of the sea. As you must have noticed, they are all furnished with wooden towers which will stand above any enemy galleys and, with the launching of our projectiles, destroy them in one sure blow. Further, Charles of Anjou will receive from his father, the King of Sicily, a fleet of thirty vessels. This, it is understood, if he is placed on the throne of Jerusalem. . . ."

That statement caused the Hospitalers to make wry faces

because of their known preference for Henry of Cyprus, nephew of Louis IX, but they held their peace.

"Thus, with mastery of the sea, once the forces of Bibars are destroyed, who shall prevent us from penetrating the interior?"

"I place myself completely in your hands, brother," approved John of Villiers. "May the heavens bless you! But you spoke of the Princedom of Antioch; it seems to me. . . ."

"We certainly must not limit our ambitions to the Kingdom of Jerusalem! All pagans must be driven from the Holy Land and the former might of the Crusaders reestablished in Syria, even to the country of Edessa. If you agree, I will leave the Holy City in your care. My forces will embark in our vessels for Tripoli. There, we will do battle against the Mamelukes, and against the Mongol Khan of Persia. Again we shall be victorious, have no doubt of it. I need not say that I will accept the aid of all those knights who wish to join me."

"By the Lord Christ, there are great adventures ahead," shouted John of Grailly. "We shall be with you, my men and I!"

"I would be ashamed not to join you," opined the Swiss Commander. "Let me at the Saracens!"

"It is understood," the sharp voice of the Master of the Hospitalers interrupted, "that you possess a large number of these magic spheres; our success depends on that."

"Be reassured," William answered with a discreet smile. "There will never be enough unbelievers to kill. What do you say, my brave Peter?"

The Marshal of the Templars nodded and growled:

"By Christ, we have enough of them to send more Saracens to hell than there are in existence from Damietta to Edessa!"

"Under these conditions, you can count on the Hospitalers. When shall we set out?" asked John of Villiers.

"The Templars are ready, good sire. It is for you to answer your own question."

"Two days seem sufficient to me. What do you say, my noble companions?"

Otto of Granson and John of Grailly agreed with their leader.

"One word more," resumed the Templar. "Your men will

have to construct some catapults and mangonels according to
our plans. They must be light and mobile. The wheels must
be such that a team of horses can pull them and always keep
abreast of our troop movements. We will place them in the
center of the forces and defend them, come what may. My
projectiles must, in effect, be able to reach the main body of
the opposing army before the enemy is too close. I should
also point out that the sphere launched by a war machine is
much more effective than one thrown by a sling. . . ."

"Lord Jesus! I shall end by pitying these infidels," muttered
Grailly.

"Along the route, all these devices will remain in the coffers of my personal luggage. My Household will guard them;
no one else shall have access to them except myself and my
Field Marshal. Any other Crusader, whatever his rank may
be, will be killed without mercy should he attempt to come
near them."

"That stipulation was unnecessary," John of Villiers stated
with a haughty air. "No Hospitaler would stoop to such trea-
son. These secrets of alchemy belong to the Temple. One last
question, brother: what does our Sainted Father, the Pope,
say about these wonderful projectiles?"

"I had an interview with the venerable Gregory X, and
told him about this discovery of a Greek Fire with previously
unsuspected power, which would allow us to drive the infidels
from the Holy Land. He gave me his blessing, promising to
keep our secret."

"And did you give him a demonstration?"

"Certainly not! Such an explosion would have attracted attention. Besides, he did not request it."

"I see," said the Hospitaler with a meaningful smile. "His
Holiness will have quite a surprise when he learns of the exact power of this 'Greek Fire.' "

Tight-lipped, William protested, "By my faith, I depicted
its effects faithfully for him."

"Assuredly, brother. Nevertheless, such a marvel must be
seen in order to grasp its true significance."

"Are you looking for a pretext to take back your word?"

"No, not at all, good brother. All the same, I wager that
the Cardinals and the Holy Father will talk of this at length
in times to come."

With these words, the meeting of the Council came to an

end. Each returned to his quarters to give the necessary orders.

One hour later the news had spread throughout the city. Comments were plentiful and unfavorable. Even the sergeants and squires did not show overmuch enthusiasm for a sortie which seemed foolhardy to all.

Still, their discipline was such that everyone made haste to prepare, furbishing armor and weapons, and loading the carts with hay and various kinds of provisions.

That night the revelry was endless: French and English knew not when they would again see their hearts' delights. Among the noble ladies, many a lovely eye filled with tears, weeping for a fiancé or a lover already counted lost forever.

Chapter II

On the morning of the third day, the ranks of the Crusaders thundered out through the Gate of Saint Anthony, and took the southward road along the seacoast.

The army was a brave sight.

In the lead the Templars marched.

First the Grand Master followed by the Marshal, the Seneschal and the Household. The Baussant banner fluttered in a light breeze, high in the clear sky.

The Commanders came next, preceded by their standard-bearers. Fifty knights, as many sergeants and squires marched in closed ranks at their heels.

The carts, loaded to the breaking point, came on behind, guarded by the Turcopoles.

The center of the troop disposition had been entrusted to the French and English knights, who followed their respective leaders. They escorted the precious catapults, whose large new wheels rasped at every turn.

Rosponsibility for guarding the rear had been placed on the Hospitalers. This was a perilous position because the Saracen horsemen were quick to harass the stragglers.

Dust raised by the thousands of marching men did little to dim the flashing of lances and helmets, but was not slow to put these valiant warriors to the test by mingling with the sweat that already trickled under their armor.

All the inhabitants of Acre were massed on the walls, despite the early morning hour.

Not a few shed tears, asking themselves how many of those who left thus in the resplendent light of sunrise would come back to their city. No one understood why the leaders advised the Crusaders to take such risks and the rumors spread rapidly from one to another of the watchers. Some declared they had learned from a reliable source that Philip the Hardy, King of France, was going to disembark on the coast with his troops. Others were assured that an enormous fleet was arriving from Sicily and that it would join the forces of the Grand Master of the Templars at Caesarea. For certain, it was the King of England who was going to come to their rescue.

In fact, no one could reach an agreement except on a single point: all bitterly deplored the sight of their city thus deprived of defenders.

But already the long column was disappearing in the ocher cloud rising from the earth. For an instant one caught again the flash of a helmet glistening in the sunlight or the scarlet of a banner whipping in the wind.

All too soon, there was nothing but a bluish line on the horizon.

The die was cast: the troops of the Crusaders went boldly forward, challenging the Sultan Bibars to do battle.

In the column itself, the bondmen, sergeants on foot and squires talked among themselves, sharing their mutual fears.

Among them there were representatives of all the provinces of France: Manceaux, Champenois, Angevins, Tourangeaux, and also some Englishmen from the counties between the marches of the Scottish border and the Gallic counties.

Among the French squires, two brothers were discussing farming. Natives of Saint-Maurice Thizouaille near Auxerre, they became Crusaders to join their elder brother, Garin, sergeant to the Templar Chapter at Saint-Maurice, who had gone out to the Holy Land.

Guiot Tholon, a robust jovial fellow, formerly a woodcutter, sported that flamboyant beard-collar known as a Newgate frill which had earned him the nickname, Guiot-the-Red.

The other answered to the name of Clement, which in no way corresponded with his hot-tempered character. One day, a Gallic sergeant had accused him of cheating at dice. Clement picked the unfortunate fellow up bodily, lifted him over his head, let him fall on his bent knee, effectively rupturing his kidneys. Suddenly, the reputation of the former scythe-swinger was solidly established and no one picked a quarrel with him.

The two brothers were impenitent whoremasters and the

elder brother often had to lecture them to lead them back on the right path.

Such as they were, with guileless blue eyes, with renown as fierce fighters, they openly grumbled but never were sullen about a task.

"By 'swounds!" Guiot swore. "I swear to you, if I had it to do over, I would never leave Auxerre. You have to be an animal to come to this godforsaken country of sweat, tears and blood on these burning trails under a sun that boils your brains. If I listened to myself, I would send all this bloody equipment packing. Me, all I need is a good ax to smash these cursed pagans!"

"You're not very far wrong! I can feel myself broiling under this whore of a coat of mail. The Saracens never weigh themselves down with any such holy scrap-iron; just a tunic, a shield and their saber. But for us, it's like being in a shell; no question of running, you have to crawl in a furnace."

"And this dust! It gets to me everywhere: it scratches as if somebody were rubbing me with a whetstone."

"If you only knew what you were going to have to face in this hellish desert! Just imagine the Grand Master and our Commanders all having to live through this dust! 'Swounds! It would be a fine thing to shelter behind the ramparts of Acre. The Saracens could lay siege to us and, for once, their heads would be broken. But no, we have to go out to do battle in open country, and they are ten times more than we."

"My boy, if the Templar were here, he'd tell you that it's to expiate our sins."

"Oh, that. Perhaps it's true. Ah, that sweet bitch, Mathilde."

"A cursed bawd for certain," agreed his brother knowingly. "But to get back to what you were saying about the Grand Masters. I agree with you, and they know better than we what the infidels are cooking up. For me, Bibars is not far away and we are going to stumble onto him without warning."

"And then what? I tell you their numbers are ten times ours. After you've killed a hundred thousand, there are just as many."

"Quite likely. All the same, I don't let it bother me: surely they have some plan in the back of their heads to expose us without cover. Me, I have confidence in them."

"Maybe you're right . . . must have a word with Garin where we make a halt. Perhaps he knows what's going on. In the meantime, I'd give plenty for a quart of good country wine. . . ."

"Don't talk about such things! You cut me to the quick. . . ."

Their throats parched by the dust, the Tholon brothers brought their interesting conversation to a close: it was a question of holding out until the evening encampment at Caipha, situated on the shore of the gulf at the foot of the Carmel Mountains.

The noon halt saw the first ones crippled giving careful attention to their bruised feet. Actually, the majority of the Crusaders had become unaccustomed to long marches. The vegetation, mostly spiny shrubs, offered little shade so that both sergeants and squires crowded alongside the carts and stretched out on the ground. Others sheltered themselves as best they could under their shields, balanced obliquely on a sword or a lance.

Fortunately, there was no shortage of water, nor of food. After taking their fill, everyone surrendered to the pleasures of a siesta, under the guard of sentinels who streamed with sweat under the fiery sun. No alarm troubled their well-earned rest, but some Saracen knights scouted the size of the Christian forces, then retired at a gallop to inform their leaders.

The strident call of horns and trumpets put an end to the sleep of the unfortunate Crusaders, who returned to their places in the column.

This start was made near the hour of vespers. The heat had not lessened at all; the gait of the foot soldiers showed its effect and the Hospitalers of the rear guard had all they could do to spur on the stragglers. Some unfortunate victims of sunstroke had been placed in the carts where they raved and struggled, fighting with imaginary enemies.

At last the glaring ball of the sun sank to the horizon, lurid in the dust and haze. Then a noticeable landswell outlined itself against the sky: the Carmel Mountains at the foot of which sprawled opulent Caipha.

Suddenly, tongues were loosened and wagging again. Everyone speculated as to whether the forces would launch an attack on the city or whether they would pass around it. The presence of the siege machines seemed to favor the first hypothesis. It was also the "version" which found most favor among the Crusaders because, once the city had been taken, they dreamed of being able to enjoy some days of carousal and repose.

With the setting of the sun, where the western sky took on tones of amethyst, William pitched camp close to the city walls, but beyond the reach of arrows.

While they were setting up the tents, the squires could see the heads of the defenders, who watched this activity with apprehension. But the multicolored banners on the ramparts were not lowered, proof of their willingness to resist. However, the city had had little time to prepare for a siege and its provisions would not last long. The inhabitants had few illusions as to the outcome of this test of strength.

Only Bibars' army could save them. Of course messengers had been sent, hurrying southward with all possible speed. Unfortunately, it would take the Mamelukes several days to assemble and come back up the coast: without a doubt the city would have fallen long before they arrived.

Women, children and old men had fled to the mountains, hoping thus to escape the fury of the Christians, but they would be unable to survive long among the barren rocks burned by the sun. . . .

Soon, the camp fires began to blaze while the blacksmiths occupied themselves with the horses and wheels damaged by rocky roads. The cooks busied themselves around caldrons that spread tempting odors far and wide. Around the tents reserved for the dignitaries of the two Orders, watchful knights mounted guard. Close by, the banners of the Temple and the Hospital flapped lazily in the sea breeze.

The night was peaceful. Only the calls of the sentinels troubled the silence, accompanied by the howls of some jackals coming from the nearby hills.

In the morning, before dawn, everyone was called to attend mass. Then the Crusaders awaited the orders that would let them know what their leaders' intentions were.

Their uncertainty was short-lived: a small contingent was designated to blockade the city, while the body of the troops broke camp to resume the march toward Jaffa.

Once the Carmel Mountains were cleared, the army again took the trail following the coast. And, stage by stage, it

came to Pilgrim Mountain and Caesarea. fording the shallow
streams that flowed down from the mountains of Samaria.
The advance across the plain of Sharon offered no difficulties;
nevertheless, the hearts of the rude knights sank progressively
as they got farther from their base: Acre.

William of Beaujeu had none of their fears. He knew that
the alert had been given and that the squadrons of Bibars
were gathering. Each day, his Turcopole spies came to report
on the situation. As he had foreseen, the Saracen forces were
gathering around Jaffa and his only wish was to cross the
Yarquon so as to assure his men a supply of drinkable water.

On the other hand, the Grand Master knew that the small
fleet had left Acre and was moving down the shore to support
his land forces.

After Caesarea, one party of the cavalry had been sent
ahead toward Arsuf and the reports from the Commanders
stated that, around the port of Jaffa, the nights were ablaze
with fires, so numerous were the Saracens.

Despite all precautions this news spread through the companies. Until then, the forces of the Grand Master had
handled themselves extremely well. They had made the usual
complaints about the heat and fatigue, nothing really serious.
Now the foot soldiers firmly refused to advance another step.

All these brave men, the brothers Tholon included, thought
it utter folly to go thus to face in open country an inestimable army which had, besides, a fortified city where it could
entrench itself and receive supplies.

For William, the situation was tragic. How to persuade his
troops to resume the advance? Must he unveil a jealously
guarded secret, thus running the risk of losing his unique advantage? Uncertain, he convened his Council in order to decide what action to take, which proved extremely fortunate.

Actually, the subtle mind of the Grand Master of the Hospitalers suggested a ruse to him which offered a good chance
of success. William of Beaujeu, therefore, made his way to
the very center of the masses of men, and in substance, ral-
lied them with this speech:

"Brothers of the Temple and of the Hospital, knights,
squires and sergeants, I know the anxiety that grips you. You
believe that we must retrace our steps in haste in order to regain the shelter afforded by the ramparts of Acre, which we
have only just left. Men of little faith! Do you think that

William of Beaujeu and John of Villiers, not to mention our noble allies from France and England, would take such a risk without sufficient reason? Know, therefore, that a vision appeared to us. The Archangel Gabriel himself ordered us to quit the city where, with heavy hearts, we awaited the assault which would put an end to our presence in the Holy Land. Verily I say unto you, we are indeed masters of Jaffa and of Jerusalem, for the Lord of Hosts will launch His lightning to assist in the liberation of the Holy Places. Some among you shake your heads in disbelief. For them, I add these simple words: they may try to get back to Acre if they wish. I know from a trustworthy source that they will never reach it, because Bibars has divided his forces in two, cutting off the route that we have followed to come here. Any retreat is, therefore, impossible. Your only hope is to defeat the army which separates us from Jaffa, and for us to take possession of the city. A fleet come from Cyprus will help us there. By Jesus Christ, our Savior, victory stands at the end of your labors!"

Only a gloomy silence answered him.

The Crusaders were pondering what they had just learned. They did not believe overmuch in that story about lightning. From olden times, their ancestors had known many a harsh ordeal, and heaven had never come to their aid. . . .

On the other hand, the news of Bibars' encirclement was a heavy weight in the balance: even victorious over the Saracens, there would have to be long marches to reach Acre, and they knew how the enemy knights would ravage a column in retreat, harassing it day and night.

Everything considered, there was actually but one conclusion: "flight" straight ahead. If a fleet was arriving—and, on this point, the Grand Master assuredly would not lie—the city attacked by land and by sea would quickly fall. Then it would be possible to breathe in the shelter of its ramparts with their five hundred battlements. . . .

In the end, whether they liked it or not, the armed forces reformed and the march to the south was resumed. With the result that, ten days after their departure, the Crusaders crossed the Yarquon, sighting Jaffa, all white under the sun, from the height of that hill dotted with tombs which overlooks it. A few joyous shouts sprang from parched throats, abruptly cut off at sight of the huge army which barred their way.

There was one poor consolation: the promised ships were at their appointed stations, blockading the small port.

At once, William had horns sound the call for battle formation. Actually, one could not ask for a more favorable location. The hill, assuredly, could be surrounded by the enemy but a sudden attack could not be launched. There would be ample time to hurl down the lightning promised to the Crusaders.

Under the careful watch of Commanders, the catapults and mangonels were immediately drawn up in a circle, and the precious coffers containing the projectiles placed beside them.

Bibars wasted no time. He knew that the midday sun inflamed these men cased in steel, and he, too, had horns and trumpets sound the battle call of his Mamelukes.

The squadrons moved off, one after the other, encircling the Crusaders with a deadly girdle. First he brought up his infantry, holding the cavalry in reserve, in case the armored knights should charge down the slopes of the hill.

On that height, Templars and Hospitalers waited, kneeling and half-hidden by their shields as protection against volleys of arrows loosed by archers to cover the attack. At that distance, coats of mail and shields sufficed to avoid serious wounds. It would not, unhappily, be long until their adversaries were at close range.

On signal, the English crossbowmen began to let fly their bolts on the advancing masses. Since the Mamelukes had no armor comparable to that of the Christians—a helmet and buckler constituting their only protection—the foremost ranks were decimated. This in no way dampened the ardor of their companions who strode unfeelingly over the bodies and continued the climb.

Statue-like, William of Beaujeu silently comtemplated the scene. He noted Bibars poised in the rear with his cavalry, there where the standards made an emerald stain. Then, starting from his reverie, he made his way swiftly to one of the mangonels, slyly nicknamed "the male cousin," and with his own hands placed one of the gray projectiles in a recess made for that purpose.

Careful aim was taken according to his direction, while the chosen Commanders busied themselves at the other catapults.

Already their assailants were close: one could see the sun-burned faces, the short beards, the grins full of hatred on their lips.

The Baussant banner dipped twice.

The levers of the war machines were freed and their deadly charges launched.

The seconds that followed were apocalyptic.

The explosion of the atomic grenades in the serried ranks of the Mamelukes wrought unbelievable havoc. Shreds of torn flesh flew far and wide. All the way to the city walls, a glaring light blinded the Saracens. Then immense clouds of dust boiled into the sky marking the brilliance of the sun. Some even thought that the luminary, reached by this dreadful explosion, had been extinguished.

Then the thundering sound waves rumbled and reverberated for a long time between the ramparts and the hill, like the beating of a million kettledrums.

When the Crusaders uncovered their faces hidden by their shields, they viewed an appalling sight. More than half of the enemy forces had disappeared. Below them, the plain was covered with pustular craters. The men and horses that had been some distance away were burned alive by the waves of heat. One could see, far off, the flash of white teeth in the blackened jumble of charred flesh.

The few survivors, shocked by this cataclysm as sudden as unforeseeable, remained prostrate on the ground. Some bushes still smoldered, giving off a dense smoke that spread close to the earth as though to conceal this frightful sight. In the distance, riderless horses galloped aimlessly. At last, a silence like death reigned.

The Crusaders, themselves, did not venture to breath a word, almost believing that they dreamed. Some crossed themselves, fearing that the end of the world had come.

Only William, a cruel smile on his lips, dared to contemplate the effects of the infernal lightning that he had unchained. All had happened as Baphomet had said and henceforth, with such weapons, who could hold out against him?

The empire of the world was his.

He had only one decision to make: did he want to reign over Europe or over Asia . . . ?

For some time, he meditated in silence, then, when he saw

that the fires, lacking fuel, were burning out and that the
smoke was thinning, he drew his sword and made a sign for
all the echelons of his forces to advance toward the city of
Jaffa.

With the Templars leading, the Crusaders descended the
slopes of the hill. There, they discovered some who still survived. But the shock sustained had been too terrible: all surrendered, begging the Christians to spare them.

Then the knights reached the points of impact. They
skirted the still-smoking craters and came upon the heaps of
dead bodies. Men and horses were entangled in an inextrica-
ble fashion, the blasted bodies giving off a nauseous odor.

Bones stabbed through the tatters of shriveled skin and it
was impossible to recognize the Sultan in such a charnel
house. Nevertheless, Bibars was vanquished. There was no
longer anyone to oppose the victorious Crusaders.

The Grand Master of the Hospital and the Commanders of
the troops contemplated this spectacle, horror-stricken. Never
had they imagined that the lightning of the Templars could
possess such power and they almost regretted having been ac-
complices in this massacre.

Before they reached the foot of the walls, the troops took
numerous prisoners who did not even consider defending
themselves. They would presently swell the number of their
fellow countrymen entombed on the hill.

In the city itself, the explosions had caused no serious
damage. Some roofs had given way, a few fires had started,
all in all nothing serious. Also, when the defenders had somewhat recovered their spirits, they found that the troops stationed in the open had disappeared, noting, on the other
hand, that the walls had played their part in protecting those
who were behind its battlements.

The leading Saracens of Jaffa consulted together and decided to pursue the action, believing that they were invulnerable behind the thick ramparts. They did not understand
what had happened but trusted that the cataclysm would not
be repeated or, at least, that it would be diminished by the
fortification of the city.

Unfortunately for them, William had foreseen this eventuality. A commander of the Temple was aboard one of the
vessels that had come from Acre. He had mangonels at his
disposal and some of the atomic grenades.

When the first projectile dropped near the mosque, an appalling panic was triggered. The bravest could not hold out against such a trial. All took refuge in the vaulted halls, the cellars and underground passages. So that, when the first Crusaders reached the base of the walls, they were able to set up their ladders without encountering the slightest opposition.

Shortly afterward, the gates were broken open with blows from battering rams and the Christian forces swarmed into Jaffa.

Foot soldiers and knights spread through the narrow streets, massacring without pity all those encountered. At last, after years of defeats, they could satisfy the accumulated hatred, avenging their brothers who had given their lives at Arsuf, Pilgrim Castle and Antioch. There was such carnage that blood ran in the gutters like torrential rain. Quickly, many soldiers turned to pillage, entering the houses and appropriating all objects of value, howling:

"Death! Death to all who live here!
Men and women, all shall perish
Who will not part with what they cherish. . . ."

Some Mamelukes, entrenched in their towers and in the barbican held out for a short time but their courage failed them: the steel-clad knights were not to be vanquished in single combat. Demoralized by the deadly fire from the skies, the last defenders of Jaffa hastened to surrender.

Shortly, Templars and Hospitalers reached the harbor. They severed the heavy chain that barred entrance to it and the Christian fleet was made fast at the quay. There were swift Byzantine dromonds, vessels with oars and with sails, galleys with rowers made up of Saracen slaves, and cargo vessels for transporting horses. In all, counting the five ships captured in the port, from which the Christian galley slaves were immediately rescued, William had a veritable squadron of thirty vessels.

When night fell on the city, stillness reigned.

For a very long time, the Crusaders had not won such an overwhelming victory. Bibars the Sultan, so dreaded and so evil, was dead. His army was in flight, dead or captured. Henceforth, no one could prevent the reconquest of the Holy

Land. Which is to say that joy reigned among the rough Christian warriors!

As might be supposed, the three Tholon brothers celebrated the occasion, each in his own way.

Garin, the Templar, attended the evening service held in the open air, at which the Grand Masters officiated, then rejoined Guiot and Clement in the snug little house where they had chosen to be quartered.

A gross, terror-stricken shopkeeper had installed them in his best room, on sumptuous carpets. Leaning on their elbows, they shamelessly devoured the extravagant feast served by their host and his three wives.

"God damn!" thundered Red-Beard. "Oh! Sorry, Garin! I haven't yet come to. When that some-kind-or-other thunder began to boom, I thought for sure the sky was falling on my head. Yes, I did. I didn't know where I was at. I said a dozen *Our Fathers* before lifting my nose out of the dirt."

"You bet!" agreed his brother Clement. "I went all of a sweat, not a dry hair—I swear it. Worst of all were the flashes of lightning, everything went white. I couldn't see a thing! Only, afterward, I celebrated. There was one of these damned Saracens on his hands and knees! He ended up as a hunk of spoiled meat on my shield. . . . You know something about all this, Garin?"

"You heard the words of the Grand Master as well as I," replied the Templar. "The Archangel Gabriel promised to launch his lightning on the unbelievers: he kept his word. God be praised!"

"Maybe so," assented Red-Beard dubiously. "Only, don't forget the gray balls that were thrown out by the mangonels. I'm pretty sure they did most of this work."

"Why not?" Garin answered stiffly. "Do you forget miracles, you man of little faith? The manna in the desert, the increase of the loaves and fishes, the walking on the water? Don't you suppose the Archangel could have entrusted these spheres to our Grand Master so that he could drive the infidels from the Holy Land?"

"What a wonderful thing it is to be a scholar," replied the scythe-swinger. "You're probably right. . . . All the same, our Lord could have given us His lightning a little sooner. That would have saved more than one brave lad."

"My brothers! The ways of the Lord are unfathomable."

"There again you're right. Me, I'm only trying to understand. The main thing is that we're all here, comfortably lodged. Well, well! Take a peek at this," chuckled Guiot. "This afternoon I picked up a few trifles. . . ."

On these words, he began removing a veritable pirate's treasure from his bag: pieces of gold, collars of precious stones, silver cups and dishes of the same metal.

"Me, too!" Clement was not about to be outdone. "Things just stuck to my paws. Between the two of us, if we get back to Auxerre someday, we can make ourselves the present of a fine farm."

"Vandals!" roared the Templar. "What is come by dishonestly is never enjoyed. What an example you are setting for these wretches!"

"Is that so? You know they weren't ashamed to do the same at Antioch and everywhere else," the two brothers protested in chorus.

"You think that a valid excuse? Of course, if these belonged to the unfortunates killed in the battle, it would be difficult to locate their heirs, so I will shut my eyes to it this time. On the condition, you understand, that you give one-tenth to God. . . ."

Whereupon, he extended his sack with a haughty gesture. Guiot and Clement glanced at each other and then, regretfully, divided their spoils of war with the Templar.

"This is well done!" grunted the latter. "You may be sure that we will make better use of this treasure than you. I shall go straight and give this to its rightful owner. And take care to remember alms for the poor."

With these words he wrapped himself in his white mantle and left with great dignity, followed by the obsequious bowing and scraping Saracen, only too happy to find himself protected by his distinguished guests.

The other Tholon brothers consoled themselves for their misfortune by gorging themselves with pastries and loukoums, greatly regretting the fact that the religion of the pagans did not permit them the use of strong drink. After that, they began to make free with the servant girls but, fortunately for them, fatigue came to their aid, the valiant warriors quickly falling into the deep sleep of the just. . . .

Chapter III

William of Beaujeu, himself, had more important things to do. The Grand Masters and the Commanders had installed themselves in the governor's palace, the fortified dwelling where the last defenders of Jaffa had put up a desperate struggle. The squires had effaced all vestiges of the combat, covering the bloodstains with rich carpets, hiding the walls with tapestries. Torches flared brightly in the secluded room to which the Grand Master had retired, still wearing his armor and his white mantle. The coffers containing the precious grenades, as well as the effigies of Baphomet, had been stacked along the walls.

William was in a good humor and, for the first time in years, his faithful servant knights, Marc and Erard, heard him murmuring Guiot of Provins' verses praising the merits of the Order:

"The Templars men of experience and integrity are;
 To them knights betake themselves from afar,
 Knights who have enjoyed the age nearly wasted,
 Who have owned, who have seen, and who have
   tasted.
 With estates and worldly goods they are done
 For there all belongs but to the Highest One.
 This is the Order of the Cross and of high chivalry,
 With great honor in Syria for many a hard-fought
   victory."

But he quickly resumed his habitual austerity and directed, "Erard, my Brother, this day will live forever in the annals of Christianity. Nevertheless, do not at any time forget our

42

motto and render homage to whom it is due. It is fitting to honor Baphomet, thanks to whom we have won this memorable victory. . . ."

At once the knight seized a filigreed key held out to him by the Grand Master, and opened a coffer ornamented with allegorical motifs, with, in their center, a heart radiating rays of light.

Inside, on a black velvet cushion, was a statue which resembled to an astonishing degree the being who still lay at the bottom of the pool in the Grand-Orient Forest.

Assisted by Marc, the Grand Master took it out and respectfully placed it on a side table surrounded by incense burners emitting a pungent smoke.

William knelt before the image and, after crossing himself, placed his hands on the short horns to put the device into operation. Almost at once, the eyes of the manikin Baphomet gave off a glow like live coals and a deep voice rang out:

"Speak, my Brother, I am listening. All has gone according to your hopes?"

"Yes, indeed, Lord Baphomet, thanks be to you: the powerful weapons that you entrusted to me have destroyed the hosts of the Saracens. Bibars is no more. Never was victory more complete!"

"Did you have doubt of it?"

"Not for an instant. Nevertheless, I swear that the outcome surpassed my wildest expectations."

"Do not believe it within my power to assist you to an absolute supremacy. The number of my weapons is limited and, to assure their wisest use, they must be launched only at troops in battle formation. Never squander them, therefore, on minor skirmishes. You know I have designs of wide intent. . . ."

"I am not forgetting that, Lord Baphomet, and I shall act according to your orders. Now the Hospitalers cannot choose but to obey me."

"That is well, brother. Do not linger in Jaffa: you must profit to the maximum from the fear provoked by this magic weapon. Follow my plan to the letter and all will turn out for the best. I have made a strategic analysis of the situation with the aid of my computer: a few years hence you should possess the most far-flung empire ever ruled by a single man."

"Thanks to you, Lord Baphomet, thanks to you I shall never forget that."

On these words, the statue became inactive.

With a gesture, William ordered his knights to replace it in its container, out of the view of prying eyes; then he had them call William of Tyre, his historian. For two hours, the Grand Master dictated for the benefit of posterity, recounting the events that marked that memorable day. At midnight, he had himself undressed and slept straight through till dawn.

The next morning he awoke refreshed and in high spirits. After attending mass, he ate with a hearty appetite and then prepared to receive the high dignitaries convoked the night before.

The Grand Master of the Hospitalers arrived an easy first. The rings under his eyes gave evidence that the Chapter of his Order had stayed up the whole night to discuss the disquieting problem posed by the surpassing power of their rivals.

However, the Hospitalers seemed affable, chatting of one thing and another, particularly of building churches in the newly delivered city. He obtained without difficulty the office of Patriarch of Jaffa for a Hospitaler, which greatly surprised him. John of Villiers, a diplomat to the bone, never accepted anything at face value.

Otto of Granson and John of Grailly finally put in an appearance: their rheumy eyes and thick tongues giving evidence of a night of plentiful libations.

With no preliminaries, William went to the heart of his subject.

"Brothers, Hospitalers, noble lords, you have seen proof that I am not a fabricator. The lightning launched through my good offices has rid us of the evil Bibars forever, and few pagan sultans have had such an escort for their entrance into the realm of Satan."

"Indeed, that's very true," exclaimed Otto of Granson. "The Prince of Shadows is going to have trouble finding punishments for him."

"Henceforth, no one will dare to confront our forces: the Holy Land will fall into our hands without a blow being struck. Jerusalem will again be a Christian city. . . . King Charles will soon arrive by sea to take his place on the throne. All counts and barons will recover their former castellanies. The convents, houses and fortresses of our two Orders shall revert to their former owners. It must be our care to restore all the castles that have been to a large extent demolished, even to the Krak of Moab near the Asphalt Lake, including that of Aila on the Red Sea. However, I forbid the annexing of any lands other than those granted to the Kingdom of Jerusalem by the pact of Jaffa. Can I count on your concurrence, good gentlemen?"

"Certainly," the Grand Master of the Hospitalers assured him. "Justice itself speaks with your lips, my brother. However, one thing distresses me: you speak as though the Templars would not participate in supreme joy—the occupation of Bethlehem, of Holy Jerusalem! Surely, am I mistaken . . . ?"

"You are not gentle brother. I would certainly give years of my life to know the Dead Sea, the Holy Temple, the Sacred Grotto, the Garden of Olives. Alas! The Archangel Gabriel has visited me again and has commanded me to leave the highest happiness to you."

"What? Would the Templars leave us alone to reconquer the Holy Land?"

"Unfortunately—yes, my dear Brother. . . . Besides, who is in a position to resist the valiant knights of the Hospital, with warriors of France and England at their side?"

"This is a greatly astounding thing. You will leave us some of your weapons at least?"

"Why should I do that, my friend? It will be enough if you take with you some of the mangonels and coffers filled with gray stones. Everyone will suppose that you, too, have the lightning of our Lord at your disposal and no one will dare to resist you."

"That is a point of view that I in no way share."

"John of Villiers, are you afraid of the infidels?"

"Certainly not! I only find the affair somewhat risky considering our total strength. What do you think of it, John of Grailly?"

The French knight pulled at his beard thoughtfully, then declared:

"By my faith, I agree with William. These dogs have been so soundly thrashed that they will not meddle with us soon again. With the reinforcement which we are going to receive, we will have no trouble in reoccupying the Holy Land. However, I would like to know the motives that incite the Templars to abandon us on such an easy path. . . ."

"That is only fair! Know then that the Archangel, from a cloud of light, commanded me with these words: "You have accomplished the first part of the task which has been allotted you. Now the Hospitalers and the Christian knights are going to achieve the liberation of the Holy Land. It remains for you to carry the True Faith to the inhabitants of the vast countries that extend behind the Kingdom of Jerusalem. Countless human beings, at this moment, are under the yoke of the Mongols. You must free them and instruct them. The Templars, therefore, will embark aboard the vessels come to Jaffa, and sail to the city of Alexandretta, where they will land. From there, across the Princedom of Antioch and the country of Edessa, they will enter the Mongol Khanate of Persia, where Abaka, son of Hulagu, reigns. When the armies of that savage Khan have been destroyed, I command you to attack the Khanate of Kaidon, which extends southward from Lake Baikal. Despite the terrible fire that you possess, you will fight hard battles. Then you must reduce the Emperor Kubla, who oppresses the empire of Cathay, to unconditional surrender. This done, when the True Faith is known from the shores of Syria to those of Cathay, you can at last enjoy a well-earned rest, but make no stop along the way for the Divine wrath will come down on you. . . .' These are the commands of the Archangel. I must obey him, and that is why the Templars are going to leave you, setting out to accomplish the mission which God has entrusted to them."

"This is an astonishing revelation, my Brother!" cried the Grand Master of the Hospitalers. "I am completely dumbfounded by it. . . . What, you dream of conquering that immense empire with such feeble forces?"

"Faith moves mountains! I possess weapons of a power unknown until now. The Mongol Khans cannot protect themselves from heaven's lightning entrusted to me, and they know the fate of Bibars. Further, word of our brilliant success will spread throughout the Christian realms. All the knights will outdo each other for the honor of joining our host."

"I already claim for myself, and for my knights, the favor of fighting at your side," John of Grailly, all fervor, enthused loudly. "Death to all unbelievers; the Truth Faith will triumph."

"I accept your offer gratefully," the Grand Master of the

Templars assured him. "We shall assuredly have formidable encounters with small groups of enemy partisans. In such cases, there must be no squandering of the heavenly lightning. Lances and swords will still have a role to play. . . ."

"Such vast designs frighten me," resumed John of Villiers. "Pacification of the Holy Land with only the troops left to me will certainly not be easy. So you will understand why my Brothers cannot join with yours. I would, however, like to be kept informed as to the progress of the operations. Will you allow our Marshal, Matthew of Clermont, to travel with you?"

"Assuredly: thus you will have a faithful report on the progression of our army. But it would be well to have matters clearly defined: the Hospitalers will be observers only and must not, under any circumstances, interfere in my affairs."

"This is as I would have it." The Grand Master of the Hospitalers assumed an offended air. "It goes without saying, on my side, that I shall direct the forces operating in the Holy Land and that our former fortified places shall revert to us in full right."

"A promised thing is a thing due! I shall not go back on the word I have given. Take note, nevertheless, that the Hospitalers must yield to the temporal authorities that which falls within their jurisdiction. The King of Jerusalem, the Prince of Antioch, the Prince of Tripoli must recover all the prerogatives they have enjoyed."

"I give my word."

"Under these conditions, good gentlemen, we are in agreement. The first thing in the morning, the Templars will sail aboard the fleet for the Princedom of Antioch. We must strike while the advantage is ours. We wager our messengers will soon bring you great news! My Brothers, noble sires, may God keep you in His Holy care. . . ."

The high dignitaries crossed themselves, then—bowing to William of Beaujeu—they withdrew to their quarters.

The next day, just at dawn, horns and drums aroused the Crusaders who made for the port in an orderly way. Once again, all showed astonishment, for they had expected to pursue the campaign on land, to attack Jerusalem. Rumors were rife and the ordinary soldiers, pretending to be well-informed, claimed that William of Beaujeu, wanting to erase the disaster of the Fifth Crusade, was going to launch an assault on

Damietta. The shame of the capture of Louis IX at Mansûra would thus be forgotten.

This illusion did not last long. Once the ships, galleys and dromonds were on the open sea, the fleet headed toward the north. . . .

During the crossing, William spent all his time in pondering the manner in which he would pursue the vast operation: the most ambitious ever undertaken by Crusaders.

He knew the strength of the Mongols. His predecessors and he, himself, had had contacts with them during that time when Saracens considered French and Mongols equally dangerous adversaries. Louis IX, himself, had hoped to form an alliance with them so as to attack the Sultan of Egypt on two fronts. Unfortunately, the synchronization of the two operations was difficult to achieve, so the King of France, having launched the assault alone, suffered a crushing defeat. Bibars himself was of Mongol origin. In 1244 his troops had struck a shattering blow at the Templars and the Hospitalers; three hundred knights of the Temple had met their death. Yes, the Grand Master knew he was facing valorous adversaries who should not be taken lightly.

William of Beaujeu and his Marshal reached immediate agreement on one point: as long as the forces of the Crusaders kept a tight formation the enemy could do nothing against it. Any large concentration of Mongol forces would be wiped out by Baphomet's weapons. On the other hand, the harassment by Abaka's swift and extremely mobile horsemen would be an ever-present danger, particularly to their lines of communication. These, in any case, risked stretching to the breaking point as the army advanced. Thus it would be necessary, come what might, to live off the land, to seize cities—if possible—intact by delivering a smashing attack. And, concerning this, it was vital to assure rapid liaison between different branches of the army as well as with the reinforcements which would be making their way from the Mediterranean ports.

William and his faithful Peter of Sevry came naturally in this way to speak of the effigies of Baphomet which could receive messages, the words of that strange creature, from the distant pool near Troyes.

"I sincerely believe that our Order is going to conquer a vast empire, thanks to the weapons given us by Baphomet," the Grand Master declared. "There is every reason to be satisfied: the meteor-borne traveler finally decided to reward us otherwise than with ingots of gold. Our riches have contributed to the establishment in all the realms of Christiandom those flourishing Templaries which have allowed us to acquire a considerable influence. However, I ask myself the same question over and over: are we perhaps the dupes of he who seems to be at our mercy? What would happen if we decided to give him no more food?"

"The same thought has occurred to me. I have wondered again and again why this stranger, exiled so far from his own kind, elects to aid us so benevolently for mean subsidies of food. . . ."

"According to tradition handed down from that time when the venerable founder of our Order encountered Baphomet for the first time, the meteor which brought him across the fathomless reaches of space had been seriously damaged, the devices which allowed him to manufacture his food destroyed. Our donation let him survive to attempt the repairs of his ship: no doubt about that."

"Yes, but what will happen if his fellow-countrymen receive his messages? We will be swamped with them! No possibility of resisting weapons as terrifying as theirs. . . ."

"Undoubtedly, my worthy Peter: I have often dreamed of it. We are—alas!—as defenseless against him as a child against a knight in armor. If we should cease our ministrations, his vengeance would be terrible!"

"We should at least attempt some remedy. It is impossible to live thus at the mercy of a creature so completely a stranger to us. . . ."

"You are right: we must, at any cost, discover the secrets of his alchemy so that we, ourselves, can make the engines whose mysteries are hidden from us. I have already dropped a hint to our chaplain. Did you know that Brother Joubert has extensive knowledge of alchemy? I will have him called in."

Some minutes later the Templar entered the cabin. He was a small, dark man who had never acquired the dignity of knighthood for his awkwardness with weapons was proverbial. But, in compensation, his lucid and searching mind made him a wise counselor, whose advice William often sought.

"Brother Joubert, I have sent for you so that you may practice an exercise for me that will demand all your intelligence."

"Speak, venerable master, I am yours to command."

"Like us, you are initiated in our mysteries and you know of the existence of the effigies called Baphomet. You cannot be ignorant of the fact that they enable us to hold converse with the true Baphomet over considerable distances. How do you explain this strange facility?"

The chaplain meditated a moment before replying.

"I have examined these statues very attentively. Their carapace conceals a delicate and subtle installation. It has been impossible to study them in detail because you have never permitted me to push my investigations further. Nevertheless, I have made some interesting discoveries. . . ."

"Speak on, my friend. You will be generously rewarded if one day you can explain how these mysterious effigies operate."

"Very well. The words of Baphomet reach us without hindrance through the air: if the statue is placed inside a cupboard, the words grow a little fainter, to cease completely once the helmet is hermetically sealed. Steel, therefore, is an impassable barrier for the messages which we receive from the Grand-Orient Forest."

"Interesting," approved the Marshal. "But where does that lead us?"

"For the time being, nowhere. Take note, however, that a huge metal wall set up around the pond would prevent Baphomet from talking with anyone."

"And consequently with his compatriots," cried the Grand Master. "You see? Already one fascinating discovery. Is that all?"

"Nay! I have also noted that when a sword is placed above the machines contained in the interior of the Baphomet-image shell, one hears the words emitted much more clearly. I have concluded that the metal concentrates the diffuse messages coming to us through the air."

"More than interesting, Brother Joubert! Proceed, I conjure you. . . ."

"Further, it is apparent to me that the force which powers the functioning of the device comes from a very heavy box, cased in lead. It contains, most surely, a substance unknown to us. To study it, I would have to be able to examine it more closely."

"You are authorized to do so: we must, at any cost, know the magic charms utilized and try to duplicate this artful engine."

"I will have a Turcopole, highly skilled in copper metallurgy, make a faithful replica of all the complex elements worked from that metal that are in the effigy. If I can pierce the secret of the box, I will undertake to produce a similar machine, all the more since that is what you wish. However, this concerns an extremely hermetic alchemy."

"You are well-versed in the arcana of that science, are you not?"

"That is true. I learned a great deal on this subject in the city of Montpellier. It was possible for me to discuss it at length with Arnaud of Villeneuve and the master, Albert Magnus. All of them think that metals are constituted from one unique and fundamental matter called sperm metal. With that is would be possible to reproduce all the different metallic structures. . . ."

"In a way, the philosopher's stone?"

"Exactly. However, their realizations are not absolutely convincing. On the contrary, during my stay in Syria, I chanced to encounter a Saracen apothecary and a story he told greatly excited me. . . ."

"Don't stop there! We hang on your words."

"Well, according to him, a meteor fell not far from Alexandretta. Its remains, deeply buried in the sands, were difficult to get at. After harsh and painful laboring, slaves finally brought to light a kind of ship, all of metal, terribly damaged by the shock and by heat."

"Does this have to do with compatriots of Baphomet?" exclaimed the Grand Master.

"There is a strong possibility of that. It is unfortunate that, unlike him, their bodies were altered beyond recognition. Everyone decided that this was an engine of the devil and the derelict was abandoned. However, this learned Arab continued the excavating and discovered a magic box which possessed the power to transmute objects placed inside it. I am convinced that this Arab understood very well the importance of this find and that he hid the strange machine with great care. . . ."

"Why didn't you seek a way to lay your hands on it?"

"Well, simply because the apothecary affirmed that the device had quickly lost its powers. But, on reflection, I am persuaded that it would now be possible to make it function again by connecting it to the box which makes the effigies of our Baphomet speak."

"Marvelous! Brother Joubert, I congratulate you: you are promised the highest positions in our Holy Order. What is the name of this Saracen?"

"Djaffar. . . ."

"If I understood rightly," the chaplain continued with a modest air, "all our problems will be solved with this machine because it will be possible to manufacture the unknown metals we lack. Thus, we will have boxes producing the power necessary for speaking over distances and even—who knows?—the means for making those spheres which contain the lightning in their bosoms. . . ."

"I must have this philosopher's casket," howled William of Beaujeu. "With it to solve all our problems, we will be free at last!"

"Brother Joubert's discourse certainly was most interesting," interjected the Templar Marshal. "Still, these are only words. There is no proof this Arab was not simply boasting. I know them: these clods always claim to be well-versed in hermetic arcana; nevertheless, Bibars' treasure most certainly never came from their crucibles. . . ."

Peter of Sevry, in fact, had always been jealous of the chaplain and claimed that a good sword prevailed over all the science in the world, which assumption had been proven by recent events to be utterly false. He wanted to oust a dangerous competitor and looked disapprovingly on so much importance being given Brother Joubert.

The Grand Master was well-aware of these battles for precedence and he curtly put the Marshal in his place.

"I am in no way of that opinion: Brother Joubert never speaks without weighing his words. This machine certainly exists and therefore I order that the course for Alexandretta be kept. There, we must lay hands on this Djaffar, and make him talk to find out where he has secreted this treasure. I hold you personally responsible for it, Peter of Sevry. We must also give our chaplain every facility that will enable him to carry on his fascinating labors. Now, my Brothers, I have need for meditation. Good night, and may the Lord bless you and keep you. . . ."

Alone, William of Beaujeu leaned his elbows on the casement of the cabin which he occupied on the poopdeck of the vessel. It was night and countless stars glimmered in the sky.

Thoughtfully, the Grand Master reviewed what Baphomet had told him. If what he said were true innumerable peoples throughout the heavens inhabited worlds similar to Earth. And the latter was only a large ball that revolved around the sun . . . a strange concept contradicting the ideas held up to that time. Most people believed, actually, that their world was flat, edged with oceans, prevailing coasts of the unfathomable deep. On the contrary, if the Earth were spherical, it should be possible to sail to the east or the west and again reach the point of departure! The empire of Cathay, situated at the end of the known world, would prove to be, in fact, halfway to France. An hypothesis easy enough to verify when that empire was his: he must equip vessels and send them across the Cathay Sea in an effort to reach France or Portugal. All these things passed understanding. . . . If they were true, mankind made up only one human race among countless others. What was an Earthly empire in comparison with the countless others existing in space? What strange creatures made up immense stellar confederations? What was their goal? Was an invasion imminent? To face such, arms as powerful as those of these creatures of the dark were needed, and craft able to navigate among the stars.

A conclusion forced itself upon him: the Templars had a sacred duty to humanity, since they alone held these formidable secrets. In the future, therefore, it was essential that scientific research of consequence be undertaken by savants of all nationalities. Strict orders must be given to spare their lives in all occupied countries and, in particular, those in the empire of Cathay who, according to many reports were considerably advanced in many fields

One man would be especially valuable in the carrying out of this mission: a Venetian named Marco Polo who had lived since 1271 in the Cathay empire. His knowledge of the people of that locality and of their civilization would be extremely useful in establishing that future university where scholars of all nationalities would be assembled under the aegis of the Templars. For the present, all depended on Brother

Joubert. That monk possessed remarkable intelligence and an alert perception. He never spoke imprudently, contrary to what Sevry thought. If he had called attention to the existence of this casket with marvelous powers of transmutation, there was no question of its reality; perhaps he had even seen it in operation. . . .

William felt weary: few men before him had borne such a crushing responsibility. If he succeeded in his task, the people of the Earth would be united and leave off fighting among themselves. The scholars of all nations would work together for their well-being and for their protection against possible incursions of beings from other worlds.

An exciting prospect. . . . However, no one would believe that the Grand Master of the Templars acted thus but for the well-being of his fellowmen and the glory of his Lord.

William knelt at the prie-dieu and murmured:

"Not us, Master, not us, but to the greater glory of Your name. . . ." Then he added: "And peace on Earth to men of good will. . . ."

Chapter IV

The fleet reached port without suffering any loss. A few fugitive enemy galleys followed at safe distances. Obviously, news of the victory won by the Templars had already reached the Mamelukes occupying the Princedom of Antioch. The stupefying power of the new weapon unveiled at Jaffa made the sultans and the Mongol Khans extremely cautious: each wondered who would be the target for the next attack.

The Crusaders were greatly surprised when they noticed that the Grand Master had secretly changed his plans: instead of casting anchor off Alexandretta, as announced, the invading forces landed at the mouth of the Orontes in the small harbor of Saint-Simeon.

William had chosen to proceed in this manner precisely because he wanted to spare Alexandretta, where the famous Djaffar must be located. It was likely that the arrival of the Templars' fleet would have panicked the inhabitants who would have fled, carrying their treasures with them. Then it would have been impossible to ferret out the precious casket.

This was a strange repetition of the past: here it was—long ago—that a Genoese fleet, bringing reinforcements to the Commanders of the First Crusade, had dropped anchor.

While the supplies were being unloaded, the Grand Master formed an elite corps equipped with numerous spare horses, slings and a few atomic grenades. His Seneschal, second in command of the expedition, took charge of this detachment and immediately set out for Alexandretta, without even waiting for the main body of the army to assemble.

The knights headed north, riding night and day. Among them were Brother Joubert and the Tholon brothers who, as usual, understood little of what was happening.

Thus, they reached the outer fortifications quite unexpected. A grenade blew down the main gate and the Templars charged into the city, surprising all the inhabitants. No one had time to flee, so sudden was the attack. However, the warriors found baggage packed and camels loaded; in a few hours many would have been miles away.

At once, patrols were sent into all the streets in search of Djaffar, each having a Turcopole translator and a detailed description of the man they were trying to find. Naturally, the soldiers would have preferred to enjoy a well-earned rest after their wild ride and did not hide that fact.

"God damn!" Guiot-the-Red swore. "What a bitch of a life! My arse is raw after that crazy ride. The Grand Master must be mad for this Djabar. . . ."

"Djaffar," his Templar brother corrected. "Most assuredly, this unbeliever possesses some important secret, since he must be taken alive."

"I wonder what it is he knows. Perhaps it's something to do with the lightning that demolished Bibars," Clement threw in.

"I would be astounded," answered Garin, "if the infidels possessed that fearful secret, else they would have used it against us."

At that moment, the patrol of which the three brothers were a part came to a halt at the mouth of a dark and narrow alley.

"Well, we're here," said Red-Beard. "Where do we begin?"

"First, we are going to search the houses on the right. Squires, guard each end of the passageway and see that no one escapes. You, Arsouf, follow us."

The Turcopole placed himself behind the Templar, who knocked at the first door. After a few seconds' wait, a frightened Saracen face peeked out. The interpreter questioned him, asking him if he knew where a celebrated seer named Djaffar lived, translating both questions and answers, as needed.

The man under questioning was visibly shaking, but was not a willing source of information.

"The name sounded somewhat familiar. He had heard of a magus who resembled the description. No, he did not know where he lived. And he, only a modest craftsman, did not rub elbows with the great ones of this world."

At last Garin lost patience, half drawing his sword from its scabbard; this stimulated the Saracen's memory a little.

"My neighbor, I am quite sure, will be able to answer your questions, my noble lords," he managed to say. "He belonged to the Emir's entourage—may Allah curse that coward who, himself, put an end to his days—and this Ghazi knows all the learned men of the city."

Thereupon, the three brothers went to the door of the indicated house. This time a servant came to admit them and conduct them to his master, in a room strewn with opulent carpets. That learned man was studying Koranic scrolls and neither showed fear nor fawned on the Christians.

To their first question he readily answered that he indeed knew Djaffar very well, a widely respected seer, who possessed miraculous medicines effective against a host of maladies. He lived close by, just at the end of the alley.

Garin thanked him politely and the Tholons made for the indicated house. The door-knocker, a copper snake biting its tail, surprised them a little, but not as much as the inside of the house. Djaffar's lair, a large cell with whitewashed walls, contained countless stuffed animals, retorts, pallets, red-hot furnaces under vessels whose boiling contents filled the air with loathsome vapors.

"A sorcerer, without a doubt," grunted Guiot, wrinkling his nose in disgust.

Bent over a ceramic container, a man still young but with a back bent by years of study and research, was vigorously stirring a greenish mixture. He did not pause when the Frankish warriors came in, but readily confessed that he was truly Djaffar. The admission caused expansive smiles to alter the faces of the three brothers. Garin asked him then if he still had the casket discovered in the desert sands. The Saracen nodded, making a sign to an assistant to watch his preparation while he moved to a coffer, ornate with allegorical designs. He pressed the central pattern—a salamander belching flames—and the cover slowly hinged upward, revealing a simple parallelepiped of silvery white metal.

"This is the marvel from the heavens," the sage declared tersely. "Unfortunately, it lost all its magic powers, so I give it to you without regret."

The Templar at once had the precious object removed by his squire, then bade the seer follow him, for the Grand Master was doing him the honor of holding converse with him. The Arab did not appear to feel especially honored by this invitation, but did not protest either, asking only that he be allowed to give instructions to his assistant for concluding the experiment still in progress. Garin willingly granted his request, but followed him closely, nevertheless, ready to prevent any rash action he might attempt.

That same evening, escorted by a part of the fleet, William of Beaujeu dropped anchor off Alexandretta, so easily occupied by the flash attack. As soon as he set foot on land, he inquired about the search and showed the greatest satisfaction upon hearing its results and learning that Djaffar, and his precious casket as well, had been found. He immediately set out for the Emir's palace, where the captive had already been taken.

The brothers Tholon were awaiting the Grand Master, all proud to have accomplished their mission so well. And William of Beaujeu praised them highly. To reward them, he declared that the brothers would henceforth belong to his House. Whenever there was a delicate mission to be accomplished, he would call on them.

This said, he dismissed them and proceeded with his interrogation of Djaffar. Brother Joubert was present and acted as interpreter whenever a word failed his leader.

"You are truly the seer Djaffar?"

"That is correct, venerable master."

"Then tell me—concealing nothing—the circumstances of your discovery of this casket and how you made use of its magic powers."

"It's rather an old story now. Some five years ago, as I was studying the constellations of the Zodiac, I saw a fiery trail in the sky. It seemed to me that it came down onto the desert, not far from here. The next day, I inquired of the guards as to the location of its impact and they led me some distance from the city, toward the west."

"Therefore, you were the first to reach the spot?"

"No, the soldiers of the guard had already tried to approach it, but the sands were so hot that they had been unable to examine it."

"This is not the way I remember it," interrupted the chaplain. "At the time I met you, you told me that you had not gone to the place until later. . . ."

"There must be some slight confusion in your recollections, my noble friend: I went to the spot several times and the excavations were carried out under my supervision, by the Emir's order."

"This is unimportant," William cut him off impatiently. "Tell me rather what you observed."

"Well, as soon as the heat had subsided, the slaves started freeing this object fallen from the sky. I recall that they had to be whipped because they thought it was a thing of the devil; I was expecting to find a stone rich in iron such as sometimes falls from the sky. Hence, I was not surprised to see a rust-colored surface when the first layers of sand were removed. But as the excavation progressed, I discovered that I was wrong: the object was, in fact, a long cylinder ending in a conical cap, which shape could in no way be the result of change."

"How did you get inside?"

"I am coming to that. Under the shock, this ship—and it was truly a vehicle that came down from the sky—was too near its pointed end. I had to wait a good hour before I was able to enter. Deleterious fumes issued from it and the interior was still very hot.

"The front part of the ship contained nothing any longer identifiable. All its contents had been flattened like a wafer. However, I did observe traces of torn flesh, undoubtedly the remains of the machine's pilot. In the rear section, the same desolation reigned. The acrid smoke choked me and the torch burned badly; but I did see the remains of living beings. They were stretched out inside long, transparent cylinders. The straps that held them were broken and they had crashed against the wall. Most of the objects in the section, also wrenched from their moorings, were only shapeless magma. On that day, I did not pursue my investigations further, because I was suffocating inside that dark box."

"But you returned again at a later time?" asked the Grand Master.

"Assuredly! Even though my friends attempted to dissuade me, and they were not entirely wrong because, during the month that followed, I suffered from a kind of consumption against which all remedies were ineffective. . . ."

"And that was when you found the casket!" Brother Joubert interrupted with impatience.

"No. That was not until my fourth visit when the debris had been cleared. It was the only mechanism left intact. It had been stowed inside a coffer welded to the floor itself and a white elastic substance had been placed around it for better protection. I put it aside, for its use was in no way evident to me at the time. For an entire week I continued the excavations, making sketches of the least damaged parts found. . . ."

"You still have them?" put in the Grand Master.

"Certainly, at my house. I have copied them carefully on parchment but it has not been possible for me to make sense of them. . . ."

"Tell me more about the casket."

"Well, when my work around and inside the ship was finished, I waited to examine it until I could do so with a clearer head. By then, I was convinced that I was dealing with a craft from out there, from across the immense distances of space, from where the stars burn. Unfortunately, the bodies of the crew began to decompose so rapidly that I was unable to study them. Therefore I abandoned the wreckage, there being nothing more I could learn from it. It was covered over with sand and the Emir pronounced the place anathema. That precaution was hardly necessary, since no one had any desire to go near it. It took many long hours of meditation for me to determine the use of the device inside the casket. Sibylline designs engraved on a metal plate enabled me to do so. The engine was composed of two parts, of a size somewhat larger than a human skull. My first experiment was simply the placing of a piece of amber in the right-hand oven, and then pushing a red button. There was a sort of humming. Soon after, both doors opened by themselves and I was surprised to see a block of amber exactly like the first. My analyses, the evaluation of its weight, everything confirmed it: the machine had produced a most exact duplicate of the original."

"Astonishing! Almost unbelievable," the Grand Master mused. "Can you prove what you are saying?"

"Certainly! After that I performed many operations of the same kind with various substances, natural and manufactured. Sand or diamond, I always obtained the same results which I could repeat as many times as I wished. These products, the fruit of alchemy, are still in my laboratory."

"We shall see them later," said Brother Joubert thoughtfully. "It appears, then, that the action of this engine is not at all like that of the philosopher's stone which transmutes base metals into gold. Its achievement seems more complete, because it contains in its core the true sperm, quintessence of all matter."

"And even living substances, my learned friend! I was able to duplicate a rat. . . ."

"But that is stupendous!" exclaimed the chaplain. "I bitterly regret that I was unable to study it with you. Alas, when I made my secret visit to you, the Mamelukes were looking for me. I had to make my escape and, I must confess, I did not quite believe what you told me. For that I now apologize."

"Is this everything you can tell me?" the Grand Master asked.

"Very nearly all, noble Sire. After that I made use of the machine to manufacture gold coins. That was the best way of hiding my secret, since I never spoke of it to anyone, except my esteemed colleague here. Unfortunately, after a month or so, my magic casket lost all its power. . . . Impossible to make it work again. However, it had enabled me to stack up enough gold coins to buy my house and be free of want for the rest of my life."

"Good!" declared William of Beaujeu. "I thank you for being so open. You shall be rewarded for it: my treasurer will give you a weight of gold equivalent to that of your casket."

"May Allah and the Christian God bestow their blessings on you, most generous sire!"

"It goes without saying that you will not utter a word of all this to anyone else. If, by misfortune, you should betray my trust, I will have your tongue pulled out."

"Never fear: I know where my interest lies and I shall be as silent as the tomb."

"Perfect! My servants will fetch all the duplicates of which you told me. Do not try to hide any. Go now: Brother Garin will accompany you."

Djaffar took his leave, walking backward and bowing deeply.

When they were alone, the Grand Master turned to

Brother Joubert. "Well, what do you think of this, learned chaplain?"

"I am convinced that what he speaks is the truth, master. If you agree, I shall begin at once attempting to repair this miraculous transmuter. Even so, it may take quite some time before I succeed."

"For the moment, it is no pressing matter. You shall have everything you require. Give the list to Brother Garin when he returns. Tell him not to say a word to anyone—him, and his two brothers. You shall have wagons fitted to house your instruments."

"Wherefore? Can I not work here?"

"Certainly not; I want you near me, you and this object with its miraculous hermetic powers. Tomorrow we leave to conquer the Khanate of Abaka and very soon we shall be a great distance from the coast. The liaison with those left behind will be uncertain. There is no need for you to run useless risks."

"True. . . . Such a marvel must not fall into enemy hands. By Jesus Christ, our Lord, I swear that I would destroy it, should we have the misfortune of being vanquished!"

"You understand my wishes perfectly, brother. In turn, I promise you a reward worthy of your merit if you are successful in your endeavor. Leave me now, and bid my Seneschal and my Marshal to come to me. We must plan the disposition of our forces during the long march ahead."

At dawn, the Grand Master and his escort left Alexandretta to join the main body of the army. Immediately the troops got under way, marching upstream along the Orontes, which they soon left, heading eastward toward the Euphrates and the city of Edessa, capital of the former country of the same name.

Antioch was occupied without a battle and supplies reached the Templars regularly. The power of their weapons was known and none cared to face them.

The Hospitalers' observers noted the interest that the Grand Master had shown in a Saracen of Alexandretta. They also remarked that Brother Joubert now had at his disposal a veritable laboratory on wheels which was guarded day and night, and in which he worked like a slave. All these significant facts were duly transmitted to those most concerned.

For his part, John of Villiers sent messages by sea. They announced that Jerusalem was occupied and that the Holy Land was again in the hands of the Crusaders. The news reached William of Beaujeu just as he reached the banks of the Euphrates, after having covered more than two hundred kilometers in twelve days. The weather had been favorable for forced marches: several thunderstorms cooled the air and there was no lack of water.

For this reason he decided to devote a day to thanksgiving, which would enable the foot soldiers to catch their breath.

The army was now at the frontier of the Khanate of Abaka and the Khan would surely attempt to thwart this irresistible advance whose aim could no longer be in doubt: after having recaptured the Holy Land, the Templars wanted to take possession of the Mongol empire.

The Grand Master called his Council into session to determine what route to follow to reach Baghdad, the capital of the Khanate. His Marshal, his Seneschal and several high-ranking officers were present. As for Brother Joubert, he stayed in his wagon, pursuing the work which was proving more exacting than he had anticipated.

"My noble brothers," William began, "I sent for you to discuss our plan of action. We have just crossed a mountainous region where our adversary, the Abaka Khan, could have attempted to halt our advance. He did nothing, and good reason: his armies are massed far from here, in the vicinity of Baghdad. In view of that fact and since we have been joined by reinforcements, I suggest that we send a contingent to occupy the city of Edessa, which will ensure protection of our rear guard. Meanwhile, the main body of our forces will follow the Euphrates, thus being assured of water and provisions. This valley is known to be richly productive and our march should be easy. We shall stop in the city of Siffin, then in Anbara, before reaching the fertile Mesopotamian plain where, in all probability, the Mongol Khan will do battle. What are your thoughts on this matter? Speak, for I shall give them all consideration."

The Marshal, Peter of Sevry, was the first to answer him.

"Venerable master, my brothers, in broad outline I approve the plan of battle just stated. The occupation of Edessa will protect our supply lines from Alexandretta, and our right flank will be covered by the arid Syrian desert. However, one

objection comes to mind: on our left will be the wealthy city
of Mosul which is protected by a strong Mongol garrison.
Should we not fear that these troops will join forces with
those around Baghdad and engage us in battle as we enter the
Mesopotamian plain? I have heard tell of some Venetian
travelers named Polo who crossed this region. They reported
that there are, not far from Mosul, springs from which flows
a black oil used in the manufacture of Greek Fire. Is it not
likely that the Mongol Kahn, knowing that we have a powerful weapon, will attack us by throwing that fire on our
columns before we descend onto the plain? The Al Jazirah
Mountains afford many rocky gorges where it would be easy
to loose catapults and mangonels. What would happen if our
horses panicked and bolted in every direction? That would
certainly be the moment for a massive Mongol attack. . . ."

"I, too, have heard of this inflammable oil," the Grand
Master agreed. "Assuredly it constitutes an important trick
for Abaka but, to ambush our troops, he would have to command the heights that overlook the Euphrates valley. You
were right to call this possibility to my attention: we have
auxiliary Turcopoles who, on their fast, high-mettled steeds
can precede our advance. These horsemen will carefully
scout the hills and report any enemy concentration."

"That seems a wise course of action," the Seneschal said
thoughtfully. "Personally, I am much more afraid of Mongol
attack on our rear guard once we leave the Euphrates valley.
There is little doubt that we shall have water available in sufficient quantity, but nothing should be taken for granted.
Quite often in June the temperature in this region is torrid.
We shall be completely unable to turn back and regain the
coast by way of the Syrian desert and our situation could become critical."

"I have considered such a possibility," asserted William of
Beaujeu, "and I—likewise—decided to follow this fertile valley rather than crossing the mountains to the north to reach
the Caspian Sea. Now we must take Baghdad and, if the enemy puts the torch to it, lay siege to other cities: Selencis,
Kashgar. If worse comes to worst and Abaka destroys all the
cities of Mesopotamia, it will still be possible for us to reach
Basra. It is a port of call for many merchant ships and we
will find abundant provisions available that will allow us to
continue our campaign."

"That is indeed well thought out!" exclaimed the Commander, Thibaut Gaudin. "There is no doubt that we shall make a clean sweep of the infidel armies. I am impatient to see the city of Baghdad; they say that its former caliph possessed a fabulous treasure which the Mongols seized. It is almost certain that we shall find vast riches still there!"

An ascetic and modest-appearing monk came to his feet: the Templar of Tyre and the Grand Master's historian. "I am ashamed to raise my voice in such a learned assembly," he said in a low tone. "In days of yore, a pagan named Alexander—the Great, so-called—conquered these lands at the head of a powerful army. It is said that he reached the faraway banks of the Indus, and then returned to die in Babylon. His empire was then divided among his generals. However, he had vanquished all those who opposed him. Alas! The Macedonians were frightened by such daring and refused to pursue his conquests further. What will our brothers say, once Mesopotamia is ours, if we ask them to push on into the Khanate of Kaidu, then into that of the powerful Kubla Khan, who reigns over Cathay? They all have a family, brothers, in the realm of France. . . . Is it not possible that they, also, will refuse to go any farther?"

"Your fears are ill-founded, brother of Tyre!" the Grand Master exclaimed. "Alexander was only a pagan and his soldiers were not sustained by our faith and the desire to bring back into the fold of the Church those Nestorian Christians who form numerous communities in places as far removed as the cities of Cathay. Christ must be known and adored from the Syrian shores to Cambaluc, where Kubla reigns! You are forgetting the heaven-sent lightning: it will dispatch to hell all infidels who dare oppose us!"

This speech more than achieved its point, and the shouts of all those present more than silenced the fainthearted brother from Tyre. The die was cast: the Templars had committed their forces to the conquest of an empire surpassing that of Alexander the Great. . . .

Everything developed as the Grand Master had predicted. Edessa was occupied without a skirmish: the garrison—weak in numbers—fled as the implacable, steel-clad warriors approached the city.

The army then moved down the Euphrates valley. However, the extreme heat made the journey an ordeal. The

shrunken stream that flowed along the riverbed barely sufficed to quench the thirst of men and horses. On the other
hand, they were able to seize abundant provisions: the harvest had been good and the granaries of the peasants were
filled to overflowing.

Almost all the knights were forced to remove their armor
and wrap themselves in the white mantle with its crimson
cross which dampened the heat of the sun somewhat.

Then the trouble began: there were flash raids on the rear
guard of the long column by Mongol horsemen. The laggards, the sick and the crippled were put to the sword.

Liaison with Alexandretta was no longer certain and the
forces could rely only on themselves.

The Templars cursed "those infidel bastards" but could do
nothing other than continue the southward march. The
progress of the column slowed a little each day, but the Mongol army failed to attack.

Anbara was taken, but it was in flames and the Templars
were unable to rest there as they had hoped. A dense, black
smoke from the barrels of naphtha that had been dumped on
the town choked them and filled their eyes with tears. There
was not one house still standing to offer shelter from the relentless sun.

Dysentery and sunstrokes slowly thinned the ranks of the
army to about two-thirds its original size. In his wagon,
which was as hot as an oven, Brother Joubert had long since
given up his research.

William of Beaujeu and his companions rode silently, their
tongues dry, their eyes burned by the glaring light. The
Grand Master had begun to fear that the brother from Tyre
had spoken only the truth: among the foot soldiers especially
there was much grumbling and mounting protests against this
mad journey.

"Never," they declared, "will Abaka face us in battle. He
will wait until we are completely exhausted and then massacre us. Of what use will the magic fire be, if we are unable
to operate the mangonels, or even to use slings?"

The anger of these unfortunate soldiers was vented freely
on the cumbersome machines which they had to drag along
with them. They swore at the engines, inventing the vilest
names for them but still not daring to abandon them, for
they alone prevented the Mongols from rushing to the attack.

This Calvary lasted two whole months.

There was no news from the Holy Land. The Crusaders felt desperately alone, forsaken, far from any possible assistance.

Then they reached the vicinity of Baghdad and, on August fifteenth, they saw in the distance the minarets towering over the wondrous city, its palace roofs, the towers of its ramparts. Still intact, the city appeared a veritable paradise: each man dreamed of its treasures, the cool shade of its courtyards, the countless delights it would offer. . . .

Alas! Between the Crusaders and Baghdad shone a forest of sabers, reflecting the sunlight: Mongol horsemen and archers, assembled in small groups, completely surrounded the Templar forces. . . .

Chapter V

There was no need for a battle call: as if this were no more than parade exercise, William of Beaujeu's troops quickly carried out the well-planned maneuvers.

The supply wagons were drawn up in a circle at the center of their stand, while squires pulled the mangonels into place behind this improvised wall.

At the same time, foot soldiers knelt on one knee outside the circle, their spears pointed forward, ready to resist any possible charge by the Mongol Cavalry.

Simultaneously, the knights donned armor which they had removed in order to withstand the oppressive midday heat.

The Grand Master had himself hoisted aloft in the basket of a ballista to survey the disposition of the enemy forces. Unfortunately, this time the Templars were unable to reach high ground, the most favorable position for defense, and William saw immediately that the Mongols most certainly had accurate information concerning the deadly lightning. They had taken care not to form any concentration of troops: archers and horsemen were drawn up in small, widely spaced formations.

In the distance, beyond reach of the projectiles, were Chinese war chariots. For the Crusaders, these were new war machines. Each was drawn by three horses and the cars held a complement of archers, their arrows ranged like ribs of a fan, while the wheel hubs were equipped with long scythe-blades. There was little defense against a massive charge of these murderous devices.

William judged by the location of the Mongol pennants that the Khan, his princes and commanders were poised to strike at any moment. Yak tails snapped in the wind at the top of the standards, which the Grand Master observed with more than curiosity as each represented a force of ten thousand men under the command of a Tumen. Counting them, he concluded that the Templars were facing close to a hundred thousand men. . . . Enough to strike any Christian with terror. Muigghams, heading a thousand horsemen and archers, were at the front of every battalion, in which Jaghouns commanded companies of one hundred warriors, while Arbans acted as sub-commanders of groups of ten.

William had made good use of the long march from Edessa to Baghdad, collecting all possible information about the enemy. He knew that the elite of these troops, chosen from the bravest and numbering ten thousand, formed the Khan's personal guard. He also knew that the preferred stratagem of these daring fighters was a cavalry charge—under cover of volleys of arrows—attempting to breach the ranks of the adversary. If this were unsuccessful, they would not give battle but retreat, trying to draw the pursuit into ambush. If this ruse proved unavailing, they still would not seek an engagement but continue to flee, only to return unexpectedly to surprise an opposition which believed itself triumphant.

Any massive attack would be wiped out by the Templars' lightning, which Abaka certainly would not risk. The only thing to do was to determine the Khan's plans and then force him to concentrate enough of his squadrons so that use of the atomic grenades would be decisive.

Lost in thought, the Grand Master signaled to be lowered from his improvised turret. At that exact moment, the horsemen sent ahead and deployed on either flank rode back at full speed in a cloud of dust. Their Commander dismounted and, in a hoarse voice, announced:

"Venerable Master, we are lost! These dogs have dug trenches on all sides which are filled with naphtha. On our right, the river is an insuperable barrier: its far bank is lined with thousands of archers. Behind us, these accursed devils have just rolled in many kegs of this oil that burns. . . ."

Silently, the Grand Master contemplated the Baussant banners waving on either side of him: his army was downwind. . . . The smoke would blanket the Crusaders, masking the Mongol operations and effectively preventing any accurate bombardment.

It was a bad beginning. . . .

And a rapid decision was imperative: ink-black clouds of

smoke already moved in on the left, reaching the farthest
ranks of the soldiers who wept and choked in the suffocating
fumes.

In this emergency, the sharp wits of the Grand Master
worked rapidly. He had already devised a new plan of action
for which he immediately gave the orders:

"Foot soldiers retreat toward the river without delay. Pull
the war machines to the edge of the water, all except four.
With two of these, start immediate grenade assault aimed at
the archers on the other side of the river. The remaining two
will launch their missiles into the river itself, downstream
from our position. All horsemen, follow me. . . ."

These orders were carried out in utmost confusion under
constant volleys of Mongol arrows. Fortunately for the foot
soldiers, the thick cloud of smoke prevented the Asian archers from aiming with any precision: however, the barrage
was so dense that there were frequent hits.

All the Crusaders took heart at the sound of the first
atomic explosions but they could not understand why they
were ordered to retreat without giving battle. Not a few wondered why the magic fire was not launched at the main Mongol forces, astonished that it was wasted on the riverbed and
on the opposite bank where the enemy troops were least numerous.

But the Grand Master had shown a remarkable competence for making the most of the slightest opportunity: the
craters resulting from the explosions quickly filled the riverbed, forming an effective dam. North of the battlefield, the
waters overflowed on the plain, miring the vehicles and
forcing the Mongol horsemen to withdraw, protecting the
rear guard of the Templar army.

Simultaneously, the knights—led by William—forded the
Euphrates and rushed the few archers who had survived the
preparatory fire. At the same time, sergeants, squires and the
auxiliary Turcopole forces formed a solid line of resistance
behind a barrier of wagons, their backs to the river.

Abaka Khan was caught in his own trap. He heard the
awesome sound of the explosions but—to his surprise—no
projectile fell on his ranks and the dense smoke prevented
him from seeing what was happening on the battlefield.

His council was quickly convened to decide what course of
action should be taken. Princes and Tumens, hot with impa-

tience, were all for charging the enemy. Abaka himself was loath to engage in any decisive assault, having the greatest respect for a weapon that could annihilate Bibars' forces. The arguments were heated, each faction passionately defending its viewpoint. Since they were wasting valuable time, the Khan finally accepted a proposal that reconciled all opinions. Half the cavalry would attack the Templars under cover of the smoke, after another massive shower of arrows.

Each Tumen pleaded his right to the honor of being part of this assault, so that the actual attack did not get under way for more than an hour after William's horsemen had crossed the Euphrates, which was now dry below the obstruction.

Unfortunately for the Mongols, this lapse of time enabled the knights to ride down the old riverbed and make a wide encircling move to the south, just behind the bulk of Abaka's forces, massed around their leader.

The planned charge of his horsemen met with a curtain of fire from projectiles launched by the mangonels along the river, under the command of Peter of Sevry. At the same instant, the ponderous iron-clad knights attacked the Khan's rear guard. Like devils surging up from hell, the Templars— riding in at full speed until they reached the right distance— launched grenades from their slings, then, wheeling away, sped back for another attack on their right. The results of this maneuver were spectacular.

The Mongols, without the slightest expectation that the Templars might pounce on them from the rear, were butchered by the atomic explosion. The war chariots disintegrated. Terrified horses unseated their riders, who were massacred by cuts and thrusts. Never had the Crusaders enjoyed such a carnival. Blood reddened the earth and their steeds trampled the guts of Mongol horses. . . .

This slaughter increased when the Templars turned back to the Euphrates, cutting off the horsemen who had been sent out to attack the ballistae. For them, no escape was possible: in front of them, a barrage of atomic explosives; on their right the waters of the river, seeking a new course and forming an impassable bog. The more courageous stood their ground, facing the Templar assault but, unfortunately for them, they wore no armor and their felt bucklers offered little protection. . . .

When night fell on the plain, the Mongol army had suffered a disaster without precedent. A few lone survivors fled what seemed to them legions of Satan, belched out of hell, followed by the garrison at Baghdad which had no wish to face warriors possessing such terrifying magical powers.

Their commanders had lied to them! Not only could the Templars call down lightning: they also had power to fly through the air. How else, when they were surrounded, could they have crossed the Euphrates to surprise the rear guard of the Mongol army?

Before entering the wondrous city where the Crusaders would finally rest from their weary labors, William of Beaujeu went to survey the battlefield where the fires set by his projectiles still burned. Thoughtfully, he surveyed the remains of the man who had hoped to close the road to Baghdad to him. The body of the Abaka Khan was almost untouched, his faithful followers having thrown themselves over him to shield him from the atomic grenades. The shock waves alone had caused his death.

The backs of his officers were charred by the heat but the Khan's thin tunic embroidered with gold was still intact. Thin rivulets of blood ran from his nose and ears.

After brief meditation, the Grand Master ordered that the Khan be taken with them so that he might be given proper burial; then, followed by his army, he headed toward Baghdad, discussing the day's events with his companions.

"Do you, dear brothers, know that in the year of our Lord twelve-fifty-five, the Khan, Hulagu, the father of Abaka, stormed this city and took it after heavy combat?

'When he entered the caliph's palace, he found a tower filled with gold, silver and a thousand other treasures. The astonished Khan inquired why the caliph, seeing that his city was about to fall, did not distribute these riches among his knights and warriors. His captive had no reply and Hulagu, revolted by such ungrateful miserliness, had him locked in the tower without food or drink. The caliph died at the end of the fifth day. Eight hundred thousand inhabitants were put to the sword. Mosques and sumptuous palaces were destroyed. I tell you all this because I want to avoid such actions when our army enters the city. I intend that all persons and properties be respected. We shall rest for a while at Baghdad and I aspire to a good relationship with its people. Do not forget that Abaka's wife is a Christian princess, the

daughter of Michael Paleologue; I demand that she be treated
with respect and accorded all the honors to which she is enti-
tled. Later, I shall create an independent kingdom here and,
to rule it, I shall name one of the knights who has served me
so courageously and faithfully."

This made the intended impression, and explicit orders
were given the Crusader troops guaranteeing that the Grand
Master's wishes would be respected.

The army reached the outlying ramparts and crossed the
Tigris. Some of the splendor that the city had once possessed
was lost forever but, in the twenty years of occupation, most
of the destroyed edifices had been rebuilt and the splendid
palaces, the mosques with their slender minarets, the well-
tended gardens won the admiration of all; so much greenery
dazzled the soldiers, who had all but forgotten the existence
of such Edens.

Almost the entire population had remained in the city, convinced of certain victory for their Khan's innumerable forces.
But, when all was said and done, the merchants and traders
were rather pleased to see the Templars entering the city,
bringing promise of expanded commerce with Christian
lands. They also believed that the Christian origin of their
princess would offer far more protection than any wall, in
which assumption they were completely right.

With the greatest curiosity, the Crusader Commanders entered the palace hall where this remote Sister-in-Christ
awaited them surrounded by the dignitaries of her court.

That Baghdad court had certainly not usurped its reputation for splendor; was it not in this very city that the most
beautiful silks in the world were spun? Dazzled, the Frankish
and English Templars were overwhelmed by such ostentation.
What a contrast was evidenced by their sand-dulled armor,
stained with dried blood, to the pomp of this court, straight
out of one of Aladdin's tales, where satins, gold brocades,
and muslins glistened in the light from countless oil lamps of
finely chased copper.

All of them felt out of place in such surroundings.

The princess, surrounded by her ladies-in-waiting and her
ministers, was seated on a golden throne set with precious
stones. Her face was partly obscured by a light veil and the
purple tunic she wore was as fine as a spider web.

No sooner had John of Grailly laid eyes on her harmonious beauty than he was swept off his feet. For him, everything else ceased to exist but this goddess sprung from some oriental fairy tale.

William of Beaujeu, on the other hand, was insensitive to her charms. Nevertheless, when she threw herself down at his feet, beseeching him to spare her and her people, he lifted her with a paternal gesture, asserting:

"Sweet daughter, I would be ashamed to behave like a brutal conqueror. It is true that I was forced to do battle with and, unfortunately, kill your husband, Abaka Khan, but I only did this to compel recognition of the True Faith to which you adhere. You shall keep the throne of Baghdad when I am gone far afield carrying on our just Crusade. In the meantime, I ask that you consider us your guests and faithful friends."

The princess appeared greatly moved by these words and tears streamed down her cheeks. At the sight of this, John of Grailly could contain himself no longer; he rushed to her and respectfully took her rose-scented hand which he placed on his forehead, crying out:

"By heaven, madam, I, John of Grailly, solemnly swear to be your faithful knight forever. If anyone does you offense, I stand ready to make him pay for it."

A faint smile brightened the face of the princess, who said softly, "Sirs, I thank you greatly. A true friendship is the most precious thing in the world. Your words bring much comfort to a poor woman in exile far from her kin. May our Lord bless you. . . ."

"Well said!" approved the Grand Master. "It is my intention to appoint a regent for this kingdom when I leave, and the grave John of Grailly seems to me the right man for the office. If such is your pleasure. . . ."

"Let us talk of this at another time, noble Templar. Now I request your permission to retire to my apartments to prepare for the mourning of him who was my husband."

"I shall certainly not detain you," said William of Beaujeu. "My courageous and ill-fated adversary deserved funeral rites in keeping with his rank and station."

The days that followed remained forever in the Crusaders' memories as the most sumptuous in their lives. After undergoing terrible ordeals, they were at last in an opulent city whose inhabitants were eager to fraternize.

Each took quarters in some comfortable dwelling and the Tholon brothers had no difficulty in finding pleasing bronze-skinned slaves who, between bursts of laughter and kisses, gorged them with sweets. The brothers from Auxerre, without inhibition, enjoyed to the fullest the cool of an inner court-yard enlivened by beds of exotic flowers. Poor Garin had to recite prayers without intermission to prevent his vow of chastity from being broken by the charms of these shameless she-devils; the Christian paradise was pale in comparison with Allah's!

The Grand Master was entirely immune to the seductive witchery of the beautiful courtesans who ensnared the soldiers weary of the bawds and other camp followers.

To secure Mesopotamia, he still had to take the city of Basra on the Persian Gulf. For this purpose he sent the valiant Otto of Granson with his English knights to capture that port, instructing him to seize all Mongol ships but cautioning him not to interfere with the free movement of merchant ships bringing the riches of Cathay and the legendary Spice Islands.

For there were two courses of action open to William in the advancement of his great design: either he could push on through the Khanate of Kaidu by land, like the affluent cara-vans that followed the silk trade route, or he could embark his army in the port of Basra and reach Kubla's empire by sea.

His choice required the deepest consideration, for there was a world of difference between an expedition to Mesopotamia, relatively close to the Holy Land, and an invasion of the Mongol empire, crossing the vast desert wastes of the Pamirs—on the roof of the world.

True, the Polo brothers, those intrepid Venetian travelers, had followed that route and in all probability were now in Cathay. According to the report of their first long journey (1260), which William had read with greatest attention, once Niccolo and Matteo reached Balghar on the banks of the Volga, they traveled in seventeen days to Bukhara, the most beautiful city of the Persian empire. There, joining a mission sent out by Kubla, they finally arrived at the Great Wall two years later. Before them, two Franciscan brothers, mission-aries from the Pope, had also journeyed to Cathay. The first, Joannes de Plano Carpini, left France in 1247 and arrived at

his destination in 1253. The second one, Willem of Ruys-
broek, a native of Flanders, left Christian lands in 1253 and
reached Karakorum in 1254. The route they followed was
known and used regularly by caravans. However, with an
army, its wagons and its precious war machines, there would
certainly be many difficulties in following in their steps. Also,
the problem of communication with those left behind at
Baghdad and on the coast must be considered. At this point,
quite naturally, the Grand Master decided to consult Brother
Joubert, who had resumed his work in complete seclusion.

The Brother promptly descended from the tower where he
had installed his laboratory. In his haste, he neglected to remove the leather apron which protected his monastic robe,
and his attire contrasted strangely with the subdued luxury of
the room where William of Beaujeu awaited him.

"Well, my dear and learned brother," William began without formality, "where are you in your work? I trust that oriental enchantments have not delayed your research. You
know how much this concerns me. . . ."

"Certainly not, venerable master! Since we reached Baghdad I have labored day and night to unravel the hermetic
secrets of this casket from another world. Unfortunately, I
have encountered the greatest difficulties, despite the fact that
I have surrounded myself with learned men expert in the art
of alchemy. . . ."

"You have not divulged the origin of our treasure?"

"I have been careful not to do so! Besides, these savants
are cloistered here in the palace and are forbidden to leave.
Thanks to your orders, we have everything we need. But the
way the magic transmuter works remains a total enigma."

"You have made no progress at all?" William asked,
frowning.

"Oh, but I have! Nothing positive as yet. The source of energy contained in the Baphomet effigies adapts well to the
casket, but it appears to be too powerful so that the operation
is overrapid and the products obtained have only the faintest
resemblance to the model placed in the first chamber."

"Therefore you will have to temper its action," stated the
Grand Master, thoughtfully, taking a rose-flavored sherbet offered by a deaf-mute slave.

"That is precisely the problem! I have tried heating it
slightly and packing it in ice; nothing succeeds. However

when I heated the metal wires that link the energy source to the casket until they became red, the operation slowed a little. Therefore I abandoned my preoccupation with the transmuter for experiments with the fluid coming from the source box by means of the conductors. This has enabled me to make some appreciable observations."

"Tell me about them. All this is of the greatest interest to me; but first have one of these delicious sherbets, a drink unknown in our countries although refreshing."

Brother Joubert, known to be something of a glutton, eagerly accepted one of the delicacies; then, sipping and licking his lips like a sensuous cat, he continued, "When a plain gold or silver wire of the kind used to embroider materials is attached to the red and black terminals inside the Baphomet effigy, it incandesces. The smaller the diameter of the metal thread, the more rapidly this occurs."

"Such unnatural fire is amazing!"

"There's more: when the wire are plunged into chalybeate liver of sulphur in aqueous solution, they produce evanescent bubbles. And, in a solution of Armenian stone, commonly called verdigris, one of the silver threads takes on a beautiful yellow color. . . ."

"Transmutation to gold!"

"No, venerable master, only ordinary copper. However, this clearly proves that each knob on the energy box has properties that are completely different. . . ."

"A remarkable deduction. By my faith, I never would have thought of that. Congratulations on your perception, Brother Joubert."

The learned Templar smirked complacently and continued with calculated humility, "These discoveries are especially important because they will help us to determine the laws governing the fluid coming from the box; and, once I am certain what it is, I haven't the slightest doubt that the transmuter can be made to operate again."

"Perfect. But hurry it up for we cannot stay in Baghdad forever and I can understand very well that such research is not easily done in a wagon. Is that all?"

"I also delved into the mechanism contained in the Baphomet effigies and made a strange discovery: I would have told you sooner but—you were always so busy with the management of this vast state. . . ."

"That should not have prevented you, brother; you must know that to you I am always available."

"You honor me, venerable master. Briefly, this is what I found. . . . Do you mind if I have another of those delicious sherbets? My throat dries up when I talk. . . ."

"Of course not. And also try one of these Turkish delights."

"Um-mmm! Excellent. These countries indubitably possess a multitude of charms. I have been told of curious substances with stranger properties which are found, so rumor has it, on the road to Cathay. One of them is similar to that substance called salamander: even the hottest fire cannot destroy it. But to return to the Baphomet effigies; inside there is a kind of metal grid with plates that slide between one another. When I changed their position in one, I could hear Baphomet's voice, although no sound came from the others."

"What was he saying?"

"Nothing understandable, since he spoke in his own language. However, because the same phrase was repeated continuously, I am convinced that it was a message meant for his kinsmen, stating his whereabouts and asking for help. Working on this assumption, a Turcopole who is expert in many languages was able to isolate several words. This will enable us to know—from now on—whether his fellow beings have heard him and are coming to his assistance."

"This is a priceless discovery! Why didn't you tell me sooner?"

"I wanted to make one final experiment, noble Master. There is also a short lever connected to this device. When I moved it and modified the position of the plates I mentioned before, by using two of the effigies, placed at a distance from one another, it was possible to hold a conversation without any interference from Baphomet's voice."

"Come here and let me embrace you. Brother Joubert: you have just given me the means I lacked. Now the several divisions of my army will be able to exchange information, even when they are several days' march distant from one another!"

After kissing the Templar seer on both cheeks, the delighted Grand Master bestowed the title of Commander of the Order on him, together with full ownership of the city of Mosul—as soon as the army had taken it. He also begged him to devote some research to the oil that burned. Then the two men went their separate ways, each greatly pleased with the other.

While John of Grailly pursued his passion for the beauteous princess, other knights carried on the continued pacification procedures at the head of the Christian army.

Otto of Granson reached Basra and a Templar bearing a Baphomet image joined him so that he was able to give immediate notification of his occupation of the port with its enormous riches and boundless supplies. In accordance with his orders, the Mongol ships were taken but vessels of other nations were left free to ply their trade.

Peter of Sevry, the Templar Marshal, was sent north to annex the Mosul region, completing occupation of the Khanate of the deceased Abaka. His troops met no opposition. The garrison abandoned the city without pretense of fighting and fled toward the Khanate of Kaidu, traveling along the shores of the Caspian Sea. They destroyed nothing before leaving because the inhabitants took up arms to resist looting and the Templars were greeted as liberators. News of this, thanks to Baphomet's transmitter, was instantaneously made known to William of Beaujeu, who ordered his marshal to make a clear proclamation that the princess, Abaka's widow, still held sovereignty over the Khanate. In this way the transfer of power was accomplished without incident.

Moreover, numerous reinforcements were arriving in Mesopotamia: troops of French, English, Italian, Spanish and German knights who had heard of the resounding victory at Baghdad and rushed to join this new Crusade.

They almost doubled the effective force of the army, but William of Beaujeu, thinking of the long distances they would have to travel to reach Peking, did little rejoicing. Feeding a large army posed serious problems, particularly when crossing arid deserts like the one which slashed Kaidu's Khanate in half. He resolved the difficulty by forming Mesopotamian garrisons from the newcomers. This retained the seasoned knights in his invasion force, and backed that with large reserve detachments. Keeping his men on the move would prevent them from growing soft as a result of lingering in the seductive oriental cities where the availability of obliging women and rich food threatened to rob them of any desire to push on with the great Crusade.

Two months had elapsed since Abaka's death and it was

now too late in the year to initiate a full-scale offensive in countries extremely forbidding in winter, if one accepted the report made by Niccolo and Matteo Polo. William, therefore, restricted himself to a limited operation, leading his army to Sava, south of the Caspian Sea. He kept the Dasht-I-Kavir, the great salt marsh, on his right and crossed the rugged Kurdistan Mountains. Squires and knights alike showed little enthusiasm for the long journey through such rough terrain and loudly lamented the comforts of life in Baghdad.

To fire their lagging spirits, the Grand Master had his chaplains tell them the history of the area. Not far from there, in the Caucasus Mountains, was Mount Ararat, where Noah's ark had beached after the Flood. From the city of Avah had come the three Wise Men, making their way to worship the Child Jesus. With them they brought offerings of gold, incense and myrrh for the Child and in exchange they were given a plain box.

On their return journey, curious as to its contents, they opened it. To their great disappointment they found only a stone, which they contemptuously threw into a well. Instantly, a huge flame sprang from the shaft, which the greatly astonished magi cupped and carried home with them. There, their descendents carefully guarded it in Galasia Castle, only a three-day march from Sava.

Was not this proof positive that the celestial lightning had always been a sign from the Lord God, and that the Crusaders were duty-bound to free these Sacred Places?

These tales spurred the Crusaders on and the army finally reached its destination at the end of October. William set up his winter quarters there and threw himself into the business of working out the details of his spring offensive.

Chapter VI

The winter proved to be comparatively mild and the knights had little time to be bored. Besides the strenuous exercises ordered by the Grand Master, they spent long hours hunting with magnificently deft falcons. The abundant game lent a pleasing variety to their usual fare. In fact, they learned to appreciate a great many things unknown in their native lands.

South of Sava there was a route frequented by caravans carrying all kinds of strange merchandise from the port of Hormuz. Spices, rare fabrics, precious stones, elephant tusks, everything captivated the Crusaders and fired them with a compulsive longing to travel to those regions where such riches could be found.

They discovered strange trees, snow-white oxen with humps on their backs and—a valuable asset for future operations—mules with unbelievable stamina. Splendid horses were also sent to them from the province of Tunocaim, just in time to replace the ones brought from Cyprus.

They learned to enjoy the taste of dates, pistachios and paradise apples, which were called *naranges* by the Persians and which had the reputation of restoring the strength of warriors after a long day's march. Naturally they began storing up all these treasures.

The Grand Marshal, who was in charge of provisioning, began assembling a great number of camels whose resistance to thirst would be of enormous value when crossing the great desert. The war machines, always dismounted during difficult stages, could be carried by these robust animals as well.

Near the end of winter, several Hospitalers arrived from the Holy Land bringing a message from their Grand Master, who congratulated William on his resounding successes and inquired as to his future intentions. It seemed clear that John of Villiers was more than a little alarmed by his rival's colossal authority. The occupation of Mesopotamia did not disturb him overmuch as long as he had the upper hand in Syria, but he feared any move by the Templars to invade Cathay, the acquisition of which would give them immeasurable power.

William of Beaujeu made as reassuring a reply as possible, leaving it tacitly understood that he was satisfied with his present conquests and had no ambition other than the peaceful administration of Mesopotamia.

One day in the month of April, however, the Tholon brothers—who were always charged with secret missions to one or another of the garrisons—captured a Venetian making for the Khanate of Kaidu. He tried to pass himself off as a merchant on his way to buy silk but, during the examination of his baggage, a coat of mail and a mantle were discovered that left no doubt as to his identity: he was unquestionably an emissary of the Hospitalers. Then, considerably more serious, a message was found hidden in his saddle. When William of Beaujeu learned its contents, he was infuriated: John of Villiers proposed a secret alliance with the Mongol Khans, promising to cut off all communications between Europe and the Templars in the event the latter attacked Kaidu and Kubla. . . .

The Hospitalers' observers were immediately thrown into the deepest dungeon, along with the messenger, and the Grand Master summoned his Council to advise them of the situation.

Unavoidably, it took a certain time for the Council members to reach Sava, so that the meeting could not take place until the tenth of May. This delay was put to good use by mustering the troops and loading the supply wagons.

So it was that all the knights who had taken part in the conquest of the Khanate of Abaka found themselves together, ready to plunge into a new adventure, though ignorant of its nature or purpose. There was the Swiss knight, Otto of Granson, John of Grailly, and all the other Templar Commanders. By then, William of Beaujeu had completed the plan of action for this new campaign and lost no time in revealing it to his staunch friends.

"Nobles, knights, my brothers. You underwent the severest of trials before accomplishing our first task; that of lifting the Mongol yoke from all Mesopotamia. Since then we have secured the peace and have rooted out those dogs who defiled this beauteous region—endowed with every enticement. Some among you, I regret to say, have succumbed to its sensuous charms, almost forgetting our mission, the propagation of the True Faith. I am more than willing to excuse such ones: human nature is weak. Did not the Apostle Peter himself thrice deny our Lord Jesus Christ? Think on your transgressions, my brothers, and say to yourselves that paradise shall be gained by leaving this instant to storm the empire of Cathay."

The craggy face of Otto of Granson, scarred by who knows how many saber cuts, was transformed by a broad grin. "Well, now, that's more like it! I was beginning to get rusty. . . . I'm ready! Down with the infidels!"

John of Grailly, on the contrary, did not like the news at all: the months spent at the court of the beautiful Princess Paleologue inspired no wish in him to return to the interminable riding and the rigors of camp life. Secretly, he hoped to persuade the princess to marry him and counted on ending his days in opulent Baghdad. And so he objected weakly:

"This is an enormous task, venerable master. May it not be one beyond our capabilities?"

"Nothing in the world is impossible to courageous defenders of the True Faith!" William retorted contemptuously. "Kubla Khan has disparaged our Holy Father, the Pope, and I intend to make him regret his words. He had the insolence to say to the brothers Polo that Christians had neither the knowledge nor the ability, to do anything supernatural; whereas, so he pretends with the help of their pagan gods, his priests have the power to change the weather whenever they wish, to foretell the future, to transport objects remarkable distances without the aid of human hands. 'Ask your Pope,' he told them jokingly, 'to send me one hundred seers, well-versed in your religion. I will match them with my own priests and we shall see who will perform the greatest number of miracles. . . .' Very well, noble sires, one hundred thousand men are going to teach this blasphemer the powers of our Savior. We shall see if he still feels like making jokes then."

His speech touched off the wildest enthusiasm. These rough men all had a profound faith which could tolerate no hint of insult. Even the elegant John of Grailly was ashamed of his thought of remaining safely in a sumptuous palace while his

Pope was being mocked by the Mongol Khan, and his voice could be heard above all the others.

"I expected no less of you," the Grand Master assured them. "Here is my plan. We shall invade the Khanate of Kaidu from the north, following the caravan track, which will provide us with many useful commodities. Samarkand, where the most beautiful carpets in the world are woven, is our first objective. From there, we move on to Kashgar, but to reach that city we shall have to cross the cold, arid heights of the Pamirs. Do I have to say that our route has been carefully planned? Passing through Kashgar and Yarkand by the way of Khotan, we arrive in Keriya. From there we press on to Tunhwang but—in order to reach that city—we shall have to cross the great desert. Have no fears, our excellent guides are used to leading caravans and will take us by the shortest way. There will be many rough days, but we shall arrive safe and sound. However, a new test awaits us there, the most serious of all for when we leave the Khanate of Kaidu, Kubla's army will be lying in wait for us somewhere beyond the great desert; the most likely place is in the vicinity of Tunhwang."

The Templar Marshal could no longer contain his dismay. "Venerable master, we run the greatest risk of arriving there with an army severely diminished by the perils of this interminable journey. When you had the noble Otto of Granson occupy Basra, I thought you had decided to enter Cambaluc by sea."

"I did have that intention at the time, brother, but several considerations led me to reject such a project. First, the wildest storms often sweep the southern waters, disabling the sturdiest ships and, further, none of us are sailors. Consequently, even with favorable weather, many might be violently ill and incapable of handling our vessels properly. What decided the matter was Kubla's powerful navy, which could easily attack us during the night when the lack of visibility, together with the heavy loads in our ships, would prevent defensive maneuvers. That is why I finally chose the land route."

"All this should be self-evident," Commander Thibaud Gaudin averred loudly. He never missed a chance to echo the Grand Master with the hope of gaining special favors. "We suffered enough only a little while ago when we sailed from

Sicily to Acre. I'm sure none of us wants to repeat that experience."

"Besides, I have some good news for you," William of Beaujeu continued. "First of all, a new sign in our favor from our Lord: it will now be possible for me to talk with all the Commanders of our Order, even though they are many a day's march away. I shall also be able to keep in touch with Baghdad to ask for anything we need. Secondly, I want you to know that valiant warriors have joined our ranks, men who know the regions where we are going like the palms of their hands. They are the loyal followers of the Old One of the Mountains, all of whom survived a massacre. But I'll let our Seneschal tell you about them, since it was he who discovered these former allies."

"They are indeed rediscovered friends," declared the giant Templar. "A long time ago, our Order was in close contact with their leader. I'm sure you all know that the Khan of the Persian Tartars, the same one that conquered Baghdad, besieged the stronghold of the Old One of the Mountains. For three years he stayed in the vicinity of Kasvin before taking it. This should give you some idea of the noble knights. Most of them were slaughtered with their master but, luckily, some were not in the castle when it fell; they survived. And they hate all Mongols with such a burning passion, they will dare anything to be revenged.

"What you may not know is that the Old One was a powerful magician who enslaved his followers with a dream of blood and carnal ecstasy. He knew the secret of a wondrous elixir: the warrior who drank of it saw the gates of paradise open to him. With the sweetest embraces, wanton houris satisfied his never-ending desires and, during his lustful dream, he sensed strange harmonies, colors, musical sounds and perfumes, all mingled with one another in dazzling convolutions. Unhappily for the dreamer, the vision disappeared all too soon. . . . The wretched warrior had only one desire: to drink this brew again. But, in order to merit another taste of it, the hashshashin must kill a specified enemy, selected by the Old One. From that moment, the successs of his mission was the warrior's only thought: if he survived, he would be rewarded with a draft of the magic beverage and if he died in pursuit of his mission, he believed Allah himself would open the gates to that paradise which he had only glimpsed, where he would live for all eternity. I possess the secret of

this elixir and have already used it to send some of the hashshashins into the Mongol empire: they traveled unrecognized
with caravans and obtained priceless information on the
preparations being made by both Kaidu and Kubla."

"Please heaven our brothers never taste this drug!" the
Templar from Tyre half whispered. "The good Lord only
knows to what ends it would lead them. Life in this fabled
Orient is too full of temptations without that."

"Have no fear: the formula for this potion is known only
to the Seneschal and myself," William reassured him. "No
Christian could indulge in such practices without the gravest
danger to his immortal soul." He paused as though struck by
another thought, sighed deeply and then continued:

"Gentlemen, my brothers, it is my sad duty to tell you of a
circumstance that has grieved me to the depths of my being.
The chance interception of a messenger placed in my hands
proof of a shameful betrayal. The Hospitalers are offering to
ally themselves with the Mongols in order to prevent us from
propagating the True Faith to the ends of the Earth!"

"What? Impossible!"

"Christians would never ally themselves with infidels!"

"Let evil days fall on those dogs! May they roast in hell
forever and ever. . . ."

"What are we waiting for? We can help them on the way!"

"We must inform our Holy Father, the Pope."

"Bastards! Sons of bitches! Without faith or loyalty."

Each, in his own way, cursed the unexpected alliance.

William of Beaujeu raised his hand for silence and said
gravely:

"God will judge them, my brothers. The renegades will answer to Him on His Judgment Day. Perhaps they have an imperative reason for this action. For the moment at least, it
does not affect my plan. I leave good, solid garrisons in the
Mesopotamian cities. Yet, I cannot understand how they,
monks like us, serving the cause of our Lord, Jesus Christ,
could fight their brothers. Thank God, I have the Archangel's
fiery sword, which—without any doubt—will bring them to
reconsider. But I spend too much time on this distressing subject when we should be thinking only of breaking camp. Let
everyone take his accustomed place in the ranks, and may the
Lord Jesus Christ grant us victory."

There was great joy among the Crusaders; after a long
period of inaction they were finally setting out on a new cam-

paign. They boasted to one another and showed off new weapons. This one had an ax with two blades curved like a crescent moon; that one, a long slash-hook for cutting horses' tendons; still another, a fine coat of mail or a shiny-new helmet with a crest of multicolored feathers.

Only the elegant, and eloquent, John of Grailly stayed away from the hubbub and confusion. He had asked his squire to bring him writing materials and was composing a poem to his beloved. In it he swore to be eternally faithful and pledged himself to bring honor to her colors, which he wore on his shield.

One hour later, the army was under way.

The attitude of the host differed profoundly from that which had gripped them when they left Alexandretta. All knew that a harsh task lay ahead and they sang psalms with solemn voices, beseeching the Lord to favor their enterprise.

Oriental splendors gave the long column an unusually colorful appearance. All the knights wore splendid silken capes and even the trappings of their horses had luxurious touches, harness traps embroidered with gold reflecting the sun. There were camels too, driven by Turcopoles, and some war chariots in the Chinese style, carrying bowmen and soldiers with slingshots. The mangonels had been reduced in size by using exotic woods and their larger wheels did not sink so deeply into the ground.

The Templars, however, had made no concession to the fashions of the hour: they kept to their sober white mantles with the scarlet cross. The only luxury they allowed themselves was the richly chased or damascened weapons they captured from the enemy. Of the leaders, only one was missing: the Seneschal. The Grand Master had entrusted to him the heavy burden of commanding the forces left in Mesopotamia. Some of the knights had hunting dogs with them, and others sported a falcon on their wrists. This was no ostentatious whim but a wise precaution: game would still be needed to vary the monotony of the daily rations.

The effective forces had been so greatly increased that William divided them in half, entrusting one division to his marshal. The vanguard was commanded by John of Grailly and the rear guard was assigned to the trustworthy Swiss, Otto of Granson.

All this multitude formed an immense iron-clad snake which gave an overwhelming inpression of power. The anthems sung by these soldier-monks could be heard for miles, clarioning the virile resolution of these Christian Crusaders.

The early stages of the journey were uneventful: after reaching Mulecte, south of the Gelachegan Sea, the knights rode through rich valleys covered with green vegetation and orchards. In six days they reached Shibagan, where an orgy of consuming cantaloupe jam was not without distressing intestinal consequences.

After that they entered a wild, uncultivated region where the dust tarnished somewhat the finery of the knights. They were easily consoled, however, by indulging in the pleasures of the hunt without restraint. Game was abundant and the loads of the provision wagons were increased with patés and haunches of venison . . .

In the market town of Talakan, they stocked rock salt, useful for preserving the meats. A little farther on, they came unexpectedly into a region rich with vineyards where the natives produced an excellent wine. That night squires and knights fell asleep with reeling heads but, on the whole, more content with their destiny.

Clement Tholon even declared, "I swear, if ever one day I get back to Auxerre, I have to take back some of these vines to get at least two or three hogsheads of this wine. . . ."

Six days later the column entered the province of Badakhstan, which they discovered to be a real treasure find. No one left without pockets filled with lazulite, silver and precious stones very similar to rubies. The expedition was turning out to be quite promising, especially since there were no signs at all of the Mongols.

From his spies, the Grand Master learned that Kaidu was by no means anxious to confront him and had pulled his troops back. He was hoping that his cousin, Kubla, occupied with fighting in China, would come to assist him in halting this iron-clad army, never yet defeated. However, the Khan of Khans, who did not particularly like Kaidu, sent his son, Momuqan, at the head of an army to fight against him. From his priceless allies, the hashshashin, William learned that Kaidu had seized Yarkand and Khotan, towns located on the route the Crusaders must follow. Further, he had met with Momuqan and the two Mongol chieftains appeared to be reconciled. After celebrating Kubla's victories in China, they had decided to unite their forces to do battle with the Templars.

The hour of a new encounter was drawing closer. The Grand Master informed his Seneschal of the situation by means of the Baphomet transmitters, so that the latter would not tie himself down with some rash sorties against the Hospitalers.

He also ordered him to occupy the rich city of Samarkand, to cover his left flank, menaced by Nomuqan's troops and those of his general, Bayan.

The Crusaders' progress was now more difficult: following the Vakhsh River, they left Badakhstan and entered the foothills of the Pamirs. The scaling of the high tableland had begun.

Not a soul lived in this desolate region; no trees, no birds. The only creatures seen were some long-horned wild sheep who kept at a great distance. Snowy summits towered above the army on every side. The cold was becoming more and more unbearable, and the waters of Lake Sirikol were frozen. For the first time the Crusaders suffered from chilblains. There was, however, enough vegetation for the horses and mules who shivered under the icy winds.

It took them almost sixty days to reach the province of Kashgar. Fortunately, the Mongols did not show themselves there, and the Crusaders were agreeably surprised by the mildness of the climate.

William of Beaujeu found himself faced with a troublesome problem of strategy: somewhere ahead of him, probably in the vicinity of Yarkand or Khotan, Kaidu's army lay in wait for him. The Khan, perhaps to deprive his troops of any hope of retreat, had mustered them with their backs to the great desert. On the Templars' left flank were the forces of Kubla's son, Nomuqan; soldiers few in number and with little experience in battle. Still, it would be better to engage them separately. To achieve this, the Grand Master ordered his marshal to pursue a northward course into Uzbekistan in order to draw Nomuqan's forces away. He also advised his loyal assistant commander to ask that more mercenaries be recruited in Mesopotamia to increase the number of his troops.

The seemingly endless trek over the high Pamirs had taken more than fifty days and had completely exhausted the Crusaders.

William studied their situation: on their right, the snow-covered Kashmir Mountains; in front of them, Kaidu's

Mongol troops; on their left flank, those commanded by Nomuqan; and behind them the Pamirs.

At any cost, the men must rest before moving on to the unavoidable encounter with Kaidu. The Grand Master, therefore, ordered that camp be set up around the city of Kashgar. Knights and foot soldiers alike rejoiced at this respite. Each hoped to forget, if only for a moment, the monotony of the long haul. The town certainly had fewer attractions than Baghdad but there was a large caravansary where merchants following the silk route broke their journey. The local beauties learned quickly enough that these rough soldiers possessed the wherewithal to buy their charms and, inevitably, a wave of debauchery broke over the town.

The white-mantled Templars, however, did not succumb and William of Beaujeu took no repressive action: he was occupied with other matters. . . .

An unsuspected affront awaited him: his need for more atomic grenades grew increasingly pressing. His stock was far from depleted but, in view of the numerous forces that might be hurled at the Crusaders, he wanted a safety margin which he hoped would be achieved by the transmuter. However, Brother Joubert did not even bring him a report. That fact, he felt, called for an investigation. The learned brother had been installed in a convenient room in the Grand Master's own quarters and when the latter paid him a visit, he found Brother Joubert drowsing with his arms around a half-empty wine jug.

"By Christ!" William thundered. "You choose a fine time indeed to turn yourself into a drunken pig, Is this your gratitude? You know how urgent it is for us to make use of the transmuter and you waste precious hours giving yourself up to tippling."

The Templar staggered to his feet. "Don't get all worked up, ve-venerable—I didn't drink that much . . . just enough to give me fresh courage for my work . . . besides, Horace said. . . ."

He belched, shook his head and took another swig from the jug.

"You drunken sot! Your breath reeks from ten feet away. . . ." Furious, William snatched the jug and dashed it to the ground. "Here I am facing further battles and with my stock of missiles that emit the lightning depleted. A way must be found to make this confounded casket function. Why aren't you working, incompetent?"

"That is going too far! Perhaps I'm not quite myself at the moment but I am not incompetent. . . . I've proved that. It's just that this devilish engine doesn't want me to know anything about it. I've spent hours pondering this cursed problem, without any result. . . ."

"But when we left Baghdad, you had plans," William said in a more conciliatory tone. "You hoped to clear up the mystery of the fluid which operates it."

"Well, yes! I worked at that, but no use, and nothing I could do about it. Besides, I prefer to look at Baphomet."

"Baphomet! And why, please?"

"He's not like you. . . . Without wanting to offend you, vene-venerable master . . . he says nice things to me. He's the one who told me to take a drink and not to wear myself out."

"What? You dare to claim he advised you to get drunk?"

"It's just as I'm telling you, venerable . . . all this is something we're not supposed to know. It's his problem, not mine; that's why he doesn't want me to work anymore. Enjoy yourself, dear Joubert. . . . Yes . . . he loves me, he does . . . Stop trying to penetrate the herme . . . hermetic . . . secrets. Finally, to tell the truth, he forbade me to touch his effigies, except to talk with him."

"Do you talk with him often?"

"Didn't I just say so? I like to do it, I do . . . First, he shows me lots of things with pretty dancing colors . . . and then I hear music, such beautiful music. . . . So, I'd better warn you, don't count on me anymore. . . ."

"Lord, help me!" William whispered. "This imbecile has been bewitched by Baphomet's magic charms. How did this devil find out that I was using his effigies for my own purposes? At any rate, there's no use in counting on the duplicator at the moment, First, we'll have to sober up this idiot, Joubert. . . ."

With a last furious glance at the drunkard, who had sprawled on a chair, singing to himself, the Grand Master returned to his quarters, to which he summoned the Tholon brothers. Clement, busy wrestling with some bawd, was not to be found, but the other two answered his call promptly.

The gloomy appearance of their leader, lost in thought, was chilling and they kept respectfully silent, waiting for him to notice their presence. "Oh yes, there you are," the Grand Master said, after some moments of abstraction. "I have an undertaking of the greatest importance for you. Already you have done me signal service and I know your discretion well. This time you must be on your guard even more than before."

"We would suffer torture and death rather than reveal whatever it may be," Garin, the spokesman for the brothers, assured him.

"I am certain you would. That is why I am confiding a secret of paramount consequence to you. Have you ever heard of Baphomet?"

"There are"—Garin spoke guardedly—"certain rumors circulating. Wild stories without any foundation. . . ."

"Not quite; he actually exists. He is a dangerous being from another world who, at this moment, is held prisoner somewhere in the Kingdom of France. However, this creature, who possesses great powers, has agreed to help us. Images in his likeness allow us to talk with our commanders over seas, mountains and valleys. Brother Joubert, charged with penetrating the mystery of their operation, had made great progress, so that I hoped the solution was near. Unfortunately, even though far away, Baphomet has corrupted our learned Brother, turning him into a comfirmed drunkard who refuses to continue his research. . . ."

Guiot, involuntarily, hung his head. How well he knew the Templar's love for the divine jug, to which Guiot often gave himself up quite willingly.

"Therefore, you are to watch him, night and day, so that he can no longer use the effigy to talk with this creature. Also, see to it that he has no wine. Aside from that, he is free to continue his research, once he is sober."

"And if he tries to escape?" asked Garin.

"Punish him well, but do not maim or kill him. I trust that he will come to his senses and be capable of rendering loyal service again. . . ."

"Won't he be able to cast some spell on us?" Guiot asked in alarm, at which he got an angry look from his brother.

"Never fear, my good man. If you watch him closely, nothing will happen. However, in case of any suspicious actions, call me. Now go and take your stations, and make sure that two of you are always at his side."

"You can count on us, venerable master," promised Garin.

Alone, the Grand Master returned to his meditation. This matter was turning out not at all well: Baphomet had discovered that William was using the effigies for his own purposes and the thing at the bottom of the tarn intended to teach the Templars a lesson by giving them a hint of his powers. Wasn't there a great risk that commanders who used effigies to communicate with their leader would be overcome by the same magic? Everything considered, it seemed best to play the game and contact Baphomet direct. It seemed likely that he was unaware of the existence of the duplicating casket and could not reproach the Grand Master with disloyalty on that count.

William stood up and returned to the laboratory where the learned Joubert snored peacefully under the watchful eyes of the Tholon brothers. He took up one of the coffers containing a Baphomet image and went into an adjoining room. After carefully closing the door, he activated and waited for an answer to his call. Only a few seconds later, the eyes of the statue lit up.

"Ah! It's you, William . . . I've been expecting your call."

A little surprised, the Grand Master asked, "Why so, noble friend?"

"Come now, don't play the innocent. I inflicted a benign punishment on Brother Joubert, who was proving too curious. . . . You both have tired, it seems, to unravel the enigma of the mechanism inside my effigies. . . ."

The Templar kept himself alert, ready to break the connection at the first suspicious sign, but made his reply carefully unconcerned:

"What harm is there in that? Brother Joubert only provided me with a means of keeping in touch with my most distant troops, which is most useful. I really can't see why you should take offense at that."

"Don't try to outwit me! I am cut off from my kind on a hostile planet and only my secrets enable me to survive. If I had wanted to reveal all the properties of my robots to you, I would have done so. You deliberately tried to appropriate them without my authorization."

"You must understand, noble Sire: my army is, at the present time, months of marching away from its base. We are ver my troops if I cannot talk from a distance with the com- surrounded by enemy forces. How can I successfully maneu- manders of each detachment?"

"You had only to discuss your problem with me. I would certainly have given you permission to use my effigies for long-distance communication. But I cannot condone such overweening presumptuousness! This time I shall be lenient. You may continue to use them, but only in emergencies. However, I warn you, if you ever again try to stick your nose into things which do not concern you, our relations will suffer a great change. You have only a few atomic grenades at your disposal and, without them, you are completely incapable of pursuing your conquests. I may, perhaps, let you have more, but I advise you to use them with great miserliness. Do you understand me?"

"I understand," William whispered, containing his anger with difficulty.

At his words, the eyes of the Baphomet image emitted blinding flashes of light which forced the Templar to protect his eyes with his hand; then the effigy became inactive.

The Grand Master remained motionless for a long moment. His head ached with a sharp torment stabbing at his brain. He was convinced that, if the blinding light had lasted longer, Baphomet would have killed him. This was a further characteristic of the strange device that would bear thinking of.

Decidedly, this otherworldly being had extraordinary powers at his disposal and it would be no easy matter to get rid of him.

Chapter VII

Brother Joubert quickly recovered all his accustomed vigor under the iron rule of the Tholon brothers. He got on very well with Guiot and Clement, who shared his taste for good living, and they made the most of the leftovers from his table. Garin, however, remained aloof. He was not at all interested in knowing the significance of the hermetic engines on which the learned alchemist was again working and he had the greatest mistrust of the Baphomet effigies, asking himself what this being from "another world," of which the Grand Master had told them, could actually be.

The Grand Master himself was now thinking of continuing his advance. He had, at first, hoped that Kaidu would move in to the attack and, for that reason, had carefully placed the ballistae in weapon-pits around the camp. But the Mongol Khan was immoderately in awe of the Templars and had no wish to face them with their positions prepared in advance. According to the hashshashins' reports, he had little inclination to fight at all after his neighbor Abaka's resounding defeat. Some of his mounted patrols kept careful watch on the outskirts of the Crusaders' encampment and his own troops were kept constantly on the alert, ready to move if the Crusaders should resume their march. Kaidu's intentions remained unfathomable and William wondered if he ever would do battle, since it seemed obvious that the Mongol had no wish to become acquainted with the Templars' famous lightning. . . .

This, in the end, determined the Grand Master to push on ahead. The tireless debauchery of his men proved that they were rested. So, in spite of the intense heat, he decided to attempt crossing the desert that stood between him and Kubla's Khanate, wiping out Kaidu's army on the way, should he decide to attack.

The long column was set in motion once more. This time there was no enthusiasm anywhere in the ranks, since the prospect of crossing never-ending sand dunes during this fiery season struck terror into the hearts of even the bravest.

Yarkand was gained without even a skirmish: Kaidu had fled so precipitously that he had abandoned some of his supplies.

In the felt tents, the Christians found dried milk and yogurt, clogs with wooden soles and leather uppers, and various spices, pepper and ginger among them. The commanders saw to it that everything was burned because they suspected some Mongol trick, especially the poisoning of any foodstuffs.

Pushing on toward Cathay, they next occupied Keriya, where squires and sergeants got their hands on jasper and chalcedony intended for Kubla.

The advance became more and more difficult: after Charkhlik, the dreaded desert began. The goods on the wagons were therefore transferred to the camels' backs. There were enough provisions for more than a month, ample for crossing the torrid expanse, according to what the guides said, on the condition that the shortest route be taken.

The Mongol forces seemed to have disappeared. Even the swift horsemen who came each day to reconnoiter were no longer seen. . . .

Before ordering the departure, the Grand Master used a Baphomet image to contact his marshal, instructing him to draw back from Samarkand, so that he could move swiftly to their assistance in case of need.

Then William of Beaujeu had the horns and trumpets sounded and the Crusaders began struggling up the sand dunes under the overpowering sun. Once more, the knights were quick to remove their coats of mail and their helmets. The horses were also stripped of their rich trappings but, in spite of this, it soon became necessary for rapid movement to dismount and lead them by the bridle because the weight of their riders quickly exhausted them.

Among the knights, Otto of Granson set an outstanding example. With sweat pouring down his face, he was instantly ready to lend a helping hand to get some camel, overburdened by too heavy a load, back on its feet or to survey the surroundings to make sure the column was holding to the right course.

John of Grailly made himself well-loved by his companions, entertaining them with his poems and songs, and never refusing a sip of his water or a share of his rations at the evening bivouac.

The Grand Master had one obsession: not to stray one step from the chosen route. The guides insisted that it took an entire year to cover the longest part of the great desert on horseback. It was his intention to follow the course marked by the water holes: after one day and one night of marching, there should be enough fresh water to quench the thirst of men and animals. However, William did not count very much on that: first of all, because of the size of his army; and secondly, because he expected some treachery on the part of the Mongols.

And indeed, at the very first halt, the spring turned out to be poisoned. This greatly affected the morale of the Crusaders: the trials suffered by the army in Mesopotamia were still fresh in their minds.

A strange phenomenon increased their fears. While they made their way under the merciless sun, the men heard mysterious sounds: sometimes the rolling of drums; sometimes the murmur of unintelligible voices. At night, this strange manifestation increased in volume. That unfortunate soldier, startled out of his sleep, who went searching for the deceptive summons, never returned to camp.

Then, too, disturbing visions appeared at sunrise: some saw verdant oases; others, streams of limpid water. Sometimes they believed that they could see a city ahead of them. But each time, when they advanced toward the mirage, there was nothing but the rolling sea of sand dunes and when their companions overtook them they found only bodies pierced with countless arrows: a sad witness to the invisible presence of the Mongols all around them.

In spite of everything, the column made progress. Provisions were not lacking and the losses of men were relatively small.

Now William of Beaujeu contacted his marshal daily to report his position. In the vicinity of Samarkand, everything was peaceful.

On the fifth day, the situation suddenly worsened: a torrid wind sprang up, raising clouds of sand and reducing visibility to a few feet. Every man veiled his face in order to breathe, but the fine dust penetrated the smallest opening, clogging

noses, ears and mouths. Gallons of water would be needed to
get rid of it and the army was already on short rations.

Moreover, the Crusaders' afflictions had only begun: when
the column came to the evening halt, everyone had to face
the evidence—nearly a thousand men were missing. Some
had lost their way, others had been killed by Mongol arrows;
the sandstorm seeming to have troubled the latter not at all.

That same night, about midnight, the dying groans of a
sentinel gave the alarm. Everyone rushed from the tents, even
before the call to arms was sounded. Then a cloudburst of arrows fell on the camp, claiming innumerable victims. Indeed,
since no one had had time to don armor or coats of mail, almost every shaft found a target. There was an even more
serious loss: many of the leather containers had been pierced,
diminishing the stock of water by a third. Many horses and
camels were also wounded.

Any random firing of the ballistae would be less than useless, so the knights quickly armed themselves and began
scouring the vicinity, without success. When they returned to
the camp, dead tired, they had not seen one of the enemy.

Deeply concerned, the Grand Master called a Council
meeting that lasted until sunrise. The tactics of the enemy
were obvious: Kaidu, refusing an open battle, would continue
his campaign of harassment with swift raids by his expert
horsemen. The Mongols knew the desert and could take what
supply they needed at every watering place, leaving the spring
polluted with the cadavers of dead workhorses.

Must they give up and retreat? Opinions differed widely
but, in the end, when an inventory of the water supply had
been made, that of Otto of Granson prevailed.

Taking into account the loss of men, there was still enough
water for thirty days, if the most stringent rationing was
maintained. The precious leather containers would have to be
protected from any similar misadventure, and the coats of
mail of the dead could be used for wrapping some, while the
others would be kept under cover. The knights would have to
wear armor and the draft animals would be protected by the
padded caparisons.

At sunrise the army resumed its march. The wind no longer blew but the heat soon became intolerable for the knights,
sweating blood and water under their armor. The column
dragged along, everyone on foot, and the distance covered
that day was a grim joke. As might be expected, there were

many cases of sunstroke, and nothing could be done for the poor wretches who bestrewed the track behind them.

That night, the exhausted men fell into a profound sleep but they had hardly closed their eyes when the Mongols attacked again. This time the rain of arrows claimed few victims but the alert was repeated many times, so that no one slept a wink.

In the morning, there was nothing to do but resume the march, which became a veritable Calvary. On that day, mirages were numerous and many unfortunates, half-crazed by the heat, floundered across the shifting sand toward the visions that faded slowly away before them the farther they ran.

Finally, for better or worse, the column reached the halfway point. Now there was no possibility of turning back. Whether they wanted to or not, they must go on. The horses died like flies. And the men were unable to quench their burning thirst. Some jealously hoarded their meager ration of water, allowing themselves only a few drops, others having finished theirs at one gulp. The latter watched for the slightest chance to steal a few drops of the precious liquid.

Otto of Granson did his best to reason with the malcontents; however, after defiant ones felt a blow from the flat of his sword, they needed no further persuasion.

His friend John of Grailly, had long since stopped singing the praises of his beautiful princess; nevertheless he often spent the night watches writing poems to console him in his solitude.

Day after day, the identical scenes were reenacted: an exhausting march during the daylight hours, and at night the Mongol attacks. The commanders tried every way they could devise to cope with the latter. They placed several squadrons at a distance around the camp. Each time the yellow demons located them and, instead of falling into the trap, rained projectiles on them from a safe distance. The Crusaders also tried setting false encampments, pitching their tents in one spot and settling down a distance away. The only result of this stratagem was a spectacular fire because, on that night, their hidden adversary used flaming arrows.

William of Beaujeu, however, had faith that the final victory would be his: he reserved use of his mangonels and grenades and refused to be disconcerted by the continued reduction of his forces, certain that the Mongols could never win a real battle. The skirmishes were irritating, tiring and they played on the morale of the Crusaders; but, after all, each day brought them nearer to Tunhwang.

Furthermore, Brother Joubert, once more sober and for good reason, had suggested an artful scheme that would assure Baphomet's neutrality. Since the latter placed so much reliance on the automatic transmissions that would signal his whereabouts to any compatriot who came within range, effective interference with them would bring him to terms. Whether he wanted to or not, Baphomet would have to let them work in peace.

The Grand Master at once gave orders for carrying out the plan, using the relays at Baghdad and Cyprus to instruct the Commanderies around Grand-Orient Forest how to accomplish the interference. . . .

Baphomet protested, flew into a rage, but was forced to let the Templars act as they pleased.

Finally, fifty-two days after leaving Charkhlik, in spite of everything, the Crusaders emerged from the hellish desert. But the city where they had hoped to find some rest was destroyed, its walls choked with debris and all the running water poisoned with decomposing animal carcasses.

This in no way deterred William from setting up his camp: the ruins of the magnificent Buddhist temples and houses provided sufficient protection against enemy arrows. The foot soldiers also began to build an emergency rampart with stones taken from the rubble, while the Turcopoles began digging new wells.

Patrols sent out did not encounter the enemy, but they brought back a substantial quantity of game which was more than welcome. Very soon thereafter an appetizing odor emanated from the spits that turned over many fires. Suddenly, morale was considerably higher. . . .

Another blessing, even more precious: the night passed without an alert and everyone slept in peace.

The leaders of the Crusade evaluated their situation: the forces were reduced to forty thousand men. All the throwing engines were intact and there were sufficient chargers and beasts of burden that could be hitched to the carts now that there were usable roads.

To the north was Qomul, capital of the province, and farther Mongol Karakorum, Kubla's imperial city. According to information from the spies, Kaidu's troops, greatly exhausted themselves from the long stay in the desert, were resting in Qomul. As for the forces of the great Khan, they were massed around Chang-Chu, north of Peking. It seemed that the threat posed by the Templars had given Kubla enough concern so that he had called up both his regulars and his reserve forces; all his supporters, in fact.

Commanders and lesser officers agreed that they should remain where they were, at least long enough for the men to regain their strength. For his part, Brother Joubert started to work again, achieving the remarkable result of duplicating a vase. It disintegrated soon afterward; however, no such success had been previously achieved: the philosopher was nearing his goal.

Then, on one fine morning, the lookouts signaled the sighting of a small group of horsemen. Some were Mongols, but there were Christians among them, for colors of Venice shone side by side with the yak-tail pennants. The order was given that they be allowed to pass, after they had been searched and disarmed.

The Grand Master at once called his Templars together, lining them along either side of the road along which the strangers must travel, with the French and English dressed in all their finery, and between their ranks the embassy made its entrance into the ruined city.

Some of the Crusaders had never seen a Tartar at close quarters, and they stared with the greatest curiosity at the slitted eyes, the brassy skin, and the peculiar helmets— pointed steel caps, encircled with a fur corona. They also admired the small horses which were known, despite their short legs, to be almost tireless.

The Mongols wore clothing of silk or fine linen beautifully embroidered with gold, their capes lined with ermine or mink. Their cuirasses, however, made of plain leather, left the Templars somewhat skeptical as to their efficiency. The bridles of their horses were magnificent but, for the most part, the horsemen rode without saddle, astride a plain piece of fur or a cloth pad. All wore large quivers, normally filled with arrows, on their backs, with the bow slung over the shoulder.

At the head of the group rode a Christian, dressed in silk and sumptuous furs. He dismounted before the Grand Master, knelt with great dignity on one knee, and introduced himself:

"Noble sire," he said, "I am a humble Venetian merchant: Marco Polo by name. That name, perhaps, is not completely unknown to you since my brothers, on their return to Italy, made a report on their travels here. However, it is not as a merchant that I pay you this visit: the great Kubla Khan honors me with his friendship and has made me his ambassador. Here are my credentials, which he was good enough to entrust to me."

The young Marco gave the Grand Master several golden tablets on which were engraved a strange script.

"Please stand, Master Polo," William of Beaujeu answered. "We agree to hear you, although it seems strange that a Christian would serve as spokesman for an infidel. . . ."

Leading the way, he conducted his guests into an almost intact room which he used as his quarters. Commanders and guests seated themselves on coffers covered with furs, then the Templar continued, "Well, young man, tell us the Mongol's message."

"The Lord of Lords, sixth in the line of succession after Genghis, the most powerful of all emperors in this world, to the Great Master, William of Beaujeu, Commander of the army which, without a declaration of war, brings destruction and death into our empire, greetings.

"Rumors of your exploits have reached our ears in distant Cathay. Now you have arrived at the gates of my empire and a confrontation of our two armies becomes, it seems, inevitable. You possess a powerful weapon which launches lightning: it proves the worth of the sorcerers who surround you and most assuredly demonstrates the power of your god. The few priests who have come before me, up to the present time, gave a poor idea of your religion, because I, too, possess a few magic secrets and not unimportant ones. Food appears in the air and comes to me without being touched by human hand. I also know how to launch thunderbolts. Furthermore, I have an army of many hundreds of thousands of brave warriors. As of this moment, a battle between us risks costing us a great many human lives without any decisive result; unless it be that the decreasing of our separate forces, to the joy of jealous rivals, counts as a result.

"Here, then, is what seems to me a wise proposal: why do we not form an alliance? You have conquered Mesopotamia and Transoxiana, and I accept you as ruler of that empire, if you will agree not to meddle in the affairs of Cathay.

"I cannot believe that a leader, as wise and valorous as you, would think that he could overcome my countless battalions, like the Persians. For every hundred killed, another thousand warriors will rush to the attack, and if you annihilate them, ten thousand will take their places. I do not, therefore, see anything to be gained by you or by me if you precipitate a fruitless struggle.

"However, if the division of lands that I propose does not entirely suit you, I agree to discuss the matter with your ambassadors, unless you prefer a personal meeting in a mutually acceptable location.

"In the strength of eternal heaven, from my palace in Chang-Chu, Kubla, great Khan of the Mongols."

The Grand Master listened to this message most attentively: he did not have the slightest intention of complying with this suggestion of partition, for his pride and overweening ambition pushed him on to conquer the entire world. Nevertheless, a delay would suit his purposes. It would, perhaps, give Brother Joubert time to produce other atomic grenades which would greatly facilitate his task. Therefore, he replied:

"Master Polo, as you are a Christian, you know that our Lord, Jesus Christ, commanded us to be merciful to poor sinners. I am willing, therefore, to negotiate with Kubla Khan and will send him messages containing my counterproposals. First, I must discuss them with my allies and with my Council. For that reason, I ask that you withdraw for a little while. You shall have my reply shortly."

"I can but agree with such a wise course, venerable master. However, before I leave you, let me give you the presents which the great Khan bade me to offer you. . . ."

He clapped his hands and some of the Mongols entered to lay a veritable treasure at the feet of the Templar. Together with the most luxurious furs and swords in jeweled scabbards were vases of sculptured jade. There were fine lacquer panels with subtle designs and basins of gold that sparkled like fire. There were also dishes of an unknown material: porcelain. One particular object caught William's attention: inside a large protecting framework, several elephants seemed to circle, each holding the tail of the one in front of him in his trunk, all carved from ivory. The Templar had heard tales of these fabulous creatures and demanded more details.

"Are these those monsters used by Hannibal in his battles with the Romans? Tell me, are they really as gigantic as people say?"

"Indeed they are," the Venetian assured him. "Nature made these animals the most formidable in all creation. With their inordinately long noses, they can uproot great trees and, with their foreheads, they can smash the strongest walls. The great Khan owns several herds. When he goes hunting, four among them carry his lodge on their backs. Furthermore, they are priceless aids to the warriors who, enclosed in a tower on each elephant's back, loose their arrows on the enemy below, while they remain invulnerable. . . ."

"I see," said the Templar thoughtfully. "That is interesting. Thank you. You may retire now."

The discussion among the Crusaders lasted an hour. The manpower of the Mongol Khan and the presence of elephants in his forces gave pause to even the bravest. Nevertheless, William succeeded in imposing his will. He called the ambassadors and, still ignoring the Mongols, he addressed himself to the Venetian:

"Master Marco Polo, this infidel seems to me to be greatly infatuated with himself. He dares to speak of magic in connection with the lightning entrusted to me by the Archangel Gabriel; this shows how firmly he is anchored to the mummeries of his sorcerers. You must know that our only thought is propagation of the True Faith to the ends of the Earth: therefore, there can be no negotiations between us unless Kubla will abjure all his errors in order to be baptized in our Holy Church. As for his magicians and his elephants, they will be impotent when my lightning strikes them from the high reaches of heaven. I am ready to give him a demonstration if he would like one—on the battlefield, but then it will be too late. . . .

"My ambassadors shall carry the details of my message to him, as well as my presents: a reliquary containing a bit of the Sacred Cross, and an illuminated manuscript setting forth the life of our Lord, according to the Scriptures.

"At dawn tomorrow, you will set out on your return to Kubla's court. Let it be known that any attempt on the lives of my ambassadors, any affront suffered by them, will be cruelly punished. May our Lord keep you and watch over you. . . ."

Marco Polo made no reply. He bowed deeply to the assembly and left the camp, followed by his escort.

And so it was that, the following day, the Tholon brothers and the Templar from Tyre, in company with the embassy, found themselves galloping at top speed along the roads of Cathay.

Besides the promised gifts, they carried one of the Baphomet effigies so that they would be able to talk with the Grand Master from any distance. This statue had been secretly modified by Brother Joubert and contained an atomic grenade: if any unauthorized and overcurious individual examined it a little too closely . . . the ambassadors, naturally, knew nothing of this minor detail.

The four messengers soon understood the effectiveness of the Mongol stage system which allowed extremely rapid communication throughout Kubla's vast empire.

They hardly had time to admire the mountaintops in the golden embrace of the setting sun, the aquamarine of torrential streams, or the verdant hills fleecy with mist: each day, about noon, they came to a relay station. They stopped only long enough to swallow a snack and change horses, then set out again, galloping on until night fell. They never saw the slightest delay: at the mere sight of the great Khan's tablets, everyone obeyed without protest. To the great astonishment of the Christians, at each stop bed and board were paid for with simple pieces of paper rather than heavy, clinking coins.

Marco Polo explained to the Brother from Tyre how Kubla operated:

"This money circulates throughout the empire. It is manufactured in Peking from the pulped bark of the mulberry tree. The resulting paste is used to make the paper which is cut into rectangular pieces of different sizes. Each bears the signature and the seal of one of the Khan's high officials and everyone accepts them without the least hesitation. They have values from the little *trunsole* to two *besants*, so that merchants can carry large sums without sagging under the weight of their purses."

"This is certainly a strange procedure, which proves the confidence Kubla's subjects have in their master, for it would be a simple matter to counterfeit these pieces of paper. . . ."

"Don't you believe it," the Venetian declared. "The seal of the high treasure is most difficult to copy and, besides, the punishments devised for counterfeiters are such that no one would be willing to take the risk."

"It is certainly a method favorable to commerce," the Grand Master's ambassador admitted. "I am also struck by the admirable provisions made along highways so that the traveler finds comfortable inns at the end of each day's journey."

"And you will be even more surprised to learn that their maintenance depends directly on the provincial and the imperial governments. Each post keeps fleet horses and racing camels at the disposal of the great Khan's messengers. The entire system is comprised of two hundred thousand horses and ten thousand relay stations which are inspected without warning once every month. Because of this, we cover in four days distances which caravans take twelve days to complete."

"Your sovereign is endowed with great wisdom. I trust that he will show the same reasoning by accepting baptism and conversion to our Holy Faith. . . ."

"He is most certainly farseeing," the Venetian replied. "You must have noticed that he has had the sides of all roads planted with trees which ensure shade in summer and indicate the roadway in winter when it is covered with snow."

"That I had observed. I also note that his subjects seem very prolific, which means many mouths to feed. Every family appears to have innumerable children."

"That is because these pagans have many wives. But they have no dread of famine. First of all, because they are very frugal, and then because Kubla has proven his foresight. When the harvest is good, his agents buy rice, buckwheat and millet, which is stored. In bad years, they are sold at low prices; actually, at a quarter of their value."

"Now that is a most charitable attitude. This infidel possesses admirable qualities indeed. He knows how to use his riches with humanity. But, tell me, at our last halt I noticed an astonishing fact: the fire that burned on the hearth was not fed by wood but by some kind of black stones. Is this some kind of magic?"

"Of course not!" Marco Polo scoffed. "These stones come from the earth. They are very difficult to light but once they catch fire, they burn for a long time and give off much more heat than wood, a quality much appreciated in winter."

"This country is full of wonders, indeed, and we have

much to learn from its people," concluded the astonished Templar from Tyre.

The Tholon brothers were not having such an edifying conversation. This frantic ride across an unknown country was sorely trying them. Clement cursed without pause.

"By God, my arse is on fire. . . . I've been through plenty in this bitch of a life, but I've never been so worn out."

"Yes," agreed Guiot. "It's damned slavery, that's what; if I had known, I'd never have set foot in this wild country. They don't even have houses; except for these inns, there are only different kinds of felt tents. . . .

"And the stuff they give us to eat: dried milk and this slop they call yogurt, boiled mutton that smells rancid, and rice."

"Don't even mention it," Clement groaned. "Especially when I am perched on one of these filthy, stinking dromedaries. One word and I'd vomit up my guts. No Christian would ever have had the slightest notion of climbing on the backs of those beasts. They're all savages. . . ."

"Now, now, brothers!" The Templar lectured them. "Think of the honor that has been done us: the Grand Master chose us from hundreds of others; a mark of distinction that will fall on our entire family. And think, too, that you are earning your place in heaven. . . ."

"Well, as for that, I should have a privileged seat for all this," groaned Guiot. "Only I don't find it all that bad on Earth. I don't feel like dying prematurely but if this continues much longer, I'll never be able to sit down anywhere. . . ."

"Yes," agreed Clement, "it's always the same ones who have the best of it. The marshal is very happy at Samarkand. Oh sure, he keeps his poor wretches maneuvering all day but that's his idea of fun: discipline. The Seneschal only thinks of how he can best devote himself to rise from the ranks and become Grand Master. . . ."

"You're right about that! But Thibaut Gaudin certainly has the same idea . . . always agreeing with the venerable master, and never failing to butter him up!"

"Bah! How about John of Grailly: scribbling poems all the time to his lady love. The only thing that counts besides that is fine clothes. You can bet he's not working his arse off!"

"But, on the other hand, you can't accuse the Swiss of being lazy."

"Maybe not; but who is always picked to travel the roads of savages? It's always us. . . ."

Despite all this invective, the convoy made rapid progress and, one fine morning, the ambassadors came in sight of Chang-Chu where the great Khan resided.

Chapter VIII

The majesty of the imperial palace filled the Crusaders with awe. The wall surrounding it was even longer than that which encircled the ramparts of Carcassonne. There was an abundance of splendid parks. And there, in the lush meadows through which a lazy river meandered, strange animals grazed. Some trim bamboo pavilions and tents of multicolored silks were reflected in limpid pools.

Marco Polo explained that the Khan often hunted with his favorite leopards in these woods teeming with game.

The palace was entirely of marble, and when the messengers found themselves inside they could not decide what they admired most: the iridescent paintings, the lacquer-ware, or the delicate statues carved from blocks of jade.

They were ushered into chambers decorated with silks and rare furs, where the Tholon brothers were embarrassed at the necessity of treading on the resplendent carpets. Above them, the fabulously high ceilings, covered with crimson and gold varnishes, gleamed like the setting sun.

Slaves immediately brought them a meal so plentiful and tasty that the men from Auxerre fairly gave themselves indigestion. When night fell, beautiful courtesans entered to disrobe the emperor's guests. . . .

Clement and Guiot, fascinated, didn't know where to look, but the whole thing became even more laughable when the visitors were in their beds: these adorable young females, with their slanted eyes, slid in beside them clad only in the briefest of garments, making it quite clear that they were entirely available. . . .

It took all the faith of Garin and the Templar from Tyre to resist this cruel temptation. They had to lose their tempers,

mixing curses with invocations to God, in order to make the
she-devils understand that it was not customary in monasteries to have beds furnished in such a fashion. Finally, the
gentle maidens fled, crying hot tears at such an insult to their
charms.

The other two Tholon brothers did not, alas, give evidence
of any such stoicism and enjoyed a night full of incident. . . .

The following morning at dawn the Templars celebrated
mass, asking forgiveness for the sins of the poor sinners; then
they activated the Baphomet effigy and sent a message to the
Grand Master, detailing all they had seen during their journey and announcing their arrival at Chang-Chu. William ordered them to follow his instructions to the letter and to
accept no compromise.

An hour later the Lord High Chamberlain came to announce that his master Kubla, Khan of Khans, was ready to
receive them as ambassadors. Silk tunics as fine as cobwebs
had been prepared for them, but they preferred to present
themselves in their customary dress: the Templars wearing
their white mantles with the crimson cross and the squires
their coats of mail. Carrying their gifts, they followed an
honor guard through the palace to the throne room; passing
through two false ones before coming into the emperor's
presence.

The splendor of the hall surpassed that of any others they
had seen and the magnificence of the court dress could not be
equaled anywhere. However, it was Kubla himself, seated on
the throne, who held their attention.

The great Khan was of medium height and well-propor-
tioned. His light-complexioned face, with dark eyes, promi-
nent cheekbones and hooked nose, gave an impression of
cruelty tempered somewhat by the acute intelligence in his intent look.

He wore sumptuous robes adorned with pearls and precious stones. His guards were dressed in tunics of the same
style, with gold belts and short boots of soft leather, trimmed
with fur. The Templars' sober habits were in startling contrast with the opulent dress of the courtiers.

The Lord High Chamberlain moved toward them and ut-
tered a few words which Marco Polo translated, "Bow down
and adore!"

The Venetian gave the example, reverently bending low, but the ambassadors contented themselves with a curt and somewhat disdainful salutation. The Khan gave no sign of offense but he treated their meager gifts with the greatest disdain. After he put them aside, servants censed him with golden incense burners; then Kubla spoke:

"So these are the Templars' ambassadors. By Tengri, they're not much to look at . . .! Is William of Beaujeu so poor?"

"Our dress is that of our Order, sire," answered the Templar from Tyre. "All our Brothers have taken vows of poverty and own nothing besides their weapons. Each of us is the servant of the Grand Master, who may send us wherever he pleases. We promised God and our Lady to obey our leaders without question and swore to reconquer the Holy Land which, thanks to the Holy Mother Mary, is now accomplished."

"I am not unaware of your rules: poverty and chastity among them. But must you also harm people who have never offended you?"

"Certainly not, sire. But Bernard, the holy monk of Clairvaux, has said: 'Knights, use your weapons to strike down the enemies of Christ fearlessly, chastise nations, punish peoples by binding their kings and leaders with iron chains and shackles.' That is why our Baussant banner is of two colors: black and white, to signify that the Templars are open and benevolent with their friends, and relentless toward their enemies. And it is clearly evident that, until now, you have refused to obey the envoys of our Holy Father, the Pope, who exhorted you to forsake your pagan ways and become a Christian. Did you not insist that your magicians had powers surpassing those of the priests of Christ? Take careful heed: the madmen who dared to stand against the Templars in the Holy Land and in Mesopotamia paid for it with their lives. The Archangel Gabriel has decided to chastise you for your presumption by entrusting his servant, William of Beaujeu, with a celestial lightning against which all pagans are powerless."

"These are most insulting words coming from the mouths of ragged dogs like you. If I had not promised my faithful friend, Marco Polo, to hear you out, I would have you executed on the spot and make sure that you suffered a thousand deaths. Be done with insults: what is your master's answer to my message?"

"The Grand Master cannot agree to leaving such a vast empire in the hands of an unbeliever: therefore he enjoins you to be baptized without delay. This done, he will—in all clemency—agree that you continue to rule Cathay, on the condition, of course, that you swear allegiance to him and to our Holy Father, the Pope."

Kubla burst into epic laughter when the Venetian had translated these words. His courtiers imitated him and, after a full ten minutes of ribald derision, the Khan regained control of himself to state:

"I have not laughed like that in a very long time. What? Your William has the generosity to offer me what is already mine? Is he mad? His lightning doesn't frighten me: I, too, have devices that can throw flames, but does he have war elephants? Hundreds of thousands of horsemen? Let him push on into my vast empire if such is his wish. Soon, not one of his filthy pigs will remain alive. I was too kind in trying to avoid the extermination of such vermin. Your William has vanquished only poor luckless wights up to now; he does not know how powerful the Khan of Khans is. Go back to him and report my words: if, within a month, he has not ceased polluting my land with his presence, my army will wipe out the last vestige of the Templars. Now there is no question of letting him have the Khanate of Kaidu, nor even the Holy Land. I swear by our mother, Etugen! I shall not rest until the last Christian has left Mesopotamia and Syria. . . ."

The Templar of Tyre made no reply: he simply nodded and, followed by his small escort, left the palace. The Tholon brothers tried to put on a bold front but knew that they were in a tight corner and kept close watch on every side.

Marco Polo made a point of accompanying his coreligionists to their horses and wished them a safe return journey, with these words, "I am sorry that no common ground could be reached. Why were you so unbending? You could at least have proposed to demonstrate the powerful weapon you possess. That might have given the great Khan food for thought. . . ."

"No, my brother," replied the Templar from Tyre. "Our Grand Master did not wish it so, for the element of surprise provoked by this horrible explosion is, in itself, an important asset. Try to convince Kubla to be baptized; that is the only chance for peace. He knows our heaven-sent lightning only by hearsay but I can tell you that he will be terror-stricken by its power."

"I am willing to try, but any chance of success seems to my laughably small. My influence here amounts to little. All my good wishes go with you. Above all, do not stray from the road followed to come here, for the Khan has given orders for you to be killed if you attempt to spy on him."

"May heaven protect you," replied the Templar. "Take care not to be with the Khan's army if he dares to send it against us."

The four Crusaders again took up their wild ride. At the first stop, the Grand Master was informed of the outcome of their meeting with the great Khan. He made no comment other than to advise his ambassadors to make haste.

At that moment, William was going through a period of depression. Without waiting for the results of his mission—he had no illusions as to what they would be—he had put his forces in motion, occupying Süchow, or at least what was left of it, for the Mongols had burned it to the ground. This scorched-earth policy was their custom: they never accepted face-to-face combat unless their chances of success were beyond question. Buddhists, Saracens and Nestorian Christians had been evacuated, but the latter were now treated as enemies and led in long convoys toward the rear.

The morale of his army and its officers was at a low ebb and William once more convened his Council, for he sensed the rumblings of revolt among the Crusaders. He did not falter or dissimulate:

"Noble sires, my brothers," he began in a scarcely audible voice, "I will not hide from you my realization that our situation is perilous. . . . What good can come of a continued advance if, at every move, we find nothing but ruins? We have no lack of water but our food supply is dwindling dangerously. There is no possibility of living off the land with food taken from the peasants, for this devil Kubla creates a desert in front of us! Hunting provides only a limited supply of meat, for the game flees at the approach of hunters and leads us always forward."

"Nevertheless, our situation is unchanged in one way," Otto of Granson exclaimed. "No one can withstand us in ac-

tual battle with the lightning we possess. So, I cannot see
what prevents us from marching right to Peking; Kubla is going to have to face us one day or another. Why should we be
demoralized by some poor wretches who are afraid of
tightening their belts? Anyway, I am certain that I can bring
them back to reason if you give me leave."

"That is all very well, my brave Otto," replied the Grand
Master. "With the exception of one point: I have come to
wonder if we will indeed be able to defeat Kubla when he
launches his troops against us. . . ."

"And why shouldn't we? We certainly defeated the Mongols at Baghdad!"

"We certainly did, my sagacious friend . . . but I have just
received most disturbing news. The great Khan has called up
three hundred sixty thousand horsemen and one hundred
thousand foot soldiers: that is more than ten to one against
us. Further, he also claims to be able to hurl the lightning. . . ."

"Oh, come now," interrupted John of Grailly. "That is
sheer nonsense. How could he possess a weapon entrusted to
us by God Himself?"

"There is no proof it is the same."

"He is trying to frighten you," Otto of Granson muttered.
"Nobody ever heard of such a thing until the Archangel gave
it to you."

"It is possible nevertheless. I must warn you that my supply is now limited. What would happen if the Mongols
charged, wave after wave, without thought of their losses?"

"Bah!" growled the Swiss. "So much the better if there are
some left; my sword is thirsty for blood. Any one of your armored knights is worth ten of these dogs!"

"If we do not starve to death before then. . . ."

"Leave that to me," said the Swiss. "Give me one hundred
horsemen and I'll make it my business to bring you back
supplies. We have only to head south, where they're not expecting us."

"That seems a worthwhile proposal," approved the Grand
Master. "What is your opinion, brothers?"

Everyone approved the argument of the valiant Swiss, and
the discussion was resumed.

"One final point remains to be considered," William continued. "My emissaries report that Kubla has in his army
those monstrous elephants which Hannibal once used against

Rome. I fear that a charge by those huge creatures could not be stopped as easily as that of horses, even with the blinding power of our weapon."

"I have thought at length on the problem of meeting these beasts," John of Grailly interrupted, smiling. "I am told that these monsters have tender bellies, and a simple fire fed by a few barrels of naphtha, of which we have a sufficient supply, should send them stampeding back toward their own masters."

"That is an ingenious suggestion," the Grand Master approved. "It seems then that we should continue to advance, come what may. Besides, no one is anxious to recross the great desert, where our losses were so great. I shall bow to the will of the majority. . . . Let those who wish to continue the march toward Peking raise their hands.

A majority of two-thirds having approved the resolution, the Crusaders left the ruins of Süchow and headed toward the large city of Kanchow.

At that time, Brother Joubert reported a startling discovery to his leader, Baphomet, still locked in the depths of his pond, had modified the text of his distress signal. It was considerably longer and a detailed breakdown of its contents enabled the Turcopole linguists to translate it. Baphomet was now relating the particulars of what had happened to him on Earth since his accident, pointing out that the Templars were making dangerous scientific progress and that it was of the utmost importance to stop them before they became dangerous.

The news sent William of Beaujeu's spirits soaring: it seemed to verify the fact that the learned Joubert was on the right track! Everything would be different if he could finally adjust this mineral-sperm generator, this super-philosopher's-stone which was capable of duplicating endlessly any kind of object.

Further, Otto of Granson's expedition proved extremely profitable and his raid on regions which appeared to be unmenaced by the Crusaders yielded a considerable stock of rice; enough to ensure a month's food for the entire army. The future suddenly looked much brighter and everyone took heart again.

Unfortunately, as they approached Kanchow, the usual cloud of smoke informed the Crusaders that the Mongols had not changed their tactics. Again gloom settled over the army.

The exhausted foot soldiers refused to go any farther, preferring to die on the spot rather than take another step.

William took stringent measures against the ringleaders. For the first time since they had set out, knights were ignominiously stripped of their rank and paraded through the camp in carts. Squires were decapitated, sergeants whipped. All this was lost effort.

Deep despair had seized the Crusaders who—lost in an unknown country, several months' march from Baghdad—no longer believed in the final victory. Besides, winter was approaching and the prospect of facing its rigors without the least shelter from the cold frightened even the bravest.

Again it was the giant Swiss who saved the situation. Always ready for a scouting expedition, he took long rides through the surrounding countryside, often meeting and doing battle with enemy horsemen. He was always victorious, for even the sharpest arrows could do little against his coat of mail. This enabled him to study the large wild oxen of the country—called "yaks" by the natives—covered with long hair and difficult to capture. They roved the plains in enormous herds. The Swiss privately decided to carry out a great roundup and succeeded in driving an entire herd back to the camp. The arrows and spears of the squires killed several hundred, again ensuring the Crusaders of food.

This time it could not be regarded as mere chance: God, most assuredly, wanted to encourage His faithful servants and William ordered thirty masses of thanksgiving to be said.

In the midst of all this, the Templar of Tyre and the Tholon brothers rejoined the army. The Grand Master immediately heard their report, which gave him much food for thought. On their way back, the ambassadors had received a package, carefully wrapped in yak hides and, when they opened it, they found the heads of the hashshashins previously sent out by William. There was no use then in counting on doing away with the great Khan and, from then on, there would be no more information as to the movement of his troops. . . .

This new setback was a heavy blow to the leader of the Crusade.

Even a visit from Brother Joubert, who came to tell him that he had finally succeeded in generating the fluid needed to operate the transmuter, gave him no joy. The Templar had strung long silver wires between the several terminals, at last successfully producing duplicates of the atomic grenades. Unfortunately, they stubbornly refused to explode. . . . There was still some detail he had not grasped.

Cloistered in his tent, the Grand Master spent his days in prayer, going out only to attend mass, refusing to speak with anyone. . . .

No one paid any heed, for food was abundant again. In addition to the yak meat, hunters were also bringing back musk deer, which tasted delicious roasted on a spit, providing the musk gland near the navel was first removed. They also killed enormous pheasants, which reminded them of other days in the pleasant realms of France or England.

While the army regained its strength, the commander in chief moped in his tent. Finally William actually fell ill, attacked by a high fever. Immediately, doctors were called but they understood little of the nature of the complaint from which he suffered. They prescribed bleeding and the application of plasters which resulted only in unbearable itching.

Everyone grieved. Masses and prayers were said for his recovery but to no avail. Our Lady seemed to have forsaken Her servant. . . .

The Grand Master was greatly affected by all this: possessing a robust constitution, he had never been ill before and thought that he was going to die at any moment. The commanders of the troops were therefore called to his bedside to hear his last wishes.

Absolute silence reigned in the camp, everyone speaking in low tones and the servants careful to make no sound in the performance of their duties.

The Commanders of the Temple, Otto of Granson and John of Grailly, knelt by the bed of this illustrious patient. They recited prayers under the direction of a Brother-Chaplain, then William spoke in a weak voice, while his clerk carefully recorded his words:

"Kind lords, my brothers, today I was heard in confession and I speak to you with a pure heart, cleansed of all sin. My greatest desire has always been to propagate the word of our Lord, Jesus Christ, and to convert pagans. That is the reason why our forces are now so far removed from our respective countries. Heaven granted me weapons of a power previously unknown and with their help I gained spectacular victories;

therefore you must by no means stop on such a promising path. I plead with you to continue our Crusade when the God of all Christians has called me to Him. The first task incumbent upon you is to choose my successor. The Chapter of Commanders will therefore meet and each of you must obey him who will be appointed as you have obeyed me."

He caught his breath and continued, "I know that this election will not comply with the rules laid down by my predecessors, for many commanders will be unable to attend. The man elected, therefore, will be only an interim Grand Master and his office will be definitely confirmed only when the dignitaries from all Christian kingdoms are able to gather in assembly. I know that he will be capable of doing what is required but his task will be most difficult, for this time the infidels are numberless. They have, besides, their monstrous elephants and we . . . we have only an insufficient quantity of the celestial weapons. . . ."

He took several deep breaths and resumed. "For a time I hoped it would be possible to acquire more by resorting to the subtle mysteries of alchemy, and our devoted Brother Joubert has spent many days and nights working to that end. That hope, up to now, has been disappointed. Therefore you must count only on your courage to win the victory. Have faith in our Lord and the Blessed Virgin Mary who will not forsake you. . . ."

This speech seemed to have exhausted him: his head fell back and he closed his eyes. Those present thought for a moment that he was about to die, but the strong chest rose and fell regularly.

With tear-filled eyes, they left the tent in total silence.

While the Crusader commanders held long talks trying to decide if it would not be better to start retreating at once, without waiting for the Grand Master's death, the common soldiers gave themselves up to debauchery. They believed that all was completely lost, for they knew what fearful numbers of troops Kubla had massed against them and held no illusions as to their fate.

The rice wine discovered in peasant huts flowed in abundance and Christian heads reeled under its high alcoholic content. But even worse, the absence of prostitutes led to a wave of sodomy in the camp. Discipline was nonexistent, and if the Mongols had attacked at that moment there would have been no doubt as to the outcome of the battle.

However, the Crusader officers shortly recovered some degree of confidence and authority. Sergeants went through the camp and threw all the drunks they found into a pit, leaving them there for several days without food or drink. The less guilty ones were simply flogged with their stirrup straps. Some Templars caught in the act of debauchery were dropped from the Order and reduced in rank to mere squires. Two unregenerates, who persisted in their erring ways, were beheaded before the whole army. This served as a lesson for the others and the situation soon became normal again.

In the meantime, William—contrary to all expectations—was slowly recovering. Brother Joubert, as a last resort, made him drink a horribly bitter concoction prepared from aromatic barks and red earth from the Indian kingdom of Multifili, to the north of Coromandel. Some caravan merchants had left these with him in gratitude for the hospitality they had received during their stay in the camp, and they had declared that this remedy was sovereign against tertian or quartan agues.

Soon the Grand Master started to eat again and the yak meat quickly restored all his vigor. The army, of course, saw this as a miracle and everyone recovered, as if by sorcery, all his previous energy. These brave souls had come to know their leader well and had complete confidence in him. Once more William of Beaujeu would lead them to victory.

It was a strange coincidence that on the Mongol side Kubla was also experiencing alternating periods of pessimism and optimism. He went on assembling his regulars and his reserves but remained undecided and could not give the order to leave Chang-Chu. His adversary's lightning worried him much more than he had let William's ambassador know.

Because of this, the great Khan summoned before him everyone who might be able to give him information on the subject. The merchants who came from Mesopotamia by both land and sea were the most explicit. Their reports all agreed: no army, however large its numbers, would have the least chance of victory over the Templars.

The lightning acted in several ways. First, the explosion threw horsemen and foot soldiers to the ground. Those near to it were simply vaporized. The others, seriously burned,

Pierre Barbet

died quickly. It also produced a wind of incredible force which could be felt at a considerable distance and which flattened everything in its path. Finally, those survivors who stayed for any time near the craters made by the explosion, even if not significantly wounded, ended by dying of consumption after varying periods of time.

However, one detail of all these reports caught his attention: it seemed to him that several times during the battle of Baghdad the Grand Master had been in perilous situations from which he could have extricated himself by a massive use of his lightning; however, he had not done so.

The unanimous opinion of his counselors was that this proved his adversary must use the weapon carefully because of limited supply.

The problem, then, was to discover how many times the Grand Master could unleash his lightning in the course of a regular battle. No one knew how to find out. . . .

As a precautionary measure, on the advice of one of his Tumens, an officer commanding ten thousand men, Kubla had ten thousand cassocks made up from salamander—asbestos—for the protection of his personal guard.

He then questioned other travelers as to the size of his opponent's army. All agreed that the Crusaders numbered no more than fifty thousand. This greatly encouraged the great Khan, for his available forces were superior by ten times that figure.

One question discussed at length in the council was that of the use of elephants in the course of such a battle. Opinions were divided: if the pachyderms panicked from the explosions and burns, would they not turn back against their masters? Taking everything into account, a solution was found: the elephants would be blanketed with salamander to protect their flanks and their ears would be plugged with wax.

It seemed that all tactical questions were resolved, and yet the great Khan remained undecided.

The reason was simple: his shamans had practiced their divinations by examining the scapulas of sheep and the results had not been at all favorable. He then called on magicians who, in a trance, communicated with the realm of the dead and their conclusions were unequivocally adverse. Some among them went so far as to claim that the Khan's ancestors were waiting for Kubla's imminent arrival. . . .

Therefore, propitiatory rites were performed. Incense was burned before the ancestor images, while priests did complicated dances around them, grimacing and gnashing their teeth. Horses and slaves were sacrificed, but the dead did not change their views.

Saracen astrologers, highly expert in that art, were then called upon. They were extremely cautious, declaring that the position of the planets in the days to come could give victory to the Templars or to the Mongols.

Nevertheless, a decision must be made for, as the days went by, an increasing number of brawls flared among the warriors of this immense army gathered from vastly different regions.

Princes, lords and Tumens therefore were asked to agree to a great sacrifice and to contribute either a beloved slave or a favorite horse. The influence of the Khan was such that no one protested: rivers of blood flowed during this holocaust. And finally the diviners declared with joy that the dead were appeased and promised success to the Mongol forces.

Thanks, in the form of sumptuous gifts to priests, were paid to Natigai, god of Earthly destinies.

All punishments, floggings, the yoke torture or the strappado were suspended. The legions began their march to the place chosen by the commanders of the army, the Noyans, to lie in wait for and destroy the army of insolent fools who dared to soil the empire of Cathay with their feet.

Chapter IX

The Grand Master had now recovered all his accustomed vigor. Because any retreat was next to impossible, the only reasonable solution was to fight—to win. He carefully studied the terrain between the two armies: the only favorable location was near Taichaohsiang. The caravans usually followed that route which passed between a swampy loop of the Hwang Ho (Yellow River) and the Hara Narin Ula Mountains. Since they would again, on this occasion, be facing an opponent superior in number, the wisest course was to position his fifty thousand knights and foot soldiers on high ground where the ballistae could be aimed with precision.

According to merchants traveling the route back to the west, Kubla had not yet left Chang-Chu. By setting out at once and pressing on in forced marches, the occupation of this key position would be feasible. However, before giving orders to break camp, William needed to consult Baphomet.

After a few seconds' wait, the device came to life and Baphomet answered the call, "Well! It's a long time since I last had the pleasure of talking with you, Earthly friend; can it be that you have encountered unexpected difficulties?"

"I certainly have had my share of troubles," the Templar informed him stiffly. "My forces melted away while we were crossing the desert. We have known famine and, to complicate matters, I was the victim of a serious illness."

"Oh? I tend to forget that your race is still subject to many maladies. Unfortunately I can do nothing for you in this area, for the small store of medications I possess would not do you any good at all. Besides, we are separated by a considerable distance and I have abandoned any hope of flying

122

through the air again. Still, you seem to have recovered complete health?"

"I have indeed, for the Lord decreed that I should continue to lead our Crusade against the unbelievers, and that is what I want to consult you about. Our enemies number close to five hundred thousand, ten times our forces, and my stock of magic weapons is now sufficient. . . ."

"Here again, I regret to say, I cannot help you. You know that when my spacecraft met with this accident I kept an absolute minimum of necessities and I cannot give you any. But you have already proven your abilities as a strategist. Using my grenades judiciously should assure your victory."

"May heaven hear you!" sighed the Grand Master. "You advise me then to seek out this encounter?"

"Most certainly! I promised your predecessors that I would give them the entire world as an empire, and you are nearing that goal. If you are victorious now, no one hereafter will be able to stand in your way."

"Have you consulted your magic devices that foretell the future?"

"Indeed I have, and you have a good chance of winning the day," answered Baphomet, without committing himself.

This evasive response did not satisfy the Templar, but he was unable to extract any further information from the creature. The conversation ended in a rather surprising way.

Suddenly the eyes of the effigy were streaked with a thousand colors and a hypnotic music filled the tent. William, transfixed, barely seemed to breathe.

Then Baphomet continued, "William of Beaujeu, are you prepared to obey me in all things?"

"Yes, master. . . ."

"You are to go forth and destroy this vermin that attempts to bar your way to the Empire of the World. Then you will govern, under my orders, for the greatest good of all Baphomets."

"I understand."

"Good. You will forget the end of our conversation."

On these words the statue became inactive and the Templar, as though waking from a dream, stretched and yawned.

Some hours later the army formed its long column and set out for Yungchang, the first city on their way to Taichaohsiang. The Tholon brothers, since they already knew the terrain, were in the vanguard and as usual—talking their heads off.

"By dawn!" Clement swore. "I was beginning to rust. I'm not at all sorry to go and give those savages a thrashing. How about you, Guiot?"

"Damned right! Let's finish them off for good. All the same, I have an idea it's not going to be easy. It seemed to me that Kubla was a foxy devil."

"Foxy he may be, but that's not going to save him from croaking just like the others. I swear to God, when that lightning goes off, there'll be meat and guts all over the place. How about it, Garin?"

"I'm not, unfortunately, as optimistic as you, my dear brothers. . . . The great Khan has a well-trained army and his monstrous elephants will be the death of more than one good Christian."

"Rubbish! Are you trying to make me believe their little beasties can stand up to the Archangel Gabriel's lightning?"

"Perhaps you're right," the Templar brother admitted. "However, we'll have to use a lot of the gray spheres to destroy those powerful brutes. Please God, we have enough to sow death in the Mongol ranks!"

"What are you saying . . . that the Grand Master doesn't know what he's doing?"

"Our venerable leader has certainly weighed every argument for and against it, but that doesn't change the fact that this battle is going to be far more difficult to win than those before."

"By damn!" said Clement dreamily. "When I remember that palace we visited, I get goose bumps all over! They say Peking is even more stunning."

"Don't be so easily tempted by the vile pleasures of this world," scolded the Templar. "You tend overmuch to forget that our only goal is to propagate the True Faith. What kind of an example will you be for the pagans if you lie around in luxury and debauchery?"

"You're right," Guiot mumbled. "We didn't behave very well in Kubla's palace. But you have to admit that those poor girls were pretty upset at the thought that we didn't want to . . . take care of them. . . ."

"Did I yield to temptation?" asked Garin sharply.

"No. Of course not. But you . . . you're practically a saint; and me, I'm only a poor sinner. . . ."

"Well, say your prayers a little more often," his brother snapped. "Wear a haircloth shirt to mortify your flesh if necessary."

"I'll try . . . but it's not my fault that I'm hot-blooded. . . . Say, getting back to the subject of Kubla, is it true that we're going to wait for him at Taichaohsiang?"

"So I've heard."

"Not a bad spot, they say. If we can dig in on the slopes, the Mongols will have a hard time driving us out."

"Provided we get there before they do. And the men are dragging their feet. Go and prod them a bit."

Guiot, the Red-Beard, obeyed and his gruff voice thundered at the laggards. He backed his words with some striking arguments and everyone was soon back in place.

And so the army came to Yungchang, where it stayed only long enough for the men to rest a little. Besides, this city too had been destroyed and had no strategic value.

The Crusaders' forced marches brought them to the Hara Mountains before Kubla with time for hurried fortification. They dug trenches at the bottom of the slopes and set the most exposed areas with long, pointed wooden shafts.

The ballistae and mangonels were placed on hilly summits where they could command all sectors. Finally, the last night before the Mongols came in sight, William ordered that hearty rations of yak and game be distributed to all. It was of little importance now that supplies were dwindling: either they would be victorious or they would die. . . .

The great Khan took his ease and hurried nothing. Why should he, when his ancestors had assured him that he would be victorious? Certainly the multitude of his soldiers, his war chariots, his battle-trained elephants carrying archers in turrets, was an extraordinary spectacle. No one, not even his grandfather, Ghengis Khan, had ever commanded such an army. There was no doubt that the Christian dogs would be annihilated. There would, of course, be losses in the Mongol ranks, caused by their diabolical weapon, but that mattered little. The empire of Cathay swarmed with people, and the death of one hundred—or even two hundred—thousand men would not be an irreplaceable loss.

Moreover, he—Kubla—had new and astonishing engines

invented by the Chinese savants, whose talents he had stimulated with generous gifts so that their ingenuity had developed fantastic weapons. They were not, certainly, as
powerful as those of the Templars; nevertheless, they were
valuable assets. Not to mention subtle ruses he intended to
use which would give the foreign dogs some difficulties. . . .

The Khan passed that night preceding the battle in his
palace at Linho while his troops took positions about the
plateau, almost encircling the Crusaders.

He honored, because it pleased him, his favorite wife and
in the morning—before daybreak—ate a hearty breakfast.
Then, donning his most resplendent robes, he climbed to the
tower carried by the strongest of his elephants. From there he
could easily survey the battlefield and have an overview of all
phases of the engagement.

The mahout started the enormous pachyderm, which—surrounded by the ten thousand men of the Khan's personal
guard—majestically took the road to the Hara Mountains.
The Khan was exceedingly good-humored: his magicians had
once more assured him of the success of this venture. It
promised to be a beautiful, clear day. Who could ask for
more? During the journey he constantly exchanged pleas-
antries with the princess who accompanied him.

When he reached the field, he had the satisfaction of seeing
the many squadrons all in their planned positions, well beyond the reach of the enemy mangonels.

A small doubt still lurked in a corner of the Khan's mind,
however. He was reluctant to launch his troops in a decisive
action unless under the most favorable omens. He therefore
called a new Tibetan magus before him, a seer of great
renown, and asked him if he thought the outcome of the
battle would be favorable for him.

The old man did not resort to any of the usual trickery of
charlatans. He was a small man with a skin as wrinkled as
that of an old apple, and piercing eyes of astonishing acuity.
It was said that he had the power to communicate by thought
alone with the lamas in the faraway regions from which he
came. He could also impose his will on whomever he wished,
and make him perform actions of which the temporary slave
had not the remembrance.

The Tibetan put himself into a trance: his eyes rolled up,
his body was seized with a cataleptic rigidity, then he rose

some distance above the ground and floated there, to the great astonishment of everyone present. Presently he sank slowly to the ground, shuddered violently as though he had witnessed mysteries too frightening for the human mind, then said in a low voice:

"Mighty Khan of Khans, you put me to a formidable test. My incorporate being plumbed the limitless spaces between universes and consulted our wise ancestors but it was almost impossible to communicate with the spirits who preside over the destinies of our enemies. A terrifying aura surrounds them. I felt the presence of a malefic creature who subjects them and whose power throws a cloud over the future. Nevertheless, I was vouchsafed a glimpse of this plain covered with dead bodies. . . . I am unable to say which side will be victorious. One thing, however, is certain: your precious days are not in danger."

"That means that we shall win," Kubla exclaimed. "These Templars would certainly not allow me to live if they won the battle. Still, this aura intrigues me greatly. What, in your opinion, is it? Could it be produced perhaps by one of their gods?"

"Absolutely not! I have never encountered such a powerful and malignant spirit: I believe that the creature is a stranger to our world."

"Is it serving them?"

"No indeed. This being serves only its own best interests."

"Good. Why then should we fear it? Go. My Lord High Treasurer will give you twenty stallions from my own stables or, if you prefer, the equivalent in pure gold."

The Tibetan bowed but without servility. Kubla climbed back into his palanquin, the elephants moved forward and the imperial standard was raised and lowered several times, a signal for the foot soldiers to begin the attack.

Each Tumen passed this order along to his own ten-thousand-man division, which rushed in a body toward the Christian positions. Like an army of ants, the warriors swarmed up the slopes.

The bravest among the Crusaders felt their throats go dry at the sight of such a multitude. And a horrifying shock was in store. Using a trick common among the Mongols, Kubla had ordered his troops to drive all the Nestorian Christians captured in the destroyed cities before them.

Men, women and children, forced to advance for they were spurred on by the pikes of the foot soldiers, called out to their coreligionists to have pity on them, to save them. . . .

Immediately advised of this, William was faced with a terrifying dilemma. Should he refrain from launching the grenades to avoid killing these fellow creatures who, although considered heretics, were nevertheless Christians?

With bowed head, nervously clasping and unclasping his hands, he remained indecisive for seconds that seemed an eternity. Then, with a sigh, he ordered the mangonel tacticians to launch the projectiles, but behind the wretched flock which, with eyes streaming tears, advanced toward them uttering piteous cries.

At once the deadly mushrooms of smoke and dust rose from among the sea of Mongols, resulting in appalling carnage. In the midst of men so closely massed, the destructive force of the grenades was unbelievable. Fragments of human flesh flew in every direction; severed limbs were thrown with such force that they fell on the horsemen waiting some distance behind the advance line.

Salamander tunics, to some extent, staved off burns, but did not lesson the shock or other effects of the explosions. When the smoke began to lift, the Crusaders saw all survivors running away at full speed, seized by uncontrollable panic. Some of them even ran past the last lines of reserves and disappeared from the plain, without anyone being able to stop them and bring them back to reason.

From the height of his tower Kubla saw everything. He had expected the enemy weapon to be spectacular, but its effect was far more horrifying than anything he had been able to imagine. The blinding bolts of lightning, the deafening explosions were something inhuman. Even the elephants trembled, despite the wax plugs in their ears and the mahouts calmed them with difficulty. As for the horses, they reared and bucked in terror, throwing the most expert riders.

Nevertheless, the unfortunate prisoners, almost all of them unhurt, except for a few burns and singed hair, rushed the Christian lines, causing great confusion. They were quickly led to the center of the defense formations where they fell prone with hands pressed to their temples. None of them felt strong enough to go through such an experience again.

For a long time the two adversaries remained alert and expectant. The Crusaders had no wish to abandon their fortified position; as for the Mongols, their ardor was definitely dampened. . . . The Jaghouns—officers commanding one hundred men—ran through the lines threatening and exhorting but with little result.

Kubla himself had to down several cups of wine to recover his self-control; then he consulted with his generals in order to determine whether or not there was still a reasonable chance of being victorious.

All declared unanimously that defeat was certain if the Templars had a large supply of the fiendish weapons. There was, however, one hope: by saturating the battlefield, William of Beaujeu could have completely wiped out the assault waves, but he had launched a relatively small number of explosives. Wasn't this a sign that he did not have many more?

Reassured, the Khan had his own fireworks technicians called to demonstrate to his followers that he, too, possessed powerful magic trickeries.

Powder, which had been known for some time, had been used by the astute philosophers to manufacture self-propelled weapons. Pressed into long bamboo tubes, it was lit at the rear, which had the effect of driving the long shafts forward. In theory, they were designed to reach the Crusaders' positions, then the front part would explode, scattering iron pellets mixed with the powder in all directions. Preliminary tests had been relatively satisfactory except in the matter of length of the slow-burning fuse used for propulsion. Having no time for further experiments, they had to rely on the results already obtained.

The pyrotechnics fired the primitive rockets which soared gracefully from their launching cradles, leaving sinuous trails of smoke behind them. Unfortunately, some stubbornly refused to leave the ground, exploding without warning and killing some of the artillerymen. Others exploded harmlessly in the air.

These projectiles generated a great deal of smoke but did little damage. In fact, the metal pellets lacked the force to penetrate mail, much less steel helmets. A few Turcopoles were wounded, since they were less well-protected; a few horses panicked; nothing really alarming. . . .

Among the Mongols, however, the effect on the general

morale was euphoric: from a distance the result appeared
identical with that of the Christian explosives, so that all were
convinced that they possessed a weapon equal to that of their
adversaries.

The Tumens were able to resume command of their divisions; Kubla, however, had no illusions, having clearly seen
the laughable effect of his toys, and could not bring himself
to order a new assault. After all, the enemy was surrounded:
they would be forced to take the initiative since they now had
many more mouths to feed, and there was no water on the
hilltops. They would have to do something about that. The
Khan therefore ordered the foot soldiers to withdraw beyond
range of the mangonels, and to wait there.

It was then that the hot-blooded enthusiasm of the Franks
and the English almost brought about a catastrophe. Seeing
the enemy retreating and wanting to distinguish themselves in
battle, they rushed to attack, riding down the slopes at full
speed. The Templars alone held their positions.

This charge was a splendid sight: their lances pointed forward, shields against their breasts, helmet plumes whipping in
the breeze, armor glistening in the sun, these men of iron appeared invulnerable. The painted coats of arms, the embroidered caparisons blazed with a thousand fires.

Far from opposing their insane thrust, the wily Khan
quickly had an opening made in front of them, so that the
brave impetuous knights suddenly found themselves far from
their positions.

Then the Asiatic artillerymen began firing their rockets,
aiming them along the ground at the legs of the horses. The
noble warriors were quickly thrown from their mounts, biting
the dust or floundering on their backs like overturned
turtles. . . .

Fortunately, they were more frightened than hurt and, by
the time the Mongol infantry moved in, the majority were on
their feet, their long swords ready for their opponents.

Yet all this seemed bound to end badly, for they were
completely cut off. The furious Grand Master was forced to
order more grenades launched at the enemy artillery positions, and then a Templar relief sortie.

Again armor glistened and unsheathed swords flashed in
the sun. With a cry of "Baussant to the rescue!" the monk-

warriors cut through the Mongol ranks like augers in soft wood and reached the Frankish and English squadrons.

Monks or soldiers, in their large white capes with the crimson cross and their square helmets, they were the incarnation of courage and gallantry. With each stroke of their blades, accompanied by a hoarse grunt, a Mongol fell.

At last, the surrounded horsemen were able to mount some of the riderless horses, or climb up behind a Templar. Then, as though on parade, the latter did an about-face, carrying the rescued men back to their own lines.

The total loss of men was negligible but one horse out of three was lost. Some, their bellies cut open by the grapeshot, were still trotting aimlessly, stumbling over their own entrails.

Again calm reigned on the battlefield. Each of the adversaries waited for the other to take the initiative. Finally, Kubla decided the time had come to send in his elephants, hoping that William would exhaust the last stock of his devilish lightning on them.

The Templar was careful not to fall into that trap. He waited until the cohort of monstrous pachyderms was at the foot of the slopes below his fortifications, then set fire to naphtha poured into the trenches dug the previous day.

His stratagem was a complete success. Panicked by the flames licking their bellies, which were unprotected by the salamander blankets, the elephants—trumpeting in pain—turned and charged the Mongols. . . .

The rout was spectacular! Unfortunately, at that very instant, Commander Thibaud Gaudin, terror-stricken, arrived to tell the Grand Master that a Mongol attack on the other side of the plateau had been launched simultaneously with that of the elephants.

This time it was impossible to resort to tricks. The ballistae again launched their deadly missiles, but Kubla intended to finish off his enemy: he had ordered his officers to kill anyone who tried to flee. The result was that his foot soldiers advanced even with terrible losses. Never-ending streams of Mongols poured over the smoking craters. For every one killed, one hundred more surged up behind him, unceasingly, without respite.

This time the stock of grenades was alarmingly low. With certain death before them, the Grand Master ordered the firing to cease. The Templars grouped together to fight hand to hand until the end.

On another side the Mongol cavalry had attacked again and the outnumbered Christian horsemen were falling back. The situation was fast becoming desperate. . . .

As far as the eye could see the plain was teeming with the enemy.

The Crusaders had only one hope left: to kill, kill and kill again, to sell their lives dearly until they were engulfed by this human tide.

It was then that one—two—ten—a hundred atomic explosions ravaged the rear lines of the enemy. One after another, without interruption, the mangonels loaded, firing as though they had boundless reserves. William thought he must be dreaming. Lowering his bloody sword, he left the front line and made his way to the mangonels.

There he found a triumphant Brother Joubert producing endless new grenades from the duplicator that at last worked again.

Now every mangonel and ballista was in action. The bravery, however legendary, of the Mongols could not hold under such carnage. The stampeded. The range of the mangonels was increased.

In the distance, the Grand Master could make out the mahouts attempting to curb the elephant on which Kubla's turret was perched, but in vain. The canopy of colored silks plunged to the ground.

A charge of knights carrying grenades forced their way through the ranks of survivors and reached the Khan of Khans. Kubla, dusty, bruised but unharmed, was taken prisoner. Completely broken by such misfortunes, he was put in chains and brought back to William of Beaujeu without having quite realized the extent of his defeat. . . .

That same evening the Crusaders discovered with delight the thousand, refinements of an imperial palace with its gracious courtesans.

Epilogue

Well-served by his good fortune and his courage, William of Beaujeu would, from that time onward, possess the most extensive empire ever conquered by a single man.

No one would ever dare to oppose him; the report of his victory spread throughout all Asia like wildfire. Kaidu and General Nayan, until then living in expectation of a different outcome, arrived to offer their submission.

The proud Sung dynasty, which still dominated the southern regions of Cathay, sent an ambassador to bring him the keys to their capital, Hangchow. The commanders of the Karakorum and Peking garrisons did the same. Now the Grand Master completed his conquests without making a move.

However, he could not keep his faithful supporters at his side, for the management of such vast territories demanded trustworthy overseers. Therefore, he put the former Khanate of Kaidu and all the realm of Transoxiana in the care of his Marshal, the valiant Peter of Sevry. John of Grailly, who seemed to be on hot coals, seized the first opportunity to board a vessel bound for Basra, where his beloved princess waited for him.

On the other hand, the fiery temperament of Otto of Granson would allow him no satisfaction in the luxury of a palace with prospects of nothing but peace. He therefore assembled a fleet and, at the head of his English knights joined by Mongol mercenaries, sailed to conquer the fabulous island of Japan.

The Templar from Tyre remained at the side of his leader to set down the chronicle of his epic crusade, already legendary.

Among all those who survived these memorable adventures, the most astonished was Kubla. After his capture the Khan of Khans expected his vanquisher to have him executed. The Grand Master, quite to the contrary, treated him with great honor, learned his language and spent long evenings talking with him. The Mongol was permitted to keep his private quarters, his wives, and was given a lavish allowance. There was a single, minor restriction: a guard commanded by Garin with the assistance of his two brothers kept the Khan under surveillance night and day.

During the course of one of their friendly discussions, Kubla asked the Templar how the magical weapons which gave him the victory had come into his possession. William hesitated an instant, then told him the exact circumstance of the finding of Baphomet, the past alliance with him and the gift of the atomic grenades, passing silently over the existence of Brother Joubert's precious duplicator.

The Mongol was extremely astonished to learn in this way of otherworldly beings who, to him, were nothing but demons inhabiting inaccessible heavenly bodies. However, the frankness of his new friend moved him to tell of the revelation made before the battle of Taichaohsiang by the Tibetan magus.

Now it was William's turn to be dumbfounded. According to this seer, he, the Grand Master of the Templars, was nothing but a puppet in the hands of Baphomet. Reason enough for him to be stunned.

Until now his relations with the creature lurking in the tarn had seemed to him to be entirely to his advantage, since he believed that he held the demon at his mercy. Actually, only the food faithfully supplied each day by the Templars of Pinay or Beaulieu allowed Baphomet to survive. The Grand Master had always believed that putting an end to that service would be sufficient to bring the mysterious being to terms. And now someone had revealed that he was the dupe, that his so-called captive held him under a spell, thanks to his astonishing psychic powers.

William could not believe it was true. Yet, turning the matter over in his mind, he remembered how Brother Joubert had been subjected. Perhaps, after all, there was some truth in what this foreign magician said. Inquiry revealed that the Tibetan was still in the palace and William sent for him that he might question him further.

As soon as he was shown in, the lama showed the perceptive nature of his mind by declaring:

"Puissant Master of the Templars, you acted wisely in calling me before you. On numerous occasions I have attempted to warn you but each time your door was barred to me. You are under the sway of a devilish creature who uses you for his own evil purposes. All your actions are directed by him, for he hopes his own kind will find him and plans for the day when this alien race will spread over all the Earth, reducing humans to slavery, as he has already done to you."

"You seem indeed to be endowed with strange talents," William mused, "but furnish no proof of your words. They amount to no more than the conjectures that any charlatan might make."

"Well, then, is it not true that you communicate with this treacherous being by means of effigies in his likeness which transmit your words over lands and oceans?"

"I cannot deny it."

"Further, do you not believe that you hold him in your power because he would have nothing to eat if it were not for your help?"

"You are quite right but, since you know it, you must have read my thoughts."

"Now that you finally recognize my powers, I am going to try to help you prevent what would be, if he is not overthrown, an appalling catastrophe for the people of this world. Each time you have talked with this alien he has commanded you to forget a part of his words, which are deeply buried in your memory. I have been able to discover what they are, in this way confirming that you have only an illusion of power: the evil mind of Baphomet holds you captive!"

The Grand Master was silent, overwhelmed. Was he indeed no more than a willing tool manipulated by Baphomet? Was the propagation of the True Faith, which he had considered his sole objective, no more in fact than a cover-up, masking a vast enterprise of conquest, the only beneficiary of which would be this stranger? Unthinkable . . . still, the Tibetan appeared to know his most carefully hidden secrets. . . . Well, then, face reality, no matter how abhorrent it might be. This did explain a number of strange facts: Baphomet's close confinement had always seemed inexplicable to him, since that accursed being could leave his protective sphere by using hermetic armor. But the creature had no need at all to move about the Earth since the Templars, no matter how far away, acted according to his will. Further, others had suspected this: the Grand Master of the Hospitalers had believed that the gift of the famous lightning was nothing but a demoniacal stratagem.

William's pride kept him from voicing his immense confusion. Then Kubla put a friendly hand on his shoulder and declared, "I know what you feel . . . believe me, it took every effort for me to accept the loss of an empire bequeathed me by my ancestors.

"Your nobility of spirit made me your counselor, rather than reducing me to slavery. You must believe this Tibetan seer and act according to his directions in order to save Earth's people. Whether they have white, yellow or black skins, their destiny lies in your hands."

"What do you propose?" The Grand Master's question was little more than a whisper.

"I have carefully considered this grievous problem, for I knew that one day you would ask me that question," replied the lama. "Your weapons, however formidable, cannot be used against Baphomet because a magic circle protects him, both him and his ship. To defeat him, there exists but one means: to subjugate his mind as he has yours, and then kill him. To that end, I have already brought together a certain number of sages, possessing—like me—great psychic powers. By joining our abilities, perhaps we can bring him to quarter. This is how we will proceed: you must contact this demon, as usual, using his effigy. Then we will make a surprise attack, following the channel of the path that allows him to talk with you. I hope to win out because he will have no time to set up counter forces. This will demand a considerable effort from us and I am not at all certain of success. However, we have no choice. . . ."

"Let us try. You have succeeded at least in convincing me: it shall be done as you wish."

The lamas then took their places in the room where the transmitter was kept. Brother Joubert stood by to cut communications immediately if anything went wrong, then William made the connection.

The Tibetans, motionless, with fixed stares, seemed lost in a state of suspended life-functions.

Suddenly the effigy came to life and Baphomet declared:

"Well, William, you have neglected me . . . but surely you are rested from your labors now. You must end your inaction and come back to France in order to let your king know that, here also, you are the master. You are going. . . ."

His speech ended abruptly on those words.

Flashes of light streaked the large eyes of the effigy.

William felt an excruciating pain in his head, then the lights flickered and suddenly went out. The Templar pressed a hand to his forehead in an attempt to drive out the stabbing torment. Grimacing in agony, he leaned toward the baleful eyes of the effigy A large room bathed in a reddish glow could just be distinguished. Its walls were lined with strange devices, completely meaningless to him. On the floor, motionless, lay a hideous dwarf with two short horns on his forehead and two wings on his back. One might have thought it a cathedral gargoyle. Suddenly he was struck by the horror of it. His liberated mind finally realized that he had indeed been the plaything of a being compared with whom the Grand Master was as weak as a child.

The Tibetans lay exhausted on the ground, suffering from the recoil of the frightful struggle. The sweat ran from their wrinkled faces. At last, their leader sat up and muttered:

"Well, the demon is dead! The struggle was more difficult than I would have believed: it missed failing by a very thin line. . . ."

"How can I ever thank you?" exclaimed the Grand Master. "You have set me free! May heaven bless you!"

"We ask nothing of you. Be lenient with your subjects and never forget that the universe is peopled with mischievous demons who seek only to delude poor humans. . . ."

And so it was that Baphomet lost his empire.

The lamas, loaded with honors, returned to their far-off native land. Brother Joubert would gladly have accompanied them, but William had need of him.

Racked by the fear of one day seeing demons arrive from sidereal space to invade the Earth, he wanted above everything else to penetrate the secrets of the spacecraft hidden in the marsh. At his order, the Commander of Pinay removed it from the muddy bottom with aid of teams of horses, and a convoy carried it to Aigues-Mortes, where it was loaded on a ship.

Arriving at Alexandretta, it was carted to far-off Cathay, as easily as the ship of the Syrian desert treads the sands.

The learned Brother Joubert, having become expert in such matters, discovered the secret of the engine's magnetic seal with little difficulty. Thanks to the remains of this second Baphomet spacecraft, he had high hopes of being able to build a vessel suitable for navigating the vast spaces of the skies, and the Polo brothers asked only to be aboard on that voyage!

Often, when William of Beaujeu contemplated the rising of the rose-colored Luna, he asked if the God of the Universe would allow this to happen. . . .

The ways of the Lord are inscrutable: thus, in a parallel universe where the sun rises in the east, the Earth has only one satellite. There, history such as that recorded by the Templar from Tyre is quite different. On May 18, 1275, William of Beaujeu was killed at Acre, defending the Accursed Tower, for he did not have access, alas, to any atomic explosives.

John of Grailly, grievously injured, embarked with extreme appropriateness on a ship, in company with Otto of Granson and the Grand Master of the Hospitalers, wounded by a bolt from a crossbow.

Marshal Peter of Sevry and Commander Thibaud Gaudin, defeated by the Sultan, perished under the debris of the chapter house-fortress of the Temple in company with two thousand Mamelukes.

STELLAR
CRUSADE

Translated by C.J. Cherryh

DEDICATION

A Donald A. Wollheim, de la part d'un modeste faiseur d'univers qu'il a mené au Royaume de Féerie . . .

Chapter I

On the eighteenth of March in the year of Our Lord 1277, the morning sun touched the massive walls of Chang-Chu Castle with gold.

A human sea was rolling toward the drawbridge. The Templars, robed in their immaculate white surcoats, on which a crimson cross showed like a stain of blood, clove the howling flood, disciplined, priestlike, on their caparisoned horses. The heavily armed cavalry followed in their wake. Peasants were there in large straw hats, dusty drovers herded their flocks and camels knelt under their loads. Now and again some Mongol astride his shaggy pony streaked through this motley crowd with the flash of silver-damascened armor.

This joyous mob had come from the four corners of the Earth . . . to celebrate the anniversary of the glorious triumph of Grand Master William of Beaujeu, liberator of the fortress of St. John of Acre—but everyone was wondering just why the ceremony had been moved up two months.

Far overhead, against the sky, the Baussant flag, black and white pierced with a red cross, cracked proudly from the crest of the keep.

At the center of the hexagonal keep a group of dignitaries was proceeding into the huge vaulted Chapter Hall.

At this hour of the morning, all the faithful followers of the Grand Master were already assembled: his marshal, Peter of Sevry, thickset and ruddy; commander Thibaud Gaudin, administrator of the vast Templar domains; John of Grailly, the gallant Frank from the distant fief of Bassora; Otto of Granson, a huge Swiss, a mercenary of King Edward I of England; Kubla, the Mongol Khan who was now an ally of the Templars; learned Brother Joubert; the brave Venetian ex-

plorer Marco Polo; the Templar lord of Tyre, keeper of the
chronicles of the Order;[1] and countless other officers—the
Grand Hospitaler, the Draper, the Seneschal, the Turcopoler,
the Chaplain, not to mention the castellan lords of fortresses.

Such was lord William's generosity that he had extended
equal invitations to his most dangerous rivals—ascetic John
of Villiers, Grand Master of the Hospitalers, along with his
marshal Matthew Clermont; and the Grand Master of the
Teutonic order, Conrad von Thierberg.

The latter kept visibly to themselves, next to their standard-bearers.

With a grand wave of his hand toward this glittering assembly, William of Beaujeu took his place on the throne under a black and white canopy. The heralds lifted their long
trumpets and sounded three long fanfares, stopping the lively
conversation.

The Council was in session. They all listened, compelled by
the solemnity of the reunion.

The Templar drew himself up to his full height, fixed his
keen eyes on each in turn, as if to assure himself that all his
guests had come. Then he knelt for the opening invocation.
As one man, the soldier-monks followed his example, signing
themselves with the cross.

"*In nomine Patris et Filii et Spiritus Sancti! Non nobis
Domine; non nobis, sed Nomini Tuo da gloriam!*[2] May the
grace of the Holy Spirit aid us, Lord Jesus, Holy Christ, Eternal Father and omnipotent God, wise creator, dispenser benevolent overseer and beloved friend, pious and humble
Redeemer, kind and merciful Savior, I pray Thee humbly
and beseech Thee to enlighten us, through Mary, Star of the
Sea. *Amen.*"

Each of these rough soldiers felt his heart strangely
touched. They remembered another Council Hall, at St. John
of Acre, where most of them had sat, and whence they had
set out on a great adventure, the conquest of the East.

William remained silent a brief moment, hands crossed on
his breast. Then he rose. "Sirs, our Brothers of the Hospi-

---

[1] This document has been faithfully edited thanks to the chronicles of
the Templar of Tyre, which faithfully record the crusade against the
vile Baphomets.
[2] In the name of the Father and the Son and the Holy Ghost! Not to
us, Lord; not to us, but to Thy Name give the glory!

talers and Teutons, I've called you here today to share with you a piece of news that has filled my heart with grief. We have scarcely escaped one terrible disaster which might have fallen on all humankind; we destroyed a demoniac creature who had us in the power of his pernicious lies. This Baphomet, this envoy of a despicable race, fell on our sweet Earth from the unguessable depths of the universe to make us his slaves. By the grace of our Lord Jesus Christ, we put him beyond any hope of harming us. But I was not at all unaware that the skies are full of treacherous demons, ruling other planets, who would sooner or later threaten our existence again. Alas, that day is upon us."

The Grand Master paused for effect, while Brother Joubert uncovered several spheres studded with countless glittering points, hidden till this moment beneath a red velvet cloth.

All eyes turned to these magical objects.

"You have before your eyes a model of the universe, copied from the one our learned Brother Joubert has painstakingly recovered from the ships which fell into our hands. Know that our sphere follows an endless track around a brazier, our sun, which heats and lights it. Our astronomers have also told us we are not alone in the universe: other fiery spheres light other balls of earth bearing other living creatures. Among them, alas, the demoniacal Baphomets, who have vowed to destroy us."

John of Villiers frowned doubtfully. "Esteemed brother commander," he objected, "these are wild assumptions. These pernicious creatures might simply be demons vomited up out of hell to destroy us. To the wisest of us, there's no proof that the lights that shine in the firmament are suns like ours, and even less proof that spheres like our Earth move around them. Besides, most scholars think the Earth is flat."

Conrad von Thierberg nodded in agreement, but did not involve himself in the debate.

" 'Blessed are they who have not seen and yet believe,' says Holy Writ. I've weighed my words carefully, brother Hospitaler, and I put nothing forward without proof. See this blood-red spot and the scarlet mark shining on the breast of it: this is the land of the invaders who are trying to enslave our earth. Our learned Brother Joubert, after long study, is sure of it. More than that, he has gained power over the talismans that let them speak through the subtle flows of the

ether, and—most frighteningly—he has overheard the clamor
of other Baphomets who have taken ship into those unplumb-
able depths. They're summoning their comrades, seeking information on our civilization, our defenses! Brothers, I tell
you the truth, a terrible danger is upon us. Someday a powerful fleet is going to drift down on us and complete the mission *one* of these monsters could not carry out. Then it's
going to be too late to stop them."

"Now, Master William," exclaimed the Grand Master of
the Teutons, "don't take us for novices. By the description of
the Baphomet's refuge in the forest of the East, that great
metal mass could just as well have come up out of the bowels
of the Earth, or out of the Tartarus of the ancients."

"Holy Spirit, give me patience," sighed the ascetic Templar. "You maintain these ships can't navigate the subtle
ethers that completely surround the Earth. Or do you reckon
that our Earth is not a globe orbiting the sun in the company
of other planets? Well, if you like, I'll prove my assertions to
you here and now."

"Faith," the Hospitaler growled, "I don't know how you're
going to convince us, but I'm quite ready to listen."

"It's not my word alone will prove your error, but the
witness of your own senses. . . . My distinguished friends,"
William went on, turning to the audience, "we're going to
leave you for a few hours and rejoin you about the hour of
nones. While you wait, I pray you climb the ramparts to
watch a spectacle I think is going to astonish you."

From his place on the dais the Grand Master signaled the
Teuton and the Hospitaler to follow him. Brother Joubert
went with them.

The four of them first passed a door concealed by a tapestry and came out again into a secret corridor lit by smoky
torches, finally arrived at the base of a tower hollowed by recent construction.

Dazzled by bright sunlight reflected in vast, mirroring steel,
the visitors could see nothing for a moment. Then as their
eyes adjusted to that brilliant light, they saw before them,
perched on a huge iron tripod, a ship in all points identical to
those the Templars had lately discovered.

"Here's the ship that's going to carry us into the skies with
incredible speed, passing all understanding," the Templar declared proudly. "By unceasing efforts, our learned Joubert has

deciphered the Baphomets' grimoire, and by using the apparatus still intact and by making the ruined pieces according to the instruction in the documents, he's put this metal globe into working order. If you have confidence in him, would you kindly trust your weight to this ladder and enter the bowels of this remarkable machine?"

"I suppose my noble brother has already tried it?" John of Villiers asked in a somewhat dubious tone.

"Of course! And I've seen wonders. That's what's given me the formal proof of the shape of our universe."

"In that case I am completely satisfied," John of Villiers assured him, and climbed the rungs of the ladder, followed by Conrad von Thierberg, who was frowning anxiously.

They all stood then in a rather large living space furnished with couches, armchairs bolted to the floor and equipped with heavy belts.

William of Beaujeu invited his guests to sit down and, providing them his example, buckled the leather strap of his chair.

Joubert, too, sat down, before a sort of ebony lectern inset with dials and buttons. His fingers plied them agilely; the door clicked shut with a dry sound while a screen lit in front of him.

"Noble brothers," the Templar declared then, "you are about to live moments which will mark your souls forever. I've already made several excursions aboard this vessel and I was in no wise harmed by the splendors it showed me. In a few moments we are going to lift into the winds and ride the pure waves of clouds, far above the Earth—around which we are going to revolve."

"This is a great magic," the Teuton said indignantly. "And why then shut us up in here? We won't be able to see a thing in this box."

"The air we breathe fails completely at a certain height," William answered plainly. "That's why we have to put an airtight seal on the entry. All the images of the outside world are going to be faithfully relayed to this luminous table."

"You take us for simpletons," John of Villiers objected. "Your so-named ship hasn't even wings to fly with. How can it get into the air?"

William smiled and simply gestured to Joubert.

Joubert slightly lifted a short lever.

A cry of shock passed the lips of the two passengers.

"Christ! We're skimming over the castle!"

"Holy Mother of God! The knights are no bigger than ants!"

At that moment the nobles the Templar had invited, faces uplifted, were watching the departure of the starship, which was rapidly vanishing from sight. They were all dumbfounded. They had seen the sphere rise from the dark bowels of the tower and the massive machine had taken off like a feather in the wind.

Aboard it, John Villiers and Conrad von Thierberg held their breath and said not a word, rubbing their eyes as if they could not accept the witness of their senses.

Now the palace of Cambaluc had vanished. Plains, rivers mountains passed under the ship, which was still climbing into the cloudless sky. The sea appeared, glittering under the sun. On its surface, thin bows of spray and a few tiny dots: the vessels which sailed the China Sea.

At last an isle grew distinct in the distant blue.

"Cipanghu!" the Grand Master announced. "The realm of my vassal Otto of Granson. We're going to veer off now to the north, and you'll see the eternal snows which cover both poles of our world. Look! already you can see ice mountains afloat on the water."

This time his guests made no protests. They were beginning to realize that William of Beaujeu was telling them the truth, that they were living moments which would go down in human history.

Now immense cottony spirals of unbearable whiteness spread beneath the voyagers' feet, clouds partially veiling the land. Through the clear spots the icepack, glittering under the sun, spread out over the pole, which was girt with an azure bow of atmosphere athwart the dark sky.

But the two soldier-monks gaped in admiration while a fairylike kaleidoscope continued to unfurl before them.

The ship lanced higher still into the firmament; the thin, fine strand of air became dappled with the ocher of continents, the indigo of oceans, the alabaster of clouds spun into fine threads.

At last the globe of Earth shone in all its glory, a sphere of lapis lazuli posed on the ebon black of the sky. The ship was now following a circular orbit at incredible speed.

The Grand Master of the Templars saw fit to give a few explanations. "We've flown over Cathay," he said, indicating a map of the world. "After passing over the pole, we'll go down again to the nadir, crossing the extreme end of the vast ocean which separates our beloved France from a huge continent hitherto unknown to us."

"What?" exclaimed John of Villiers. "There are unknown lands between Europe and Cathay?"

"Indeed. If a ship went west from the shores of the kingdom of France, it would meet a territory which extends for vast distances. After crossing mountains and valleys, the voyager would have to set out again to cross a vast stretch of sea, and finally arrive at Cathay."

"I'm quite overcome," said the Teuton. "Faith, learned brother, I repent me of mine unbelief. We're actually creeping round on a globe hung in the sky."

"But," asked the ever-practical Hospitaler, "is this unknown continent inhabited by creatures made in our likeness?"

"Assuredly it is. I've met there men not only like ourselves (except that their skin has an ocher tint), but they're much more like our race than the ebon black folk who live in Africa. Yet the animal species are different. I saw there cattle with massive foreheads, deer with huge racks of antlers, birds colored like the rainbow. Strangely enough, these primitive people have no horses at all."

"Then they are to be pitied," John of Villiers said sententiously. "Without that noble animal they couldn't cross those vast distances."

"So our globe has three inhabited continents?" asked Conrad von Thierberg.

"Precisely. More, there are countless isles beyond Cathay, eastward, and they're inhabited by savages too, while another very large island extends to the south in the same ocean. But that's of no import. Now we're going to fly past Luna, which is nothing but barren, arid rock."

Brother Joubert moved several dials again and the sphere angled up and shot toward the star-scattered sky.

William of Beaujeu's two guests, dumbstruck, watched the Earth shrink until it became nothing but a ball, while on another screen the pink surface of the moon grew in their view.

"Mark you," said the Templar, "the soil of this sphere

bears countless craters like the ones the explosions of our fireballs made. Djaffar and Joubert have taken long thought on
the matter. They've come to the conclusion that these are not
the effects of a war. Well, then, these impacts could only
have been made by projectiles out of the void, centuries past.
Their precise origin is still a mystery. A few of the steeper-
sided craters seem recent; others are more or less eroded.
You will also see tall mountain ranges, dust-covered plains
and a few tracks like the beds of ancient rivers."

"Here's something to think on," said the Grand Master of
the Hospitalers. "The Holy Scriptures must be able to shed
light on the matter. Isn't it reported that the forces of the
Devil once fought against the archangels and seraphim? Lucifer himself rebelled against his Creator and met defeat; then
he was thrown into hell. Maybe we see there the traces of
that fierce battle."

"A very attractive hypothesis," the Templar applauded
him. "But I would beware of getting into a biblical exegesis
on that theory. Whatever it was, dead stars have no interest
for us. Now I mean to give you a glimpse of the unbearable
fires which burn at the heart of our sun, while we approach
the two planets which orbit between it and our own Earth."

The pilot executed a quick turn of the ship without otherwise affecting his passengers and the machine rushed headlong toward the brilliant star, which grew in their sight and
transformed itself into a furnace of unbearable power.

Special panels then slid over the outer hull and the image
on the screens darkened, letting them see a spotless white
image close to the ship.

"Vesper, our nearest neighbor," William declared. "Thick
clouds mask its surface. We plunged into the heart of them
and couldn't see the surface of the world. So we have to conclude that this star has no inhabitants. The temperature must
be very high on the continents and all the water must be rendered into vapor—hence these impenetrable clouds."

The two other soldier-monks said not a word. The majesty
of the great universe filled them with wonder.

Again the metal sphere rushed toward the solar fires, but a
miraculous sweet coolness persisted inside the ship.

Then the screens showed the burning surface of Hermes,
on which flowed rivers of molten metals that made shining
lakes undisturbed by waves.

A new climb into space let the passengers admire two giant planets where gaseous spirals—purple, amaranth, rust and saffron—intertwined in an awesome ballet. One of the stars was girt with an amethyst ring like a priceless crown.

William of Beaujeu meant to go farther still, to the very frozen limits of the solar system, but his passengers declined the offer. They professed themselves satisfied with the experience and fully convinced of the possibilities of the wondrous ship taken from the Baphomet.

For the several minutes of their return trajectory, John of Villiers, who had recovered some of his self-possession, still expressed reservations on the theories his rival set forth. "Dear friend," he began in a categorical tone, "I must yield to the evidence. Our Earth is truly round and she orbits the sun in company with other planets which hardly look like her at all. That's precisely what leads me to wonder whether these other stars that spread across the heavens as far as we can see can possibly have intelligent creatures created in the image of our God. It seems to me even more untenable that within this hypothesis, you have to suppose that these hypothetical brothers, these quasi Adams and Eves, challenged God's goodness by picking the fruit of the Tree of Good and Evil. Then, like us, they would be tainted with the same original sin and on that logic, they must be redeemed by Christ. Now if there do exist, as that theory suggests, billions of inhabited planets, there must have been billions of Christs, billions of Virgin Mothers, and even billions of popes. Redemption could not be reserved for humans alone since God is good. Alas, the Holy Scriptures only mention one Christ, one Mary, and one sole pope!"

The Grand Master of the Teutons cast an admiring glance at his companion. The argument was a telling one. Only the subtle Hospitaler had a quick enough wit to raise such objections. Triumphantly John of Villiers folded his wrinkled hands and with a smug smile on his lips waited on his illustrious rival's answer.

"And very well might there have been billions of Christs!" William exclaimed. "The Divine Power which created this unfathomable universe—couldn't it be sufficient for the Savior to manifest Himself on each world in the image of its inhabitants? So why *couldn't* there have been a Messiah among the Baphomets? And, my brothers, I strongly advise you meditate on these words, which you will grant me *are* in Holy Writ. . . . Didn't Our Lord say, 'I have other sheep which are not of this fold . . .'? So that is plain proof that there are other creatures in the universe endowed with intelligence. And don't go telling me that the sacred texts only speak of one Christ. Have you found in the Holy Bible any passages saying the Earth is round? That it spins round the sun? That there are other planets near us? No! The dogma is then in no wise opposed to the plurality of inhabited worlds."

Conrad von Thierberg assumed a worried look. This rough, brave soldier was more at home on a horse or in battle than in verbal fencing. He left John of Villiers the honor of pursuing the argument.

And John refused to own his defeat. "Your facile sophism doesn't convince me in the least. St. Thomas says in effect: 'The Earth is the center of Creation and all the stars were formed to let man know the seasons.' And St. Paul for his part declares that there is no other world but the Earth, that the stars and the heavens were made for the Earth and for man. No mention of extraterrestrials there."

"But Jesus clearly said, 'In my Father's House are many mansions,' " the Templar fired back. "What about the existence of angels, archangels, thrones and powers, dominions, seraphim, virtues, principalities and cherubim? Do the nine choirs of angels indeed live in the sky? These are by definition . . . extraterrestrial. The Christ is universal, and He affirmed it. Listen to St. Paul. 'When the time is accomplished, I will bring all things under one head, that is, Christ, the celestial beings and the terrestrial.' All creatures are mortal and only a Redeemer can give them eternal life. It's no lessening; on the contrary, it expands His love to legions of beings like or unlike us."

This time the Templar's two opponents gave no answer— not that they were convinced, but that the Earth's ocher surface was rushing toward them as if the machine were about to crash. Were they about to pay for this mad temerity with their lives?

The ship made a dizzying nose dive and under the bewildered eyes of the witnesses perched on the ramparts neatly came to rest on its three feet in the hollow tower.

"Well, noble brothers," said William with a smug smile, "what say you to *that?*"

"Faith," replied Conrad in his thunderous voice, "no problem for me. Our Eart' is round just like a ball, and the sun holds the center of our system."

"What has me worried," John of Villiers said in turn, "is that I can't deny that this quite wingless ship sails at an insane speed. If we only took aboard enough provisions, it could surely carry us to the farthest stars. But I still have to voice one objection . . ."

"Do," the Templar replied. "I'm here to give you all the explanations you could want."

"So. Well. Before we left, you were talking about the possibility of an attack of similar vessels launched against the Earth. So you think that the Baphomets have a large fleet. Now evidently you have just the one ship. So it's impossible to expect to overcome an opposing fleet if—by some misfortune—you ran into any of them en route."

"A perceptive objection. I'll give you my answer, but before the Council of nobles which is so impatiently awaiting us."

The four passengers left the ship then and, following the route by which they had come, they reentered the vast hall, where they were assailed by a deluge of questions.

William resumed his place on the dais and, lifting his hand to restore silence; "Messires," he said in a loud voice, "brother Hospitalers and Teutons, I understand your curiosity. Patience. I am going to pick up the thread of my story, which we broke off for that little voyage with my noble friends. I had to convince them of a few facts of dire importance: the fact that the Earth is round; that it belongs to a system of planets orbiting endlessly about our sun; and most of all—to convince them of the extraordinary abilities of the Baphomet ship, which can sail immeasurable distances. This was, I believe, accomplished."

John of Villiers and Conrad von Thierberg, to the vast surprise of their brother knights, nodded in agreement.

"—These points have been established," the Grand Master of the Templars went on, "our assembly has to resolve some other problems of vital importance to our race. The Baphomets, as I have told you, know of our existence, but they don't know how we dealt with the emissary they sent to our world, and that must throw them into a grand confusion. Surely they're wondering if they ought to leave us in peace or attack

us with a powerful fleet. Their hesitations leave us a little
breathing space in which to act. The noble John of Villiers
justly and forcefully reminded me a moment ago that we
don't have enough strength now to fight in space. So an alter-
native suggests itself: brace ourselves and wait for the Baphomet attack—asking our friend Houen-Lun to gather a
number of Adepts to repulse our attackers by means of their
psychic talents. Second possibility: seize the offensive and
launch an attack on the planets occupied by the Baphomets
with a powerful fleet capable of beating these cruel adversaries. After careful reflection, the venerable Tibetan chief,
our esteemed Djaffar, our learned Joubert and myself
succeeded in setting a reasonable plan into motion. Houen-
Lun has told me that the powers of the Wise Men were inop-
erative when they were shut within a metal vessel. At one
stroke—our main weapon, out of action. But fortunately, after days and nights of research, Brother Joubert has found a
means to get around that difficulty. He states that the Tibetans' brain waves can be propagated over an apparatus which
exists on the Baphomet ships—the antennae they use for
speaking long distance, which receive certain impulses. . . .
The Baphomets in charge of receiving messages aboard the
enemy ships could thus easily be deluded by one of the lamas. Thanks to his remarkable powers, the Adept would have
the Baphomet believing he was talking to peaceful merchant-
men. So one of the Tibetans could corrupt the judgment of
officers and crew; one of us could finally get in through an
airlock to spy on our enemies."

"Noble brother," muttered John of Villiers, "you're telling
us marvels, to be sure, oh yes, but not enough to win a battle
if the course of events should lead us to one. Surely it would
be a good plan to send spies among the Baphomets . . . but
our looks would have to be compatible with those of those
sky-dwelling races or the men you send are going to be unmasked very quickly."

"I've foreseen that eventuality. A goat's hide and head
would be enough to disguise one of us."

"Let's admit that there's one remaining problem," the Hospitaler said in a deathly silence. "That our forces are a joke
and that we can't fend the advance of a powerful fleet away
from our planet."

The audience was sitting as if paralyzed. All in the hall felt that they were dreaming. Even the most learned of them needed all their faculties to follow the debate, the import of which they did, however, realize.

"Have I ever," replied the Templar, "pretended to have ships as numerous as our armies? Our numerical disadvantage will be largely offset by our experience in the art of war."

"Ve'd still haf to be able to make these demoniac machines," Conrad von Thierberg grumbled. "So far as I'm concerned, I don't understand a bit of it."

"Our learned Joubert and the wise Djaffar have made astonishing progress," William replied, "in mastering these esoteric sciences. They now understand the operation of most of the machines equipping these ships—that, in large part thanks to the tiny crystalline charts which carry all the instructions meant to teach ordinary folk among our enemies the arts of alchemy. Still, it took a powerful intelligence to gather the very elements of these understandings, and our ablest workmen would be helpless to reproduce the delicate mechanisms which move these ships through the ether."

"Then it is impossible," John of Villiers cut in dryly, "to beard the Baphomets in their lair."

"You omit one simple factor, noble brother," the Templar returned with a touch of malice. "No need, you see, of master artisans when one has a duplicator which faithfully reproduces all the pieces—even the tiniest—just so long as we feed the right metal into it. So then, our alchemists are quite capable of that much. Now, already, I have a dozen ships in perfect working order and I'm continuing to produce them."

A long silence fell on the crowd.

Hospitalers, Teutons and Templars reflected on the vistas opened by that unexpected revelation.

Conrad von Thierberg, always full of fire, exclaimed: "Ah, vell, in that case, no problem. Let's go get those demons!"

A good section of the crowd agreed with that proud sentiment. But John of Villiers was still thinking. Finally he decided to give his opinion. "Noble William, your words, I admit, are full of sense. It would be mad at this point to launch a blind attack on an enemy we scarcely know. So let's pursue the construction of a great fleet, and meanwhile, let's send spies to give us valuable information on our enemies."

"I thank you for your support, gentle brother. That solution seems wisest to me, too. Sirs, brother Hospitalers and Teutons, I appeal to you—all who approve this project, raise your hands."

They all knew the wisdom of the Grand Master of the Hospitalers. As for William of Beaujeu, he had the greatest empire on Earth, and he had won countless victories, so almost all the soldier-monks approved the proposal. Only a few Teutons abstained, more out of jealousy than on real conviction.

"Noble brothers, thank you for your confidence," William concluded, and rose to show that the audience was ended. "Let us thank the Lord that we were warned of our danger in time and let us pray Christ to bring this Crusade to victory! May this be a battle of the forces of good against those of evil. The Baussant flag will once more go in the van of the host which leads the holy war!"

The crowd dispersed then to enjoy the merrymaking which marked this holiday. Tongues wagged freely.

But the Grand Masters, meeting in a private chamber, went over the details of the future expedition in secret.

By nightfall, they had reached agreement.

Each withdrew to his own apartment, while the officers of the three orders passed their instructions to their subordinates. The crew of the ship which was to set forth into infinite space (until then the sole possession of the Baphomets) then gathered at the castle to be prepared for the mission by Joubert and Djaffar.

Chapter II

While the duplicators worked ceaselessly under the supervision of Joubert, Djaffar and their assistants, William put a finishing touch on his expedition to the stars.

The Grand Master needed a reliable man to run his empire during his absence. He chose his faithful commander, Thibaud Gaudin, whose courage and honesty he respected. Under William's eye, the Templar learned to manage the various factions which set Khan against Khan, to supervise the harvests, the extraction of minerals needed for the manufacture of the spaceships. He gave him precise instructions, too, regarding the agreements the Templars maintained with the Eastern Kingdoms. There, as it happened, the Commanderies flourished, ships and caravans brought in gold, spices, rich brocades, incense, perfumes . . . which attracted rich burghers and noble lords.

The Templars had become bankers to kings and emperors, with whom they dealt as equals. No one could make war without their approval. Ambassadors came to seek their advice. French, English, Germans and Italians must reckon with the wealthy soldier-monks, wielders of the thunderballs. Pope John XXI himself dealt carefully with them, for they were on their way to becoming masters of the world.

Power, alas, begets hate.

The kings were jealous of the Grand Master, though they dared not admit their hostility openly. They employed multitudes of spies in the Commanderies and even at Chang-Chu. Hospitalers and Teutons, reduced to a supporting role, were only too eager to aid their rivals' enemies.

So Thibaud Gaudin faced a very delicate task. Impossible to use the thunderballs against Christian kingdoms. John XXI had let it be understood in so many words that this devil-weapon must never be used except against infidels, on pain of excommunication.

Any attack on the Commanderies of Europe had to be met with less baneful weapons, and Templar companies scattered over the face of the world were incapable of meeting any opposing coalition. It would be worse yet when the fleet took to space, taking with it the flower of the soldier-monks.

Only the posts in America gave them no trouble. The Templars, dug in behind the thick-walled castles they had built along the majestic rivers of the New World, had nothing to fear from the natives, who had no warhorses and whose arrows could not penetrate the plate armor and the mail shirts. Sachems and chiefs knew that these newcomers wielded the thunder. So they traded with these demigods whom they had learned to fear and took no chance of offending them.

It was the same situation in China and on Cipanghu. Only the maharajahs preserved a certain independence, limiting themselves to the payment of tribute to their powerful neighbors.

At least the main expedition would not be leaving Earth for several months, if everything went as planned. Thibaud Gaudin thus had all the time he would need to serve his apprenticeship in that crushing power.

For their part, the high officers of the Order never stopped working. William's two lieutenants, Peter of Sevry and Otto of Granson, tirelessly scoured the Templar Empire to gather the elite of the soldier-monks. Some arrived at Chang-Chu along the caravan routes, leading countless quite useless horses; others used the flying ships to reach the army's camp.

The Grand Hospitaler gathered drugs, opiates, elixirs and narcotics, along with wadding and linen bandages for the wounded. Djaffar the Wise had also supplied certain powders sovereign against infections, which they had found in the Baphomet ships. They had not yet fathomed the secret of their manufacture, but they had been faithfully reproduced thanks to the duplicator.

As for the Draper, he gathered cottes, surcoats, armor, chausses and helms. He also had recourse to the duplicator to assemble strange airtight armor, to let the men breathe in the void of space. With these there was no fear of suffering cold or heat; the marvelous devices assured a moderate temperature under any circumstances.

Provisioning the ship with food was under the supervision of the Seneschal. The Templars, it developed, did not fare well on the fetid broth produced by the strange alembics which equipped the ships. These hardy warriors needed meat when they fought and even had a papal dispensation to eat meat on Friday and other fast days. So they had to alter certain ships to provide stables where they could raise cattle, pigs and chickens.

Stocks of jerky and smoked fish had been put aboard each ship to allow a crew to survive for several weeks if it found itself cut off from the rest of the fleet. The American possessions furnished an abundance of buffalo meat prepared in strips—the natives called it *pemmican*. And from Cipanghu came delicious, perfectly preserved fish. From China, bushels of a grain capable in itself of assuring the warriors' survival for months, if they added a kind of condiment called soy sauce.

The Chaplain installed portable altars aboard each ship and collected countless ciboria filled with the Host.

Finally the Turcopole received some light, fast ships, which had been mostly stripped. They were to play a role derivative of the light cavalry, making lightning strikes on enemy lines. Their hand-picked crews underwent intensive training on the Earth's moon.

Meanwhile the ship meant to spy on the Baphomets was checked over with the utmost care.

Marco Polo, freshly arrived from his commercial chicaneries in foreign lands, took command of that.

The crew consisted of the lama Houen-Lun, Brother Joubert, Djaffar the Wise, and three brave lads with nerves of steel: the Tholon brothers, natives of a hamlet near Auxerre.

Garin, the Templar, was the intelligence in the family . . . had the knack of involving himself in the subtlest intrigues and enjoyed success in discovering the best guarded of secrets.

Clement, a giant of a man with a wild temper, was a former woodcutter. His strength was incredible. He had amazed the army by carrying on his back an Arab horse with a wounded fore-pastern. The big fellow had quite cheerfully gotten under the poor animal's chest and walked the brave beast along on his hind feet. The Mongols, horrified at this centaur, had let him pass unhindered, and Clement, whom they had all given up for dead, had appeared in the camp at daybreak.

Guiot, called Red Guiot because of his flamboyant beard, had the craft of a fox and a thief's quickness. He had no equal at discovering provisions hidden by peasants and treasures concealed by nobles. That won him a comfortable purse which he dissipated shamelessly in endless partying.

The three had one thing in common: aquamarine eyes and an astonishingly keen stare.

Garin was sorely aggrieved by his brothers' immoderate affinity for escapades, but for all his threats and exhortations he never succeeded in setting their feet on the straight and narrow path, and he said ceaseless prayers for the salvation of their immortal souls.

Despite all differences the three brothers got along like thieves at a fair, and their signal bravery had gotten them assigned to go with Marco Polo.

" 'S blood," Guiot swore, wolfing down a mouthful of grease-dripping mutton. "Here we are in another damn mess. I heard what the Venetian said, I heard it every bit. I know how to use a sword or a good axe, a point, that's all . . . and here somebody wants to shut us up in some flying pot to go God knows where in the clouds. Garin, you're smart, you've got to explain it to me."

"May the Holy Spirit help me illumine your obtuse brain," the Templar groaned. "You've naturally heard about the Baphomet who gave us the fireballs."

"Sure. I even saw drawings of him—a goat's head with big horns, black fur all over his body, clawed hands and a pair of blue breasts. Man'd think he was seeing Lucifer in person."

"Good. Well, these devilish creatures came to conquer our Earth. Our reverend Grand Master, Lord bless him, unraveled their subtle tricks and killed their envoy. But there's still a threat hanging over Christendom. That despicable race surely won't stop at one check. One day or another the Baphomets will return in force to enslave us. So William of Beaujeu has decided to anticipate them and create a powerful fleet to destroy the enemy in his lair. . . ."

"I've got it. Only why are we going to go with the Venetian in just one ship?"

"To spy on them, for pity's sake! Marco Polo has long experience in trade with foreigners, and we're going to pass ourselves off as peaceful traders come from another planet."

"Huh, I don't get it," Clement grumbled in his turn. "They're going to see in a minute that we're not Baphomets."

"Indeed they are," Garin growled with a weary sigh. "That's why we're taking along a Tibetan to deceive the enemies who may observe us with his psychic powers. He'll read their minds and we'll disguise ourselves to look like traders from some race accustomed to deal with the Baphomets. So we'll be well received and we can spy on them."

"But I can't say a single word in their damn language," Guiot objected.

"Don't fret yourself. All that's been taken care of. The learned Brother Joubert has been able to make adaptations on the talismans from the captured ships. We'll undergo a treatment that will let us speak their language."

"Hah, I get you. We just have to get into one of their fortresses to know what they might be cooking up, right?"

"Right, my dear brother."

"Botheration, we got to go fly in the clouds and fight with funny-looking pipes that spit fire. Me with no axe, I'm good for nothing."

"You can still carry it off. As for the new weapons, you've learned to use them. Besides, in the events of the tourney we're giving tonight there're going to be prizes for the best shots. You can show off your skill."

"You think we can be in it?"

"Sure. Our ship doesn't leave until tomorrow dawn."

William of Beaujeu, as it happened, had reckoned that the best way to occupy these warriors who had come in from the far horizons was to offer them one of the entertainments they so prized.

A tourney would be a choice attraction for the army—acquainting them all with the new machines that Djaffar and Joubert had set up.

Of course there would be some classic sword bouts. The knights, clad in the new armor, would meet in a closed field. But even more ambitious maneuvers had been arranged: bursts of real fire where the crews of mangonels, catapults and firetubes could set off their shells with a full charge of powder and test their versatility. (The latter weapons had been devised by the Chinese. They let them hurl the Baphomet thunderballs far afield.)

Most of all William wanted to test the knights' reaction to the explosion of the fireballs, which they had never had to face, and he also wanted to test a new battle tactic. In a real encounter the Baphomets would have a profusion of various explosives, and any wave assault would amount to suicide.

Under the guise of a preventive crusade aimed at enemies of the Holy Church (with papal approval) the Grand Master was actually hiding vast ambitions, ambitions which would have horrified any who might have plumbed the depths of his soul.

For him the universe was a new prize dangled before his rapacity. The empire of Earth no longer satisfied him once he realized the existence of stellar kingdoms much more vast. He would never, of course, openly admit his desire for hegemony: the prayer "*Non nobis Domine, sed Nomine Tuo da gloriam*" eased his conscience; he had almost succeeded in persuading himself that he was acting purely for the cause of the Lord and the True Faith.

So on this clear morning, when a stiff breeze was lifting the proud gonfalons, banners and standards, a huge crowd had gathered on the plain as well as in the silken and tapestried galleries.

Noble ladies and almond-eyed princesses arrayed in their most beautiful finery entered upon a battle no less fierce than the knights—oriental belles opposed to occidental. Each combatant had chosen a lady whose colors he bore, and she would become queen of the tourney should her chosen warrior gain the victory.

All over the camp, knights and squires were polishing their weapons. A melee of combatant troops were to meet afoot, after the joust which opposed the two men armed with lances.

Then would come the gauntlet of fire, and after that, a mock combat with Baphomet weapons. Finally, at evenfall, the victors would meet at a banquet, if their health permitted and they had not broken too many teeth.

The honor of directing the tourney fell to marshal Peter of Sevry. His blushing broad face showed that he must have poured himself a few libations, but that hardly stopped him from having a lordly bearing when he headed for the Grand Master with all his house about him to ask permission to have the knights enter the lists.

William drew his sword, the heralds blew deafening fanfares and the marshal lifted his baton.

The future adversaries lowered their visors and entered the closed field, which was divided into twenty parallel strips.

Hospitalers and Teutons prepared to meet Templars, while Kubla's warriors met French, English and German knights.

The Mongol chief was sitting in the gallery overhanging the lists, beside William, John of Villiers and Conrad von Thierberg, which was evidence of the esteem the Grand Master had for him.

The laws of the joust provided that the combatant must strike the opponent on shield or helm. Blows below the belt were forbidden. Arbiters would watch to see that these rules were scrupulously observed.

In a thunderous racket, the destriers' shoes hammered the earth; the plumes of the crests streamed like living birds as the combatants lowered their stop-ringed lances, gathering speed.

Although the armor was the new model, they had all charmingly modified the helmets with allegorical figures and monsters to such an extent that the brave jousters looked like creatures from another world.

In the first shock of encounter, nearly half the knights bit the dust. Some got up swearing, stalking off to hide their shame in their pavilions, others staying flat on their backs while their squires came running to attend to them. Happily, a few of them were seriously hurt, for the strange metal of the armor had an exceptional resistance. On the other hand, more than one man hit on the head had cracked incisors and molars in a flood of blood.

The survivors went back to the starting point.

Among them stood all the officers of the Templars, Hospitalers and Germans. This time the victors were going to meet new opponents. So John of Grailly found himself face-to-face with a giant Teuton, Siegfried von Orselen.

As for Otto of Granson, he was going to have to meet Godfrey of Antioch, a Hospitaler of wide renown.

For the second time the horses stretched out at a gallop,

the shock of lances resounded like the axeblows of woodsmen in the forest, the earth shook under the impact of unseated bodies.

This time four knights alone stayed in the lists, Otto of Granson, John of Grailly, Siegfried von Orselen and Thibaud Gaudin. As it turned out, the Frenchman and his adversary had broken their lances in vain.

Finally, after a last engagement, a single combatant remained ahorse: Thibaud Gaudin, who proudly took a little trot around the enclosure to lift his lance to the chosen of his affections and to come to receive the palm of victory from the hands of William of Beaujeu.

"Surely, noble friend, no more valiant warrior could receive this reward," the Grand Master exclaimed, delighted. "With you, I am assured that my empire will be in good hands in my absence."

John of Villiers and Conrad von Thierberg paid him compliments too, but with teeth clenched. Assuredly, they took no pleasure in the defeat of their own party.

But the melee which followed let the Hospitalers and the Teutons distinguish themselves. After two hours of merciless combat, in the course of which helmet plumes flew in the wind, armor was hammered, shields battered until their devices were rendered illegible, the two victors received in their turn the prize they had so painfully gained.

Now the sun was high over the horizon and hunger and thirst made themselves felt. Everyone went back to his quarters to gather strength for the struggles of the afternoon.

This time it was a very different entertainment. The armies united around Chang-Chu were split into two groups, mixed companies of Chinese, Tartars and the three rival orders of soldier-monks.

The point of the maneuver was this: the blue army had to try to cross the river under the fire of the red army, which was dug in on the plateau.

A spectacular innovation: judges and observers flew over the field of combat in the ships at low altitude to gain a better view of the whole, to appreciate the results of fire and to decide at a glance on the number put out of action.

Of course, the site of these war games had been chosen at a far distance from the palace, and the wind direction care-

fully studied so that the pernicious emanations might be rapidly dispersed far from the combatants.

William and the two other Grand Masters stood on the
peripheries of the battle aboard a vessel with the Baussant
arms painted on its hull.

The blue army followed Conrad von Thierberg, while the
red drew up under the banner of Marshal Peter of Sevry.

Before and behind the lines, the company flags served as
targets for heavy missles. The light arms were trained on the
combatants, who found themselves spattered with black paint
mixed with Chinese powder. These were judged out of action.

From the start, it appeared to the observers that the warhorses could not be used in this kind of encounter.
Frightened by the unaccustomed explosions, they reared and
fled in every direction. Kubla's elephants mirrored the panic
in the ranks of the blue army.[1]

William seemed to have foreseen these incidents. His orders urged the knights to scatter themselves wide and to get
down in the individual holes dug by the squires the moment
fire began.

The soldier-monks judged such a position unworthy of
them, so they remained in the open, but when the horses and
elephants came rushing down on them, they plunged head-
first into these despised refuges.[2]

But as a whole the maneuvers eloquently demonstrated
that the knights did not have sufficient training to fight enemies using explosive weapons.

When the first wave of attackers crossed the watercourse,
the defenders, instead of staying in the trenches and
maintaining a fire supported with light arms, rushed to the assault waving their swords. A number of them were mowed
down—or rather spattered with paint—which in no wise hin-
dered them from continuing to fight, contrary to all the rules.

Some, having regained their horses, even led a heroic
charge, making an ideal target for the fire of the arbalesters.

All of it ended in a total muddle, which brought mocking

[1] Marginal note of the Templar of Tyre: This definitely put them out
of the expedition. Besides, they were too heavy for the ships.
[2] It must be admitted that a few inexperienced marksmen had put in
real charges. The army mourned about fifty dead. The disaster was
hidden from the soldiers to preserve their morale: they were told the
missing had been sent on a long reconnaissance mission on the borders.

smiles to the faces of the Grand Master of the Teutons and that of the Hospitalers, while William's countenance grew longer and longer.

His armies had decidedly forgotten the things they had learned in previous campaigns. They had to be completely taken in hand regarding land encounters as well as the ship-board combats which would surely bring more disappointments. . . .

By heaven's grace, William had time enough to attend to it. He thanked the Lord for having gone ahead in training his army, because if the Baphomets had attacked Earth at this moment, they would have won an easy victory over these poor simple souls who still believed in the power of the sword.

"All that must change," William said dryly to his officers and the other Grand Masters, at the banquet which found them together again that evening, under the vast tents set up in the open air of the palace gardens.

Only the dignitaries shared in this communal feast. The infantry, on the other hand, was in a sad state. Deafened by the explosions, half strangled by the dust clouds, their legs incapable of carrying them, and their eyes burning, the unfortunate Tholon brothers had thought their last hour had arrived when a heavy missile fell a little short and exploded not far from them.

"God's blood," Guiot swore weakly, "I really thought I was in hell. Now I know what chastisement's awaiting me for my sins. Garin, you were right to tell me not to go running after bawds—"

Whereupon he swallowed a cupful of spiced wine, which put a little heart into him, while Clement took up the refrain.

"Holy name, I still see the fires dancing before my eyes. Say, Garin, you really sure we ain't dead?"

"My brothers, I tell you in all truth: born of God, dead in Jesus, we rise again by the Holy Spirit. Repent your sins and you will inherit eternal life. Sin no more and ye shall know peace of soul. What matters then the loss of a mortal body? William—bless him—preaches a Holy Crusade which will give you the means to redeem your faults, by traveling infinite space to serve the cause of the Faith. During our voyage, we will have no chance to be tempted by sins of the flesh, far less to be moved by foul perversions. So we shall be meeting creatures whose sex is surely not like ours, and all fornication will be forbidden you under pain of revealing your earthly nature. So you will have occasion to make a virtuous and complete abstinence. . . ."

"God!" sighed Guiot, dazed. "I never thought of that. That's true. We're going to have to give up women for a damn long time."

"That is exactly the truth," the Templar assured them with an ironic smile. "If we meet other star folk, they're surely going to have a shape different from ours."

"Holy name," Clement swore. "What a bore! And what do you think, we going to have to stay very long in that purgatory?"

"Hard to say. The equivalent of one or two of our months no doubt about it. Lord Marco Polo has to make contact with other merchants, get information out of them, maybe even enter one of the cities occupied by the Baphomets. Then we go back to Earth, taking the long way home so as not to draw attention of enemy patrols. Surely a minimum of two months, granted nothing unforeseen comes up. . . ."

"Ah, well, that's promising. Garin, my brother, thanks for letting us know. I'm done in, I'm going to bed. You coming, Clement?"

"I'm there. Night, Garin."

"The Lord protect you and grant you edifying dreams," the Templar wished them, astonished to see his two comrades become so virtuous.

He stayed musing a moment, staring into the glowing embers, wondering why his miscreant brothers had suddenly lost their appetites. Was it the prospect of leaving Earth that led them finally to think of their salvation? He shook his head, knelt for a brief prayer and, wrapping himself in his great white cloak, prepared to sleep the sleep of the just.

As for Guiot and Clement, they seemed to have forgotten all their fatigue. The moment their brother fell asleep, they went wide-striding along the road that led to Chang-Chu.

At the end of a quarter hour, they reached the drawbridge, identified themselves and entered the city by the postern gate.

There they followed a dark lane about fifty meters and reached the front of a brightly lit shop. Songs, cries, oaths rang far down the lane. The sign hanging over the door illustrated the name of the tavern. The Four-Day Drunk.

Through the upper-story windows came women's laughter.

The two brothers looked at each other with a conspiratorial grin. Before suffering a forced continence of several weeks, they were going to give themselves memories enough for this disturbing voyage, and even for several future ones.

Next morning, Garin found Clement and Guiot sleeping nearby. He recited his matins, prepared breakfast with the leavings of the last night's supper, then, as his brothers still kept snoring, hands curled, he decided to shake them, gently at first, and then more roughly.

The sleepers turned back over, grumbling.

Confronted with the futility of his efforts, Garin scratched his head thoughtfully, leaned over Guiot, sniffed his breath and straightened with a grimace of disgust, for his brother reeked of wine.

Suddenly he snatched a waterskin, emptied it into a shield and poured it liberally over the luckless fellows who came up like the devils they were, cursing and blaspheming.

"For sure," the Templar growled, "you'll always be impossible. Where did you spend the night?"

"Well, we thought we ought to say good-bye to our friends," muttered Clement, snorting. "Then we went to town. . . . Suddenly everyone was drinking our health, and we had to answer that. Couldn't offend them."

"Yeah," said Guiot. "Couldn't let old buddies down like that. . . ."

"Oh, yes? And then?" asked Garin, taking out of the rascal's pocket a red silk scarf. "A farewell gift, I suppose?"

"Right you are," said Clement. "Out where we're going, the nights can get cold."

"Cease your lies, you filthy sinners! You were sunk again in orgies and debauchery. I don't know what keeps me from giving you up to your sorry fate. . . ."

"You know, we were thinking about you," Guiot murmured, all abashed. "We were going to bring you a relic, a tooth of St. Agatha, because it would bring you luck, and you can't be wounded when you're carrying it on you."

So saying, he rummaged in his purse and brought out a yellowed stub that the Templar hurled far from him with a ringing slap.

"Stupid yokels! They'd have you believing any kind of

flummery when you're drunk. Eat and get dressed. We're supposed to be on board in an hour. . . ."

"All the same," protested Red Guiot, "you're going too far. A tooth that cost me thirty sols. . . ."

The Templar shrugged and, paying no more attention to them, turned back to his affairs, then brushed his white cloak meticulously and polished his armor.

At the appointed hour, the Tholon brothers presented themselves in front of the reconnaissance ship. Clement and Guiot were yawning fit to unhinge their jaws.

Lord Marco Polo walked up and down before the ladder to the lock.

The Venetian was a very handsome man. A large cap of red-striped velvet crowned his black, almost crinkly hair. His deep-set blue eyes enlivened an energetic face, full of health, tanned by his endless ridings forth. His short curled beard, which he frequently tugged, but half hid his bull's neck, which marked an uncommon strength. His wide shoulders were clothed in a spotless ermine mantle, which cloaked a fine figure well set off in a broidered pourpoint.

His piercing look, of astonishing keenness, passed over the members of his crew. Then he talked to them in his musical voice, with a slight Italian accent.

"My friends, we're going to live together a dangerous adventure. I know your bravery and I haven't any worry about your behavior if we run into a fight. But it will be your cleverness and your adaptability we need most of all. We're going to be staying among hostile populations and we have to watch moment by moment how we act and what we say. Be cautious: a casual gesture could be fatal among strangers. The secret of our success rests, then, in our constant care. Thanks to Brother Joubert's talismans, you will be inspired by God and speak fluently the language of the people whose look you will assume. The wonderful gadgets of the learned Joubert work marvelously, I'm sure of it. The wise lama who is going with us will keep us safe from all surprise by his power to compel souls. It is imperative for the safety of Christendom that we conduct this mission well. You'll be merchants, so no quarrels and no stealing. Only one thing matters to you, to sell your goods at a good price. Keep your ears open at all times and make your friends do the talking; be generous. Don't be stingy with gifts; keep an open table.

Most of all, don't ever let yourselves be rash in eating and drinking strange food and liquor; we'll inform you of the danger of certain items, but we could forget some details. So it's up to you to act with prudence. Be wise also in mistrusting others' generosity. Don't let people get around you. I don't know what the women of the other worlds may be, but the female kind always brings the most extreme danger! Now we're going to board. You'll get the rest of my instructions on the ship. Know finally that I have the utmost confidence in the success of our mission. You'll be equal to your job."

So saying he agilely climbed the rungs of the metal ladder which led to the lock, and his companions followed.

Besides the Tholon brothers, there were only two other passengers, Djaffar the subtle, the only one who knew precisely how the esoteric engines aboard worked, and the wise lama Houen-Lun, on whom rested the whole success of the expedition.

There was no lack of room. The ship could accommodate ten men. Everyone settled in comfortably.

The ships meant for William's army had been faithfully based on the Baphomet ships, the sole difference being that they could easily hold a hundred armed men.

The size of those ships might seem strange to the extraterrestrials, so Joubert had given the spies a ship similar in every detail to those of their enemies.

When the thick hatch clicked shut on its mountings, the Tholon brothers felt a little uneasy. They were going to face unknown dangers. And would they see the sweet Earth again?

But when the screen in front of Djaffar came alight and William wished his mission good luck, the men of Auxerre felt all cheerful and full of pride. Had not the Grand Master said that on them rested the destiny of all mankind?

They swelled with pride and swore they would accomplish their mission without fail, come what might.

Chapter III

The ship took off like a feather, headed for the light clouds which drifted lazily in the blue.

In bewilderment Clement and Guiot saw the green countryside shade off and disappear in the bluish haze, while the thin clouds unraveled themselves across the viewports or, at least, what took the place of viewports.

The sight became even more impressive when the Earth dwindled to become a plain blue-haloed sphere nestled in the ebon sky.

"God's blood!" Red Guiot gasped, "that's climbing."

"And our moon," raved Clement. "Look at that! You'd think it was a princess' jewels. . . ."

But the ship was still gathering speed. Djaffar stopped checking the instruments. Everything aboard was automatic, or practically everything, and his role was limited to watching the behavior of the whole.

The ship exited the solar system perpendicular to the plane of the ecliptic, so that they could hardly tell the other planets in the star-studded sky.

"My friends," Marco Polo said then, "our voyage is going to last several weeks. We'll pass close to several stars like our sun. Most of them shouldn't have any planets. But all the same, our wise Houe-Lun will proceed with a psychic broadcast when we cross the vicinity of those stars. Of course, the nearer we come to the land of the demoniacal Baphomets, the more careful we have to be. In the event we met another ship en route, Djaffar knows the procedure to follow. Our lama will try at that point to dominate the minds of the crew to get information on the way the extraterrestrials conduct their commerce. That will be one of the most dangerous moments of our voyage. You will have to be quiet and not interrupt his spiritual concentration. He'll share with us then what he's learned and advise us the best behavior to follow. For the moment, don't fear that you're going to suffer from idleness. Doctor Djaffar is going to teach you our enemies' language, by means of a marvelous talisman. Every day you'll wear that network for an hour. You may perhaps feel a few headaches from it, but that won't last. At the end of a fortnight, you'll be speaking the language of the planet Baphom as readily as your own. You'll also know the Baphomets' usages and customs, which will keep you from making mistakes. Finally, if we make contact with a different race, your apprenticeship must be much more rapid, a few minutes, no more. Djaffar will give you a medication then that will ease your fatigue. Now, take your places for your first lesson."

The three brothers, a little reluctantly, took their places on the special seats, after which Marco Polo assured them that he had undergone this treatment himself with no hurt, and so had Djaffar and Houen-Lun.

This lesson went very well.

At the beginning they sat there with their mouths open. A thin voice whispered incomprehensible words in their ears. Little by little they relaxed and the murmur became inaudible.

Their lesson finished, they had a little liberty, and then, it being dinnertime, the Auxerre gourmands had to content themselves with a thin broth doled out by a mysterious machine. To quench their thirst they had nothing but water, a very poor beverage in the reckoning of Clement and Guiot, who were beginning to dream of the food of the good Earth. . . .

But they put a brave face on it, keeping their opinions to themselves. Marco Polo, Djaffar and Houen-Lun were under the same discipline, so the Tholons would have been churlish to complain. As for Garin, he was taking great delight in his two miscreant brothers' pretense.

This monastic life was going to last for days and days.

The Tibetan spent most of his time crouched on his mat, surrounded by a gold net, his skull shining with grease. Djaffar undertook regular examination of the strange instruments situated in the console before him, and he concocted unguents in his spare time. As for Marco Polo, he ceaselessly compared the configuration of the constellations which shone on his screen with those depicted on a crystal sphere.

The Tholon brothers unenthusiastically submitted to their daily seances. Only Clement complained of headaches and nightmares. Djaffar gave him several drops of a bitter mixture and everything settled back into order.

The sun had long since become only one tiny ember lost among countless other stars.

One morning as Garin wakened he pronounced a few words in a strange language with harsh accents. Amazed, he finally understood Djaffar's maneuvers, discovering suddenly that the ship, driven by immaterial waves, was navigating in an environment without regard to their own, following a trajectory precisely determined by an automatic system. He realized that the images he was seeing on the screens were only a rendering in a spectrum of light perceptible to his eyes. Strange details came into his mind, visions of a ruddy planet with a sky streaked with amethyst cloud, or titanic cities lifting towers to assault the clouds like the towers of Babel. He knew, too, the unnatural customs of the perverted Baphomets, who committed fornications among themselves with males and females. From these monstrous unions were born little monsters which would be brought up en masse in warm incubators. Horrified, he perceived thousands of foul mouths suckling hungrily at the plastic tubes which dripped a foul green broth.

The Templar learned, too, that there existed besides the Baphomets three other races of aliens. First, the graceful Ethir with frondy plumage and vast wings, who had led a peaceful existence on their own planet, nesting in the great branches of the trees, feeding on grain and tiny insects. Then the Baphomets had come and the gentle flying-folk lived now in slavery. Certain of them, expatriate, served as household servants. Their long broken wings trailed sorrowfully behind them. The ones who stayed on Eth had been provided with tiny brain implants and worked without letup, cultivating the wondrous flowers which they distilled to produce a rare essence. This they saved in crystal vials and sent by entire shiploads to the Baphomets, who drank it prodigiously. This drug plunged them into an incomparable ecstasy after their interminable couplings.

The Orpheds, on the other hand, were insects like huge

praying mantises. They were expert in the making of strangely convolute horns from which they drew melodious sounds, and they had besides a marvelous gift for musical composition. Their race had been decimated by the Baphomets and the survivors were brought into captivity on Baphom. There, to soothe their masters, these poor creatures must play their inexhaustible repertoire without cease. They suffered from the climate of this planet of exile, which was too cold for them, and they died very quickly. Fortunately their race was very prolific. Each female laid about thirty eggs, which were hatched in artificial incubators. The little ones were then fed by metal creatures, which gave them the juices of the plants indispensable to their growth, especially imported from Orph.

The Odeous, the only race with an advanced civilization, had been enslaved after harsh combat which had ravaged their homeworld. Their bodies would have been very much like those of Terrans if nature had not given them an iridescent skin of changing colors. Their vast, translucent eyes were full of a marvelous tenderness. The Baphomets, lacking pity, made these spacefarers prisoners eternally chained to their ships.

These slaves had an inborn talent for electronics, chemistry and mechanics, which rendered them irreplaceable. They did ceaseless commerce on the planet Baphom, crossing immeasurable distances to make contact with other distant stars and to furnish their masters with new sources of nourishment and the psychedelic drugs of which the Baphomets were inordinately fond. Impossible for these ships of the damned to escape the despotic lords of Baphom: a special device inexorably brought their ships back to this planet, as a lodestone draws iron. No hope either of ending their pitiable lives, for tiny electrodes implanted in their brains rendered every attempt at suicide impossible. So for all the course of their existence, the Odeous gazed on one another with their vast, wide-pupiled eyes, slaves forever imprisoned within the hulls of their ships. Their females, beautiful as goddesses, knew a fate even more pitiless. The foul Baphomets, avidly seeking after new pleasures, appreciated their delicate bodies, their graceful beauty, and filled their harems with these unfortunate creatures.

All this the Templar learned without surprise, as if he had

always known it. Before his departure from Earth, he would have had difficulty absorbing these gifts, so strange to his mind. But thanks to the magic apparatus, he took in this information as if it were ordinary.

His brothers acquired these revelations almost at the same moment and painlessly assimilated them. As for the other passengers, they had undergone the treatment before their departure and already knew these details.

Marco Polo still had to give them some supplementary information.

"You know now what is the aspect of these creatures that we will meeet on this voyage. Unfortunately, we don't know their language at all. The Baphomets despise their slaves and few among them speak the idiom of the enslaved races. Our wise lama will therefore have a very hard task if we chance to meet a ship inhabited by Odeous. Once the initial contact is established, we will disguise ourselves so we don't attract attention. Everything necessary has been foreseen. You just have to carry out your role. The most painful part of it is doubtless going to be enduring the lenses which will make your eyes like those of the Odeous. Come, I'm going to teach you to slip them under your lids."

This unexpected masquerade added a little charm to what had become a wearisome voyage. Clement dissolved in an attack of mad laughter when he saw Guiot looking at Garin with a dove-eyed and tear-streaming stare.

Happily, their long campaign across Asia, while William's army, coming out of Palestine, had warred against the Mongols, had taught them to live with people of customs often quite strange, and for them, an Odeous was not so very different from a citizen of Cipanghu.

On the ship, life went on afterwards with its accustomed routines. Djaffar passed most of his time watching to be sure the ship was behaving itself, kept taking notes and consulting the microparchment images, transparent as glass, which could be enlarged on a special screen. He even consented to give several cursory explanations to Garin, who was now capable of understanding these grimoires. When Djaffar went to his couch, he dreamed for long hours with his eyes wide open. Then he saw again the countryside of Alexandretta, his distant homeland, its blue sky, its long pebbled beaches, its dunes simmering with haze, its gardens of palms and gnarled, centuries-old olive trees, the multicolor clumps of fig trees and pomegranates, the groves of aromatic gums.

He never missed his hour for prayer, for turning toward the pale and vanishing star where lay the tomb of the Prophet. This in no way prevented him from joining in the offices which the Templar recited faithfully each morning. The Turcopole seemed to have constructed a religion all his own, in which he mixed in perfect harmony the teachings of Islam and of Christianity.

Houen-Lun, now, lived apart from everyone.

Sometimes he exchanged rare words with Marco Polo or Djaffar, and spent the rest of his time in strange positions, his limbs bizarrely contorted, his spirit stretched out to seize upon the faint murmurings which he alone perceived, coming out of the infinity of space.

Once Garin, intrigued by this apparent indifference to the outside world, dared ask him what he was doing.

"Making progress," replied the monk.

"What do you mean?"

"I'm learning not to be troubled with human emotions."

"Is that all?" the Templar pursued, a little taken aback.

"No, I'm also losing the sense of my body and the perceptions that disturb it."

"But how do you do that?"

"I forget it by not moving it. I've stripped off my body, rejected the form of my intellect, driven off every preconception. So I can live in harmony with the universe and be one with it."

Garin went no further. Apparently the Tibetan through his long asceticism and draconian disciplines of physical control, had arrived at a mode of existence different from that of other human beings. The Templar would have liked to try it, but Houen-Lun seemed too far advanced in his practices to bother himself with a disciple. Besides, Marco Polo had warned him: the fate of the expedition rested on Houen-Lun. The first contact with the aliens would be decisive.

The ship thus stayed to its course for interminable days. Without the magical clepshydras aboard, they would have all been incapable of realizing the passage of day and night.

Now the Tholon brothers had accustomed themselves to their disguise, they had learned to anoint their faces and hands with a rainbow ointment the shades of which changed subtly in a cyclic rhythm. Thanks to a salve also concocted by Djaffar, they could bear the presence of the lenses in their eyes without any irritation.

The Venetian spared them no compliments. According to his plans, the Tholon brothers would serve as his escort if perchance they had occasion to leave the ship. Djaffar could not leave the vessel, for he must defend it from all unexpected intrusion, and as for the Tibetan, he preferred to be alone, ready to probe minds, rather than mix himself in a crowd.

Now Baphom was clearly visible. The star appeared on the screens like a little red sphere. And so far its demoniac inhabitants had not manifested themselves.

But one day, when Djaffar was at his ritual of prayer, the Tibetan came out of his priestly immobility.

Without showing the least emotion, he said simply: "My spirit is in contact with strangers aboard a ship like ours. . . ."

Then he fell back into his habitual silence, while his companions scanned the screens in vain and Joubert feverishly worked over his several instruments.

A few instants later, Houen-Lun declared: "There are several Odeous traders. Four, in all. You're going to locate their ship in a moment. Brother Joubert, you'll send a distress signal, requesting their escort to the nearest spaceport. At the moment their minds are conditioned to this. They won't be amazed at anything."

While the passengers quickly put on their disguises, Joubert was still examining his detectors. Finally a tiny bright point appeared on a luminous plate. Almost simultaneously a message echoed through the ship, asking its identification.

The Templar was long prepared for such a meeting. He activated a tape which sent back a recording furnishing the requisite information.

Almost at once the communications officer asked for precise information on the breakdown which was afflicting their ship. Joubert nervously turned to Houen-Lun. The Tibetan went to the transmitter and snapped off several phrases which seemed to satisfy their questioner completely, for a few minutes later a metal sphere stopped several cables distant from the ship occupied by the Terrans.

"Brother Garin, and you, Guiot, get into your suits," the

Tibetan said then. "You're going to pay a visit to these strangers so that you can pick up some metal jars containing air, which is what they think is the matter with us. Take these here and have the Odeous examine this object. That will impress on their minds what they must know."

So saying, the lama handed Garin a bronze cylinder on which were strange, twisting ideograms. The Templar took it in his fingertips, studied it distrustfully, a brief glance which served to awaken in him curious hallucinations. A choir of crystalline voices repeated a monotone and ceaseless litany. He turned his eyes away and the noise ceased. Garin put the malefic object into a leather bag, then the Templar and his brother placed the magical networks onto their heads, which gave them a violent headache, but a swallow of syrup eased that quickly. Joubert and Clement then helped their friends get into their cumbersome suits. Finally the two envoys entered the airlock and manipulated the wheel on the hatchway. A few seconds later they found themselves outside. It was a breathtaking experience to find themselves so isolated between the two vessels in the face of starry infinity. The Terrans underwent a brief moment of panic.

But they quickly recovered their wits. The two ships were close, and the crossing was easy. They maneuvered themselves carefully with little rockets which let off tiny jets of air. Little by little they approached the lock of the second ship, and when they had grappled to it their anxiety much eased. Now it only remained to learn what manner of welcome was awaiting them.

The opening of the lock posed no problem, and when they had gotten the second hatch to work, they found themselves in the presence of the occupants of the other ship.

The network had conditioned them and they should not have felt any surprise, but the reality far surpassed the images their minds had received.

The two couples who regarded them with those immense eyes, eyes imprinted with a poignant sorrow, were of a breathtaking beauty. The graceful bodies of the two women, tightly fitted with translucent suits, were of rare perfection. And when the Odeous spoke to them in a musical voice, Garin and Guiot were mute, struck dumb with admiration.

Happily, their friends, thinking that they were suffering from oxygen deprivation in their ship, made haste to open the visors of their helmets, asking with infinite tenderness: "Do you feel better now?"

"Thank you," Garin sighed. "Our strength is returning." And his brother was casting avid eyes on the two alien women, marking small pointed breasts under the bronze tunics, slender legs, impudent mouths, red as fruits, saying to himself that if all the Odeous women were so wondrously lovely, his mission was going to be ridiculously pleasant.

"What happened?" asked one of the athletically built Adonises.

"Our air tanks were filled wrong," said the Templar. "So we were trying to reach the nearest base, but, without you, I don't know if we would have gotten there."

"The Ethirs who tend the ships are getting more and more careless," one of the women agreed. "We've had some problems too. A food synthesizer broke down, that's why we've had to cut our voyage short. What was your destination?"

"Orph," Garin said. "Our friends are impatiently waiting for our return. We're going to reboard. . . . Do you want us to come back and bring you some food?"

"No. Our backup synthesizer is working, thank you. We've prepared four cylinders for use. Will they be enough?"

"More than enough. The base isn't very far."

"Two hours of flight time, about. You can just follow us; we'll advise the satellite authorities that we're coming in. But I'm uncommonly rude. I forgot to introduce myself. I'm called Ildes, and my companion is Ilea; and he is Wrer and she Wrera."

"Heaven save you," Guiot wished them, quite naturally using the formula ordinary in such occasion. "As for me, I'm Guioult and my friend is Garoun."

"Have you been long captives?"

"Alas, I was quite young when the Baphomets imprisoned me on this cursed ship," Guiot lied boldly. "How can I thank you?"

"Isn't it natural that companions in misfortune should help one another?" Wrer sighed, sadly smiling. "Death alone will bring us deliverance. Forgive us for prolonging your ordeal."

"I've brought you a gift," Garin said then, bringing out the cylinder Joubert had sent. "Quite a small thing, but this object will help you bear the long hours of captivity."

"Thank you from the bottom of our hearts!" Wrera exclaimed. "How marvelous. Just looking at it makes me already forget the monotony of my poor existence. Here are your tanks. We're going to help you fix them on your back."

The two Terrans then reclosed their visors and let themselves be harnessed up, bending under the weight. Then they worked their way back into the locks while their hosts made the hand sign for good-bye.

The return crossing was a little more difficult. Because of their burden, the projectors were less effective, but once they were launched everything went well.

Stopping was a little delicate and Guiot had to deaden the shock with his hands as he came in, but the contact was not too brutal.

The four Terrans found themselves a few moments later in the living quarters of their ship.

"Everything went all right?" Marco Polo asked anxiously, the moment his envoys had taken their helmets off.

"No problem," Garin assured him. "The Odeous are charming folk who are very willing to help their neighbor."

"Ah, yes, and their women have no equal," Guiot exclaimed lyrically. "My word, I've never seen such girls. . . ."

Marco Polo gave them a bewildered look. He was apparently expecting a different kind of report. But Joubert put the tanks in the place reserved for them. To render his story believable he had emptied the main reservoir of its contents.

"Good. Now we just have to board one of the space castles built by the Baphomets to protect their planet. What did the Odeous tell you in that matter?"

"Just that they would show us the way and announce our arrival," Garin answered.

"Perfect," the Venetian replied, rubbing his hands. "So the garrison won't suspect us at all. Let's hope it isn't too well manned and that our friend Houen-Lun can control their minds without difficulty."

"The prospect looks good," said the Tibetan, lapsing from his silence. "My talismans have completely dominated the crew of this ship. They've just destroyed the cylinder according to my orders, leaving no trace of it. As for the garrison they call satellite 289, it comprises about ten Odeous. I shouldn't meet any difficulty getting them to swallow our story."

"So much the better," Marco Polo rejoiced. "Let's follow our guides. They're going to our next destination."

After a short journey during which the Terrans watched neighboring space very attentively, the satellite they had been told of stood out against the inky sky.

Strange castle in truth, this glittering torus bristled with vanes—antennae, in the Odeous tongue—which turned slowly in space. About its circumference, several platforms had been set up to receive and refit the ships from space. All, luckily, were empty.

Joubert replied to a message demanding the ship's identification, and then the voice of the communications officer invited them to dock at berth four.

The learned alchemist programmed the autopilot for that maneuver and the ship grounded itself on the shining surface without so much as a shudder.

At once two dish-ended arms came to lock it in, and a supple tube adjusted itself over the outer hatch of the airlock.

For the first time since their departure, the Terrans found themselves in enemy territory. Marco Polo looked anxiously at the Tibetan to assure himself that all was going as it ought, but Houen-Lu stayed quiet, fixed in his priestly posture, his eyes glazed in mystic contemplation.

The inner lock opened then with a dry click; the passengers felt a slight pain in their ears while a light fresh breeze swept pleasantly through the living quarters, chasing away the stench which had accumulated there.

"Let's go," Marco Polo ordered in the alien language, and they went out through the brilliantly lighted tunnel.

His companions, save for Houen-Lun, followed him with a hesitant step at first, then with more and more confidence.

The Terrans, taking the ramp provided for that purpose, reached the passage which ran around the satellite. There was in effect an artificial gravity nearly equal to that of the Earth, so they walked without difficulty up to the section where the crew of the other ship was waiting for them, along with about fifty other Odeous.

With a signal, they bade them sit down. "Wrer," one said, "told me that you had trouble with the ventilation system."

"That's right," Garin said shortly. "The Ethir are getting more and more careless."

"Alas, they are slaves as we are. Their life is a long wait on death. But I found no trace of your outward voyage. Where are you coming in from?"

"We left from Baphom by the nadir lanes," Joubert explained, "with Orph for our destination. Happily, we had gone through a routine check which saved us from asphyxiation."

"But a very painless way of getting from life to death," the officer murmured. "So. . . . Since you seem to cling to life, we're going to fill your reservoirs. That will take awhile. You can go then and finish your mission, unless you'd prefer to go back to Baphom for a general refitting."

"What matter?" Garin said laconically.

"Of course, it doesn't help you," the Odeous agreed with a look of understanding. "Yet, I have here a cargo jettisoned by a ship in trouble, and you could take advantage of that to get back to Baphom. It's a matter of supplies coming from Lyzog, a newly discovered planet, drugs for which our masters are so eager and a few instruments of undetermined use."

The Templar thought but an instant. He had in his hands an unexpected chance to introduce himself into the enemy fortress, and Houen-Lun would surely find a way to get interesting information out of their enemies.

"All right, Baphom," he growled. "There is as good as anywhere."

"You want help to load this cargo?"

"No. We'll do it alone. It's our business."

"Very well. Wrer will show you the way."

The Terrans rose then and followed their guide along the passages. He, luckily, did not seem at all talkative.

He brought the pseudo-Odeous to a room where about ten small cases were stored, then, considering his mission accomplished, withdrew to rejoin his companions.

Garin and Guiot gathered up the cargo without difficulty, using a small cart. Apparently the muscular strength of humans was superior to that of the Odeous. Then they set the machine rolling over the ground, which was covered with an amazing carpet, soft as velvet, with no seam; and they all regained the lock. In two trips the cargo was loaded.

There remained the business of taking their leave. The Terrans went back to the room where the guardian of the castle was always to be found, and Garin announced simply: "Finished. Can we go?"

The technician cast a glance over the various dials. "The pressure in your reservoirs is normal," he replied. "You can put out." He consulted several forms. "Ah! I've found a record of your ship. The microfilms regarding you were lost. You are indeed Guioult and Garoun?"

"That's right," the Templar agreed.

"Sign these releases," murmured the Odeous, handing them a transparent rectangle and a stylus.

The Terrans did so, wondering all the while if their initials might not arouse the supervisor's suspicions.

Apparently the education they had received was perfect. The supervisor glanced rapidly over the documents. "Everything in order," he said. "May death free you soon."

"Wish you the same," the comrades said in unison, walking out without asking further questions.

They were all sweating liberally and feared their makeup might run.

On the return walk they met Wrera, who gave them the sign for farewell, but she spoke not a word to them. Guiot turned back to look at the graceful silhouette, but his brother dragged him along rapidly. The moment seemed ill chosen to be counting the flowers.

Once aboard, Marco Polo and Joubert closed the lock and the alchemist proceeded to the routine operations of undocking. The ship took off then, headed for Baphom.

"Well," said Houen-Lun, "did everything go all right?"

"Absolutely. You had the guard officer's mind in perfect control. They even trusted us with a cargo for Baphom. We're properly listed on their parchments."

"And what is this cargo?" asked Marco Polo.

"Drugs the Baphomets use," Garin replied, "and a variety of instruments from Lyzog, a planet recently discovered."

"Joubert will examine them. Perhaps he'll find some interesting information."

"The minds of these poor folk have already given me an abundant harvest," the Tibetan interjected softly. "These satellites, like formidable barbicans, defend the access to Baphom. Nothing can reach this planet without being found out at once by sensitive detectors. What is more, the space forts are covered with demoniac weapons. They can vomit hellfires capable of melting the thickest hulls, and swift rockets equipped with thunderballs far more powerful than ours."

"And if we snatch one of these cursed weapons to make copies?" the Venetian suggested.

"I thought seriously about that," replied Houen-Lun. "Alas, we wouldn't know how to use them and those ogrish fellows who guard the fort don't know the secrets of their manufacture. We'll have to try to capture a Baphomet versed in these arcane magics, unless I can read into the soul of one of their scholars. Once on Baphom, it will be an easy matter. . . . But I still gathered some interesting data on our adversaries. These miscreants are unbridled libertines who seek pleasure above all else. Drugs, talismans which stimulate the senses, lascivious music, everything of that sort they enjoy. These androgynes copulate and fornicate without letup. Luckily they aren't fertile except at infrequent seasons, so their race is not numerous. Their perversion will surely be a precious help to us. Being of extreme sensitivity, they fear all pain. Being devastated by the least discomfort, these cowards seek tranquility by recourse to all sorts of calming drugs. Moreover, if the drugs should prove ineffectual, they'd not hesitate to suicide, preferring death to suffering. Ceaselessly they explore new planets to gain new pleasures to sate that inexhaustible thirst for pleasure. . . ."

To the vast disappointment of his companions, the Tibetan fell silent again and plunged back into his meditative state.

Marco Polo, Joubert, Garin and Djaffar entered long discussion of this intriguing information.

Clement and Guiot had better things to occupy them. Seated apart from the others, they discussed in low voices the exotic charms of the fascinating Wrera. The two of them would have gladly stayed some time on the satellite to make a more intimate acquaintance with her.

Chapter IV

While the ship headed toward Baphom, Marco Polo, Joubert and Djaffar hastened about in the process of a minute inventory of the cargo.

They carefully deciphered the grimoires which gave the use of the strange elixirs, the odoriferous unguents, the multicolor powders. All of them were supposed to give the Baphomets paradisiacal visions, marvelous dreams, subtle pleasures.

Certain of these drugs must be burned in incense burners, others swallowed in little cups containing a dose which must never be exceeded under pain of severe intoxication, and still others were meant to be consumed in long, curiously curved pipes.

In certain boxes were unknown pieces of apparatus which drew the attention of the alchemist and the learned Templar. Most acted directly on the nervous system, increasing sensory perception, transforming the least music into a celestial symphony, or the foulest broth into refined nourishment.

That gave Joubert an idea. "Why not," he suggested, "take advantage of these filthy Baphomets' inexhaustible thirst for pleasure? The Baphomets aren't familiar with these machines yet, since this cargo is coming from a recently annexed planet. With the help of Djaffar and Houen-Lun, I might make bold to arrange a talisman which will plunge these vile beings into such an ecstasy. . . ."

"But to what purpose?" Garin wondered. "How will that lessen the power of the Baphomets?"

"I shall explain. If the virtues of our talisman can far surpass those of these Lyzogan machines, the principal dignitaries are going to want to get one."

"Of course, but how does that profit us?"

"Suppose that we add to it a second effect, a delayed effect which will activate at our command. For example, an atrocious sensation of pain. We could then put our adversaries beyond harming anyone, at the moment we choose."

"That's not at all a knightly method," Garin muttered. "Until now we've always fought our enemies honorably. Our Grand Master would never condone the use of such vile tricks."

"What scruples, my friend! This demoniac race has never hesitated to enslave peaceful people, and it desires to reduce our compatriots to slavery, don't forget that. The Odeous undergo such moral tortures that they hope only to die, to put an end to a hopeless existence. So why have scruples in fighting the Baphomets by taking advantage of their vices?"

"Joubert is right," Marco Polo broke in. "I don't see how the tactic would be more damnable than the use of the thunderballs which themselves risk killing innocent slaves. In all probability, when we fight the Baphomet ships in space they'll not be guided by those vile cowards, but much more likely by the poor Odeous, incapable of disobeying their despotic masters. So this solution offers then an immense advantage of getting at the ones really to blame. It only remains to know if the adjustment of such apparatus won't present insurmountable difficulties."

Houen-Lun came out of his trance. "Once for all, I can assure you that we lamas can control pain at will, as well as the rhythm of our breathing, the beating of our hearts. To do that one has only to educate the mind to let it command the bodily organs. Certainly the Baphomet mind is different from ours, but we have sufficient knowledge of it to try to make the project work."

"Yes," said the learned Joubert. "We've studied the minute waves emitted by our brain by means of magic boxes in which there are woven threads as thin as spiderweb, fashioned after the documents aboard the ships which came to Earth. On a magic window, Djaffar and I could see the materialization of three sorts of waves, one corresponding to sleep, one to conscious activity and the third to meditative thought, prayer for example. The last lets us command the organs of our body, and our Tibetan friend has gained an extraordinary mastery of it. So we know how to act on the

Baphomets' sensations, and therefore these demoniac machines can be turned on their own thoughts."

"In my opinion," Djaffar remarked, who had remained silent thus far, "we have to use Tibetan methods as much as possible so as not to risk having our secret discovered—should the Baphomets be moved by these unfamiliar contrivances to start an investigation. The mechanism which reverses their action, in particular, must be commanded by human thought, and not by techniques known to our enemies."

"That's possible," Houen-Lun agreed. "But we may run into trouble if our devices are put in places inaccessible to my thought waves—underground, for example, or even in the middle of a metal fortress."

"Doubtless," muttered Joubert, "we won't reach perfection on the first try. At least nothing is stopping us from trying."

Everyone agreed with the Templar and he set to work, aided by Djaffar.

Both of them occasionally asked Houen-Lun his opinion, and he briefly interrupted his meditation to give them advice.

So the voyage seemed very short to the learned Terrans. After having worked out this Machiavellian plan, they helped Houen-Lun create the marvelous device which would subjugate their enemies.

Prudent addition to their plan, Marco Polo had decided to use one of the trinkets they found in the cargo and modify it, retaining its original shape, so the object seemed to come from the planet Lyzog, and would arouse no suspicions.

This solution offered the advantage that they might introduce a new twist, intercepting ships of Lyzog origin and adding to their cargo a few utensils adjusted by brother Joubert.

Clement and Guiot had acquired some gifts of science during the recent weeks, but these esoteric discussions were still clearly beyond their comprehension.

Houen-Lun had them undergo several seances of hypnosis, and the two brothers then found themselves able to fill in for Joubert at the controls of the ship. Their role was limited otherwise to watching the sighting apparatus and the luminous serpents which twisted across the screens, to give the alert if they took on certain configurations.

Whatever else, they showed themselves enormously proud

of their promotion and accomplished this new duty with the greatest seriousness.

While Djaffar and Joubert were proceeding with their delicate experiments, Marco Polo was studying the best means to get this malefic talisman accepted among the highest Baphomet dignitaries. Would it not provoke their mistrust if they attempted to sell it? After all, the plunder came from an enslaved planet. . . . It would be more likely to offer it without compensation. But according to Houen-Lun, the despotic Baphomets respected their new subjects' commercial practices. The best course then would be to pass himself off as a merchant anxious to improve his standing by bringing the most precious Lyzogan merchandise, while getting some reward out of it. . . . That would not quite match the observations of the occupants of the satellite, but the Tibetan could remodel their memories when they came back. The more the Venetian thought on the matter, the more he was seduced by this project. It only remained to take on the appearance of a Lyzogan. That did not present any insurmountable difficulty. These aliens had a look near that of Terrans, close except that their skin was olive green. The disguise would be easy. Whatever the risk, the stakes were worth playing for. The Venetian rogue then shared his project with his companions. Joubert, always full of good sense, advised him to declare that the apparatus would only work for a year. Then it must be recharged by Lyzogan specialists. Marco Polo was only a modest merchant and would pretend to be ignorant of the secrets of this delicate technique. So he would have the opportunity to leave on a mission, first to go find other such instruments, then to put the first ones back into working order.

The folk of Lyzog were apt to blow the lid off it, of course, but they had to hope that William of Beaujeu would hasten his offensive rapidly, so that the Baphomets would have other matters to occupy them.

Garin still raised a timid objection: could Christians act on the souls of other creatures, perverted ones to be sure, but created by God?

Joubert swept his scruples aside. The Pope had not settled the question and nothing proved that the Baphomets ever had been endowed with an immortal soul. Besides, it was no time for waffling. The ship was reaching its destination.

A little later, the heralds of Baphom made contact with the

arriving ship. Joubert gave the requisite information and sat down at the controls.

Thank God! The satellite had announced the arrival of the ship with a cargo coming from Lyzog, and the vessel was authorized to land at once. Then it was taken over by long-distance commands and began its descent toward Baphom. The scarlet sphere grew in their sight. The Terrans put a last touch on their makeup, all of them looking like Odeous except Marco Polo, Guiot and Clement, who were disguised as Lyzogans.

The Venetian had judged that it was appropriate for his person to be escorted by servants who would serve as his bodyguards. Besides, the ships' crews seemed usually to have four persons: the crew would thus be reduced to the normal figure.

The vessel did a long spiral orbit to the level of the atmosphere, then plunged toward the surface, passing through red clouds which, under the rays of the scarlet sun, gave the planet its fiery look.

Soon the surface of the earth became visible.

Its aspect was astonishingly like that of Earth: continents covered with luxurious vegetation, snow-crowned mountains, oceans, lakes, rivers, vast deserts. In sum, without the ruddy tint over the whole, the passengers of the ship would have believed they were coming home.

As they descended, details sharpened. They spied other ships leaving a vapor trail behind them, and then cities took form.

This time the Terrans fully realized that they were very far from their homeworld. The houses reached an incredible height, thrusting toward the sky until some of them brushed the clouds. These immense towers were walled rather like the walls of a medieval city, but not walls of stone. A moiré veil of light played between them, closing together into a dome over the city to form a glittering vault.

The sites designated for ship landings were outside this luminous dome; each site was provided with a pylon crowned by countless dishes, which the Terrans knew now to be antennae for scanning and communication.

The ship, in an impeccable parabola, came to rest quite gently on a semispherical cradle.

When that was in place, the whole contraption started to

move and the vessel stopped near several other ships, sitting near a dome provided with long appendages.

One of them came to place itself over the lock, repeating the operation done on the satellite, and the hatch opened on a long, brilliantly lit passage.

"My friends, let's not keep our hosts waiting!" Marco Polo exclaimed in the Odeous language. "Stay on your guard constantly. Houen-Lun is going to stay on board alone. I don't think he'll have problems with the crew that will come to refit the ship. He'll keep in contact with us and advise us of his location so we can rejoin him if the need arises. Don't forget that you're slaves, and that I'm only a merchant. Scrupulously obey the orders given you. If you are at a loss, Houen-Lun will help you. I'm taking our apparatus with me to present it in person to the Baphomets. May the Lord aid you and His Holy Mother guard you."

On these words, the Venetian went bravely into the long tube followed by his friends, who, to tell the truth, did not go with enthusiasm. . . .

Apparently the masters of this planet did not suspect their visitors in the least. They had no men-at-arms in view at all.

The little group thus reached a room where an Odeous slave was waiting on them.

Joubert, who was reckoned as the captain of the ship, handed him one of the tiny parchments given him on the satellite. The officer examined the document in a scanner and with a weary gesture gave them a sign to pass on.

Marco Polo obeyed and calmly opened the door before him. A curious vehicle formed of little carts attached one behind the other was drawn up along the dock. They all took their places on the seats, and the whole machine rolled at once on a hissing air cushion, to plunge into a tunnel lit by luminous plaques in the walls.

The cars, following a pronounced slope, plunged deep underground. The convoy thus made a long passage at great speed. The wind whipped the faces of the passengers, who sat plastered against their upholstered cushions.

Finally after a spectacular climb up again, the machine stopped at the end of the line. There, guards outfitted in metal armor ranged themselves on one side and the other of the guests, and escorted them through several corridors.

Marco Polo and his companions quickly ascertained that

they were dealing with automatons and not with living beings.

They arrived finally in an austere room where sat a Odeous and an Ethir, the first representative of that race the Terrans had met.

The birdman looked them up and down a moment in curiosity. "Well," he exclaimed, "the folk of satellite 289 were right. You have been roughly handled. You are hardly recognizable. No question, under the circumstances, of trusting you with another mission. I'm going to advise the personnel center to put you on rest and recuperation until further orders. But who are these three strangers?"

Joubert stepped forward a pace. "We were given the mission," he said in a dull voice, "of contacting the natives of the planet Lyzog, recently discovered. We took on a cargo and brought back three native specimens. One is a trader who desires peaceful commerce with our masters. He calls himself Polo; his companions are Garoun and Clem."

"Surely, noble stranger," Marco Polo agreed, expressing himself unasked, and in a strong accent. "Our friend says aright. I hear tell that their lordships the Baphomets are eager for new toys, amulets, talismans and drugs which refine the pleasure of the senses. So I made it my duty to bring my most precious samples to acquaint them with the use of them."

The Ethir with broken wings gave him a curious look, as if he could not believe that a being in possesssion of good sense could deliver himself voluntarily to their tormentors, but he limited himself to piping: "You are well informed. The powerful Baphomets do adore this sort of novelty. One of them will receive you soon."

So saying, he pointed out a chair, while the robots surrounded the rest of the crew to take them to the Odeous barracks, where they could wait for their next assignment.

"Many thanks for your help!" Marco Polo called. Then, turning to Joubert he added: "Thanks for the excellent voyage, captain. I'll see you again, perhaps on my next voyage."

Joubert gave no answer. He followed his guides with the downcast air which suited an Odeous.

The Venetian and his two companions then found themselves alone with the slaves, who regarded them with a puzzled air, leafing through several dossiers to cover their confusion.

The ambiance of the Baphomet residence was vastly different from that of Terran castles. The smooth walls bore no ornament, not the least picture or tapestry. The costumes themselves presented a drab uniformity. The most humanlike were, paradoxically, the automatons of metal armor who, from a distance, might have passsed as knights.

Gloom and sadness reigned here. The slaves did their duty without sloth, but without enthusiasm. Yet the scribes showed a certain compassion regarding these strangers who would soon be slaves like themselves and who seemed not at all to suspect the fate which awaited them.

A luminous signal lighted on a table and put an end to the Odeous' reflections. The door had just opened and two robots were waiting.

"Our lords the Baphomets are disposed to receive you," said one of the slaves. "Follow these guides. They will take you to their apartments."

"Many thanks for your courtesy," Marco Polo exclaimed. "Can I allow myself to offer you a little souvenir of our meeting?"

So saying, he held out one of the numerous amulets which Houen-Lun had sent with him.

The Odeous contemplated it in astonishment. Such an attitude was certainly not usual in these places. But the object pleased him. It gave off a disturbing harmony which seduced him, and he gave a faint smile. "I accept this gift," he said, "with great pleasure, stranger, and here's some advice in exchange: our Baphomet masters do not put up with much contradiction. Do what they ask you and don't expect to discuss it."

Marco Polo bowed in thanks and, followed by the Tholon brothers, trod in the footsteps of the two priestlike creatures who waited his pleasure.

This time the Terrans were invited to take an elevator, an apparatus strange to them, and when they got out at the top of one of the gigantic towers, they found themselves facing a decor quite different from that of the subterranean halls reserved for slaves.

Marco Polo had admired countless palaces in the course of his earthly wanderings, but never had he contemplated such a mass of riches. The palace of the caliph of Baghdad itself, reputed for its treasures, could not be compared to this unheard-of treasure-trove, this veritable galactic Eldorado.

The antechamber opened on a vast salon full of marvels: furniture wrought by the most skilled artisans in the rarest materials, unknown jewels casting a thousand fires, living pictures wherein the colors mixed ceaselessly in a harmony always new; multicolored lights; graceful moving sculptures changing shape at the whim of breezes; statues of perfect realism where the fleshly hue of the skin made one believe them somehow alive; shapeless forms the sight of which plunged the viewer into ineffable bliss, and delicate curios of sometimes inelegant aspect, which could capture and magnify the senses to transport one into a paradisiacal universe peopled by visions and matchless sensations.

The Tholon brothers stared, mouths agape, at this incalculable wealth, not knowing where to look next. Marco Polo did not let himself be overwhelmed by this opulence. He wondered simply if the talisman adjusted by Joubert and Houen-Lun would meet with any chance of success competing with all these objects, these fruits of a science far in advance of the Terrans'.

The visitors' surprise increased still more when they were let into the salon, after having undergone a detection scan apparently meant to reveal any hidden weapons.

Before them, clad only in a diaphanous tunic with metallic highlights, a Baphomet softly lounged on immaterial moiré spirals, contemplating Odeous dancers, who were performing a lascivious ballet to the sound of ethereal music.

Within reach of his clawed hands, a cylinder starred with precious stones (a weapon surely), and a platter filled with unknown substances, dainties the monstrous creature crunched nonchalantly.

Marco Polo and his two companions remained standing a long moment, before the Baphomet lord deigned to perceive their presence.

Finally the ballet drew to its close and the dancers eclipsed themselves behind a gold curtain, leaped with unequaled grace which somewhat turned the Tholon brothers' heads.

The perverse being then turned his head, looking disdainfully on the strangers who had come, staring at them with lively eyes as if he were sounding the very depths of their

souls. Finally he belched loudly and croaked: "So you are the
natives of Lyzog, the newly found planet. To judge by your
hideous appearance and your stupid faces, there's not much
to expect from you. But you claim that your artisans made
remarkable devices that enchant the senses. I have a few
minutes. Show me your knowledge."

Marco Polo, nothing daunted, declaimed with the volu-
bility of a brave trader determined to have his merchandise
well esteemed. "Noble lord, your subtle wit surely knows that
one should never trust appearances. A doltish looking fellow
can make objects of utmost delicacy, and a stupid looking
one can turn out to be unbeatable in the most esoteric games.
It happens that we Lyzogans have some talent in engineering
mechanisms which can charm the senses."

"Your chatter is wearying me. Get to the point."

"Most puissant lordship, here then is the quintessence of
our art: the treasure, fruit of interminable research and
worked out by our most clever specialists. No one of its users
has ever been disappointed and, moreover, it has no danger
in it, not the least addiction."

"That remains to be seen," growled the Baphomet, and
seized the bronze cone on the velvet cushion which the
kneeling Venetian offered him.

For a few moments the alien remained silent, contemplating that object at all its seams. Then two knight-robots made
their appearance, bringing a Baphomet whose arms and legs
were confined in thin chain.

"Have this marvel tested on the condemned prisoner," the
master of these places ordered. "He has nothing more to lose.
So far as you're concerned, you can pray your gods, if you
have any, that you were telling the truth."

"Heaven forfend," the Venetian protested, "that I would
have wished to offer some trap to a representative of so powerful and respectable a race. This instrument is very easy to
operate; just fit it on the crown of the head with this lacing.
Then the user finds himself transported into a fairy world
where there's nothing but beauty and total sensory pleasure."

So saying, Marco Polo placed the cone between the
prisoner's horns. At once the fellow changed his manner,
which had been up to that point tense and anxious. Now his
features reflected ineffable bliss; his eyes, plunged into
nowhere, appeared to contemplate visions of paradise. All an-

quish, all fear had fled him. He wagged his head gently as if he heard a symphony of rare perfection.

That lasted for long minutes, and as the prisoner did not seem at all incommoded by the experiment, the first Baphomet growled eagerly: "Take that apparatus off him and give it to me."

Marco Polo obeyed. "You have been able to tell," he said, resuming with some energy, "noble lord, the complete harmlessness of this precious houbit. You can use it without the least danger for hours, during which . . . . It brings to a quintessence all sensation: the sensory pleasures, with it, become incomparable joys. It increases too the joys of music, and those which go with the good life. But it is perhaps in the amorous pursuits where its action is most perfect. The most expert houri will never bring you such full. . . ."

"Are you going to shut up, cursed chatterer?" the Baphomet growled, snatched the object from the Venetian's hands and placed it feverishly on his head. "Your verbiage annoys me and I wonder what restrains me. . . ."

A blissful smile suddenly appeared on the hideous creature's thin lips. He heaved a groan of satisfied ecstasy and sprawled lasciviously on the couch.

The guards had taken the prisoner away and the Baphomet was alone with the supposed Lyzogans.

Marco Polo gave a sigh of relief. Evidently the talisman had worked perfectly. It remained to persuade the masters of this planet to let him leave again.

For interminable minutes, the alien stayed thus, eyes half shut, in the most total euphoria. A few dancers, curious, had put their noses out behind the curtain and were amazed to see their despotic sovereign so at ease.

Apparently, invisible observers also had some suspicions, for a strident alarm echoed out. Six guards in metal armor came rushing into the room, waving short weapons like that within arm's reach of the Baphomet.

This sudden interruption drew the pleasure-seeker out of his nirvana. He took off the device. "Out!" he screamed. "Stupid robots, I didn't call you! Who's the cretin who gave you the alert? Who sent you in here? I wanted to be left alone with these fine Lyzogans. I have to have a serious talk with them. Cut off those cameras at once. What I have to say is no one's business."

The guards vanished as suddenly as they had come and the delicate, frightened dancers vanished again behind the drape.

The Baphomet rose then, studying the marvelous cone from all sides, then, ignoring the Tholon brothers, took Marco Polo by the arm like an old friend and drew him into the corner of the room.

Some downy chairs and a marble table materialized before them and the door of a credenza opened, revealing appetizing food which surrounded flagons filled with various liquors.

"Sit down, my friend," croaked the Baphomet, signaling his guest to be seated. "Chose what pleases you and serve yourself."

The Venetian served himself moderately, while his host declared with a blissful smile: "Faith, I thought for a moment that you meant to fool me with fancy words. The impostors who've tried to slip us drugs or apparatus claiming incomparable qualities are . . . legion. But regarding you, I recognized that you were telling the truth. This houbit, as you call it, is a true marvel. I could have stayed for hours under its control, and feel no weariness; to the contrary. Have you more of them?"

"Alas, no, noble lord. That's the only sample in my possession. But that's of no matter. If it pleases your Magnificences, I can get a quantity from my planet."

"You don't know how to make them here?"

"I'm only a poor merchant, Light of the Universe, and only the most skilled artisans of Lyzog can make these marvelous devices."

"Pity. I would have given you a laboratory with all that you might have asked to make one. It's so long since I've felt such pleasure, and I would gladly have shared my plenty with my subjects. I am the master of this city, and in such cases as this, I have at my command vast authority and riches of which you have only the most feeble idea. . . . Let's be practical, what do you want in exchange for this little device?"

"Not much, in truth, Your Lordship. Quite simply the exclusive right to sell in the city and in the empire."

The Baphomet frowned somewhat. "So far as Tekaph goes, I gladly give you an exclusive license. But it's not in my power to give you an imperial carte blanche. With my influence, you can hope to obtain that monopoly. Of course, it will require that you make gifts of several of these marvels to our emperor and me. . . ."

"May your Serenity be repaid for his kindness," replied the Venetian. "But I must advise your Mightiness that these houbits don't work but a single year; after this period, they have to be recharged by our specialists on Lyzog. To tell the truth, that would scarcely present any difficulties if regular relations were established between our planets."

"Relations for which you would probably have exclusive right?"

"Your Grace is getting ahead of my words. . . ."

"Well. I'm going to relay your desires to our Venerable Zolial. If he feels as I do about the use of this toy, no doubt he'll give you satisfaction. While you wait on his answer, you'll lodge in my palace. Go!"

Marco Polo and the Tholon brothers retired with much bowing and scraping. The Baphomet, without further ado, voluptuously replaced the cone on his head while two graceful Odeous slaves, robed as princes, timidly made their entrance.

Four metal creatures came to surround the Baphomet's guests as they departed the hall, guided them wordlessly toward the lift, which descended several floors and stopped at the door that opened onto apartments reserved for Lyzogans.

Without attaining the luxury of the apartment of the city's master, these rooms were still more sumptuous than those of the palace of Chang-Chu, and throughout equipped with an incredible number of refinements which delighted the Tholon brothers.

Foremost, they had eyes only for the six lovely Odeous who welcomed them, showing them about the place: three bedrooms with as many baths, a salon and a dining room.

Marco Polo let himself (without raising an eyebrow) be disrobed by two slaves, who replaced his clothing with a spidersilk tunic. They sat him down comfortably on a sofa, then knelt at his feet to await his pleasure.

The Tholon brothers had been treated in the same way and looked at the moment like two pashas.

"Tell me, lovely child," Marco Polo said then, stroking the nearest slave's long hair, "I'm a stranger to this planet and I'd like to be informed on the habits and customs of its inhabitants. Can you get me some works dealing with the Baphomet nobles?"

The young woman rose, joined her hands in respect to him and took a box set on a pedestal, pressed on the reliefwork; and a square piece of furniture silently moved across the onyx floor, stopping in front of the Venetian.

A laquer panel slid back, revealing a screen and a keyboard with several buttons.

"You only have to push this green button for a detailed list to appear on the screen," the adorable creature explained in a musical voice. "Then you feed in the number of your choice and you'll receive all the information you want."

Marco Polo, eager to know the extent of the Baphomet empire, its history, its resources, performed the requisite operations without further waiting.

Images in three dimensions and in color materialized while the musical voice of an Ethir commented on the scenes as they appeared.

The Venetian stayed thus in contemplation for long hours in front of this magic mirror, unable to sate his thirst for knowledge.

When fatigue settled on him and he cut off this marvelous dispenser of wisdom, the Tholon brothers had been snoring for a long time, stretched on their downy couches. The Odeous, lying on quilts, were also plunged into profound sleep.

The pseudo Lyzogan let them rest. He ate a modest meal, contenting himself with the remnants of the gargantuan meal his companions had eaten, then let himself down into his bed with a satisfied smile. The results of his research already surpassed his expectations.

Chapter V

The sweet caress of a slender hand wakened the Venetian. His mind still fuzzy with sleep, he sought the sight of a window to know if it was daylight; not the least opening in the walls. Suddenly memory came back to him. Of course, since he was in the depths of the Baphomet palace.

But suddenly a terrifying thought sent him leaping out of his ethereal couch. During his sleep his two libertine squires must have committed considerable lecheries on the lovely Odeous. Surely those imbeciles would never have thought of their anatomical differences. Everything might be ruined.

In haste he pulled on his shirt, his breeches, his tunic, and flung himself into the dining room where the Tholon brothers were peacefully munching delicacies, stuffing themselves with many-colored jellies and beguilingly perfumed fruit juices.

"Did you sleep well, lord?" Clement asked courteously.

"Too well, I don't doubt. And you? Your companions didn't disappoint you at all?"

"Certainly not," Guiot replied with a beatific smile. "These poppets are delectable, sweet, sensual. . . ."

"They didn't make any disagreeable remarks?"

"Ah, no, we completely satisfied them, if that's what you're asking."

"Perfect. I'd prefer, however, that from now on, you don't give yourselves over to these romantic adventures; abstain. God will thank you for it."

"Well, now," protested Red Guiot. "It's not Lent, after all. . . ."

But the Venetian signed him to shut up. Two slaves made their entry carrying platters with shining vases. They poured the three men great cups of spice-smelling brown drink, then retired, all blushing, with a conspiratorial wink directed at the Tholon brothers.

This copious breakfast done, the charming Odeous came to propose to the Baphomet's guests a massage and an anointing with aromatic oils after their bath, but Marco Polo refused them very shortly for all the disappointed looks of his companions.

All three of them then went then to the bath, a new luxury for them, and opened the taps full. A warm perfumed water flooded into the opaline tubs.

"Watch out; don't dive in there," the pseudo merchant warned them. "Our makeup could wash off. Let's just take advantage of this to make a few repairs." And so saying he drew a vial out of his pocket and all three of them repaired the night's damages.

Clement was busy fussing over his brother's face when he heard a light rustling. With a bound he leaped to the door and opened it wide. Behind it was one of the slaves, still bent over to look through the crack in the door. The Terran seized her by the arms, dragged her brutally into the steamy room.

"Little whore!" he growled. "You were spying on us."

"Aiii," the pretty child wailed, fighting and scratching like a crazed cat. "Let go of me, let me go, will you, you brute?"

"Let her go," the Venetian said. "Useless to hurt her. She's going to tell us very nicely what she was doing. Were you spying on us, gentle damoiselle?"

"Of course I was," the girl laughed, as if this question seemed to her the depth of stupidity.

"For the sake of the Baphomet lords, of course."

"Of course," the gentle creature laughed, and came to him and murmured in his ear. "Take me in your arms, you great simpleton. . . ."

So asked, the Venetian did so while the slave overwhelmed him with disturbing indelicacies, all the while hissing into his ear: "Listen, stupid! You don't realize it, but this palace is loaded with microphones. I'm going to pretend to fight; use that to give a hard kick at the head of the sphinx that decorates the side of the bath. . . ."

And she began to twist in every direction as if to escape the embrace of that great clod of a merchant.

Marco Polo had now understood the Odeous' cleverness.

He pretended to hold her clumsily, slipped, and with a blow of his heel, sent the appropriate image flying in pieces.

The slave immediately dropped her pretense, set herself in front of the three men. "Be constantly on your guard," she said quickly. "The Baphomets have placed devices to spy on you everywhere. Are you really Lyzogans?"

"Well," Marco Polo hesitated, "that seems evident to me. What do you expect we are?"

"I'm not too sure; and at any rate, I don't care. They only charged to warn you: the Baphomets are fearful tyrants who have but one desire, to enslave all the peoples of the galaxy. We don't know you Lyzogans at all, but if you have means to defend yourselves, fight to preserve your freedom before it's too late. Even if you have no hope of winning, fight to the last. Believe me, we Odeous have been through that frightful experience: death is preferable to slavery. Now let's go back into the apartments. You mustn't arouse their suspicion."

On these words, the graceful child fled, light as a doe. The three Terrans stared at one another. What must they think of this warning?

The Venetian in particular was asking himself anxious questions. Was it an insidious trap laid by the Baphomets? Was it possible that the slaves had set afoot a clandestine resistance movement?

He followed his two companions, leaving the bath, and started at the sight of two metal creatures which waited grimly silent in the salon.

"Our lords the Baphomets summon you to their apartments," one said. "Follow us, please."

The Terrans walked in their tracks, wondering if this visit had some connection with the events preceeding.

Their host's manner somewhat reassured them.

"Ah, here are our brave Lyzogans," exclaimed the Baphomet who had seen them the day before, smiling broadly. "Tell me your name, merchant. I forgot to ask you."

"Polo, at your service, noble lord."

"Well! my dear Polo, you seem to be born under an excellent star. I shared your coming with our emperor, the Venerable Zolial, and he has expressed the desire to make your acquaintance. Follow me. We must be punctual."

A lift then brought the three Terrans and their host up to a terrace where a flying machine waited on them. It looked like

a great bird with a hideous head, and its wings were only useless ornament. All of them took their places in it and the apparatus lifted at a dizzying speed, then slanted off toward the
sun, which was still quite low on the horizon.

During the passage Marco Polo admired the layout of the
city, more than he had been able to do on their arrival. Each
tower was decorated with terraces, wondrous gardens, often
linked together by footbridges adorned with flowering bushes.

The machine then flew over a smiling countryside of
forests and luxurious vegetation. At last a crystal mountain
sketched itself on the horizon.

"What splendor!" Polo exclaimed. "I have never seen the
like on my planet."

"What do you expect, merchant? We are esthetes, syba-
rites, artists who adore beauty. It's natural that our emperor
have a marvelous palace. This mount has been rebuilt piece
by piece, from its origins on the planet of the Ethir. Those
folk had no use for it, so we moved it here. It has the advantage of being incomparably resistant, and consequently,
offering an excellent protection. The towers which top it are
telescopic and they can, at need, retreat into the bosom of the
mountain."

"Very useful precaution, when one fears attack," Marco
Polo observed conspiratorially.

"Ah, it's practically a superflous measure. We have nothing
to fear here. Our squadrons are powerful, our satellites control neighboring space, and no one dares attack us. Quite to
the contrary, we're ceaselessly increasing our domain. Soon a
new planet will be added to our empire, I don't speak of
yours. It goes without saying that we're going to have peaceful relations with a people who produce such useful artists."

"Thanks be paid you, noble lord," Polo chimed in. "My
compatriots' only desire is to trade profitably with the mighty
Baphomets."

"So, we understand each other very well, be sure of it. But
here we are at our destination, and in a few minutes you're
going to have the very rare honor of being presented to our
emperor."

Now the machine had slanted for the summit of one of the
adamantine towers and came to rest like an eagle in its aerie.

The four passengers climbed out and were led by a squad

of four robots into a little room where all of them had to submit to detection scan.

"Simple precaution," said the Baphomet. "See, I'm subjected to it too. Our Venerable Zolial never leaves anything to chance."

By now their clothing, the tiniest buttons, their shoes, the houbit itself were scrutized from all sides. Apparently everything looked harmless, for the visitors recovered their goods without any of them being the least damaged.

When each of them had put his clothing on again, a door opened on a lift and the Baphomet guided his companions to the secret place where his sovereign sat. This time they saw absolutely nothing of the maneuvers it underwent, for thick shadows enveloped them during the whole descent.

The opening of the hatch revealed a glittering scarlet light which somewhat blinded the Terrans. They recovered normal vision very quickly, and on leaving the machine saw a magnificent spectacle.

The entry hall had the height of a vast cavern with insubstantial walls, all chatoyant light whose colors fused, constantly making new forms, complex and rainbowed spirals. The ground itself appeared transparent, so much so that the Terrans no longer knew whether they were walking or flying. The lessening of gravity, which rendered their movements easier, contributed to this troubling impression.

Contrary to the Terrans' expectation, no eager courtesan attended the pleasure of the sovereign. A few Odeous slaves slipped furtively amid the furnishings arranged tastefully in the room, while an orchestra of Ethir, set apart in a loggia hung along a wall, was playing a melody of touching beauty.

Marco Polo, for the first time since his arrival, felt an uncontrollable anxiety gathering in him. If by misfortune the master of the Baphomets revealed their origin, they would never see their homeworld again. Assuredly their disguise had been done with all desirable perfection, and each button of their costume, the very patterns of their robes, constituted a psionic screen established by Houen-Lun himself, but how to be certain of their effect on such alien beings?

Of course the guards had found nothing out of the ordinary, and they must have incomparably good equipment. So why would Zolial show himself more perceptive?

An opening which showed suddenly in the wall put an end

to the Venetian's self-posed questions. An enormous Baphomet, big-bellied as a buddha, gently reclined on a gilded couch, awaiting them.

"Prostrate yourselves," chirped their guide, providing them the example.

The three Terrans let themselves fall to the floor in a single motion, arms extended. Then a deep voice said, "Rise and draw nigh."

They all gathered themselves up and with lowered heads took a few steps in the direction of the august sovereign.

"So, my brave Fizzur, these are the Lyzogans you told me about. You say their artisans surpass us in the creation of psychedelic stimulators to take the senses away."

"To be sure, Your Majesty," replied the Terrans' companion. "I myself have used it to assure myself of its harmlessness and the results have surpassed all my hopes."

"They don't appear highly evolved," growled the emperor. "Recall to me what is their stage of civilization."

"Eighth degree, Your Plenitude, with a rather strange asynchronism of maturation. They have gone very far in the study of biology and yet haven't reached the stage of star travel."

"Normal if they had stimulators capable of bringing them to a state of full contentment. What would they need to seek in space?"

"Your sovereign intellect sees it quite correctly. If they can attain to happiness, their civilization would be strongly introverted. According to the information we have from the crew of the starship which discovered their planet, they don't have any weapons, at least in the sense we understand them."

"Perfect. So, merchant, you come here to sell your famous devices. How does it happen that you've brought only one sample?"

"Your Serenity," Marco Polo squeaked slavishly, "the reason is that we're dealing with objects of great value and I didn't know if their effect would be adapted to your psychic makeup. My cargo is a sample of our production, so how could I know what your race would most prize? Now I know that our houbits work perfectly and I am completely at your disposal to bring as many as you may desire to your planet."

"You have set several conditions on your offer, Fizzur tells me."

"I limited myself to asking for a charter assuring me of a monopoly on the sale of this apparatus."

"And for what price would you expect to sell them?"

"Your Majesty will decide that himself."

"Well. We'll see later. Unhappily, these devices are relatively fragile, so it's necessary to recharge them at the end of a year?"

"Indeed. And only our able artisans can do that work. I'm incapable of it."

"Would you be suggesting that our own technicians couldn't succeed in putting them in order?"

"If they try to discover the method of function themselves, I fear, alas, that they will get no result. But our Lyzogan specialists will be happy to teach them the method to use, which demands a very long apprenticeship. . . ."

"We will get into that problem later," growled the master of the Baphomets. "If these houbits are as marvelous as Fizzur pretends, I will allow my most faithful servants a reward. Now, enough talk; put that gadget there and depart."

The four visitors withdrew backward, and well escorted, were led back as far as the lift, then from there to the terrace.

An hour later, Marco Polo and the Tholon brothers found themselves again in their apartments, easing their waiting by enjoying glasses of a wondrous-smelling topaz liquor, without worrying about the lascivious Odeous stretched at their feet.

The Venetian, plunged into his meditations, did not even see the delicate hand which caressed his body and set on his chest a little beauty patch.

Suddenly a screen lit and the image of Fizzur appeared like an incredibly real nightmare.

"I have excellent news for you," he announced jovially. "His Serenity has been fully satisfied with the test he had made. He allots you a monopoly on houbit trade for two years. You are going to leave immediately for your world and bring back five hundred of these wonderful devices. Have you any favor to ask?"

"Faith, no," replied Marco Polo. "I will act diligently to satisfy his majesty and I thank him from the bottom of my heart for his goodness. . . . Would it be possible to use the same ship on which we came? The crew seemed to me very competent and they knew Lyzogan regions well, so I would be more reassured, for, I confess it, these voyages in starry immensities frighten me."

"That seems easy to arrange. Moreover, while we have no well established routes, we would prefer to use the services of the crews who already have experience in the regions of these new planets. Tell me—I am in a hurry to use this marvelous instrument again—will your artisans be long in making them?"

"I think they are already made," replied the pseudo Lyzogan. "I only have to go and return."

"For security reasons, you'll deliver your merchandise on satellite 289."

"Can I ask the price I'll be paid for each houbit?"

"It's true, I forgot. It appears that crystallized carbon is highly prized on your world; you'll then receive an eye-sized diamond for each apparatus in good working order."

"Excellence, you heap upon me. . . ."

"Fine. Now, go. Each instant delays the moment I can use this extraordinary stimulator again."

Marco Polo bowed deeply, hesitant to ask his host to make him a gift of the slaves which were lent to them, but he dared not for fear of awakening suspicion.

The three Terrans then returned to the car which must take them to the starport, and they were agreeably surprised to find that the Odeous went with them.

"Will we have the pleasure of having you as traveling companions?" asked the Venetian.

"Indeed," his companion replied in a breath. "Our lives depend on it. If you refused us, we would be reduced to the most painful duties. Never would a Baphomet lord deign to use the services of a slave polluted by a barbarian."

"Well, we are delighted, believe me," the three men said at once.

The starship was resting peacefully on its cradle, where the Terrans had left it a few days before.

Marco Polo, Guiot and Clement entered the lock and had a joyous reunion with their companions, still made up as Odeous. Houen-Lun, for his part, remained motionless in a corner of the cabin.

"Well, old man, it's a pleasure to find you again," exclaimed Guiot, giving the Templar a friendly slap on the back. "But we were welcomed like princes. We even brought back souvenirs. But you. . . ."

So saying, he motioned at the slaves who were coming in to join them.

"Passengers for Lyzog," Clement laughed. "The return trip will be more pleasant than the one coming."

Joubert, the ship's captain, did not intend to risk trouble. "My compatriots are going to sit in front," he ordered. "Gentle damoiselles, would you sit on the back seats? We're taking off in a few moments."

They all obeyed. The lock closed and the Templar sat down at the controls. The ship nosed toward the wide sky, the bow toward satellite 289.

Houen-Lun then came out of his trance. "All went very well," he declared. "I had no trouble controlling the mind of the green Orpheds who came to set the ship in order and I could follow part of your peregrinations, except of course when you visited the Baphomet leader. Speak; you have nothing to fear from the Odeous. They are sleeping at my order."

"The emperor seemed enchanted with the houbit. He entrusted me with bringing back five hundred from Lyzog. I have to set them out on satellite 289. Do you think it will be possible to get such a quantity of them?"

"Once we return to Earth, that will be easy. It's not a question of complicated mechanisms, but rather of configurations harmonized with all the senses through the medium of sight. Did you get the other information?"

"Indeed, and in quantity, thanks to a marvelous device which told me the history of the Baphomets and furnished me all the details of their empire. Alas! I was not able to obtain any details on their crews, not much more on the placement of their squadrons."

"I know," interrupted the Tibetan. "I too did not discover much, for these questions seem jealously hidden and only the highest dignitaries must have knowledge of them. Pity."

"And these charming slaves," asked the Venetian. "What are we going to do with them?"

"I could prolong their sleep for the duration of the journey," murmured Houen-Lun, "but they seem desirous of talking to us, and maybe they have information of interest. I'm going to wake them."

The three Odeous stretched and yawned, and their immense eyes opened, looking about them.

"Well, we're now departed far from Tekaph," murmured the one who had spoken to Marco Polo. "I can scarcely believe that we're delivered from these monsters."

"What monsters are you talking about?" asked Joubert.

"The filthy Baphomets, of course! But you must know them if you're a slave as I am, and condemned to live lodged in disease-ridden barracks when you're not traveling in space. Surely your passengers are still ignorant of what's awaiting them, but I've warned them."

"Indeed," said Marco Polo. "But Emperor Zolial showed himself very courteous to my way of thinking. He promised to limit himself to establishing peaceful commercial relations with my Lyzogan compatriots.

"Give up playing this farce," cried the slave. "If you are a Lyzogan, why are you wearing makeup? My companions quickly unmasked your friends; you're lucky we hate the Baphomets so. I don't know who you really are. I suppose that you belong to an unknown race and that you came to spy on these demons. Please heaven that we never come back to Tekaph."

Marco Polo looked at the Tibetan.

"You've guessed aright," he said then. "You can see me now as I really am and my friends look like me, except they have white skin. We are inhabitants of planet Earth, and we fear that the Baphomets are going to invade our world. Can you help us fight them?"

"Indeed. We Odeous only live in the hope of someday regaining our freedom. For generations we have been gathering secrets in the hope of giving them someday to our liberators. The blessed day has finally come."

So saying, she approached Marco Polo and, opening the collar of his shirt, passed her gentle hand over his chest. The Venetian let her, not very well knowing what to think, and then the slave drew back holding a finger on which one could see a little dark spot.

"See this beauty mark. It contains in the form of microfilm . . . invaluable information. All the sites of bases and satellites are on it, as well as the total strength of the fleet of this cruel race. The miserable Baphomets are accustomed to discuss things among themselves when they have sated their pleasure, without paying the least attention to us. For them, we are nothing but insignificant creatures, almost cattle. So from year to year we have gathered a mass of information. Our race is expert in electronics and mechanics, and it was easy for us to make this tiny disc which contains all our knowledge. I feared being searched in detail before my departure. Our foul masters would not have missed it, but I had had the time to put this microdot on Marco's chest."

"Delightful," Djaffar chortled. "If this houri tells the truth, our mission will have been a success."

Without further waiting, he put the disc on a special reader and plunged himself into the reading of that document.

Joubert and he, with the aid of Aira, the Odeous slave who confessed to a remarkable education, passed long hours in transcribing it.

The ship stopped near satellite 289, and Houen-Lun altered the memories of its inhabitants without the learned Terran scholars even interrupting their work. So the ship could change its heading and veer off straight for Earth without arousing the attention of the Baphomets.

After a peaceful voyage the travelers, mad with joy, saw the increase of the azure world from which they had set out some weeks before. Now, thanks to the golden nets, the Odeous spoke fluent French.[1]

Before landing, the voyagers could admire the countless vessels parked around the castle of Chang-Chu.

The escort which had followed them since their arrival in the solar system left them then and the ship settled gently into its berth, in the interior of the hollow tower.

Peter of Sevry was waiting for the envoys of the Grand Master and escorted them as far as the Chapter Hall, where William of Beaujeu, surrounded by his principal officers, gave them warm welcome. "Welcome to you, valiant Marco Polo. Your absence has been long and we feared that the Baphomets might have captured you. Speak, I'm anxious to hear the news you bring us. But first of all, tell us what are these angelic creatures I see beside you?"

---

[1] Marginal note of the Templar of Tyre: For the reader curious to know the fate of the Odeous, I owe to truth to confess that they quickly died, except for Aira. Taken with a painful languishing they could not be cured despite prodigious care. Incapable of feeding themselves, they became like skeletons and died after being given last rites.

"Noble Grand Master, these are slaves of the Baphomets, of the Odeous race. Two other peoples have been enslaved by these demons—the Ethir, like great birds, and the Orpheds, who look like insects. Aira here with me has confessed herself possessed of vast knowledge in the sciences of our enemies and she has given us priceless information. But without the sage Houen-Lun, we would never have gotten our mission that far."

"Tell me your voyage without leaving out a single detail. I'm very eager to learn more about our fearsome foes."

The Venetian furnished a detailed account of his adventures, and then got to the information of a technical sort.

"The upshot of this all is that the Baphomets don't like to expose their precious persons. When one of them runs a risk, it's because he's been condemned for some grievous offense. We were able to confirm that when we tried out the houbit. The visitor who came here to Earth recently surely must have transgressed imperial edicts. Usually the ship crews consist of Odeous, who have been reduced to slavery, and these poor folk scarcely have the heart to fight for their implacable masters. The only thing that can incite them to fight against us is the device which kills them if they disobey . . . although they hardly cling to their lives. Many of them, and Aira will confirm it, only hope to quit this hopeless life. But the women in their harems have organized into a secret resistance movement, and they now know of our existence, which will inspire them to survive and help us set them free. Thanks to them we have a plan of the Baphomet empire defenses. As for the Ethir, they're hardly warlike; they're set over domestic tasks and the organizing of their masters' amusements. And the Orpheds . . . they do the most menial labor and their minds are vastly different from ours."

"Let's get down to purely military considerations," the Grand Master broke in. "In the light of all this information, what do you advise me, Brother Joubert?"

"Surely our houbits are going to be valuable in disorganizing the Baphomet hierarchy when we decide to use them. Their emperor intends to lend them out to his high chiefs as a reward, so delighted he is with the joy he's gained from them. When the delivery we promised is made, we'll have a trump card in our hands."

"No, I refuse to trust these little toys," Otto of Granson's voice rang out. "These Baphomets aren't stupid. If they get onto the trick, they'll destroy these trinkets and we'll be up a creek! Nein, we got to run headon at the enemy aboard our ships and land on their planet by the strength of our right arms."

"Well said!" Peter of Sevry applauded proudly. "The Temple must fight for the holy cause of Christ as it has always done, striking point and edge!"

"We all agree on this point." William of Beaujeu cut them off. "But neither is it unfitting to use subterfuge against such implacable enemies. So Sir Marco Polo must diligently deliver those talismans to our enemies. We will take advantage of this brief delay to train our troops in tactics very new to them. For the first time, they will have to cross the defenses of fortresses set in space. These fortresses are guarded by Odeous, but also by metal automations which are going to obey their masters scrupulously. So we have to expect strong resistance. According to this young slave, we can't expect to blow them up with the thunderballs, because the Baphomets have devices that can explode them prematurely. Is that not so, my dear child?"

Aira answered the question at once, amazing those present with her knowledge. "According to our technicians, the antimissiles aren't infallible. They pursue attacking rockets by the heat they give off. You can trick them by either of two means: first by firing before and behind your projectile devices, giving off even more heat, which will invariably draw them off. Or your gunners might fire their rockets in pairs and make their trajectories intersect. When the Baphomet projectiles get to the intersection point of the two missiles, they'll hesitate and lose themselves in space. I don't at all claim that these measures would be effective on every occasion, but they'll let a good percentage of your rockets get to their targets."

"I admire such knowledge in such a beautiful creature," exclaimed John of Grailly. "No one would have thought such a lovely girl could teach such learned scholars! But I still have a fear at the bottom of my heart . . . . Will these measures be useful when our ships are in combat with the ships of the Baphomets?"

"Certainly," the Odeous assured him. "But these perverse creatures are full of tricks and they won't be slow at all in

finding some countermeasure. We'll be well advised to anticipate a second series of machines guided to their targets by
the transmissions that let ships receive orders and communicate among themselves."

"Now those are wise and prudent words," Joubert said.
"But can we be skilled enough to work out such delicate
machines?"

"Your race has all the necessary intelligence," Aira assured
him. "And as for the knowledge, I'm here to give it to you.
My people have not been slaves but for about a hundred
years, and before we were exiled on Baphom, I was considered one of the foremost experts in physics and cybernet-
ics. I still carry in my heart the image of my dear planet. I
was giving up hope of seeing it again, but since your arrival,
I feel a wild hope reborn in me. That's why I devoted all my
strength to aid you in your noble cause."

"Now be you thanked, gentle damoiselle," said William of
Beaujeu. "We Terrans have valor, but what can that do
against magical arms? That's why we will have great need of
your help. We're going to postpone our offensive so our crews
can familiarize themselves with the use of these ships that are
so new to them. Once we've destroyed our enemies' armada,
we'll have to fight on the very soil of the Baphomet planet.
Assuredly the battle will be hard fought, and our scholars are
going to be of great help in putting these miscreants forever
out of condition to harm anyone. The day that the Baussant
banner flies over Baphom, your compatriots, I swear by
Christ, will regain full and complete independence! Noble
friends, it's late. Let's go rest a little. There's a difficult task
ahead of us, in the face of which the combats we fought
lately against the Mongols were only children's games."

On those words, the assembly adjourned. But William
stayed awake a good part of the night in the company of his
officers and the wise Houen-Lun, to make all the necessary
arrangements for the rapid manufacture of the houbits
promised to the Baphomets.

When the cock crowed to herald the new day, the Grand
Master finally rested from his labors, but only for a few
hours.

Chapter VI

William of Beaujeu had wisely decided to wait until his troops were trained before throwing them into an assault on the Baphomet empire; but he had omitted one important factor.

The troops assembled around Chang-Chu Castle were wallowing in idleness. Jousts, tourneys, shipboard training, mock combat around the Earth's satellites no longer satisfied them. Lordlings, knights, squires fretted with impatience. The soldier-monks themselves recalled their glorious ride across Asia, and dreamed of meeting new worlds, this immense space where they were going to carry the Holy Faith.

The arrival of the gentle Odeous ladies put the finishing touch on the impatience of the Frankish knights, the English and the Germans, who had had no expectation of such things. They had heard about savage worlds, monstrous races, and the image of the Baphomets was not exactly one to tempt them, but lo and behold, it turned out that these famous extraterrestrials had women of incomparable beauty. A little disturbing to be sure, with those immense eyes, but did not the Arabs use kohl to elongate their lids? All these rough warriors were conquered by the voluptuous beauty and the exotic charm of the Odeous. In that case, why not dream of settling up there? Of carving out at sword's point some duchy or barony? Assuredly, William would reward his faithful servants, and more than one family's second son, fated for Holy Orders and without expectation of lands, looked to the future with a wild hope in his heart.

Tartars and Mongols too, seized by an ancestral dream of conquest, were only waiting on a sign to hurl themselves madly into space.

Otto of Granson, John of Grailly, Peter of Sevry, Conrad von Thierberg, John of Villiers, and even Kubla, came then to intercede with William, complaining that they were no longer masters of their forces and that any moment some impetuous madman might be on the brink of convincing his vassals to go rushing off with him to some distant planet in space to carve himself out a kingdom there. So the effect of surprise, which was one of the main weapons the Terrans had, would be canceled.

Instantly the Grand Master flew into a towering rage, swearing that any rebel would be followed pitilessly and killed by the patrols which watched the borders of the solar system, but Kubla's intervention made him stop and think.

"Noble lords, it seems to me that we haven't at all taken into consideration a new element which does have importance," declared the Mongol Khan. "This war will have but few things in common with the wars we have waged on this, our planet. The weapons which will give our side victory are not those which we are accustomed to use. Strange, alchemical . . . we have learned that these purely mechanical engines of destruction have an overbearing importance. Now, the gentle Odeous damoiselles have told us that their compatriots were learned scholars expert in such subtle magics, letting them make destructive engines until lately unknown to us. Then why not modify our initial plan and change our first objective? Surely, it is tempting to strike the enemy to the heart and attack Baphom, but to take it all, is that not a mistake? Our troops aren't used to space combat, and the first engagements with experimental crews could bring us some serious reverses. The planet Oddh should not have any garrison as important as the one at Baphom, and in choosing the objective for our first assault we can test our crews and get what we most critically lack: scholars perfectly familiar with the alien alchemy that lets them make these ships and equip them with these terrible engines of destruction. And besides, we will attract the attention of all the races the Baphomets have enslaved, which can then bring us new allies. Beyond that, it would certainly be very useful to have an Odeous technician aboard each ship, because if the situation arose, he could then make needed repairs."

William was proud, hotheaded, but his extreme intelligence overcame his faults. He recognized at once that the arguments Kubla set forward had weight. But they did not affect the sending of Marco Polo with the promised cargo. The Grand Master himself was beginning to weary of these endless maneuverings, of these jousts which only served to diminish his forces. He too had felt the seduction of boundless space, which stretched before him as lately he had seen the vast plains of Asia when he had just beaten Bibars. . . .

After a brief thought on the matter, he straightened, drew his sword and saluted the Baussant banner which hung above the seat of state: "Down with the infidels, good sirs! You've convinced me. Now we have to get to action. The army will leave tomorrow to board the ships and take off for the world of Oddh! Marco Polo will accomplish his mission as decided; two Templars and one of the Tibetans will go with him. Houen-Lun and Joubert the Wise will be part of my company aboard my flagship. So will the Odeous damoiselles, whose advice will be precious to us when we make assault on their world. Now and henceforth I pass my earthly power to my faithful servant Thibaud Gaudin, who will be my lieutenant on this world, awaiting my return. Come near, my brother! I must give you with my own hand my seal and my ring so that they may not fall into blaspheming hands. They give you supreme authority over all the Commanderies and Territories of our empire. You may dispose of our goods, lend gold and silver, and if I should not return, there will devolve upon you the honor of convoking the Council of thirteen member knights, priests and brothers of the various provinces who will discharge or continue you as my successor before God and men."

William's secretary then carried in on a black, white-barred cushion the two priceless symbols which would make the Commander the most powerful lord on Earth. Henceforth he would have the right to an attendance of fourteen squires, two knights and a brother as servants, to a secretary, a Turkish scribe, two stewards, two valets, four Turcopoles, a courier, a chamberlain, a cook, a fourth of whom carried lance and shield. They were all already assembled behind William's attendant when he touched knee to earth to receive the insignia of his new charge, while the Templars intoned gravely in unison:

"*Non nobis Domine, non nobis, sed Nomini tuo da gloriam.*"

Having made that transition of authority, the Council adjourned. Everyone ran to his tent to pack his baggage. A feverish activity seized all those who were about to hurl themselves into this glorious adventure.

William had gone back to his private apartments and prepared three letters. The first was addressed to Pope John XXI. This learned doctor, known under the surname of Petrus Hispanus, and a very enthusiastic supporter of this Crusade, looked on the expedition with a favorable eye. This was the gist of it:

"Most Holy Father, Pontiff of all the Earth, bearer of the papal crown by the dispensation of God, your humble and faithful servant William, Grand Master of the Templars, makes you to know that, on this day, twelfth of the month of May in the year of our Lord 1277, the army of Christ's faithful servants has left our sweet Earth to root out this vile brood which opposes the heavenly Kingdom of our Lord Jesus, to make known the only True Faith, that of the worshipers of the Lord, to the very edges of the universe. May the Savior of the world have mercy on His soldiers! While we carry on this Holy combat to enter into possession of the heritage which He has given to mankind, God will see to the defense of the earthly goods that each of us leaves behind. All of us, servants of the Holy Cross, depart under the Baussant banner. Alas! we shall not all return from the unfathomable space where we are going for the glory of God. Be the defender of my brothers. Never suffer that they be despoiled or unjustly treated. My wise and faithful Thibaud Gaudin has received from me all authority to administer the worldly goods of the Order in my absence. Deign to be for him a Father and a Counsellor. Your faithful servant in Christ: William of Beaujeu."[1]

The Templar sanded his ink with a sly smile. He did not at all begrudge papal sovereignty over the planets and territories he envisioned conquering, knowing that John XXI was going to give him the lion's share.

The second letter was addressed to the King of England.

[1] Marginal note of the Templar of Tyre: This letter could not have reached the Holy Father, for God saw fit to recall him on May 20, at Viterbus. He met a frightful death, crushed by the fall of a platform. His successor, Nicholas III, elected November 25, was not at all as well disposed toward our order.

"To my very dear lord Edward I, illustrious King of the English, Duke of Guyenne, salutations in Him on Whom depends the life of all creation! On this twelfth day of May in the year of our Lord 1277, the army gathered about the castle of Chang-Chu launches forth to distant stars to dislodge from them the vile and faithless villains who oppress the peaceful creatures engendered by Our Lord, God of the Universe. Otto of Granson, your faithful vassal, is accompanying us along with the English Crusaders. I have no doubt that they will show their valor as they have done already on preceding campaigns, in the course of which we have brought to the True Faith Tartars, Mongols and Cipanghi. In my absence, Commander Thibaud Gaudin will enjoy all rights and prerogatives in the management of my earthly goods. I am assured that he will find in Your Majesty a counsellor and a true friend. May the Lord bless his humble servant, William of Beaujeu."

Finally, the third letter was addressed to the King of France, Philip II the Strong, its tenor, like the preceding, indicating that John of Grailly and the Frankish knights who had taken the Cross were going with the army, having left in a war against distant infidels.

In conclusion, the Grand Master drafted a proclamation to his troops. It would be read that very evening in every camp.

"Brother knights, squires and men-at-arms, the time has come to serve the Eternal God. To you, the valiant, the brave, the glory of your battles will open wide the portals of heaven! You are going to war against the minions of Satan, who have enslaved divine creatures, issue as you are of an Adam and an Eve, whatever the aspect God saw fit to give their bodies; they the weak, the oppressed, are your brothers. We are going to bring them the Light of the True Faith for the salvation of their eternal souls. You know the dangers, the evils, the perils that await you. The vile Baphomets are, alas! expert in the malefic sciences which birth flames, death and destruction. But God will have you in His Holy keeping. Be ye not dismayed, for He has taught us the art of war through His archangel Gabriel, conqueror of the Evil One. You are going to voyage in unknown space, battle against powerful nations. If we win, you will hew out a new empire, and some of you may perhaps even settle beyond the Earth. If we are defeated, there will be no retreat, for the miscreant

Baphomets will come to invade our dear homeland. Never forget that you fight for the glory of Our Lord Jesus and His gentle Mother who will bear your sorrows. You have left friends and families; many of you sold lands and houses. Religion and honor are now your only possessions. But the power of the Baphomets reaches its end, for it is no other than that of the beast of the Apocalypse whom the Most High has determined to put down! May the Lord Jesus bless you! Always follow the Baussant banner. It will show you the way to heavenly bliss. Angels and archangels will help us in our just war."[1]

After polishing his speech, the Grand Master changed his mind. Rather than trust that exhortation to the heralds, it would be much more impressive to have it proclaimed using the magical loudspeakers that would let them all hear it at one place. So he called in brother Joubert, who gathered the necessary equipment for him.

So William's voice echoed as far as the farthest edges of the camp, to the vast astonishment of the Crusaders, who saw in it a new demonstration of the astonishing powers conferred on their leader. More than ever they felt assured of conquering a fairyland flowing with milk and honey, where friendly peoples would welcome them with open arms.[2]

In all this business, the three Tholon brothers had been forgotten. They did not know whether they were to go with Marco Polo or go with the expedition.

Garin went to find Joubert, who gave him reassurance. The Venetian was in charge of delivering the houbits, but with other companions. The Grand Master wanted to have them on his own ship, as soldiers who had already had practice in the alien language. He had therefore ordered that Guiot and Clement should go with him on the flagship.

He himself was to stay a certain time on Earth to finish the manufacture of the apparatus promised to the Baphomets,

[1] Marginal note of the Templar of Tyre: William was surely thinking then of the Ethir, whose physical appearance is very close to that of the celestial legions, but he was going too far in attributing to them a soul, for the matter is still quite strongly debated, even among Templars.

[2] Another note from the Templar on the spirit of that day: This was, practically speaking, rather far from the truth.

but then he would join the host in the vicinity of the planet Oddh.

The cosmopolitan legions, gathered under William's banner, began their embarkation in good order. Thanks to the training they had undergone during their months of waiting, each man knew in what ship he must take his lodging. There was a clear majority of Templars and strong contingents of Hospitalers and Teutons whose crests in the likeness of monsters and chimeras dominated the crowd. Mongols and Turcopoles were also there in good number. There were even folk of Cipanghu with their strange black lacquer armor, swords which bore guards with minutely engraved motifs.

All of them bitterly regretted not being able to bring along their faithful steeds, which had been turned out to pasture in the prairie grasslands. Henceforth their mounts would be metal engines that would carry them across infinite space. When they reached the soil of a world, these valiant horsemen would not rest content until they had domesticated some kind of steed to replace their brave Terran horses.

In spite of brief jostlings and shovings, everything went as smoothly as possible and the various ranks of the army went into space one after the other, to gather in the vicinity of the moon. Near Chang-Chu, the squires were putting aboard four destriers, for William of Beaujeu, John of Villiers and Conrad von Thierberg, the fourth being held in reserve.

From the height of the keep, Marco Polo was watching the ships of the armada lift majestically, each ship easily identifiable by the heraldry of the corps to which it belonged.

Suddenly, for an unexplained reason, one Templar vessel lost altitude and, completely helpless, crashed to earth not far from the castle. At once, rescue squads directed themselves at full speed toward the crash site. They could only, alas, recover poor bodies, frightfully mangled, impossible to identify. This was happily the only accident and it passed unnoticed by the majority of the armada. By the grace of heaven, it was not the flagship.

Finally the last ship containing the destriers disappeared into the blue sky and the Venetian was alone with several Templars and Commander Thibaud Gaudin.

The latter crossed himself piously. "Please our Lord," he murmured, "that His faithful servants someday see their dear

Earth again. The noble William is taking on a grave responsibility."

"Christ have them in His Holy keeping," sighed Marco Polo. "The Grand Master has weighed heavily the pro and the con before lauching this attack on the Baphomet empire. This expedition is going to season his troops and our houbits will be a great help to him when he launches his attack on the main fortress: the planet Baphom. In four days, I too am going to travel to these far countries. Don't forget me in your prayers, for I have a hard part to play in this."

Far away in the skies, the armada was veering off toward its objective. The men had watched amazed as the Earth grew round as a ball, then Luna appeared, riddled with craters. Now they saw nothing but infinity studded with pale stars, and their hearts shuddered at the thought of their smallness before the immensity of the universe.

William had split his armada into three squadrons: the left wing was the English; the right the French; and in the center, a little withdrawn, the elite of his troops was composed of his faithful Templars, Hospitalers, and Teutons. Far ahead, a few fast ships commanded by the Turcopole Gerard of Tours blazed the trail for the fleet. They used particularly sensitive scanning apparatus, tuned by the learned Aira. The rear guard was under the command of Peter of Sevry.

Finally the Templar of Tyre had begun to move his finest pen over a parchment illumined with golden stars, to record this memorable expedition.

In the flagship, William of Beaujeu, standing before the spheres which represented the constellations, revealed his plans to his allies.

"The Odeous planet," he declared, indicating an orange dot, "is located rather far from Baphom, and, unlike Baphom, it isn't protected by a belt of satellite fortresses. There exists only a garrison meant to prevent any slave rising. It's commanded by Baphomets, but it's principally crewed by creatures in metal armor, the robots. The base of the ships that control space traffic is on Lyzar, Oddh's large satellite. We know the exact location of it, but it's likely that the ships will prefer to fight in space. Once these ships have been eliminated, we'll have to use main force to take the citadel near the Odeous capital, where their oppressors are well entrenched. In the beginning we won't rely on any help from the natives. Their demoniac overlords have given them a damnable talisman that will kill them outright at any act of disobedience. Most of all it's important to preserve the installations where the Odeous alchemist scholars work. We have the utmost need of them in what's to come. Now I give you the words of our dear damoiselle Aira who, far better than I, can tell you about her homeland."

"Oddh is located near a tripartite nebulosity and a very dense mass of stars. Its sky is thus very different from that of Earth, for countless stars light its nights. By day, the light from our sun is much weaker than on your world, for dense clouds surround our planet. But the climate there is rather gentle, for a greenhouse effect stops heat from escaping. Our eyes, more sensitive than yours, see at night very easily, a trait we inherited from our ancestors who were hunters at night. Our vegetation is like yours, but it will surprise you by its scarlet color. Be careful: there are many carnivorous plants, and they are rivaled in ferocity by the azgar, a swift, six-footed beast, one of the most dangerous flesh-eaters known. Luckily the beast hardly ever leaves the mountain regions, except when its favorite prey, the elur, grow scarce. At any rate, don't ever let an unknown creature approach you. It's better to kill a peaceful herbivore than to be eaten by some monster. I do not have, alas! much information on the Baphomets, for they hardly ever go out of their fortress. From the age of one year, all our children must be brought to the genetic centers to be numbered, and the males are given that cursed device that they must wear all their lives. Some of my compatriots still live free, hidden in mountain caves. The bird-robots, drawn by their bodies' heat, track them without ceasing. Add to that the azgar, and you understand that it's useless to count on their help. As for the Baphomet fortress, it's surrounded on all sides by an energy dome. It will be very difficult to penetrate. But I have heard that there do exist secret passages that will possibly let you get in there. A last detail will be pleasant for you to hear: my compatriots breed herds of domestic elur that will remind you of horses, except that they have six legs and a horny shell that protects their flanks from azgar claws."

The Odeous bowed sinuously, joining her slender hands to salute with infinite grace and retreated modestly behind the

Terran leaders while the knights and soldier-monks meditated on what they had just heard.

For the first time they had real knowledge that differences existed between Earth and Oddh.

The armada followed its course without unlucky meetings, though sometimes Aira pointed out some curious stellar object—the blue gaseous clouds where stars were born in a fiery furnace, dark nebulae where the horrified eye believed it saw monstrous faces, sometimes some double or triple star system, giant stars, blue or purple, and the veritable lighthouses of space, the pulsing Cepheids and the dwarf stars, deadly traps that one dared not approach for fear of being sucked into some unknown universe. Fortunately, these maelstroms in space were carefully marked on the spherical charts the Terrans used.

After ten days of voyaging, Houen-Lun, far before the scanners, signaled the presence of an enemy ship. It happened to be a ship making the regular run between Baphom and Oddh.

Prudently, William had his armada come to a stop, while the wise Tibetan waited for the moment that the crew would use its transspace communications to control their minds more easily.

The flagship approached its prey as near as possible, while staying outside scanner range. Finally, after an hour of waiting, the Tibetan announced that he was in control of the aliens. The reconnaissance vessels could then board the ship and capture the crew.

The Odeous were then brought aboard the Baussant ship, and the remarkable Djaffar began to work at once, guided by Aira. They had very rapidly to remove the implants with which the crews were equipped. Only the female slaves meant for the harems did not wear these explosive devices, for it might provoke some little damage to a Baphomet if his companion of the moment grew restive.

The principle of this vile device was simple. The young underwent a hypnotic treatment which disposed them to obey the despotic Baphomets implicitly. When one of the subjects refused an order, there was a mental conflict and the emission of a certain form of brain waves, and these, being detected, acted on the detonator of a tiny explosive capsule lodged under the scalp. No direct connection existed with the brain.

A simple skin incision at the base of the skull delivered the poor fellows. There was only the physical conditioning, which was the lama's business, and they were rather numerous aboard the ships, to treat all the prisoners.

The operation was quickly completed and the captives regained consciousness.

They were surely frightened to find themselves surrounded by strange beings, but after a rapid conversation with Aira, a wide smile brightened their faces. They automatically brought their hands to the backs of their heads, touched the dressings Djaffar had put there, as if to reassure themselves of the truth of what their compatriot had said. Then Sonz, the ship's captain, cried: "Thank you, Terrans! We can never give you sufficient proof of our gratitude. And here we are free! We are finally going to be able to fight these despotic masters who have oppressed us. Tell us . . . your wishes will be our commands."

"Surely you can do us great service, being current with the customs and habits of the Baphomets," William of Beaujeu replied. "At this very moment we're bound for your planet to free it from the yoke of these devilish creatures. According to the gentle damoiselle Aira, there is no belt of fortresses in that area of space, and the crews based on your satellite are weak. We therefore plan to attack that base and destroy the ships that land there."

"Excellent," the Odeous applauded him. "And what armament do you have?"

"Thanks to your compatriot, we have rockets to strike the enemy ships, guided by the faint waves they emit. For our part, we're protected from their impact by devices that give off heat, since it seems that the enemy projectiles are attracted by them."

"That's so, but what have you done against the vortex mines?"

"Excuse me, learned friend," said the Grand Master, "I don't know these machines at all."

"What?" the spacefarer exclaimed. "You're going straight in without knowing about that trap?"

"I never heard them talk about it," Aira confessed.

"That doesn't surprise me. It's a secret device and very new. Our ships carry broadcasters that neutralize those mines. Failing that, they'll provoke a titanic explosion that will destroy any ship in the vicinity. By the cosmos! you were lucky to meet me. I worked on the laying of that mine field and I know where they are. We'll use the disconnector that's on my ship and we'll sweep ourselves a path. Later, we'll make copies of this device to equip your ships. One thing more. Do you have quark cannon?"

"Of course not, my son," growled William. "Is this another new Baphomet magic?"

"Ah, yes. We have been compelled to install them for these devils. These arms project elemental particles that tend to destroy the equilibrium of the atoms of the hulls, making the metal lose all cohesion. There's no defense against it, except the emission of antiquarks that annihilate these particles and make them explode. Our physicists don't know the secret, nor do I. So we have to confront it without protection, but you do have other weapons, don't you?"

"Surely; that's what let us take your ship without striking a blow. We can act on your mind by the use of the antennae that you use in communication."

"Excellent," said Sonz. "But that won't work against the robots. No matter. That ought to sow a grand confusion in the enemy ranks, at least. When you've taken Oddh, our scholars will give you antiquark devices. What forces do you have?"

"More than two thousand ships."

"That must suffice to attack this objective. Well! I suggest you get your advance underway, until we start the minefield. I'll send you a purple flash. The passage will be marked by green beacons to starboard and red to port. Whatever you do, don't get off the beam."

On those words, the starfarer, with four Templars for companions, went back to his ship, but his companions stayed near their new allies to advise them.

William at once called in Gerard of Tours to give him the order to get underway in the wake of Sonz's ship, and the armada followed slowly.

Now the Odeous' star was clearly visible and it was a matter of waiting till the enemy scanners signaled the unaccustomed presence of a fleet in its territory.

Luckily the promised beacons did not delay their appearance, detaching themselves near the base of a nearby tripartite nebulosity, visible only on the Terrans' course.

The Turcopole, assisted by Kubla, immediately put his swift ships on through and disposed them at the far opening of the breach in a fan formation, ready to defend the passage.

The enemy had still not reacted.

The blue squadron starboard, formed mostly of French, threaded through rapidly; then it was the turn of the English on the red side, and finally the mass of the Templars.

Scarcely had they run the gauntlet when Houen-Lun signaled the presence of a cloud of swift ships.

The Mongols under Gerard of Tours darted toward them, following their favorite tactic. Scarcely arrived, contact made, they discharged a spray of missiles, then fled as if seized by panic.

This trick had the calculated effect. Some of the squadrons rushed to pursue them, and then they fell among the French, who acted quickly to put them out of action. Until now the enemy had used nothing but missiles and the defenses Aira had arranged had worked marvelously. Few of the Terran ships had been touched, while numerous enemy vessels had been destroyed.

Houen-Lun and his fellow Tibetans stayed alert. They had a great deal of difficulty locating their enemies amid the countless mental contacts they were receiving.

The Baphomet squadrons, having gained prudence in the first engagement, concentrated then into two compact columns that headed in, with the evident goal of catching their enemy between their fire.

William then ordered Peter of Sevry to stay close to the open passage in the minefield to control a way of retreat, and signaled Otto of Granson and John of Grailly to maneuver so that their squadrons came at the enemy from above, crossing the T, which let all the Terran vessels fire their missiles, while only the ships at the head of the Baphomet lines could open fire, for fear of wiping out their friends in front of them.

William plunged under the opposing squadrons while the vanguard came back to range themselves in front of him.

These maneuvers were executed perfectly. The long months of training had paid off.

At the outset, the Terrans had gained a marked success. The enemy, crushed under a deluge of missiles, saw the head of his columns founder, turn face about and take flight, followed by the Terrans who kept contact with them.

But far from flowing back in a rout, the enemy squadrons were departing in good order toward the nebulosity, to hide there.

As the Mongols of Gerard of Tours and Kubla pressed them too close, the Baphomet ships had recourse to a secret weapon, but, all their vessels were not equipped with it. In a scene out of nightmare, the hulls of the brave pursuers eroded, the crews vaporized; certain ones, thanks to their suits, scattered out miraculously and drifted off in the icy void. Some could be recovered at the end of the battle.

William, always master of himself, had his squadrons stop, let his battered enemy escape to find refuge in the dark windings of the nebulosity.

The Grand Master had acted wisely. A frontal assault on an enemy at bay would have been fatal to the Terran ships; by his action he brought his forces under control.

In fact only about a hundred ships had found refuge in the gaseous cloud. The Terran squadrons, firing volley after volley, had already won the victory, and it only remained to hunt the enemy out of his refuge.

Now it was the Tibetans' turn to prove their efficiency. They had only to fear the confusion of the ships, and their delicate waves could easily find their adversaries, putting one after another of their maddened crews out of action, for they were using their communications constantly to keep contact with each other in the labyrinth.

In a little while Houen-Lun and his adepts were in control of the minds of the enemy leaders, making them give an insane order to the bewildered armada.

"Abandon the shelter of the nebulosity!"

One after another, the vessels then came to expose themselves to the Terrans' fire. As the admirals alone had the secret weapon, the enemy destroyed only a few of the ships, and soon the Templars could enter the nebulosity in their turn to board and seize the ships under the Tibetans' control.

Ten hours after the beginning of the engagement, the last ship of the squadron defending Oddh was put out of commission.

Although the Odeous on those ships had died, still William's tactic had let him use the Tibetans' psi attack under the best conditions, and he had saved almost all those who were on the flagships.

Six Baphomets were captured too, and chained in the hold of a ship prepared for that purpose.

The hardest task was accomplished. Now it remained to gain the base located on the satellite, then to land on Oddh. Now, without the use of his ships, the enemy would have the hard task ahead of him.

Chapter VII

William of Beaujeu was not accustomed to rest on his laurels. He ordered Peter of Sevry to leave the post he had filled during the battle—he was fretting with impatience in that position—to procede to the rescue of the scattered and shipwrecked crews. He lent him several Tibetans to stop the surviving Odeous from suiciding or being killed by their cursed implants.

Sonz had appreciated the progress of the battle like a connoisseur. "Lord," he suggested to the Grand Master when calm was restored, "we've made some good catches. The ships the Baphomets were on had quark devices and these cowards were so afraid that they didn't even sabotage them. Let's use them against the satellite base."

"Is that really necessary?" the Templar objected. "We'll need them to attack Oddh. What forces do the defenders of your moon have?"

"Now they aren't numerous at all. Fewer than a hundred, half of which are robots. Instead, the base is equipped with a powerful antiship defense—automatic missile launchers buried in the rocks of the mountain."

"If you know where they're placed, it will be enough to pepper them with our thunderballs. We have a lot of them."

"Excellent tactic. The explosions will ruin the mechanisms that let them uncover the silos to launch. Only you'll have to rout out the defenders buried in the tunnels."

"That's no trouble for my troops. They're more at ease fighting on solid earth than in the sky. Let your companions take one of the captured weapons. We'll make copies of it with the duplicators. The others can stay in reserve in the case of some ugly surprise."

"I'll get busy about that at once. But it's still possible that these delicate mechanisms aren't going to be easy to reproduce."

The Grand Master then asked Houen-Lun to probe the minds of the Baphomet prisoners to get all the information they had on Oddh's defenses. Then he regrouped his squadrons and turned his bow toward Oddh's moon, whose crater-pocked face seemed to smirk at the inky depth of the heavens.

Blue squadron was charged with the sweep operation. It met missile fire, but thanks to the thermal devices, most of that was lost in space.

In answer, Terran missiles came crashing down with full force on the silos where the enemy launchers were buried and quickly destroyed them. This base was of minor importance, and the disproportionate number of forces present let them saturate each device so thoroughly that the antiship defense was promptly silenced.

John of Grailly split his forces, one part staying in orbit as emergency reinforcements, the other landing at the starport, which had been spared destruction. It went without saying that the hot-tempered Frenchman was one of the first off the ship.

His forces met little opposition. Only a few robot squads launched a counterattack. The knights' training had taught them to disperse and hide, using all the resources of the terrain. They became invisible in no time.

The Baphomets did not appear to have given such prudent instruction in programming the metal beings, who were battered down one after another by the steel projectiles from the powder arquebuses.

A second wave met the same fate and the French then began a methodical advance by successive squadrons, each covering the other while they progressed out of cover.

The port installations were quickly taken. They were in perfect condition. Apparently the Baphomets, never having envisaged the possibility of a defeat, had never provided any mechanisms.

It remained now to get the missile silos lodged in the mountains around the base. The ground was poisoned at surface level by the residue of the nuclear explosions. John of

Grailly decided to use a classic tactic for assaulting fortified
castles: sappers.

Assuredly the exits of the tunnels leading to the silos had
to be strongly guarded, and a frontal assault would cost them
very dear. Then the clever Frenchman discovered in one of
the rooms of the starport a detailed plan of the underground
retreats occupied by his enemies. With the help of the Odeous, he moved out the earthborers stocked in the hangars, the
very ones which had permitted them to build the silos, and
pierced vertical wells to the tunnels.

One after the other, the companies of space-armored
knights, carrying shield in one hand and short arbalest in the
other, descended into the holes.

They began by routing the robots who guarded the entry
ports, taking them from behind. Then reinforcements flowed
into the tunnels. In a few hours all the installations had fallen
into the hands of the French.

In all, few Odeous were captured—only five, freed thanks
to the Tibetans who disconnected their implants. The defenses
were practically automatic, robots rather than slaves assuming
the maintenance and defense of the whole.

As soon as the victory was won, John of Grailly ordered
his men-at-arms to go back to their ships, only leaving a
hundred to clear the tops of the silos buried under the rubble,
using the machines they found on the site.

The whole operation, from start to finish, had only taken
about a dozen hours, and soon the batteries of missiles could
be turned against the planet.

During this time, William had massed his squadrons in the
stratosphere of Oddh, at the other side of the world from the
capital, the Baphomet den wherein these perfidious creatures
were entrenched.

The Grand Master, concerned not to damage the precious
factories, had decided to launch a land attack with his Templars.

They had still to destroy the energy dome which protected
the fortress the tyrants held. Houen-Lun had painlessly
probed the captives' minds and William knew perfectly the
defense forces, the armament they had at their disposal and
the configuration of the tunnels linking them with the castle
outside. He thus learned that they were full of deadly traps
letting them make bloody defense of the walls in case of in-

vasion. No question then of using the strategy which had lately worked so well for John of Grailly.

Instead, Sonz, the Odeous spacefarer, gave him precious advice. "In theory," said he, "this energy dome is uncrossable. Of course, it would be possible to lay siege to this fortress. Its provisioning would hardly let the Baphomets hold out more than a month. But our principal advantage is surprise. We mustn't give the Baphomet squadrons time to intervene. Let's use the few quark cannon we have to wear away the soil, just under the energy dome, so our troops can slide under and make a direct attack on the inside of the fortress. Your knights have a crushing numerical advantage. Using a simultaneous assault from six different positions, you can very quickly overwhelm the robots and get yourselves into command central."

This proposition gained the agreement of all the Terran leaders. Templars, Hospitalers and Teuton knights then left the ships out of range of the defenses and began their march toward the city in dispersed groups.

Some batteries opened fire but they were quickly silenced by the ships' weapons. The Terran groups reached their objectives without excessive casualties.

In the capital, everything remained calm. The Odeous, obeying their masters' orders, remained cloistered in their residences. A sporadic fire broke out at times, coming from the robots. Might the Baphomets have begun to mistrust their slaves? No Odeous contingent opposed the Templars.

It was an unhoped-for chance for the city; its architectural marvels would surely have taken a great deal of damage in a fight in the streets.

The citadel was set on an eminence dominating the capital, which it controlled in normal times by its batteries of weapons, but the force field had one inconvenience: it did not let them use those batteries, for it was impenetrable from either direction.

The Baphomets' devilish tactic seemed simple. Believing themselves invulnerable in their lair, they were calmly waiting on the help which would unfailingly be headed their way from Baphom.

Fate had decreed otherwise. The ships bearing the quark cannon had just made a rapid passage above the protective dome, aiming at ground level.

The dense rock eroded like sand, leaving large holes. At once the Templars brought up metal plates, platforms, putting them on the yielding earth as they advanced.

Very swiftly, the attackers reached the other side of the translucent wall. They saw then the massive palace of the governor, a baroque masterpiece of chiseled stone.

Trusting to their dome, the Baphomets had hardly bothered to fortify the castle. Flowered gardens and pleasant woods surrounded it; a few domestic animals which looked like deer and birds with fairytale plumage sported there.

The Templars, taking advantage of the cover, were able to thread their way up to the gate without hindrance. There, it was quite another matter. The massive portcullis with bronze engraving was closed and the robots posted behind its ogive windows met their assailants with heavy fire.

But the rough warriors were in their own element. While the arbalests cracked clouds of explosive projectiles that were swallowed by the openings, Conrad von Thierberg, at the risk of his neck, attacked the thick panel that closed the entry with blows of his axe.

In a few minutes the giant German had gotten it down, and followed by his Teutons, broke into the castle. For their part the Templars were not idle. Using ladders, they entered through the windows, while John of Villiers directed the fire of his Hospitalers toward the roofs where the defenders had fled.

Without regard for the rare wood furniture, for the thousand treasures gathered in the vast halls, the soldier-monks broke through, sweeping all before them.

The Tholon brothers, always riding on their luck, broke into the harem. They had to face the eunuchs, who hurled at them incongruous missiles: fruits, vases, amphorae, incense burners. The Odeous slaves, bodies shining with perfumed oil, scattered in all directions, dismayed, with a clicking of their bracelets and collars. Some dived into a pool of bronze fish, sinking among the lilies and lilypads floating on the surface of the water, which wound like jade serpents round their wet bodies. Others huddled as much as possible behind the huge porcelain vases, or under the piles of cushions, even behind the spidersilk curtains suddenly rainbow glittering with a thousand reflections that played over the sparkling gems adorning the lovely harem servants. All of them were chittering and chattering, frightened by these metal-covered giants who had broken into their luxurious though well-guarded prison. They quickly realized that the palace had fallen to assault by considerable forces, come to set them free. Pressed with questions by the Tholon brothers, they gave all their information on the placement of the command devices in the dome, and even offered to guide them there.

The boys from Auxerre climbed four abreast up the stone staircase, disdaining the lifts, and came rushing into the room where four haggard Baphomets watched in anguish the screens which showed them the invasion of the domain they had believed impregnable.

Seized with abject terror, they hurled themselves at the feet of the Templars, begging them not to torture them, and they were content to get them on their feet without touching them and order them to cut off the protective field. Immediately the vile creatures obeyed them. Then taking advantage of the Tholon brothers' instant of inattention, they swallowed vials of poison. This was the end of the fortress. The armies of the French, the English and the Mongols in turn broke into the castle. A half hour later the last robots were destroyed and William triumphantly entered the fortress over which the Baussant banner was already flying.

It was from the command post the Tholon brothers had captured that the Grand Master directed his operation of liberation for the world.

The few garrisons scattered over Oddh were destroyed without difficulty by ships flying at ground level, and occupation forces were brought into each major city.

The Terrans' first objective was to free the male Odeous from the deadly implants which had enslaved them to the Baphomets. That took a long time, for the overburdened Tibetans could not treat them all at once. At any rate, there was no haste, for, at least the moment, there was no threat hanging over the planet.

On the night after the end of the fighting, William gathered his principal officers in a vast hall of the Baphomet palace, which was covered with a film of shining tissue with strange scarlet arabesques. At one end began a monumental stairway of wood veined with black serpents. Purple cushions fringed in gold covered the massive chairs.

On the immense tables were spread strange foods, birds.

served in their bronze plumage, game baked in cinnamon-per-
fumed sweet sauce, fried insects floating in a mellow sauce,
mounds of pâtés stuffed with spices, vessels filled with crèmes
mixed to make a subtle design on their surface, veritable
works of art, cakes with crackling crusts or covered with
smooth glazes in rainbow colors. Voluptuous Odeous
presented the platters to the guests. Each of them, robed like
a goddess, had put on her finest dress in honor of the liberators. Some wore gold bands confining their thick hair; others
had thrust carved insects in the metal behind their heavy
chignons. Diaphanous tunics of pastel colors reflected the
light of the crystal and emerald chandeliers, and all were
anointed with the same heavenly smelling ointment which
filled these rough warriors with dreams.

In finely turned flasks, transparent liquors of heady aroma
were ready to quench the warriors' thirst.

French, English, Germans and Mongols were honored at
this celebration.

When they had finally finished, the Grand Master, who had
hardly touched these tempting offerings, rose and summed up
the situation. "My brothers, let us give thanks, let us praise
and give glory to Our Lord for having given us the victory!
For the first time, the host of the Crusaders has met the
miscreant aliens and given them a sound thrashing. Now
these creatures born by the will of God are going to know
the True Faith and regain their freedom. In sum, our losses
have been few and we must congratulate ourselves on having
so easily eliminated enemies who had devilish weapons
hitherto unknown to us."

William was silent a moment while he drank a mouthful of
water from an engraved cup. Then he continued. "But we
will make a great mistake if we think we are invincible.
Formerly I thought long on the use of the starships and of
likening them to sailing vessles. I have read and reread ancient texts recounting history's naval battles: Salamis, Ac-
tium, Bravalla, Constantinople . . . and I have discovered
there not one valuable instruction to help me work out a
battle tactic for space. Our recent campaign was a succession
of improvisations. How to liken ships that fight far from one
another with vessels of sail, with galleys which meet and
board? The fire missiles have no proper comparison with
Greek fire; and magic circles, like that which protected this

castle, bear no resemblance at all to the stone walls of our strongholds. For awhile I hoped to find advice among the Odeous, whose practice of alchemy is very old. Alas, this peaceful people has never worked out a specific tactic for this kind of battle. We must then rethink this problem entirely, thinking soberly on the possibilities offered by the new machines we have at our disposal. Let's not forget: we have only met a small portion of the forces opposing us; the effect of surprise was working in our favor, but now we can't count on it. Before ending his life, the governor of this planet sent out alarms in all directions, signaling our attack and asking for help. We're going to be meeting squadrons equal if not superior in number to our own. What must be our objective? To try to liberate the Ethir and the Orpheds? Or, instead, to go to Baphom to engage in decisive battle? We have to broach that question without delay. I am open to suggestions."

That declaration threw a pall on the party. They had all, in the euphoria of the banquet and the victory, forgotten reality, and the Grand Master had reminded them of the precariousness of their position, nothing held back.

A heavy silence reigned for a moment. Their stomachs were full of strange food, tender meats, succulent vegetables, plump, juicy fruits, all of which had all been tested by Brother Joubert on Turcopole slaves, which guaranteed their partial harmlessness, but not their easy digestion by a Christian stomach. On top of that, one had to add the consumption of volatile liquors, quite pleasant to the throat but tending to befog the celebrants' brains somewhat.

Ascetic John of Villiers had not particiated in these feastings. He drew himself up to his full height. "Are we bloodthirsty wolves," he growled crossly, "or Christ's soldiers? I've not heard anything here but talk of fighting and conquests, while problems of primary importance are passed over in silence. As far as I understood, we still came here to bring our brothers of beyond the Earth the True Faith. Well, no one seems to be worrying about learning whether the Odeous have souls, if they knew a Christ, and how they worship the Divinity. So far as I'm concerned, I refuse to go any farther in this universe before having raised that question. So I demand that we immediately call in the leaders of this people to listen to them and to decide what our response should be toward them."

All the Hospitalers earnestly applauded, while William of Beaujeu sat with a scowling face. These theological discussions could go on forever, while he had to seize the advantage the Terrans had won to prepare the next course of operations. Nonetheless the Templar assumed a more pleasant expression. He could not leave aside a question of dogma without risking having himself disowned by the Pope and abandoned by a portion of his forces.

"I was meaning to address that problem after the purely strategic questions were settled," he avowed, "but since our brother John of Villiers wants to discuss this major point first, I am glad to support his opinion. Let someone bring in the Odeous."

A few moments later the heralds brought into the hall four aliens of very saintly age, eminent scholars, secret leaders who had escaped during the painful years of enemy occupation. All of them had a rather disturbing look, with their vast eyes, but their features reflected an extreme intelligence.

"My brothers, be welcome," William of Beaujeu exclaimed. "We have called you to this place before our assembly to enlighten ourselves on various points of utmost importance. Please be brief in your answers, but conceal nothing."

"We take the greatest pleasure in answering your questions," replied the eldest of the Odeous. "Before anything else, I shall make myself interpreter of my people in thanking you from the bottom of our hearts for having freed us from the foul Baphomets. I was elected leader of this planet during the days of the underground. I'm named Adoos, and my companions have asked me to speak in their name. I think that it's an opportune moment to normalize our relations so that no shadow will remain between us. My fellow citizens are aware of the immense service you have done us, and we're ready to work with you in all areas."

"Perfect. We're certainly going to understand one another. Our wise brother John of Villiers, who leads the Hospitalers, is going to ask you some questions."

The Grand Master turned to the Odeous, looked them up and down for a moment in some disdain. "Your folk are very civilized. They tell me you've existed for some number of years. So you have a religion?"

"Of course," said Adoos. "It has, of course, evolved over centuries, but our present belief is simple. We worship the creator of the universe, who manifests his power at every moment through the harmony that exists in the world."

"And this divinity is unique?"

"In a certain sense unique, since it is the universe, and the universe is in it. God is everywhere."

"How do you worship him?"

"Very simply. In each family, the father is the priest and he dedicates a few moments each week or each day, as he can, to teach his family about the double nature of the universe, of the necessity of good and evil, the smallness of our individual selves, the duties we owe to our fellows."

"Dualists of some sort," John of Villiers replied, and framed another question. "Do you believe in life after death?"

"Our poor self must rejoin the universal Intelligence and merge with it, if that is your meaning."

"But your body. Is there a resurrection?"

"How could the atoms which compose it reunite after being scattered over our planet? It would take a great pride to think that God could bend to regard folk as unimportant as we are."

The Grand Master turned toward his people with a venomous smile. "Of course," he pursued, "you are entirely ignorant of original sin?"

"I don't understand what you're referring to. Why should our origin be stained with sin?"

"Consequently, you are not awaiting the coming of any Redeemer?"

"We hope to be free of the Baphomets. You are our liberators. The exact meaning of your question escapes me."

"Have you holy books that recount the creation of the world?"

This time Adoos seemed to doubt his questioner's sanity. "Do you not know that the universe began its existence in a titanic explosion billions of years ago? No Odeous was in existence then. How could we have works reporting such ancient facts?"

"Quite simply, by the voice of prophets speaking in the name of the Lord," John of Villiers returned, annoyed. "Of course, you don't have any prophets?"

"Faith, no, our philosophers have never had the signal honor of entering rapport with the Divinity."

"Consequently we can't find among you any trace of the holy Word, no hope of a Redeemer. Have you heard tell of angels, and of Lucifer who revolted against the Lord?"

"Absolutely not. The words I have heard you use make me think of winged beings . . . maybe you mean the Ethir. As for Lucifer, would he be the father of the Orpheds?"

"Useless to follow this idle questioning," the Grand Master said without answering. "It's self-evident that we're dealing with obstinate pagans. That's nothing very surprising, though, since on our Earth itself many peoples have never become acquainted with the Truth without the Crusaders and our missionaries. Our task is considerable, but with the help of Christ, we will lead them to the good. If our brother William sees no inconvenience in it, my Hospitalers are going to begin work as soon as possible and teach these infidels the catechism. I think that half our force will suffice to preach the good word. I'm going to send a brief to His Holiness at once to advise him of the deplorable state in which these poor folk exist and ask him for the creation of bishoprics and parishes, as well as the dispatch of an ecclesiastical court to take care of rebels, apostates and magicians. Thanks to us, to our Crusade, these poor sinners can learn about salvation."

So saying, John of Villiers sat down again. William seemed somewhat in disagreement with his conclusions, especially with the unilateral decision that deprived him of a part of his forces, but he wanted most of all to get back to strategic questions. "Thanks to our brother's foresight," he said, "we've now settled that thorny problem. Does someone else want to ask other questions?"

"Certainly," trumpeted John of Grailly. "First of all, I'd like to know if the Grand Master of the Hospitalers intends, by leaving half his forces here . . . to claim this planet?"

"This is a question only for His Holiness the Pope, who will allot these newly discovered territories to whoever seems good to him," the Hospitaler replied hotly, applauded in that by Conrad von Thierberg.

This time too, William made no reply, although he had some few motives for bitterness.[1]

---

[1] Note of the Templar of Tyre: Messengers had now reported the

"May I know what your form of government is?" the Frenchman asked then, addressing the Odeous. "Do you have a king, an emperor?"

"We've long had a democratic government elected by the sovereign people. An assembly designates a president, who chooses his ministers from among it."

"But the land. To whom do the lands belong?" wondered John of Grailly, somewhat horrified.

"To the people, of course, who work it by communities. It's the same for our factories and our residences. Each citizen receives a salary proportionate to his work. In the case he's temporarily unemployed, the community gives him half his highest salary; if he's sick, he's cared for free. But why such questions? Is it different in your world?"

The Frenchman did not answer. He sat down with a profoundly disgusted expression.

"And your armies, whom do they obey?" asked Otto of Granson, who despite his well-lit and swollen face, had kept his clarity of wit.

"Primarily the chief of state, myself currently, and then their generals and officers of various rank."

"But who pays them?"

"The state! How could it be otherwise? A fleet of starships costs a fortune."

"Who directs the work of your scholars?" Djaffar the Wise asked then.

"The one among them they've chosen as most apt to direct the course of their research. No one obliges them to do something they don't approve. But the Minister of Science can, in time of need, mobilize scholars of various disciplines to examine an urgent problem. Credits are voted them by the assembly in either case."

The remarkable Arab seemed quite interested in this system, since all his life he had had to finance his own works himself, but he made no comment.

"I ask you in my turn, since I have satisfied your legitimate curiosity," Adoos said. "You have delivered us from the yoke

accidental death of John XXI. The Council gathered at Viterbus was under pressure from monarchs jealous of the Templars and the other monastic orders. Papal candidate Cardinal Gaetano Orsini, ex-inquisitor, was jealous of William, and once elected, lost no opportunity to advance his rivals.

of the Baphomets, but what will be our status henceforth? Will we be free or will we simply have changed masters?"

This time William found himself caught short. For him, cast into a new universe, the temptation was great. After having carved out a vast empire on Earth, why not reign as all-powerful master over these infidel peoples? After all, as John of Villiers had remarked, these people might be compared to the Mamelukes or the Mongols. They did not practice the True Faith and so they could be made slaves without the Pope seeing any impediment. . . .

But in fine diplomacy he gave a shaded reply. The Odeous scholars were indispensable to him in conquering the Baphomets, and consequently he had to handle them cleverly to make them his allies. There would still be time to change his manner later.

"Your question surprised me, I confess." he said. "That's why I didn't answer at once. It goes without saying that you'll remain leader of the Odeous and that you'll govern your world as you see fit. We only ask you to listen to our priests, who'll teach you our religion. Besides, my Hospitaler brothers are going to leave a garrison here, but only in the intention of defending you against a return of the Baphomets."

"And when you have finished with these demons," Adoos insisted, "will the Terrans leave our planet?"

"That goes without saying. When all danger is removed, we will limit ourselves to establishing fruitful trade relations."

"I am happy that you've given me that assurance. Certain of us feared that we might have escaped the Baphomets only to fall under a yoke even worse than theirs. Under those understandings, we are quite disposed to work with you."

"And I'm quite happy with your statement," William exclaimed. "We have great need of your scholars to give our ships powerful armament, in particular to install on them the quark devices. I would also like to have your opinion on the strategy we should adopt to beat the Baphomets once for all."

"Our specialists will gladly help you. I'm going to give orders for them to put themselves at your service at once. But I fear I can't be of any help to you so far as your second demand is concerned. You see, the Odeous are a peaceful race, and we've never practiced the cursed art of war. That's also why the Baphomets conquered us so easily, for our technology is far in advance of theirs. But I can give you a bit of advice: the Orpheds are much better in space warfare. Unlike us, they have only a rudimentary science and yet the Baphomets had great trouble conquering them. You must then turn your ships toward Orph, to use that race's experts. Their aspect differs greatly from ours, and the Orpheds look even rather hideous, but they hate the Baphomets from the depth of their hearts, even more than we, for they have been slaves longer."

"Thank you for your advice. We'll deliberate the matter. My wise brother Joubert is going to go with you; put him in contact with your scholars so that work can begin with the fewest possible delays."

"Thank you, Lord Templar. We'll do everything to your satisfaction."

So saying, the Odeous left the hall with Joubert.

"Well! my brothers, what do you think? Must we follow the advice of that stranger and turn our ships to Orph, or meet the majority of the enemy forces near Baphom?"

"No hurry about that," exclaimed John of Grailly. "These demons have a training we lack. The Orpheds might give us precious advice."

"Zo let's get moving," Conrad von Thierberg broke in. "A miscreant rabble has no weight before the Knights of Christ. Let's crush dese barbarous Baphomets."

"Vell spoken," thundered Otto of Granson. "After all, we just won a battle; why not follow up our thrust? We'll make a mouthful out of those infidels."

"We only met weak forces," Peter of Sevry remarked then. "If we attack Baphom, our adversaries will fight with the energy of desperation, for if their planet falls their hegemony is finished. No! We must limit our ambitions for the moment and go against Orph."

"The cunning of the fox is equal to the strength of the lion," Kubla remarked, smiling. "Our adversaries don't know our intentions. Why not lead them to scatter their forces by threatening to attack the satellite barrier that surrounds Baphom, with weak forces, then draw those that follow us near the main part of our strength?"

"That's an interesting idea," William applauded. "But I don't intend to do it in the near future, because our troops aren't seasoned enough. We wish fighting against too important forces. Orph is not far from that world. If the Baphomets launch a counterattack, we'll be warned by our scouts and we can get back in time to make sure our garrison isn't overwhelmed. Let's take the Baphomets' empire before facing these demons in their own domain where they are powerfully entrenched. Our losses will be few and our armament will be increased by the aid of the Odeous. I propose to attack Orph without further delay. What say you to that, my brothers?"

John of Grailly, Peter of Sevry and John of Villiers allied themselves at once to the Templar's proposal. Only Conrad and Otto refused their agreement. But when John of Villiers had murmured a few words in the ear of the Grand Master of the Teutons, he finally acquiesced.

Then it was agreed that, as soon as fifty ships had been equipped with quark weapons, the squadron would take to space and head to Orph.

The dignitaries scattered then, casting a mistrustful look on the drunken soldiers who sported with Odeous women, with no regard for the salvation of their immortal souls.

Outside all was quiet in the camp, lit by braziers which heightened the scarlet tint of the neighboring woods, making them look like flaming torches.

Chapter VIII

William was satisfied with having gotten a decision which left him all his freedom to maneuver. If by chance the Baphomets attacked Oddh during his absence, that would only be half a misfortune, for they would be rid of allies who were becoming more and more troublesome. The Templar had no intention of turning to a hostile pope to distribute the fiefs his own troops had won. Besides, time was on his side, so Marco Polo would have more chances to carry off his mission to good effect. He could even bring other houbits, since Lyzog was not in the neighborhood and its communication with Baphom remained free. He only had to hope that the clever Baphomets would not discover the trick.

Finally, the Grand Master hoped that the Orpheds could lend him precious advice on the way to handle a war in space.

The fleet turned its bows toward Orph four days later, proceeding at cruising speed. John of Villiers stayed behind with half his forces.

The armada found itself thus stripped of a goodly number of ships, but in their place it now had quark cannon, which made up for this loss, at least in some measure. In sum, William, the soldier, had reason to be satisfied; but the monk, the Templar, the servant of the living God, sensed a great deal of trouble in the offing. When, long ago, he had discussed with John of Villiers, had he not assured him that there must have been Christs on other worlds? Well, for the Odeous, there had not been. Must one believe that only the Earth had been so chosen? That only men were the sons of God? In this case, no alien would have knowledge of the True Faith, and Terrans must carry the Word across the universe—an immense and somewhat frightening task! But on Earth itself, not all creatures believed in the existence of Christ. Houen-Lun, for example, had a philosophy quite different from that of Christians. For him, all living creatures were sacred; he killed no animal; he ate only vegetables and boiled cereal. He was one of the only humans who regularly ate the mixture the ships distributed, for, he said: "It doesn't come from any living creature." Contrary to Djaffar, who had within broad lines, adopted the Christian religion, the Tibetan had refused to have himself baptized, and the Hospitalers had often brought that matter up with the Grand Master.

But the Grand Master had a practical mind. Houen-Lun had rather frightening powers, which had let him overcome the Baphomet who had come to Earth. Now the Asians constituted the armada's shield, for they alone could overcome the aliens' minds, using powers which were reserved for prophets in the Bible. Surely the wise men had secrets the Odeous themselves did not know, so William was very careful not to provoke the wrath of his old allies by trying to catechize them contrary to their will. Later, when peace reigned over the interstellar empire of the Templars, it would be time to take up that delicate problem. Houen-Lun, for reasons known to him alone, served him loyally, so why ask more for the moment? Surely hate of the Baphomets was the main reason for what Houen-Lun did, and his faithfulness to the Templars would not likely be forever. The future would tell what attitude to take with him. At any rate it was useless to think too much on it, for after all, that devil of a man could quite well be spying on the thoughts of the leader of the armada.

The soldier-monks, aided by the Odeous, began to accustom themselves to handling the ships. Their maneuvers were more rapid, their evolutions more precise, and they all found this space navigation exciting. They fearlessly watched the stars pass, crossed nebulosities as if they were some sort of marshland, and began to discover by instinct the multiple ambushes of space without even having recourse to the delicate instruments with which the ships were provided.

All that augured well for the future.

It remained to learn how to attack Orph. William called in

the Odeous to get some few bits of information from them. Captain Sonz furnished it to him quite gladly.

"The situation on that planet is quite like that of Oddh, except it has no moon. The Baphomet ships are therefore stationed near the governor's palace. We have to fight in space to eliminate them, then we have to cross an energy screen the same as on our world, passing under it by using the quark cannon. As for the forces there, they're not numerous, not more than a hundred ships."

"And the Orpheds . . . what will be their attitude toward us?"

"This race has hardly any points in common with us. Once they lived in common in immense pyramids, veritable mazes. Most of the individuals were asexual and only the royal pair engaged in procreation. The warrior castes assured the protection of the city. The workers gathered the necessary food. Altogether, they did not have a very advanced civilization, except in the field of music. The central hall of the pyramids used to contain titanic organs, and all the Orpheds would gather there to perform enchanting symphonies. They played strange instruments only they knew how to make. At present the Baphomets have suppressed the royal couples, and all the individuals are sexual, but the tyrants carefully control their reproduction. Only the best musicians have the right to breed. That way the Baphomets hope to get from their unfortunate slaves more and more refined music. But don't mistake it, the Orpheds are brave and even cruel. Each fertile female can lay up to thirty eggs a season, which is why their masters saturate them with contraceptives. The young reach maturity quickly. The Orpheds will be valuable allies for us, although they are sometimes difficult to understand and don't readily form bonds of friendship. One more bit of information. If you trace a circle taking Baphom as the center, Oddh and Orph are just about an equal distance from the Baphomet planet. It's the same for Eth, the homeworld of the Ethir. Only Lyzog is much farther removed. That's why it was only recently conquered."

"Well, we are advised. The business will be delicate, at least if we want to spare the natives. So I'll adopt a different device for our fleet: instead of putting each ship behind the file leader, I'm going to shift them in space, each locating itself in a different plane from the preceeding. Thus, whatever quarter the attack comes from, our firepower will be equal, without our ships risking running into each other. No nebulosity near Orph?"

"None. The planet is isolated in space with its four companions, which are not inhabited, and only infrequently visited by prospectors."

"Perfect. We'll arrive above the equatorial plane, so we will have a much greater freedom of movement. Let each man go to his post. In five hours, we'll be starting the operation. We can't let ourselves suffer heavy casualties. Consequently, we'll have to win a quick victory. Let everyone do his duty for the glory of Our Lord."

The leaders of the various squadrons went then to take the positions assigned them in the new plan. They all watched the screens anxiously to spot the Baphomet ships.

The Baphomets remained invisible, and when the armada came in sight of Orph, the enemy had still not manifested themselves. They discovered no mines at all.

William, worried, feared a trap. His enemies were surely advised of his arrival, so why did they not try to drive him back?

Houen-Lun, questioned on the matter, could not give any answer. He did not perceive any mind touch in space. Must he then conclude that the Baphomets had abandoned their conquest? After all, this planet played but a minor role in their economy, and they knew that they must go into combat for it with a very clear numerical disadvantage.

William sent his Turcopoles in on reconnaissance near the planet. They met no opposition. Growing bolder, they descended then into the atmosphere, but no one attacked them.

Kubla made an orbit of the planet at low altitude and then sent this message to his leader: "Noble Lord, there is not a single important city here that is not in flames. Apparently, your adversaries have used a scorched earth policy. They leave you a planet on which all installations have been destroyed to stop you from using it. That appears to me a good tactic and we Mongols are accustomed to use it. Some hordes of natives are still wandering here and there. They seem to be in the greatest poverty and apparently have no weapons. But the palace section is invisible. A shining dome like that of Oddh is covering it. Your enemies have probably gathered all their troops there, and we will have to use main force to get them out."

The Grand Master was rather discomfited by this news. He would have liked very much to destroy some enemy ships to diminish the Baphomet forces.

These demons had delivered him a planet void of all interest, more, they risked having been tricked, drawn off to Orph while the Baphomets destroyed the Odeous factories, which now took on a vital importance.

Without further delay, William ordered blue and red squadrons to go back to Oddh with all possible speed. John of Grailly took command of them with the express order to alert his leader if he met enemies on the way.

But no message had been sent by the Odeous. Maybe the French and the English would arrive there in time to save them from the fate of the Orpheds.

Thus, having taken the risk of dividing his forces, William bore down toward the nest of Baphomet resistance with the intent of finishing it as quickly as possible.

This time his ships were caught by clouds of missiles launched from the ground. They were almost all intercepted, but this defense forced William to abandon his projected air attack.

Furious, the Grand Master had to resort to debarking his troops all around the fort, out of missile range.

Orphed was in no wise similar to smiling Oddh. This world had a luxuriant vegetation more like terrestrial jungles.

The Templars, cursing and swearing, saw themselves faced with the obligation of breaking a road through immense trees, in stinking marsh, infested with insects of all kinds, from which the Orpheds were moreover descended.

Only the leaders had mounts, the six-legged elur, whose horny carapace shrugged off spurs and who must be guided with reins fixed in their ears.

The squires gritted their teeth and built carts to carry the quark cannon and the firetubes to hurl the thunderballs, an innovation they owed to the Odeous and which weighed considerably. To that they had to add the victuals, munitions, and to undergo the damp heat which reigned under these thick leaves. The very air was almost unbreathable due to the strong content of carbon gas and its mephitic odor. But the Crusaders must count themselves lucky not to have to suffer the continued fire of enemy missiles. Sometimes one of the projectiles got through to the ships which were patrolling at low altitude and the green hell transformed itself into a volcano, knocking down all the trees within a league about.

Of course, the Tholon brothers were part of the foot contingent who dragged themselves through the mud, having lost all sense of direction in these dense thickets.

But sweating and panting, they drew on the cords linked to the carts, following a narrow road opened by the woodsmen whose axes hacked through the brush, after explosive charges had destroyed the largest trees.

Luckily, they had not so long a road to go, and the column of which the boys from Auxerre were part reached the edge of the forest at nightfall.

In the distance, before them, they saw the shining dome which shielded the enemy fortress.

By way of prudence, William ordered his troops to stay under cover and to fortify the strip along the edge of the forest.

That was hardly business for tired infantry who had had to struggle a good hour with their shovels to dig out individual trees.

Finally, when they were able to take a little rest, it was night. An almost total darkness enveloped them, for no moon rose to lighten the shadows. Water seeped into the trenches, legions of big insects like giant mosquitoes gnawed in vain on their spacesuits, but they all slept a leaden sleep, while sentries surveyed the area about them and while patrols walked between the lines, exchanging passwords.

The Terrans thus slept a good part of the night. A few hours before dawn, flashes streaked across the jungle. Coming from before and behind, a heavy fire fell on the positions of the Templars, who wakened with a start.

In the light of the explosions, they could see their enemy, robots in dark armor who were attacking them from cover, without concern for the losses they suffered.

William learned later that these implacable warriors had used underground passages and come out in the forest to catch his troops from behind.

At the moment the Templars had to get themselves out of this one alone, for the melee stopped any intervention from the ships. The training they had undergone on Earth saved them from destruction. In their shelters they could locate their enemies without difficulty by the fires in the brush, while staying under cover themselves.

The robots used a fire that acted as far as arrow range, which pattered down and set aflame the trees it touched.

In this furnace the Terrans' position very quickly became untenable, while their attackers had no worry about the devouring flames.

For good or for ill, the survivors had to leave their individual holes to reach the plains around the forest.

A few carts could be saved, but most had been destroyed by the fire. Yet as a whole the situation turned in favor of the Templars, who had done slaughter at the start of the attack while the robots were attacking on open ground.

When the glow of dawn lighted the woods, they could train their fire on their enemies who were cornered against the fire in the forest. These demons could certainly bear passing through the flames, but they could not stay there long, so that when the emerald star of Orph arose, the battle was won.

But at what cost! Now the Templars had no more heavy armament to attack the dome, for most of the quark cannon had been destroyed.

William, on Sonz' advice, decided then to drop the necessary machines by parachute, while his fleet opened a concentrated fire on the missiles vomited forth by the fortress.

Toward noon, everything had settled into order.

The Templars, well sheltered in new diggings, had set the firetubes and quark projectors up in a battery.

All of them took a little snack and drank a few gulps of wine, which had become a rare treat.

Now it remained to get the enemy out of his lair.

As the message receptors stayed silent, the Grand Master decided to participate in the final operation in person.

Accompanied by Conrad von Thierberg, whose height and broad shoulders gave him the carriage of a giant, he debarked from a small ship in a forest clearing. William stolidly adjusted the straps of his cuissards and, digging in the spurs, forced his destrier at a gallop through the thickets.

A few moments later he reached the front lines.

Garin Tholon and his brothers, who looked like living statues of filth, for their armor was coated with grease, met him there.

"Well, my dear fellows," their leader said, "how are we doing?"

"It's been a hot time, noble brother," replied Garin the Templar. "But we gave them a good thrashing and they haven't come back from it. The attacks of the metal creatures have stopped. Now our weapons are set up in battery and we can open fire against their fortress."

"Perfect. Fire the quark cannon to weaken the soil at the base of the dome. Then wait on new orders before the attack."

Garin went to pass those instructions and soon the luminous beams were digging at the earth, without reaction from the enemy.

"What does it seem to you, Brother Conrad? Apparently our adversaries haven't anything left in there but a garrison of robots to slow us down."

"That seems likely to me. These cowards don't dare risk their precious necks, nein. But I wonder if their crews are reduced to nothing. The way I see it, they're vaiting in the castle enclosure to fight der last battle."

"Maybe. At any rate, I don't want to take any chances. We have to finish this fast, so much the worse for those inside. I'm going to blow their fortress."

Now a few openings gaped around the dome and Garin came back to receive the Grand Master's orders.

"My brave friend, I forbid you to go into that hole. There's no Baphomet there and I fear some trap. Train our cannon on the openings, and use the largest caliber and the most powerful thunderballs. Go."

Again the Templar went and the servants of the firetubes charged the guns which opened fire in unison, while all put themselves under cover, including the two Grand Masters who had made their precious destriers lie down on the ground.

Everyone waited for a powerful explosion, but the reality was even worse. A conflagration of titanic force deafened the besiegers; an immense column of smoke like a black, twisting mushroom shot skyward, making the daystar dim, settling its shadow over the battlefield.

The first trees of the forest were laid low to the earth, while the burnings were snuffed out like candles.

When the dust settled, the Templars got up, staggering,

shaking off the bits of earth that covered their suits. They saw then that the dome had disappeared, and an enormous smoking crater gaped in place of the fortress.

"My vord," exclaimed the Teuton. "They must have had a stock of thunder material our spheres exploded."

William did not answer. He was in shock from the explosion, tottering. He put his hands to his ears, forgetting his helmet.

"You're vounded?" asked Conrad.

"No. Just shaken up. Help me get my helm off."

The Teuton undid the straps and lifted off the confining headgear, observing that a thin thread of blood trickled from the ear canal, but the hemorrhage stopped very quickly.

"Ah, vell, you got off all right," the German said.

"Yes, our enemies must have had explosives gathered there, or maybe it was a trap meant to blow up our knights if they risked going in. We'll never know. But here's a new proof of the demoniac cleverness of the Baphomets. We must constantly be on our guard."

William and Conrad climbed back onto their mounts, which had not suffered too much from the shock, and went to review their troops. Thanks to the individual holes there had been only a few deaths, those when blocks of stone had fallen right on some unfortunate occupant.

The knights and the squires gathered to go back aboard the ships, which had set themselves down nearby. William was in haste to leave this cursed planet, which could no longer be of any use to him now that its installations were destroyed.

"Look, my lord, there's a column of knights coming down the hill."

William turned. Truly, a line of gray dust marked the advance of knights arriving at a gallop.

At once the Templars set themselves in battle array in front of the ships.

They all saw quickly that they had little to fear, for the arriving forces were not numerous, not more than fifty.

When they were in firing range, the Terrans were able to identify them. They were Orpheds. These strange green creatures rode on bronze beetles quite like the noble Terran scarab. They differed little except in one important point: being warm-blooded rather than cold-blooded, which meant they could reach the size of small horses.

The aspect of the newcomers created a stir of panic among the soldier-monks. These beings looked irresistibly like grimacing cathedral gargoyles. For these devout souls, no doubt at all, these Orpheds could not but be demons spawned by Lucifer, the fallen angel who had rebelled against his Creator. It needed all the authority of the Commanders and the discipline of the Templars to avoid a massacre.

William himself sketched the sign of the cross and sent for Sonz to ask him if these were really the natives.

When the captain answered in the affirmative, he ordered him to go ask their intentions.

The Odeous, mounting an elur, galloped as far as the strangers, with whom he carried on a moment's discussion, then came rapidly back to the Templars.

"Well?" asked William. "What did you learn from them?"

"Nothing very disturbing, my lord. They belong to a little community that lives in the mountains and escaped from the Baphomets. They ask medicines and weapons. They don't lack food, being vegetarian. You have nothing to fear from them."

"Do they know whether there are other fortresses on Orph?"

"I questioned them on that subject. They answered in the negative. As we supposed, the Baphomets left some time before our arrival and destroyed all these installations. Only the robot legions had hidden under the fortress that we destroyed. The Orpheds are certain we've destroyed the whole planetary garrison."

"Good. Have them given what they want. Go tell them I don't want to talk with them. They look too much like demons vomited up out of hell. Even the Baphomets aren't so hideous."

"Will you leave troops in this place?" Sonz asked then. "Will you not ask them strategic advice?"

"A company and four ships, useless to leave more. I want nothing more to do with this planet and these people. Go talk to them if your stomach can stand it. They turn mine."

The captain saluted and went back to the insectoids, while William and his officers boarded the flagship.

It took to space at once and was soon joined by the rest of the squadrons, which gathered in battle formation, waiting the orders of their leader.

The Grand Master was entirely undecided. Without any news of Oddh, he did not know whether he should go back to that planet or make a rapid raid toward Eth to gain it instead.

A message from Otto of Granson put an end to his hesitation. The giant Swiss reported that blue and red squadrons had reached Oddh without hindrance. The planet had not suffered any attack. Elsewhere, space seemed empty. The Baphomets had apparently retreated to Baphom. He added that the Odeous were working around the clock and that in a few weeks the Templar forces would be doubled. Finally, he concluded, without giving more details, he had to announce the arrival of a legate of the new pope, Gaetano Orsini, elected under the name of Nicholas III.

William took in this information in particular, and it sent him into a towering rage.

"What have I to do with that brainless chatterer?" he growled. "By the Glorious and Blessed Virgin Mary, there's no fat glutton courtier of His Holiness going to tell me what I'm going to do. These worlds are mine and I'll allot them to whomsoever I like! Ah! I'd laugh if somehow the Baphomet fleet turned toward Earth. Sure, they'd be praying to me then and begging me, if I let that pernicious horde go. When I think that they never even sent me reinforcements . . . !"

"Good sir," the Templar of Tyre broke in, "it's not fitting for a servant of Christ to say such things. Anger has gotten the better of you. His Holiness is the representative of our Lord in this world and nothing escapes his authority."

"You forget the prerogatives of our order!" William returned, red-faced. "We constitute an independent power which enjoys the protection of Rome without accepting its guardianship. Who has worked more than I for the Glory of Our Lord? Thanks to me, the Holy Faith will be spread from one end to the other of the Earth and of the universe. I laugh at papal bulls and I account for my actions only to the Master of the World, the God of the Cosmos who created all the stars and those among them. But after all," he noted, sweetening his tone somewhat, "I am very wrong to give such importance to cowards who came to feast on my conquests. We're heading for Eth. Then we'll go force those demoniac Baphomets out of their lair. Now let me alone."

All those present, far from eager to run afoul of the Grand Master's temper, retreated at once.

William went and knelt before a shrine and submerged himself in his meditations.

Surely, if the Grand Master's faithful could have read into his thoughts, they would have been dismayed, wondering if their leader had not fallen prey to a demon.

Happily, only Houen-Lun could enter minds, and the Tibetan stayed mute as the grave.

Plunged into an abyss of desolation, William felt his faith waver. Lately when he was still on the sweet Earth, had he not stated to John of Villiers that the power of Christ was sufficient so that He could incarnate on every planet, bringing about the redemption of sinners? Well, on Oddh and on Orph—Sonz had assured him—no native had ever been moved to die to assure the salvation of his brothers' souls. It was for that reason, rather than for military motives, that the Templar wanted to go to Eth. There, finally, he might discover the traces of a local Christ. If he did not, what must he think? That beings of such demoniac aspect as the Orpheds might never have known original sin? Come now! What, would man be the only bearer of that stain? Surely even on Earth, quite a good many nations had not known Christ, and it was precisely his role, as servant of the Faith, to spread it among them. But why did the Son of Man not manifest Himself to give him a mark of his power? After all, the business at hand was worth it. Never since Moses had any human had so much effect in increasing the kingdom of God. Why would he not also have right to a message? To tablets of the Law? On Oddh and on Orph, soldier-monks already worked to convert the infidels, but could the rules of the Ten Commandments and the Gospel be applied to creatures as different from men as the Orpheds, who laid eggs like serpents, or even to the androgynous Baphomets? William did not know what to think. His brain was overwhelmed. For the first time since his childhood, the proud soldier felt tears flow over his seamed cheeks. The Templar wept for himself, for the shattering of his universe, for after all . . . If this multiform pantheon discovered on Earth and in space implied that beings rampant over the worlds created gods at their own need, and if, in fact . . . He did not exist . . .

Little by little, the Grand Master felt his reason totter, for these problems were impenetrable, and he hardly had the gift to resolve them.

Gradually he slid into a deep sleep.

The soldier-monk rested long in that state, his head on the rail bench of the prie-dieu. During this time, the ships lanced through the infinity of space, tiny dots carrying aboard them weak creatures driven by insatiable pride to desire unfathomable secrets that their tiny souls could scarce conceive.

William was not the only one who plunged himself into esoteric meditations. The wise lama also had his problems.

Of another sort, of course, but still painful. Convinced that beings reincarnated after death as other living creatures, Houen-Lun saw no obstacle that Terrans should not reincarnate as Orpheds, Ethir, Odeous, Baphomets, and vice versa. That increased the stretch of the cycle each must run before reaching supreme felicity. Again, his benevolent inaction regarding the world and its inhabitants found itself in shabby state by now. Houen-Lun had succeeded in unifying the mysterious supernatural power which manifested itself in nature; he had now added to that the stars and planets, but how to excuse his acting in complete contradiction of the maxims which bade him kill no living thing, not to do harm to any, neither to birds nor to beasts, not even to flowers and plants?

Once, he had acted to kill the Baphomet who had come to Earth, by telling himself that these pernicious creatures abused the world's harmony. He had held the same rationale then in agreeing to help the Grand Master of the Templars in his crusade against the Baphomets. But were not these perverse creatures too born of the Master of the World, Adibuddha? Then why destroy them, since the mountain tiger too has a right to exist? The world, surely, is only illusion, but where is reality in the immensity of the universe? Was it necessary to give up helping these western warriors, these rude-mannered folk and their primitive faith? Such an abandonment meant, pure and simply, their ruin. Without the psychic activity of the lamas, they would only be playthings in the claws of Baphomet tigers. In sum, which was the greatest risk of disturbing world harmony? The Baphomets, to be sure. But the proud Templars, the Hospitalers, the Teutons, were they not also greedy and despicable as these filthy beings?

Houen-Lun, torn, realized that he was very far from realizing his supreme disinterest, for close ties still bound him to this vile world he thought he had rejected.

His heart thrust him toward aiding his fellow humans.

His reason told him that by doing so he would intervene still more in the disturbance of events, flagrant contradiction of his doctrine.

Powerless to make a decision, the lama drove all thought from his mind.

So the time rolled past rapidly.

The Templar and the Tibetan were both surprised to learn that the fleet was approaching the world of the Ethir.

William leapt to the command post, forgetting his problems to plunge himself into action.

Houen-Lun waited and watched.

Chapter IX

The planetary system of the Ethirs had ten planets. Notable fact, two of them were capable of sheltering living things, but they were vastly different. The first, nearest the white star, enjoyed a tropical climate. Covered with jungles of luxuriant vegetation, it sheltered an abundant wildlife, often dangerous, somewhat like that which existed on Earth in the Cretaceous period. The Ethir had only arrived there recently, having constructed ships capable of space travel only within a mere hundred years. That world had served primarily as a hunting preserve. Only a few posts had been put there. Since the conquest of the second world by the Baphomets, it was completely abandoned.

The civilization of the birdmen was widespread in the temperate and serene climate of Eth. It was far from advanced compared to the Odeous. The Ethir still lived in fortified cities girt with high walls, and covered with a transparent roof. The castles, the houses in which they lived, still had an access mechanism high above, pierced through that sturdy roof.

Their owners had easily flown great distances. They had sometimes used balloons to transport heavy weights, dirigibles drawn by powerful birds, petrels. Animal evolution had followed a special course on Eth. Almost all species were capable of flight.

Besides their powerful wings, the Ethir had thin arms ending in a slim, four-fingered hand with an opposable thumb, which let them do all manner of work.

To prevent these unfortunate folk from flying, the Baphomets had broken the humerus, which healed crooked and prevented the wings from extending; but these cruel masters took great care not to damage their hands, which were indispensable in the playing of musical instruments.

The Ethir, of a peaceful disposition, had let themselves be conquered almost without striking a blow. They had been slaves for only about thirty years, gentle and graceful slaves, with their downy, almost immaculately white plumage, remarkable musicians.

William had learned all these details through Sonz, but for the moment he had no concern for them, for he was only looking to know if Eth had been provided with defense systems.

The detectors had found no mines, and as for the three moons, they proved deserted. Evidently the Baphomets had not had time to fortify them.

Examination of the planet showed that it had been evacuated. There was only a garrison of robots charged with watching the slaves and taking care of rebellion.

The summit of the hill supporting the fortress was protected by a vast shining dome.

This time, however, the Baphomets had not indulged in systematic destruction. Eth, the flower planet, produced heady essences much prized by these demoniac creatures. They had left intact those vast plantations with specimens lovingly selected over many years. Only the factories near the cities had been leveled.

All that pleased William considerably, for he did not even have to worry about attacking the enemy fortress. His troops knew the tactic to use backward and forward, and they had quickly eliminated fort and garrison.

When that was accomplished, the Grand Master went to Ethor, the planetary capital, in order to deal with the lord of these lands.

He then had leisure to admire the delicate architecture of the city, flying at low altitude. The streets, useless before the coming of the Baphomets, were teeming with an awkward crowd. Only a few despised collaborators had kept their wings unbroken.

As a priviliged distinction, the collaborators had also had the right of flying the transport dirigibles. Since the arrival of the fleet, the majority of these cowards had fled into the planet's desert regions. Without weapons, they represented but a small danger and they would be quickly obliged to surrender.

Sonz assured the Templar that it would be easy to heal the unfortunate victims of the Baphomets. A very simple surgical operation would let them recover the use of their wings.

William was welcomed on the platform covering the palace by musical trills of an orchestra and a choir singing the praises of the liberators of the planet. Then he was led into immense high-ceilinged halls, the walls of which were decorated with silver perches and soft nests of velvet, now unused.

Arros, the venerable Ethir who had once been governor of the planet, welcomed him with the greatest marks of deference. He and his ministers cast themselves at the Templar's feet, kissing his hands in token of thanks. William gave himself over to this effusive welcome for a moment, then lifted Arros impatiently to his feet and asked Sonz to translate what he said.

"Don't abase yourselves so," he ordered. "Such acts are for gods alone, and I am only a humble creature of the Living God, Master of the universe. Don't you have any god, that you worship his work in this fashion, like as you are to the angels of our religion?"

"Of course we do," answered the old Ethir through the Odeous' translation. "We believe in a supreme creator who reigns over all the universe, but we do not deny him in any way by thanking him for his grace through your agency, for you have chased away these monsters who oppressed us."

"Tell me, old one," the Grand Master pursued, "has your God sent onto this world the incarnation of His beloved son who, taking your carnal form, came to set you free from original sin?"

"Assuredly!" Arros replied with an astonished look. "How could you know that, coming from a distant planet? Dhret took on flesh several centuries ago, to give our people the teachings of religion that conformed to the desires of his Almighty Father."

This time William felt himself seized with joy. Finally he had found the proof he searched for so hard. Earth had not been the only place chosen for the Incarnation. A Christ existed on this planet. All his doubts were wiped out in an instant. Neither the Odeous nor the satanic-looking Orpheds had yet reached the stage of their evolution when God judged it right to send His Beloved Son to bring them His Holy Word, but these angel-like Ethir were, like Terrans, redeemed by Christ, who had taken on the form of the inhabitants of this world.

"And how did He die?" the Templar asked anxiously.

"Covered in years and revered by our people," replied Arros. "How could it be otherwise? We owe him great gratitude, for he gave us the Holy Precepts, the models of all our life, which will let us pass after death to supreme happiness."

William suddenly went white. Without the pain of a shameful death, how could this Christ be able to redeem these creatures?

"And what are these teachings that He gave you?"

"Never to kill those like us, never to eat flesh, only grains and vegetables, to leave the family nest to make our own at the age of fifteen, to rear our children and care for them, to receive those whose parents have died, to marry our brother's widow, if perchance he should have left this world untimely, to despise wealth and abandon the quest for material goods save as we need them, to praise the God of the universe twice weekly by our songs, and to gather on the anniversary of Dhret's disappearance to glorify him, to take only from the rich, to charitably smother our brothers when they grow old . . ."

"What?" gasped William. "That impostor preached euthanasia and polygamy, by Christ! You're making fun of me, old one. Take care!"

"Don't get so angry, my friend. Each race finds appropriate a different moral code. What is good for us birdfolk would not necessarily be suitable for you other folk, you warriors come from the stars. So it is forbidden for us to fight to take the goods of other folk, while your God surely orders you to fight without mercy against the peoples of the universe to increase your domain. For I have no illusions, stranger, we have simply changed masters and we thank you for it, for you seem much gentler and kinder than the foul Baphomets."

An amused light shone in Sonz' eyes as he translated these words and William almost choked. "You are completely mistaken, old one," he assured him. "The Templars never enslaved anyone. They limit themselves to teaching the universe the True Word."

"Under constraint, for it in no wise corresponds to what we follow."

"Your doctrine, true, does differ markedly from ours, but you venerate a Redeemer and it will be easy to explain to you the errors in the Dogma that your people have followed until now. For example, it's not at all right for you to marry a brother's widow when you're already married, for it's forbidden to have more than one wife."

"In your world, perhaps, if your race were prolific, but we, who only lay a single egg, hatching after an incubation of two years, how could we perpetuate our race if all the marriageable females were not fertilized?"

William gave a vast sigh. "The ways of God are inscrutable. I see now how an alien could differ from a human. His needs, his moral code, his soul . . . are not like ours, so how could a religion be universal? Already on our Earth, there are numerous ways of worshiping the Lord, and how to know which has the Truth and, especially, if there exists a Dogma applicable to all . . . you appear moved by good intentions when you preach polygamy. Among other peoples more prolific than either of us, there is a selection of births they call eugenics, which is I believe the case of the Orpheds, who smother all the subjects that have flaws or deformities. All that is forbidden by our God. But how to know if we must impose His Laws on peoples like yours?"

"You are surely understanding and good and you realize that any intervention in our ancestral inheritance would amount to a new slavery. Yet you must decide and you seem torn."

"Certainly, I am facing formidable problems, but I pray God to enlighten me to act according to justice and according to His desires. For the moment I'm going to leave you a little garrison on your planet. You'll be free to practice your religion your way. Later, when the war against the Baphomets is finished, we'll have time to reflect soberly on the attitude we should adopt. Go."

The Ethir withdrew, his great wings trailing behind him. He looked clumsy and awkward, but what must be his lightness and his grace when he glided through the sky on his immaculate wings!

William went back to his flagship without delay. He wanted, before leaving this solar system, to take a look at the

neighboring world to be sure that no enemy troops had taken
refuge there. The squadron then made a rapid turn and the
Grand Master stepped out on this new world of a luxuriance
and savagery unimaginable.

Voracious lianas had already invaded the precarious Ethir
installations, breaking the walls with their weight.

The Templar and his escort perceived monstrous trees
whose trunks and branches were covered with foot-long
spines. According to Sonz, the Ethir had used these sharp
darts as daggers in preference to better steel, for they contained a deadly poison which killed in a few seconds. Men-
at-arms gathered a great number of them, in spite of the
trouble they had detaching them from the trees. In this woods
also lived countless plants with saps that intoxicated, irritated
or poisoned, of which the Baphomets had made once an
ample harvest.

There also he found strangling vines the quickness of
which defied imagining. Countless skeletons of animals, hung
above the ground, marked the presence of these implacable
green killers.

William quickly understood that no garrison could survive
in these places, at least without having major means to fight
against the vegetable assault that each night regained the territory of the clearings made the day before.

So he left these cursed places after having consulted his
oracle Houen-lun, who confirmed his impression. Outside of a
legion of beasts and insects, no being with a brain could live
there.

Reassured, the Grand Master then turned their bows for
Oddh, to concentrate his forces for the final assault.

On the way, he received excellent news from the message
darts. The enemy fleet had disappeared from space.

This was reassuring for the moment and disquieting for the
future. The Templar disclosed this information to Sonz,
whose intelligence he respected, and Sonz confirmed his fears.

"I discussed that with the Orpheds at some length," the
Odeous assured him, "and here is what they conclude: the
Baphomets are cowards. They gladly annex planets when
they face only a feeble resistance, which has been the case
until now. They surely reckoned that your Earth would be ill
defended, and their surprise was considerable when they
found themselves faced with a people resolved to fight with

all their resources. Since you have at your disposal, besides, technological means equal to their own, these cowards have adopted the tactic of walls. Only their planet has a power device behind which they can find shelter. Their satellites constitute a sealed enclosure which few ships can face and even in the event attackers succeed in making a breach, they will have to defeat the massed squadrons behind them. On Baphom, there are food supplies and minerals which must let them hold out for years. What matter if they have to sacrifice a few slaves?"

"We know that tactic very well," William murmured, mechanically stroking his black beard. "Our kings have fortified cities, and their dukes and barons have mighty walled castles, very hard to destroy, except with our thunderballs. We are expert in the art of siege and we are well experienced in tactics that require this kind of fighting. So then why can't we come at the enemy in his lair when we have forces enough at our disposal?"

"There's a good reason, noble lord," the Odeous said. "When you fight on Earth, your troops can feed themselves on the land. In space, it goes differently. How can your ships stay near Baphom without provisioning with fuel and food? You have to divide your forces, one part coming back to Oddh to take on supplies, while the other maintains the ring around the strong place. Then the enemy will have a hard time making sorties en masse, but you will be numerically inferior, and for all the courage of your warriors, you will sustain serious losses, maybe even disastrous ones. Then when your crews are reduced, the Baphomets, assured of combat at odds of ten to one, will only make a single mouthful of your ships."

Those were the right words to make all the soldier-monks stop and think, accustomed as they were to the art of war.

William himself could not but recognize the correctness of his ally's opinion. Of course it was possible to leave the Baphomets in their lair and exploit the planets they had liberated, increasing the squadrons with new crusaders. But for their part the demons would surely take advantage of this to reinforce themselves, and the installations on Baphom were intact, while the Templars could only count on Oddh. Time was surely in favor of the besieged, who someday would break out in force.

So it was necessary to make a choice: to protect Earth, without great strategic interest, since its science, still in its infancy, could not let them build vast factories; or Oddh, the only world capable of furnishing a great quantity of indispensable minerals to the duplicators and to the alchemists who worked out the delicate mechanisms of the ships and weapons.

Thinking well on the matter, the Baphomets had the master cards and only Marco Polo with his houbits could change the course of events.

Now, the dart messages had not furnished any clear information on the Venetian. Had he been unmasked or had he indeed found himself quite simply walled into the enemy fortress?

Houen-Lun would perhaps have been able to answer these questions, but the Tibetan wise man, plunged into a sort of catalepsy, had escaped this world and its intrigues.

William was thus alone, face to face with his dilemma, while the unbeaten armada turned toward Oddh.

Marco Polo had kept his promise faithfully. He had left Chang-Chu four days after the departure of the Grand Master's squadrons, the lama Tarim, Brother Berard and Brother Montclair going with him, all of them, of course, made up like Lyzogans and speaking the language of those aliens fluently.

The route followed by this cautious ship drew off to one side, away from that followed by the invasion fleet, so that the pseudo merchants arrived unhindered at satellite 289.

There, things became a little more complicated. The garrison had been relieved and none of the new people knew Marco Polo. Surely the memory of the central computer kept a record of the passage of the Lyzogans, but the Odeous captain in command of that station demanded the arriving ship stay in orbit, waiting on precise instructions. A state of war had been declared, and no ship could get into the fortifications of Baphom without a special safe conduct.

Marco Polo and his companions must then wait patiently for the requisite authorization to arrive. Evidently the Baphomet leaders had other matters to occupy them, for the Terrans stayed in that condition in range of the satellite defense for five interminable days.

The Venetian, worried, racked his brain to discover some subterfuge which would let him carry off his mission, but in vain. He could not help but alert the Baphomets and compromise the success of an operation of extreme importance for the Terrans.

He had, besides, other worries, for Tarim did not prove very cooperative. The Tibetan disliked to leave his meditations to probe the minds of the occupants of the satellite and the Venetian was not very sure how to bring him out of it. The two Templars were hardly better recruits, being unbridled loudmouths who constantly talked about the fine points of swordsmanship and tricks of war, making ceaseless fencing passes in the narrow living quarters.

Marco Polo paced like a fox in a cage and was beginning to wonder if his trick had not been discovered, when the satellite finally gave him authorization to approach.

Each occupant of the ship put a final touch on his makeup and when the Odeous captain made his entry, all was ready to welcome him.

The Odeous looked the Lyzogans over arrogantly, comparing them against pictures previously taken of the visitors to Zolial without their knowledge, then inspected the cargo in detail and finally deigned to growl at them: "All of it looks all right to me. You're going to take yourselves directly to Baphom. You see, our emperor fears our fortifications may be the object of an attack and he wants the houbits to be turned over to him in his palace. You'll land directly at the imperial starport; there, they'll give you new instructions. Two starships will escort you as far as Baphom as a security precaution. I warn you to obey these instructions strictly. It's worth your life, if you value your lives at all."

Then the Baphomets' slave turned his back without further civilities and went back to his post.

Marco Polo easily found the two ships indicated to him and put himself at once at the disposal of their commanders. They had come to guide the ship and the three vessels veered toward Baphom.

The Venetian, during the passage, did not fail to look carefully at the borders. He could thus observe that countless patrols were cruising about, making any invasion impossible. The convoy was checked more than ten times before it arrived in Baphom's near neighborhood.

There a grand and frightening spectacle was awaiting the
Terran spies. As far as the eye could see extended clouds of
ships of all sizes, well arranged in squadrons.

Their forces matched the size of William's armada, and
they still had to reckon with countless ships stationed on the
satellites and on Baphom itself.

Berard and Montclair were seized with an understandable
dismay and Marco Polo had to reassure them, reminding
them that if they succeeded on this mission, all these fine
vessels would be without leaders to command them. That
cheered the Templars somewhat, little accustomed as they
were to such sights as this.

Before entering the planet's atmosphere, the ship underwent a new inspection, made this time by Orphed slaves.

The two monks had the utmost difficulty mastering themselves, for these creatures reminded them of the demons of
hell, minions of Lucifer. But the Terrans underwent this last
test successfully, and a few minutes later they were authorized to set down before the palace, but on automatic pilot, like all the other vessels, doubtless to avoid having
candidates for suicide missions hurl their ships onto the defensive installations.

Finally, after a perfect landing, the hatch opened and the
four passengers found themselves in the presence of a squad
of robots. This time it was quite necessary that Tarim follow
his companions.

Marco Polo, anxious for his cargo, went back for several
checks. Ethir slaves were already proceeding to off-load the
precious houbits into vehicles ranged beside the ship.

The Venetian heaved a sigh of relief. Apparently the
Baphomets had no doubts and were taking the agreed delivery of the precious devices.

Nothing had changed since his last stay. The patrols were
better equipped, the checks more frequent, but the palace was
still thrust toward the clouds. The emperor had not yet
judged the situation grave enough to hide the high tower in
the entrails of the rocks.

The Terrans' escort followed the same route as they had on
the Venetian's first visit. As far as he could judge, the lift led
to the same floor, and they let them into an apartment identical to the one they had previously occupied.

The moment he knew they were not headed for some dark

dungeon, Marco Polo found himself perfectly satisfied. But as his guards were going to leave without uttering a word, he made up his mind to question them.

"Can I know when it will be possible for me to meet a Baphomet lord?"

"Question without answer," replied the robot in a rasping voice. "Our lords know your presence in these places. They will call you when they deem fit. I advise you the danger of crossing the threshold without being asked. You will receive very disagreeable shocks to your organism, which will become fatal if you make a second attempt."

Then the metal machine turned its back and walked out.

Marco Polo's first concern was to put a finger on his lips to signal his companions that all conversation would be overheard.

Sulking, the Templars went to lie on the downy beds while Tarim cast a psychic message to his companion.

"I don't particularly approve the object of our mission," he stated. "This interference in the existence of creatures endowed with reason does not please me at all, but Houen-Lun has charged me to guard you. So then here is what I could learn. The Baphomets have detected the fleet of the Grand Master of the Templars. They have decided to remain on the alert and to retreat behind their powerful defenses where they enjoy a crushing superiority. So far as concerns us directly, I have not noted any particular distrust."

This information was of the greatest interest, and Marco Polo would have given a great deal to send it to William, but that was unhappily impossible.

So he asked in his thoughts:

"Do you think they will let us leave their planet to go get other cargo?"

"I don't know. Emperor Zolial is presently in conference with his generals. He scarcely has time to concern himself with us. Now leave me to my meditations. I will advise you if something unforeseen comes up."

The Tibetan then broke off all mental contact and Marco Polo, for all his attempts, could not get further information out of him.

But the Lyzogans appeared still to enjoy certain prerogatives, for scarcely had the robots crossed the threshold than

four slaves with slender bodies and small high breasts slipped
furtively into the room.

Pertly they came to size up the guests, curious to look over
their anatomy. To judge by their frowns they were not
seduced by the virility of the Lyzogans, for they went off into
a corner of the room, squatting on a rug of long downy fur,
and began to babble and whisper in each other's ears com-
mentaries which made them laugh like little mad things.

One of them, though, came to Marco Polo, whose breadth
of shoulder seemed to impress her. She planted herself in
front of him, hands on hips, the tips of her breasts thrust forward under the diaphanous tissue of her tunic, and smiled at
him quite wickedly. Then she drew closer to him, slid her
hand under his shirt to caress his neck, and breathed in his
ear: "You're the stranger that left with Aira, aren't you?"

"Indeed," the Venetian agreed. "Was she a friend of
yours?"

"My sister. I'm called Daicha. What happened to her? Pretend to embrace me if I don't displease you too much. You
know that they spy on us."

"You're even prettier than she is. I take the greatest
pleasure in covering you with kisses." So the Venetian assured her and set to work. This lasted some few moments.
"Your lips are soft as velvet," he said. "And your perfume
drives a man mad."

"Tell me about Aira," the slave insisted.

"She's getting along well," Marco Polo replied evasively. "I
left her on my planet."

"You aren't Lyzogan. I know you're in disguise. Tell me
where you come from. Is your nation powerful and well
armed?"

The Terran hesitated a moment. Such confidences risked
compromising all their plans. But on the other hand, he was
alone, without ties with the Templars, and an ally was not to
be rejected. Besides, the female slaves wore no implant. "I
come from Earth," he answered. "We have a powerful fleet
which is right now not far from Baphom. That's why the
Baphomet emperor has decreed a state of emergency. An attack against this planet . . . would it be possible?"

"Alas, its defenses are impenetrable. I heard Fizzur talk
about it. The Baphomets have decided to retreat behind the
wall of satellites and wait till your people come here, then

destroy them. Now your people are attacking my homeworld of Oddh. I hope they free it! Then your people will doubtless attack Eth and Orph, but you must warn them not to go up against the defenses of Baphom."

"And how might I do that?" Marco Polo asked. "Normally I would have set my cargo out on a satellite and gone back to Lyzog, but the Baphomets decided otherwise, for all ties with other worlds have been broken."

"We're going to think on this problem," whispered Daicha, who made herself quite small in his arms, groaning with pleasure. "Take me. I want you . . ."

Surprised, the Venetian carried her to the bed and let her down delicately. At that moment a robot entered.

"Lord Fizzur," it said, "is waiting on the Lyzogan Polo."

The Terran straightened, straightened his hair and clothing, then followed his guide. He knew that the Baphomets did not like to be kept waiting.

The governor of Tekaph received him in the same luxurious apartment he had occupied when the pseudo Lyzogan had made his last visit.

"Salutations, my dear Polo," he exclaimed jovially. "I have to congratulate you. Your houbits are marvelous. No psychedelic drug ever gained us such a quintessence of pleasures. The emperor is enchanted. I learned that you have faithfully discharged your mission. Perfect. We love faithful servants. Alas, due to a slight mishap, we can't let you go back to bring a new cargo. Pirates are menacing our communications lanes and we can't let you run such a risk. Don't worry. This incident will be of short duration and we'll soon resume fruitful exchange with your planet. Tell me. Have you had any difficulty on your way, met any fleet?"

"No, your lordship, everything went as fine as could be, apart from the usual small incidents, we met a magnetic disturbance that shook us up a little, but nothing serious."

"I was only wanting to be sure that the pirates hadn't sent some ships toward Lyzog. Apparently they haven't done anything of the sort. That confirms our information. Well! my dear merchant, go back to your apartment. You have to rest there a little while, but we'll give you all you desire to entertain you. The slaves do seem to be to your taste."

"Indeed, sir. Daicha is a marvelous creature. I was going to try her out when your robot came to get me."

"Perfect. Go back to her and avail yourself of her till you've had enough. When you tire of her we'll find you others."

"Thank you, thank you, munificent highness. Your humble and obedient servant only asks to be useful to you."

"You please me. I think we're made to understand one another. Go. If I need you I'll send for you."

Marco Polo withdrew, bowing liberally. He reentered the lift and went back to the gentle Odeous, who was still lying on his bed.

In a corner the Templars were devouring the tempting food, while the Tibetan stayed in lotus position on the carpet.

The Venetian took off his boots and lay down near Daicha.

"Everything went all right?" she asked in a low voice.

"Yes. He only wanted to ask me questions about my voyage and to tell me I was going to be here a little while. In one regard, that isn't displeasing to me, although the place does lack privacy."

"Don't let that bother you," said the Odeous.

So saying, she pushed a button in reach of her hand. A bronze curtain at once isolated the bed from the rest of the room.

"Now I think we are going to have to make love." She smiled. "If you're not too tired, that is."

The Venetian's fervent grip left her no doubt on the subject. As for Fizzur, if he was watching the scene, he was going to be satisfied.

Chapter X

During the days that followed, William's envoy lived the life of a pasha. He did learn interesting details on the slave organization. They had a well organized information service. They had even succeeded in stealing some very useful instruments, several devices to command the robots, devices that looked like little cylinders, that one could slip into a pocket; and even the pen-shaped weapons which gave off a killing ray. The most precious was beyond a doubt the electronic key that disconnected the energy screen at the doors. All these objects had been stolen from wastebaskets, for they were broken equipment that the slaves had patiently put back in working order.

But for the moment the Venetian could only wait. He was still without communication with the outside world and Tarim was not at all cooperating.

That lasted several weeks.

During this time, William of Beaujeu also was fretting, without pastimes as agreeable as Marco Polo's.

The voyage to Oddh had not posed any problems. They captured one enemy ship damaged by an antimatter particle, but its occpants had not possessed any interesting information.

A patrol of Hospitalers came to meet the armada which had settled on the moon Lyzar, and the Grand Master rejoined John of Villiers in the capital of the planet Oddh.

This time he had considerable reason to forget his military worries.

When he made his entrance into the hall of state, he found the Grand Master of the Hospitalers enthroned on a chair bearing the emblem of his order. At his right sat a bishop in a scarlet robe, at his left stood a monk with a weasel's face whom he had no difficulty identifying as a Dominican of the Holy Inquisition.

Knitting his heavy brows, William of Beaujeu marched toward his ally, who was flaunting a wicked smile.

"Welcome to my domains, noble brother. Your expedition was successful? Permit me to introduce you to His Holiness' legate, Bishop Liccardi, and to the President of the Holy Ecclesiastical Court, Father Evrard, who has already done an excellent work in my estates."

"Salutations to you, my brothers," grated the Templar, lips taut. "Can I ask the reason for this little joke? Especially when has John of Villiers arrogated to himself the right to give orders on my lands?"

"That demands a few explanations, I do concede," the Hospitaler said in a mocking tone. "If Your Eminence would read his papal bull. . . ."

The bishop stood up and drew from his long robe a parchment bearing a lead seal at the end of a ribbon. He unrolled it and read in a loud and solemn voice.

" 'To my loyal servant in Jesus Christ, William of Beaujeu, by the grace of God Grand Master of the Templars, I Nicholas III, Universal Pontiff by the decision of the bishops and cardinals meeting in Council at Viterbus, under the Inspiration of the Holy Spirit, do order and require the Grand Master of the knightly brothers of the Temple as follows:

" 'Upon reception of this bull, John of Villiers shall be recognized as legitimate and absolute sovereign of the Planet Oddh, of its dependencies in its star system, and of its inhabitants.

" 'Conrad von Thierberg shall receive the same rights and prerogatives on the planet Eth, in the name of the Teuton brotherhood. These rights shall be transmissible to those who succeed them in their courses in the dignity of the Grand Mastery of their orders.

" 'We declare the Planet Orph a papal domain and install as governor our loyal Paolo Liccardi, who will be recognized by all as papal legate in outreTerre.

" 'We allot to William of Beaujeu for the services rendered to the cause of the Holy Faith the Planet Baphom, with all authority over its inhabitants, the Baphomets, and this donation shall also be transmissible to his successor named lawfully with pontifical approval in his charge of the Grand Mastery of the brother knights of the Temple.

" 'We give all powers and competence over these four planets to the Reverend Father John Evrard at once President of the Holy Tribunal of the Church, agent of the Inquisition, who will judge, condemn all apostates, backsliders, magicians, sorcerers, and blasphemers belonging to the peoples of these aforenamed planets, herein comprising all miscreants of Terran race who, overcome by the devil, might show themselves rebel against the orders of Rome or fall into criminal error touching the domain of the Faith.

" 'We are assured that our faithful servant William will show himself loyal and obedient, and that he will not raise any difficulty or any objection of any sort in the application of our desires, this on the salvation of his soul. If however he show himself reticent and rebel, we would be led, not without deep sorrow and regret, to abolish the aforementioned order of Templars, to declare all its members subject to the Holy Tribunal of the Church which might render in their case, with our approval, any sentence upon its members. It goes without saying that, henceforth, all his temporal goods, Commanderies, domains, fields and forests, moneys of gold or silver, precious objects, be they on Earth or on other planets, would be immediately and without delay confiscated and remanded by us to whomsoever would be judged worth of possessing them. Ships and arms of all sorts would be sent to the Hospitalers and the Teutons.

" 'In the name of the Most Holy Virgin Mary, pious and full of glory, of her Son Our Lord Jesus Christ, our defender, creator, redeemer, merciful and beloved Savior, of the Eternal Father and of the Holy Spirit, *amen.*' "

If lightning had struck William he could not have gone whiter, while his rivals looked him up and down triumphantly. He seemed to become smaller, as if crushed by the weight of adversity.

Behind him, his faithful companions, haggard of face, had set hands on the pommels of their swords.

The Grand Master was thinking. In fact they gave him nothing but a domain still inaccessible, taking from him the indispensable alchemical treasures of Oddh. They even threatened him with stripping him of his earthly possessions.

They were going to burn and torture aliens to whom they had promised freedom.

All this under pain of damnation and destitution for him, who had always been a defender of the Holy Faith. Him who had conquered the Holy Places, protected Earth from a frightful invasion.

A wave of rage overcome him.

One moment he thought of spitting his spite in the faces of these jackals, but he did nothing of the sort. Turning his back, William drew himself up to his full height and, flanked by his brother servants, quitted the hall without saying a word.

While stalking back to his ship, he pursued somber thoughts. After all, this was what he might have expected. Like the emperors, could the kings and the pope himself have endured that the representative of an order of soldier-monks should become the most powerful lord the Earth had ever known? These cowards owed him everything. Without him they would be nothing but dogs fawning at the feet of the foul Baphomets, and behold how they showed him their gratitude. Was this the image of Christ? The accomplishment of His word, of His justice? How could the just and good Lord allow such exactions? Unless of course, the Holy Trinity was nothing but a false image and the real God of the universe laughed at the weak worm that he was? All his old doubts came flooding back. But if this were a testing? If he found, he, William, found himself in the position of Christ tempted by the devil on the mountaintop, faced with the riches of the universe? Must he like Jesus, turn the left cheek when someone had struck him on the right? Could it be a question of saving his immortal soul? He must think it through, but the power he held had drained his spirit and he had seen himself complacently becoming the richest of the rich. How to reconcile power and asceticism? And if the order must die by his failing? Proud and brave, the Templars had been praised and adored, and now all the world was jealous of them.

Without even realizing it, he reached his flagship, his soul afire, without having made a decision. Then he saw an elur racing up at full speed, ridden by his faithful marshal Peter of Sevry.

Peter leapt to the ground and crossed himself, groaned in a strained voice: "Good brother, I have sad news. A ship has

just come from Earth with a message from Thibaud Gaudin.
Here it is. I know its tenor from our brothers in the crew,
who told me the terrible happenings. . . ."

"Faith, they couldn't surpass what I've just heard. Follow
me. We're going back to Lyzar at once. All the brothers must
leave Oddh without delay to come to join us."

Without a glance at the marvels which spread across the
screens aboard, the two Templars, seated in the command
post, waited until the ship had taken to space before they
spoke again. During that time, William had carefully read the
report of his representative on Earth.

Surely what it reported in no wise helped the already em-
broiled affairs of the Grand Master.

Thibaud Gaudin advised him that the kings and emperors
had not waited for the papal injunction to rush to the spoil.
All the Templaries of lesser importance, in France, in England and in Germany, had been attacked and seized by
royal or imperial troops. In France, the Templar domains
had been confiscated. Only the fortified Commanderies were
holding out by passive resistance. Well shielded behind their
thick walls, the Templars feared nothing in the near future,
at least while they had provisons. Already the situation was
worrisome in certain Templaries and Thibaud Gaudin had to
use ships to reprovision them.

The besiegers, however, appeared still undecided. They did
not rush to all-out assault, probably waiting for the papal decision to abolish the Order of the Temple.

Thibaud Gaudin refused to use the thunderballs against the
troops of their suzerain without express order, for each Templar carried graven in his heart the motto:

My body is the king's;
My soul is God's;
My honor is mine own . . .

So he asked William to let him know quickly what he must
do.

The Grand Master, when he had taken in this terrible
message, buried his head in his hands. His reason tottered.
Everyone had turned against him. The pope, supreme authority of Christian folk, representing Christ on Earth; his king to
whom he had always been faithful, making him many loans

of money; his very allies to whom he had trusted his ships, his thunder weapons . . . and they owed him everything!

But his pride quickly got the upper hand. No! He, William de Beaujeu, would not fail his brothers who had entrusted to him the supreme title of Grand Master; they expected salvation from him; he would save them, though they all denied him.

The high dignitaries of the Order were now at his sides, anxiously waiting for his decision. John of Grailly and Otto of Granson were there, and they were also torn between their duty as vassals of the kings of France and England, and their friendship for their comrade in arms. They must decide quickly.

"Noble brothers," declared the Frenchman, "I have never received any order enjoining me to withdraw my troops from your fleet. Consequently, you can still count on the men of France."

"Dose vords are trut' for me too," the giant swiss Otto of Granson assured him. "Besides, I am a mercenary who sells his services to whoever he likes; and I haf decided to stay true to your cause. My men at arms will continue to fight at your side."

These words went straight to William's heart. He sighed deeply, signed himself with the cross. "Thank you," he said, "my brave companions, for not abandoning me in adversity. May the Holy Spirit inspire me, for on my decisions depends the future of the order. We see things before us, and what remains for me at the moment? My fleet is still powerful, even if it's stripped of Hospitaler and Teuton forces. Kubla too remains loyal to me, and I can count on his Mongols. The situation is then grave, but not desperate. After all, we still have the houbits . . ."

A deep voice then made itself heard. Houen-Lun, coming out of his meditations, had decided to intervene in the debate. The Tibetan had played a major role in the success of the Templars, and all of them began to hope.

Alas, he had quickly to disenchant them.

"Noble William, I must, to my great regret, tell you that you can no longer count on my help or that of my companions. I have thought carefully before taking this decision. My convictions forbid my actively intervening in the unrolling of events in this world. The houbits therefore will not be activated to kill the Baphomets. They will keep their euphoric powers for a few years, but they will not become deadly traps for their minds. You must fight henceforth without relying on our psychic powers. But I shall not abandon you yet. I am waiting for the return of Tarim, who is on Baphom. I will relay you his messages, if need be. Later I will ask you to set us out on Lyzog. There is no ecclesiastical court there to condemn us. The Lyzogans have beliefs close to our own. They will let us create a community and recruit adepts. My decision is without appeal."

So saying, the Tibetan went back into lotus position and his eyes went into the beyond, contemplating visions he alone could see.

A deathly silence fell over the gathering. The soldier-monks dared not look at the Grand Master any longer.

But this news did not seem to surprise William overmuch. He had always known that the Tibetan's position was in contradiction with his belief and one day or another he would desert the Templars' side. Alas, everything was crumbling about him. Without seeking to draw Houen-Lun back from his decision, the Grand Master began in a brittle voice: "Well, the situation is no longer grave, it's desperate. I refuse, you see, to fight the Hospitalers and the Teutons. They are, like us, Christian, and they're only obeying the orders of the sovereign pontiff, even if the terms of the bull are unacceptable to us. I can't make up my mind to give the order for my loyal Thibaud Gaudin to use the ships and the thunderballs. The kings are our suzerains and we don't know how to deny the oath that binds us to them, even if, instead of helping us, they crush us . . . Have a letter sent to Thibaud at once by message dart, and bid him gather all the Terran ships and put on them all our brothers who are still free, without forgetting our stocks of thunderballs, and head for Baphom at once. All the documents regarding the alchemical secrets and those having to do with the making of starships have to be burned to the last. We must not have these terrible arms serving our human brothers to commit massacre among them."

Brother Joubert went off in a hurry to execute that order, while William went on.

"I don't have much choice left, actually. My heart is broken at the thought of leaving the poor Odeous, the Ethir and the Orpheds in the hands of the Inquisitors, who are going to hunt them and burn them at the stake, but I have no choice. My honor is in question. I've lived all my life fighting for the Holy Faith. Like Christ in his passion, I cry my despair, aye, my God, why hast Thou forsaken me? Thou who once saved St. John at Acre by giving us weapons that let us defeat Bibars? But Thy designs are inscrutable and I must doubtless rejoice in my misfortune, for it assures the salvation of my poor torn soul, crushed by a dire destiny . . . Well, now, my brothers, there's nothing more left for us, but to finish our existence as we began it, and the way we would have wished when we pronounced the vows to join our holy order; then you knew the great disciplines of the House and its inflexible commandments you swore then obedience to your Grand Master elect and promised not to abandon your brothers. Remember on this day of trial the words of St. Bernard: 'The knight of Christ kills in conscience and dies at peace. Dying, he works out his salvation, in killing he labors for Christ. Doubtless he should not kill the pagans at all if he had another means of stopping their invasions, but it is better to commit massacre than to let the menace of sinners hang over the head of the just.' So down with the filthy Baphomets. Death surely awaits us, for we will have to face satellites that vomit terrible walls of fire, but your honor will be safe and your salvation assured. For myself, I look upon the end of my days in this vile world as a deliverance.

> "This age is too vile and low;
>   Yea, I fain would go;
>   when I think on the lords
>   And their deeds and their words
>   dead, now, long ago!"

William fell silent, his face reflecting vast sorrow. For him even the hope of gaining a day of the heaven promised the faithful servants of Christ was only uncertainty. His faith wavered under his experiences and only despair possessed him.

But he lifted his head when his faithful companions drew their swords and thundered out a hymn in their rough voices.

> "God Almighty and Eternal
>   Who guided good St. George,

Thy knight and holy martyr,
Gave him grace and merit
In martyrdom and passion;
By him and Virgin Mary,
Most Holy Mother, She,
For Christ's sake grant us strength
To keep our vow and laws.
May we win to Heaven,
Thou God forever King:
*Non nobis, non nobis Domine,
Sed Nomini Tuo da gloriam."*

A few hours later, the ships of the fleet came to rest on Lyzar, one after the other, to complete their refitting in arms and munitions.

Their hearts were heavy, but the soldier-monks' resolution was well and deeply anchored in themselves. They could not hope to destroy the vile race of infidel Baphomets, but at the least they could fend invasion away from Earth and let the Hospitalers and Teutons gather their forces, giving them a chance to survive.

The former would stay on Oddh, without expecting to oppose the movements of their ex-ally's squadrons. John de Villiers had been advised of the decision his rival had taken and could only congratulate him on it. Evidently, William was not contesting the papal division and was going to seek a glorious death. Good riddance. This Templar was becoming altogether too bothersome. It did not stop the Grand Master of the Hospitalers and that of the Teutons from putting their own squadrons on a war footing, for they had not forgotten the power the Baphomets had, after all, being filthy and very fearsome miscreant creatures. They had no intention at all of stopping the Templars from destroying themselves in an attack on the barrier of satellites protecting Baphom. But they wanted to be in the immediate neighborhood to watch the peripheries of the drama, and, one never knows, to participate in the combat. After all, French, English, and Mongols remained faithful to William. The Tibetans seemed to have abandoned him, but, with that astonishing man, anything was possible. He was capable of succeeding against all probability, in getting control of Baphom and its treasures—which had been imprudently allotted him by the Pope.

The old lion's rivals were still mistrustful of his leaps.

William, shut in his cabin in the heart of the flagship, spent long hours in meditations and in prayers, waiting for Thibaud Gaudin to join his fleet before attacking with maximum strength. He did not worry much at all now about strategy, seeking to strengthen his shaken faith and to die a good Christian. He at least had no illusion of his chances of success. Without the houbits, his ships would be massacred.

The Tholon brothers, crowded in with the others in the scant quarters of the base installations, had not even the chance for one memorable binge before hurling themselves into this suicidal attack.

"Ah, well," sighed Clement, "I don't understand how we got into this mess. William conquered three worlds and he finds himself robbed of them."

"Our Lord means to test our faith," Garin replied. "We Templars came to the height of power; now we must pay for our pride. An old saying has it that the Tarpeian Rock is near the Capitol. We aren't the only ones to know disillusionment. Many others before us have conquered vast empires and lost them."

"All the same, the Pope has gone too far," growled Red Guiot. "Give a planet to the Hospitalers and the Teutons, that's bad enough, but to keep one for his personal use . . . Not to mention those filthy monks of the Inquisition, who stick their noses in here wanting to rule everything on Oddh. There've already been twenty so-called heretics burned by those butchers! So far as I'm concerned, Christians or not, I'd throw the scum out!"

"Mind your words, my brother," the Templar chided him. "You owe complete obedience to our Holy Father the Pope, even if his decisions seem debatable to you. You're only a worm without great importance in the eyes of Our Lord. How could you judge then, when you're ignorant of so much?"

"S'death! maybe I don't know everything, but I'm sure that without William, no one would have these damn planets, and I'm sure that the Baphomets would have invaded the Earth a long time ago. So all that's platitudes and we . . . we're going to lose our heads for it."

Garin did not answer. In spite of himself he could not stop thinking that his brother was right, only he owed a blind obedience to the Grand Master of the order, and if William ordered him to die in battle, he would throw himself blindly into the fray.

A week later, the fleet lifted majestically into the starry heavens. Each vessel had been prepared for this last battle. Certain of them, crammed with explosives, had been devised as fireships to try to blow up a link in the chain of satellites, thus opening a passage to their attack, but no one had much confidence in it.

Thibaud Gaudin was headed directly toward Baphom and must arrive near the Baphomet fortress almost at the same time as William's squadrons.

Behind the armada as it left Lyzar, John of Villiers and Conrad von Thierberg followed at a distance, like jackals shadowing a caravan to eat the dead.

The voyage was dotted with various unimportant incidents. A few ships collided and a nervous Templar fired a salvo at a Teuton ship which was following a little too close for his liking.

The armada then arrived in sight of the fortifications around Baphom. Their configuration was simple: the satellites were set in a quincunx pattern circling all parts of the planetary system of Baphom, forming a sort of saucer above and below the plane of the ecliptic.

The direct path to the lair of the demoniac Baphomets consisted then of attacking head on into the plane of the planetary system. Of course, that would be the sector best defended, five successive lines of fortified stations barring their way.

But it was there that William chose to make his first thrust, for behind the satellites, the enemy fleet would only have a narrow area to deploy and all their fire could be concentrated into that mass.

But before launching his ships the Grand Master must handle some preliminary operations. He must in particular sweep the vicinity of mines.

The quark cannon were very useful in this task. They let them work outside their range of the defenses and reduce these deadly machines to dust, making large gaps in the mine field.

A brave enemy would have tried to engage the

minesweepers with swift ships, but the cowardly Baphomets, trusting in their defenses, let it go on without reaction.

When that work was finished, William prepared for the attack. The ships of Thibaud Gaudin had rejoined him, and his forces were now complete. The Grand Master listened to the grim report which his faithful friend made him on what had happened on Earth. As it happened, all the kings, all the emperors had decided to make an end of the Templars, deeming that they would never dare turn their thunder weapons against Christians, and the Pope not only let them do it, but secretly encouraged them.

There was now left only one outcome for the honor of the soldier-monks: to die fighting the miscreant Baphomets.

The Grand Master had the attack order sent to his squadrons. This time there was no question of sending the Turcopole and Kubla's light ships in first.

These were the Templars themselves, supported on either wing by the French and the English, who met the deluge of projectiles belched out by the satellites.

Conforming to the established plan, several fireships were among the contingents in the van. This tactic proved double-edged. Sometimes one of them exploded prematurely in the heart of a formation and the neighboring ships, gravely damaged, became an easy prey to the guided missiles. But from the fact of the abundance of targets, the fire coordinators found themselves swamped and could not recognize these fireships in the heart of the mass of Terran vessels. So almost half these destructive engines reached their targets and a breach was opened in the barrier.

Seeing this the Templars gathered hope. Now in place of undergoing fire of powerful armored forts, they were going to be able to fight against other ships on equal terms.

The brave soldier-monks plunged into the gap. Their assault was so headlong that the vessels at point came within firing range of Baphom and got off several missiles that hit the capital, sowing consternation among the Baphomets, who had thought their city invulnerable.

At this instant if the Hospitalers and the Teutons had rejoined the Templars, the battle would doubtless have been won. Alas. John of Villiers and Conrad von Thierberg did not judge their rivals diminished enough to come to their rescue.

The squadrons of the Baphomets then had the chance to regroup and to launch three counterattacks, one frontal, meant to protect Baphom, the other two in a pincer movement to cut off the Terrans from their rear guard and encircle them.

This time too the combat was long undecided. Before them the Templar lines bent under the shock, but held. Clouds of missiles and antiquark beams made ravages among the two adversaries without deciding the encounter.

On the flanks, French and English had to bend back, then reestablish new lines where they could hold without retreating an inch.

From one side and the other, however, the losses were considerable and finally the Baphomets, more numerous, were winning the encounter.

William, whose ship at the heart of the combat set off volley after volley, was wondering if he should not retreat. He still had his light ships in reserve, which might break the deadly circle, but the Grand Master hesitated to use his last reserves.

Then Houen-Lun, who was still aboard the flagship, came out of his silence.

"Rejoice, William!" he said. "Tarim has just entered contact with me. We are now quite near to Baphom, where he is in Marco Polo's company. Your faithful Venetian has learned some news of import from the harem slaves. Zolial the Baphomet emperor has become rather talkative under the influence of a houbit. He revealed a fearful secret. There exists, at little distance from this solar system, a sort of maelstrom in space, a microscopic black hole, infinite access to unfathomable depths. Once it menaced Baphom, but Baphomet scholars succeeded in stabilizing it without being about to get rid of it. Here are its coordinates. If you succeed in passing the installations which maintain it, you can cast it onto the planet of these pitiless creatures. But you must act quickly, for some few enemy ships protect that place."

The Grand Master saw at once the advantage he could get from that incredible information. He immediately ordered Kubla to disengage his rear guard while he himself maneuvered as if he were beating a retreat.

Thanks to heaven the Templar forces were still sufficient,

and soon all the survivors were back at their starting point,
outside the belt of satellites.

There William established a solid line of defense composed
of Templars, French and English to block the gap.

He then sent commands to his faithful Thibaud Gaudin,
and he himself with the Turcopoles and Mongols peeled off
at all speed toward the site Marco Polo had told him of.

Soon the Baphomets' secret installations appeared on the
screens. They faced satellites bristling with antennae, set in
an octohedron in the distance. Of the black hole he saw nothing. In his delirium, had Zolial lied?

Sonz hastened to explain to William that that was no wonder, that these strange formations, tiny objects of incredible
density, trapped all material objects, all radiation passing near
them. Once plunged into that vortex, they disappeared forever and no one knew exactly where they went. It was always
a black hole of small dimensions. One could pass through a
world, making a tornado at its point of impact and another at
its exit. And in that there was a slight problem . . . for if the
course of this black star by some ill chance were stopped at
the heart of a planet it would see all the matter in it absorbed
like water by a sponge, and the world would disappear, leaving nothing but a tiny navigation hazard of enormous density,
a deadly new trap of slightly increased dimensions.

But already the enemy ships charged with its defense were
rushing toward the Terrans.

A merciless battle ensued.

The Mongols' swift ships did wonders. They whirled
around their adversaries, feinting, threatening to flee and returning to the assault on an isolated enemy, turning with a
mad address to escape opposing fire.

This time numbers were on the side of the Templars, for
the Baphomets, trusting to the small size of the black maelstrom, had never thought that their enemies could discover it,
and they had only gathered light forces there so as not to
draw attention to it.

In a little time the last defenders were put out of action
and Sonz, even before it was all over, took over the controls
of the installation.

These had not been destroyed for a good reason: they
alone kept the black hole at a distance from Baphom.

The Odeous signaled William to move all his ships out of a

direct line with the foul planet, then with a grimace of hate, he hit the controls, changed their settings to aim the monstrous projectile to its objective, and put the whole device into motion.

At once the black maelstrom shot inexorably toward Baphom. Only special instruments let them see it, for its intense gravitational field was not visible to the naked eye.

Paradoxically it seemed to distort space and time, for it went at a truly incredible speed.

Epilogue

Directed by the sure hand of the Odeous, the deadly object headed right for the cursed planet. In front of it, the Terran ships, warned by William, headed out of its way, but the enemy ships had no time to react.

Suddenly seized in lightning-fast turbulence, Baphomet satellites and ships were hurled one after the other into that gaping maw where matter compressed to infinity and infinite depths.

On Baphom, the emperor, warned of the cataclysm, hastily embarked in vessels loaded with treasure which had been prepared to such an end, and the foul lords tried to take to space and flee.

Unhappily, their ships, slowed by their heavy load, could not get far enough fast enough. Already the dark mass, momentarily surrounded by incandescing clouds and lightnings, was rushing down on them.

William, who had followed near the whirlpool, watched the end of the enemies of the human race.

Then the malefic object struck the surface of Baphom. A cyclone devastated the neighboring countryside, while at the antipodes, a similar phenomenon was in action.

Now the black micropoint, restrained by its traverse of the planet, had clearly slowed, and was traveling less swiftly than a ship.

In the command station of the flagship, the Templars were ecstatic. Against all hope, the Lord had decided to save them! It was a miracle like that at St. John at Acre. When they were about to go under, Almighty God had helped them.

They all looked toward William of Beaujeu. On him devolved the glory of the victory.

Suddenly the rough soldiers blanched. The Grand Master had vanished.

A telltale winked on the control panel, revealing the terrible truth at once. The brave Templar, his mission accomplished in this lower world, had taken his place in a lifeboat and was headed right for the maelstrom.

All appeals were vain. The ship's communications were disconnected by William, who was relentlessly set on his fate.

The screens showed him in his mad course, looking with a gaze of ecstasy on the clouds which still surrounded the black hole. A few shining atoms whirled in a dance before falling forever into the abyss.

The nightmared eyes of the hero's faithful stared also at the strangely twisting clouds.

Then for a brief moment, they had a fantastic vision, as a cross of light shone out in space.

It vanished so fast they all wondered if they had been dreaming. William had seen it before dying. For him it was a sign: his sins were forgiven. An expression of peace touched his face before he vanished forever.

The dark meteor quite swiftly departed the area and vanished into the infinities of the heavens.

The surviving Templars, assisted by the Hospitalers and the Teutons, quickly destroyed the few enemy forces remaining in space.

Thibaud Gaudin, accompanied by John of Villiers and Conrad von Thierberg, left his ship then on Baphom. The devastation the black hole had made was fortunately localized. Few of the slaves were dead, and Marco Polo and his companions had not suffered from the cyclone, for they had been sheltered in the palace, which remained intact.

Thibaud Gaudin solemnly took possession of Baphom in the name of the Order of the Temple and this time no one dared contest his decisions.

But John of Villiers and Conrad von Thierberg still had doubts about the death of their rival. Sonz assured them that the ship, though caught in the whirlpool, had escaped the deadly maelstrom: William might have survived. The Odeous thus proposed to guide them to the very place where, he said, they might find the Grand Master, shunted off in space.

The squadrons of the Hospitalers and the Teutons left Baphom. Before leaving, John of Villiers declared he would soon see on this place the representatives of the Holy Inquisition.

Thibaud Gaudin had been astonished by Sonz' insistence, but he had not the technical knowledge of the Odeous and he dared not contradict him; since Sonz affirmed that William's lifeboat was still wandering in the void, he must be telling the truth. Thibaud accordingly sent a powerful squadron in pursuit of the Hospitalers and the Teutons.

The ships went off on the track of Sonz and his companions; suddenly they all vanished from the screens.

Thibaud Gaudin then understood the Odeous' stratagem. Devoted to freeing his people from the yoke of the Inquisition, he had led the torturers of his people right into the dark whirlpool.

The Chapter of Templars, reunited sometime afterward, confirmed Thibaud Gaudin as successor of William, and the new Grand Master made some important decisions.

The Templars had finished their crusade. The foul enemy had been destroyed.

On all the freed worlds, the tribunals of the Inquisition were abolished. Odeous, Ethir, Orpheds and Lyzogans recovered their ancient liberties.

The Tibetans, the papal legate, the Hospitalers and the surviving Teutons were brought back to Earth, where they were traded for imprisoned Templars, and then the ships left again for Baphom.

On that return, Thibaud Gaudin took with him all his ships. He directed them into the shape of a cross around the Baussant flagship and the squadrons disappeared into the infinite heavens.

On board echoed a chorus of deep voices. *"Non nobis, Domine, non nobis, sed Nomini tuo, da gloriam . . ."*

Outstanding science fiction and fantasy

To order these titles,

use coupon on the

last page of this book.

DAW PRESENTS MARION ZIMMER BRADLEY